Beastly Cycle

A Quiet Tale of the Soul

L. R. M. Pilcher

Cover Artwork by Yves Münch

To Mom and Mom P. Thanks for cheering me on through the good and rough times of both writing and life. This one is for you…

Love can be one of the most powerful forces in the world, turning the meek into warriors and humble into royalty. It is not always easy to find or even see, but it can surprise in most unusual ways…

Prologue

Quiet Hopes

The almost fully grown man stood beneath the rising half-moon on the grounds near the vast tangle of roses and the small garden adorned with statues of purest crystal. The warm night air brought great promise with it. The ancient stone castle loomed overhead like a sentinel, silent and watching. He was quiet amid his thoughts. He had grown to love the human-like creature he had named Kilda over the past several months, of that he was certain. One kiss and declaring his honest love was all that was needed to break the curse hanging over her, which kept her in the form of a hawk-like human without wings. That was what he had discovered in the last scroll, which he had found half hidden in the lowest library. She was not able to give him the answer herself. Her curse prevented her from speaking of it. The same held for her actual name. He smiled at the thought of her freedom, both of them fleeing from this wretched place and living their lives in the same town far away until they could be together in marital bliss. If she would consent to his proposal after the curse was lifted, of course. He was not one

Beastly Cycle

to force such a thing on a lady, if she did not desire it as well. Too many other men that he had heard of had done exactly that, and it never ended well. He would rather remain alone than trapped in an unhappy marriage.

 The full moon crested the tall trees in the distance. She had agreed to meet him here when it was almost at its zenith. He did not know how he would be able to get through the remainder of the night with his stomach in knots from nerves. He wished for his plan to be done, and quick, but he had to wait until the perfect time, or the cure, for lack of a better word, would not take. He had an hour, two at most, to complete it once the moon was in position. Otherwise, he would have to wait three or four more months for everything to be right again. He gazed at the darkened sky again. The moon was almost in place. He heard the snap of a twig behind him. He turned and smiled at her approach. The butterflies in his stomach were going wild! She looked lovely, caressed by the moonlight in her flowing dress.

 "Kilda… There's something I need to tell you," he hesitantly explained.

 The fleshy corners of her mouth along her curved beak raised into a smile. "I'm listening…" she purred in her velvety voice.

 He gazed into her green eyes, and his carefully chosen words seemed to vanish to his dismay. He

Quiet Hopes

shook his head, forcing himself to continue, despite his rattled nerves, "I… I've fallen in love with you… and… I hope that… you feel the same for me."

He could see the sheer delight in her eyes! He had a foolish grin on his face, but he no longer cared. He placed a hand on her brown feathered cheek, guided her face a little closer to his, and planted a single kiss on top of her beak, near her eyes, lingering for a second…

Suddenly, he felt something slam into his stomach, throwing him off his feet! Bewildered, he rolled onto his knees, face to the ground, and his head curling to his chest. He grunted and gasped to catch his breath, one hand wrapped around him, while the other propped him up. He heard a chuckle above him. He peered upward. Kilda was laughing with glee! He could see no humor in his pain. Then, one by one, her feathers began to fall, floating gently down and turning into a clear, icy dust glittering in the moonlight on the grass.

He groaned and doubled over, his nose almost touching the ground, his hurt from her merriment forgotten. Stabbing pains, like several hot knives, began in the flesh on his face and within the depths of his stomach. It spread throughout his body within seconds. It then sank deep into his very core. His skin suddenly began itching fiercely! He clawed at his arms where it was the worst, shredding

Beastly Cycle

his sleeves in the process! Longer, black hairs sprouted from his elbows to his hands, while orange-ish red ones, like copper, began to cover his upper arms. He could feel his skin crawling with more emerging on the rest of him. His face shifted as his nose lengthened, and his ears shrank. His light brown hair fell onto the grass beneath him. Some other kind of hair quickly replaced it on his head. A pair of something sprouted on the top of his head. He watched his fingernails stretching, turning into short, thick, dark claws. Bare human lady's feet, a flowing brown skirt, and the ends of long brown hair then slipped into his view.

"You pathetic fool," Kilda sneered at him. "My thanks for freeing me. A great pity that my prison is now yours!"

She danced away from him toward the garden of crystal statues beyond, roaring with laughter. All of a sudden, he heard a sound of stone grating against stone near her, a sharp icy crackling, and her gasp of shock that quickly turned into a piercing scream of loss as a strong wind gusted by briefly! The world then dimmed before his brown eyes as he fell mercifully into unconsciousness…

Chapter 1
~ Beauty ~

The Carriage Returns

Rennora sighed contently, a dreamy smile dancing across her face, and lost herself once again in her favorite tale. She had reached the page where the heroine was rushing back to the dying creature's side in order to break the curse on him with a kiss on the cheek, which would return him to a human prince and free the cursed people-turned-animal inhabitants as well. She had read and reread the book so many times now that she could almost have recited the entire thing backwards. She did not care though. She still hung onto its every word as though it was the first time. The pale, nineteen-year-old girl leaned back against the tree and closed her gray-blue eyes, savoring the warmth of the afternoon sun. She slipped into her dream realm where everything was perfect and wonderful. Her eyes opened a bit, absorbed the wide array of colors within the little corner of the vast garden hiding her, and finally came to rest on the shadow of the oak tree along its edge where she was very comfortably seated under.

Beastly Cycle

It then took her a moment to realize exactly what she was seeing. It was three hours past midday! She leapt to her feet, dusted the loose grass off her brown, plain dress and apron, which was tied on her slim frame, scooped up the book and cap that had tumbled off her lap, and charged back toward the large stone manor, quite frantic! Several wavy brown locks of hair slipped loose from the braid at the back of her head, but she could not fix it and run at the same time. It would have to wait until she had a chance, preferable *before* the head cook, Madam Tisza, realized that she had lost track of time and was two hours late. It was a first for her. She was not certain if she would be dressed down something fierce, like the repeat offenders, or simply given a strict warning. She dearly hoped for the latter. There had been recent talk of dismissal as punishment!

She threw herself at the frame of the open doorway, using it to halt her momentum, and quickly caught her breath. She straightened her hair, tucked the braid under her cap as she replaced it, hid the book in a large pocket on the underside of her apron for safe keeping, slipped into the cavernous kitchen, wound her way through the other servants without a word, and dove into the large room that housed her assigned profession. The fire under the large cauldron had died down during her absence. She tossed on a few more logs and stirred

The Carriage Returns

it back up to bring the water inside the cauldron to a boil again. While she waited, she wrenched the plug out of the bottom of the first stone basin that she worked in, draining the dirty water through the pipe on the underside and well beyond the edge of his Lordship's land. She dipped her large ladle into the cauldron of cold water beside her and used it to rinse out the last of the soap and lingering scum from the bottom. She replaced the plug, hacked a new chunk off her current soap block, dropped it into the bottom, filled a bucket carefully with the very hot water, poured that into the basin, added enough cold water until she could stick her hands in without scalding herself, and began to work her way through the vast stacks of filthy dishes on the counters and floor within the room.

    She despised her job, scrubbing away with a coarse brush and rag. However, until she could finally prove her worth, she could never even hope for a better position. The trouble was that no matter how hard she scrubbed or how well she cleaned them now, she never was acknowledged for her improvement. The first couple of years when she began, she alternated with other girls. If anyone fell behind, the person scrubbed for an extra day for each day she fell behind. She had fallen behind so much then that she became constantly stuck with the unsavory task more often than not. Then months rolled by, the other girls were given new, better positions, and she was still the scullery maid. She had been at the position for seven years. Other girls came to assist when there was far more work than she could handle, or it was her resting day. There were a couple of girls that dried and put the various items away, but otherwise, she alone carried the responsibility of the detestable suds that left her hands cracked and sore at the end of the day.

However, today she was thankful that she had been able to resume unnoticed. She worked quickly to catch up where she thought that she should have been had she not been late. She was halfway through the current load, when she heard the clatter of more dishes at the end of the counter. She dried her hands and began to shift the remaining stacks closer to her basin, in order to make room for what else was still to come, when she spied Madam Tisza standing with her arms folded in the doorway to the kitchen. Rennora gasped, then hung her head in shame and braced herself for the unknown punishment that she knew was coming.

"Ella will take over," Madam Tisza firmly stated. "She will get your pay for today as well. You're done. Be late again, and you'll be dismissed permanently."

Rennora could hardly believe her ears! "But the others who have been late repeatedly only received a warning each time!" she pointed out.

The Carriage Returns

"And they will receive the same treatment if they do it again from now on," the head cook sternly declared. "Understood?"

Rennora nodded in defeat. It was most unfair, but it was her life. She was the bottom of the serving ranks and easily replaced, while anyone else's position would take time and training. She began to leave, when she remembered the book that she still had tucked under the safety of her apron.

She showed it to Madam Tisza and shyly asked, "May I return this to the lower library before I go?"

The older woman snatched it out of her hand with a firm, "*No*. I will. No more books for two weeks."

It stung. Yet, Rennora said nothing. What could she say? Anything that came to mind would simply make matters worse. She headed through the kitchen towards the outer door. She could feel all eyes on her as the whispers of what had occurred followed her. She dragged her feet across the extensive grounds, sore at the injustice of it, and through the small gate that bordered the land. She sighed heavily once she came to the small town that lay about a mile from his lordship's house. She resolved not to be late ever again. It seemed like a simple enough solution to her trouble, but she would wager that it would not be the end of the matter by far.

Beastly Cycle

As Rennora passed by the market, she heard a commotion in the town's square. She joined the crowd gathering around the founding father's tall statue of stone, curious as to the source. The other townsfolk were in a bustle over the news that *the* carriage had been seen on its way to town. She hoped that Conadora, a wealthy merchant's daughter, was safe. She made her way to the front of the crowd where she waited and watched beside the worried parents clinging to each other near his lordship's eldest children. The prince and his carriage that the girl rode in were not ordinary, or so everyone had been told Rennora's entire life. The legend that spoke of his cursed predicament had fascinated her for years, but seemed so muddled with each person or chosen lady's telling. It was so terribly similar to her favorite book that she was almost certain she could assist the next lady chosen. She only wanted a bit more information to be completely sure…

Every several months or so, an unadorned black carriage, drawn by four horses with no driver or attendants, came to one of the villages or towns surrounding the forbidden forest, seeking that single, fortunate lady that would have her turn in attempting to break the curse on the ruler-to-be. Otherwise, he was doomed to never claim his throne and die a monster of some kind. The carriage had favored this town once again, over the last two

The Carriage Returns

years, taking a total of three ladies thus far, with Conadora as the latest. Each time, the girl was returned unharmed and dressed in the clothing in which she had left. The odd thing was the story each one had told upon her recovery. They ranged from being locked in a small room and given little to eat to attending a grand ball in rags with no one else there. Two things they both agreed on though, the ruined castle was perched on the edge of a cliff, ready to fall over at the slightest wind, and there were no riches to be found anywhere. The structure, height, and even the layout of the castle itself changed with the teller. Rennora was determined to hear what Conadora had to say for herself this time, since she had not been present at any of the previous girls' journeys or their returns.

    Rennora spotted the carriage entering the main thoroughfare! A hush fell over the people. The transport maintained a steady pace until it drew closer. It then slowed to a halt on the edge of the square, while the people remained near the statue. It was not very large, only enough room for four people to sit comfortably inside, nor was it in the best of shape. It had signs of wear all over. Yet, the wheels were sound, and the horses appeared well cared for. Her eyes shifted to her fellow townsfolk. The people watched and waited in the mounting tension. They did not dare approach it, or it would rip the girl off her feet and back inside with an invisible force, then bolt with its precious cargo. The family would have to wait another two weeks for her next attempt to return. No one wished that.

The carriage creaked open. A set of small folding stairs at the bottom of the doorway flipped down of their own accord. A girl of seventeen with green eyes, long brown hair, and slightly tanned skin, dressed in a pale yellow dress that brushed the ground, descended from it. She took a couple of steps towards the crowd, then simply stood there in a daze, her eyes unable to focus on any one thing, while the stairs retracted and the door closed behind her. The poor girl seemed like she was ready to faint. Rennora shifted her weight, so she could rush to her aid if needed. She knew that the girl did not care for her much, but Conadora appeared to require all the assistance that she could get. The horses must have sensed Rennora's intent. All four heads turned and gazed directly at her! She froze under their scrutiny for several minutes. They then slowly scanned the crowd. The strange thing was that all of the horses' eyes seemed gentle towards her. To everyone else, they cast a steely gaze, challenging even a single person to make one tiny move as they met each one straight in the eye. She wondered why that was, when a sudden movement caught her attention!

Conadora took one shaky step in the heavy silence. Then another. She continued staggering

The Carriage Returns

forward until she was within arm's reach, well away from the carriage, and then paused, swaying on the spot. The horses stamped their hooves and promptly charged off down the road. The spell over the town shattered in an instant! Conadora's eyes rolled upwards, while her legs collapsed from under her. Her mother stood there with her hands over her mouth in horror! Rennora snatched the girl's arm as her father caught her body before she could crash onto the hard, stone road. The satin brocade of the girl's dress made it difficult for him to scoop her up into his arms. However, he managed. Yet, her fuller skirt still trailed on the ground and threatened to trip him. Rennora gathered it up and carried it as she kept pace beside them all the way back to the family's house. The crowd followed at a modest distance, eager to hear whatever story the poor girl had to offer. Rennora bit down her irritation. Could they not give the family some peace, for pity's sake?! She then recalled her own reason for leaping ahead of everyone to assist. She blushed in shame, knowing full well that she had no right to berate them.

    The merchant kicked the bottom of his door a couple of times to announce his presence, since his hands were full, and slipped inside sideways the second it was opened, with Rennora and his wife close behind. He snapped at the steward to impale anyone that dared to invade his threshold uninvited, send for a healer at once, and bring up a hot drink for his wife, before he fought his way up the wider stairs that led to the upper level of the family's home. The additional weight of Conadora threatened to send the pair crashing back down! Rennora noticed his predicament and freed up a hand from the bundle of skirt so she could steady him by his arm. They made it to the upper landing where he continued his mad dash into what Rennora guessed to be Conadora's personal chambers and a second large room within. There, he gently laid his poor daughter on a pink satin coverlet on her large bed. Rennora released her self-appointed task and slipped to the side wall without a word, fully expecting to be thrown out at any moment. She watched him pat Conadora's hand and cheek in turn as he tried to wake her or show some sign that she was unharmed. Nothing. Her mother tried as well, but had no more success than her husband. She fell apart over her daughter's still form, unable to maintain any semblance of composure for a moment longer. The merchant then spied Rennora's silent form. He hauled her firmly over to the bedside.

"Watch over my precious jewel until I get back," he commanded.

Before Rennora could answer, he gathered the hysterical woman tenderly into his arms and guided her through the outer doorway. After a few minutes, she could hear him thundering down the stairs.

The Carriage Returns

"Of course," she told the empty hallway.

She sighed and straightened the slumbering girl's skirts, then sat on a nearby padded bench. It was a pleasant room filled with elegant, sturdy furniture, some of it covered in elaborate brocades in a soft pink or cream, and two other doors on the far wall. The afternoon sunlight streamed in the clear glass window, framed by soft curtains of pink and edged in a delicate cream embroidery. She was out of place with her simple clothing and lowly station in life. She hoped that the merchant would return quickly and both ladies would recover well from their ordeal. Her wait had not been long, when he returned with the local healer. She darted back to the wall to remain out of the way while the elderly man set to work. He felt the unconscious girl's brow, pried her eyelid open, and then held her wrist in his gentle hand for a couple of minutes. He pulled out a strange tube-like thing from deep within his large bag and used it to listen to Conadora's shallow breathing and various places on her chest. Rennora and the father waited patiently.

The healer then traded his instrument for several glass jars, a few smaller pouches, a mortar, and a pestle. He added different amounts of assorted dried herbs, liquids, and other things from the jars and pouches into his stone mortar and ground them together into a thick paste. When he was done, he scooped a generous helping of the

Beastly Cycle

mixture on his first two fingers and held it under Conadora's nose without touching her. It must have been a very potent aroma, because before Rennora could count to three, Conadora suddenly heaved, her green eyes popped open, and she flung his hand away! She coughed and gasped a few times, fighting to gain her breath back! Everyone else was relieved to see her responding. The girl collapsed onto her pillow, breathless and exhausted. It took a couple of attempts for the older man to gain her full attention.

"Mademoiselle?" he addressed her firmly. She stared into his light brown ones through glassy eyes of her own. "How are you feeling?"

"W…where am I?" she stammered, looking quite perplexed.

The merchant shifted closer. "You are home, my blossom."

The thought seemed a difficult one for her to grasp. "Are you certain? He promised me a safe journey home after my stay in the village was complete."

"What village?" her father demanded.

She opened and closed her thin mouth a few times, lost for words. She breathed deeply and tried again. "The village outside of the castle's lands, where all the nobility rest when they are recovering from their exotic or extensive traveling. I have to remain there until the carriage comes for me! I must

The Carriage Returns

return to the village, or I will not be able to journey home!"

She attempted to rise to her feet, but both men gently pushed her back onto her soft bedding.

"No, no, ma petit," the father insisted. "It has already brought you back! You are safely home with me."

She stared at him, shocked, for several minutes. Rennora could feel the awkwardness from the men as they waited for the girl to come to her senses. She hungrily licked her lips a couple of times. Her expression shifted from confusion to hopeful.

"Y-you mean I made it?" she asked, desperate and clinging to her father's outstretched arms.

He nodded earnestly. She gazed at the floor, stunned, then collapsed, sobbing hard onto his elaborate green velvet tunic. The healer whispered something into the merchant's ear, packed up his bag, and slipped out to leave the girl in peace. Rennora stood forgotten against the wall. She shifted her feet to leave as well, when Conadora raised her head.

"Oh, Papa!" she wept. "It was awful!"

He stroked her hair. "There, there my heart's delight. Tell me all about it…"

"I remember going to the castle like I was supposed to, because I did not wish for anything to happen to you and Mamma. It was horrid! It was

Beastly Cycle

crumbling away before my very eyes! There had to be only the entrance hall and a few rooms left! There was no reason that anyone could possibly have declared that would have forced me to remain there any longer! Not with the upper floors missing, and the rest ready to collapse on my head at any moment! Oh, I could not do it for more than two nights, Papa!"

"Of course not! No one with any sort of sense would ask that of such a delicate flower as you. Did you speak to his highness of this? What did he say?"

"I informed someone and then…" She stared at the floor again. She seemed to be groping for something that was not there anymore. "I think he understood and… something about an apology… There was a brilliant green light within the flawless facets. I remember the carriage taking off again to somewhere nice, I think. There was some sort of ball with an orange, hairy animal man of some kind presiding, but no one else attended. He never danced with me though. He simply stood there, watching… So terribly heartbroken… A song that tore my heart in two and vanished before I could locate who was playing…" She rubbed her head, a single tear trickled unchecked down her cheek. "I am sorry, I do not recall anything else." She was so desperately lost again.

The Carriage Returns

"Did you see the prince?" Rennora suddenly inquired without thinking.

The merchant glared at her for daring to interrupt! She promptly fell silent again.

"The prince?" Conadora said. She thought deeply for several minutes before hesitantly responding. "I do not know. There was this person coming out of the castle, but I never got a good look at him, or at least," she paused once more before continuing, "I do not think I did…" She rubbed her forehead. "I am sorry. It does not make any sense to me either. I do not wish to discuss it any further. My head is paining me very much."

The ache and tears evident in her eyes tore at her father's heart. He nodded, kissed her on the head, settled her back onto the bed, and promised to send her maid to her to tend her. He slipped out of the room. Rennora curtsied and promptly followed after him.

He closed the door softly behind them and snapped at Rennora, "Do not speak a word of this to *anyone*! Do you understand?"

Rennora promised without hesitation. No one would listen to her in the first place, and she loathed gossip, unlike many others in the town.

"Good," he replied, satisfied. "My poor girl has already been through enough without the entire town adding their damage to it as well. This could ruin her chances of a good marriage if it was known

Beastly Cycle

that the prince refused to even see her, or her mind has been addled from all of this. Not a single word, or I will have you before his Lordship and locked in his prison before you could blink. Understand?!"

Rennora nodded.

"My steward will see you out the back way," he dismissed her with a wave of his hand and left her to it.

Chapter 2
~ Beauty ~

Broken Heart

Rennora meandered toward the edge of town to give herself time to mull over what Conadora had said. She wondered why the prince had not allowed the girl a true chance at freeing him. Could he see into her heart and was disappointed at what was there? Did her beauty not appeal to him? Did her criticism of his home offend him so terribly? Did she not have the right air about her? A few more potential reasons presented themselves as well, with each one more outlandish and ridiculous than the previous. She paused in her thoughts when she came to the founder's statue and turned her gaze down the road that led out of town. In as little as two days, or as long as several months, the carriage would return. Its door would open on its own once more. Not even a tiny gust would stir within the town's borders. A single, deep red rose petal would drift out, carried by a soft breeze to land on the next lady who was destined to try breaking the curse, no matter where she was. The carriage then would charge away, allowing her a limited time to prepare

Beastly Cycle

for her departure. Once it returned, the fortunate one would have two days to enter the waiting carriage. Not a second more. Otherwise, someone dear to her would be struck down sick for each day that she kept the prince waiting. Rennora wanted to hope that she would be chosen, but it seemed that his highness had a taste only for ladies of at least some rank and quality. She sighed, letting her wistful thinking be simply that.

    She turned toward the lane that would take her to the house where she resided, when she heard a loud snorting laugh. She stiffened as multiple feminine giggles joined in. She glanced around and spied two of her fellow servants amid a small crowd of friends from various low ranks in town. They had fallen silent at the sight of her gazing directly at them. The girls were knowingly smirking in her direction. One of the boys around Rennora's age was eyeing her appreciatively, until the girl beside him kicked his shin. He quickly averted his eyes with an innocent look to his square face. The other boy bore a melancholy expression in Rennora's direction. Rennora could not recall his name, unfortunately. He was one of the few that was kind to her on the sparse occasions that they had spoken. Her fellow female servant from his lordship's house nudged him angrily to divert his attention away from Rennora. She promptly snapped something at him! However, the male servant heatedly retorted

Broken Heart

as he glared viciously at each and every person within the group in turn. They stood frozen, shocked and indignant! He pointedly turned and stormed away. The girl resignedly called for him to wait. He simply dismissed her plea with an angry wave and continued up the main street! The other girls closed in and began talking over each other to the injured female servant. The furious servant then glared vehemently at Rennora as though placing the blame for the boy's angry departure entirely on her.

    Rennora quietly left, confused and saddened herself by what she had seen. She was quite certain that she had been the subject of the crowd's conversation. They were quite delighted in her reprimand. That was clear. However, she could not understand why. She was not the favorite and had never done anything vicious to any of them. She pulled out of her dismal musings when she noticed a couple dressed in their finest, clearly members of nobility, heading her way in the lane. She stepped to the side and curtsied low as they passed to show her respect and lower station. The gentleman nodded in her direction briefly, then ignored her further. The lady on his arm sniffed, tightened her grip on his arm, and increased their pace until they turned the corner into the town proper. Rennora sighed heavily. The nobility were far more civil to the other servants than to her, with both lords and ladies nodding their heads and smiling in polite

Beastly Cycle

acknowledgement to them. Why was always the question. She had no answer to that and no one to confide in for answers. She continued to the house where she resided once more, heartbroken.

It did not take her much longer to reach it. It was a sturdy place with stone walls that contained just three rooms, a matching floor, and a thatched roof that kept the weather out. Flowers bloomed on either side of the doorway with a vegetable garden, a berry patch, some other flowers, and a few nut trees in the moderate land behind it. She slipped through the shabby front door, past the modest main room, and fled straight to the smaller room she shared with Arissera to avoid speaking to anyone. She knew that if she paused for even a moment, she would be severely berated over what had happened, along with a probable beating by Mistress LaZella, the older servant woman who had taken her in when she lost her parents many years ago. The woman was due home any minute. Rennora could not bare anything she had to say right now.

She let the thin curtain over her doorway fall closed behind her and flopped down on her straw stuffed mattress on the floor, which occupied one side of the room. She stretched herself out with her head in front of her small box, which contained what few treasures she owned, with her feet at the rear wall, so she could gaze at the pink cloud painted sky beyond the window in the center. Her thoughts drifted like the setting sun, inch by inch, first touching one thing and then another, until the sky began to darken. She then rolled onto her side with one last thought flitting through her mind before she dozed off. She was going to see Fistorik tomorrow. Perhaps he had changed his mind about his desire to remain only friends. All she could do was hope and be patient. Perhaps, things would go well for her with him. After all, things could not possibly become any worse than they already were. Right?

    Rennora awoke early the next morning coated in a heavy sweat, trembling and panting for air, like she had run several miles instead of just slumbering in her bed. She wrapped her blanket tighter around her, seeking some form of comfort from its rough presence, until her shaking ceased. Her dream had been so vivid! This mysterious being, draped from head to toe in a dark cloak, stood before her, ominous and silent. She was absolutely petrified in its presence, unable to move in the slightest! It slowly drew a familiar sword and pointed the weapon right at her heart, the tip barely touching her lace up bodice.

    You will be mine! was the forceful thought that entered her head! She was certain it had not come from her!

Beastly Cycle

She swallowed against the lump of fear within her throat. She tried to shift her weight and found the task quite simple. She promptly bolted! She did her best to maintain as much distance between her and her human pursuer as she could, or to lose it by suddenly changing directions. However, it kept up with her easily every step of the way! Then, all of a sudden, a large, coppery orange creature flew out of the forest and slammed into the person! She watched, frozen and horrified, as the human fought the creature for its life! She screamed when the orange thing drew first blood from the being's outstretched arm!

She clasped her head in an attempt to force the gruesome images from her mind, stumbled to the sink in the main room, and splashed some water from a waiting bucket onto her face to refresh herself. Feeling better, she debated on more sleep until she noticed a touch of color that caressed the horizon outside. There was no time left for such a luxury. She took a rag, moistened it, and washed all of the sweat off of her as best she could before she dressed for the day in the fading darkness.
Grabbing a hunk of bread and cheese, she set off for his lordship's manor. She slowed her walk through town and savored not only her meager breakfast, but the chirping of the crickets around her as well, serenading anyone that cared to listen to their sweet sound. She reached the servant's entrance nearly an

hour later. She brushed off any lingering crumbs to make herself more presentable and hurried straight into the kitchen where the dishes from the early working servants' breakfast awaited her. She began without delay. She continued without pause until well after the main house had had luncheon. When it was the servants' turn for the midday meal, she halted.

    After a word from Madam Tisza forbidding her to leave the house for her meal as an additional punishment, she joined the others at a long, well-worn table in the kitchen and ate in silence. The talk around her this time was, of course, Conadora's return and who would most likely be the next lady. The other girls teased and speculated, each suggesting someone with a merry laugh, until Rennora was snidely informed that she should be next, since no one desired her presence in town in the first place. Madam Tisza curtly admonished the offender! However, Rennora kept her silence as she shut out the voices within the room. The words slashed through her like a hot dagger. What hurt the most was that it was true. None of the other girls cared for her or anything that interested her, such as books, fact or lore, gardens, and music. They preferred the latest clothing stylings, who was courting who, who was still unattached, and whose courtship had turned for the worst and why.

Beastly Cycle

Rennora ate quickly and returned to the dishes until her turn for a rest late in the afternoon. As she dried her hands, she was glad that she had Fistorik's company to brighten her day. They had been courting until about two months ago when he ended it for some mysterious reason. After she had gotten his heartbreaking letter telling her so, she had confronted him. He had quickly explained his desire to remain simply friends. She did not want to make a fool of herself over him, especially knowing others' great delight they would take in her humiliation, but she still harbored a secret hope that she would eventually win him back. For now, she was content to be his friend.

She soon darted out the door and headed to her favorite oak tree to find Fistorik already waiting for her. Her heart leaped at the sight of the twenty-year-old captain in the local guards. His dark blonde hair, carelessly tossed to one side, made him look mischievous and dashing. His green eyes, however, were somber this time instead of playful.

"Something wrong, dear captain?" she asked him, concerned.

"I've, uh, something that I need to tell you," he replied in a gentle voice.

This was very unlike him. He usually had a ready smile and good cheer. As he lowered his gaze, she felt a tingle in the pit of her stomach, a fear mingling with nervousness rising to her throat.

Broken Heart

"Is it something I've done?" she asked.

He shook his head, refusing to meet her eyes.

"May I ask what then?" she cautiously dared.

Fistorik opened and closed his mouth a few times, reminding her of one of the many fish that swam in his lordship's beloved pond. She stifled a merry grin at the thought and waited. He tried one more time, but could not bring himself to say it. He handed her a small scroll with a shaky hand, whispered a desperate apology, not quite meeting her gaze, then thundered away. Puzzled, she read it. There, in his untidy writing, he apologized over and over again for most of the parchment's length. He then explained that he had been courting another girl for the past six weeks, and she had accepted his proposal of marriage. They planned on wedding within three months.

Rennora's world, her hopes, her dreams shattered in those few words! She collapsed to her knees, devastated! She gazed up in time to see a lovely girl slip her arm into Fistorik's. He beamed warmly at her as they stood on the edge of the estate, his heart in his eyes. They soon walked away together in joyful bliss. Rennora's vision blurred. She sat there, tears streaming down her face. She then quietly sobbed into her apron, the wretched parchment crumpled in her fist. After the space of what felt like many lifetimes, she heard footsteps approaching her. She hurriedly dried her eyes and

Beastly Cycle

rose to her feet. She never liked people seeing her so upset.

"What is wrong?" a pleasant, baritone voice asked.

She saw a pair of well-made, tall boots slip into her view. She kept her head down and shook her head, refusing to speak to Wescar, a minor lord's son.

"You know you can tell me anything," he pressed.

She almost snorted at his words. She could not tell him anything without the entire town hearing about it. He never had any discretion when it came to keeping secrets, even when they were courting a few years ago. She watched him shift his feet slightly. He then softly chuckled.

"I told you that he was horrid for you," he firmly stated. "He left you first chance he had for the next girl that crossed his path. I would never do that to you. You hold my heart still… You know this."

She could hear him grinning at her misfortune.

No, you simply lie, can't be trusted, and try to gently force me into things that I'm not ready for, she thought.

Wescar stepped toward her. "My offer still holds, my sweet wady," he whispered in a high, baby-ish voice that he thought was endearing.

Broken Heart

She, however, found it quite irritating. She had asked him nicely, even told him sternly, to cease in the past, but he never listened. Yet another reason that she had ended their courtship. It did not matter to her that he was low nobility, set to inherit everything. He was not the kind of person with whom she wanted to share her life. She dearly wished that he would turn his persistent affections and attentions elsewhere. She had no desire to even speak with him with the gaping hole persisting within her chest at the moment. She certainly could not manage the demands of both and maintain any sort of hold on her sanity, so she fled toward the manor and the solitude of the dishes. She could feel him charging close behind. He called her name! She stubbornly refused to answer him. He caught her arm just as she reached the kitchen doorway.

"I've given you my answer already," she reminded him, through frustrated tears. "It *has* not and *will* not change."

"Bear in mind, my sweet wady, that no one will ever cherish you like I do." He leaned in closer as he whispered, "You are within a few years of reaching the age where no one else will consider you for even courtship, let alone marriage."

"Is there a problem?" she suddenly heard someone demand sternly!

Beastly Cycle

The pair leapt apart at the sight of Madam Tisza, the manor's cook, and Quorrick, her husband, standing within the kitchen entry.

"I ask again, is there a problem?" the large groundskeeper rumbled in his deep voice, glaring at the young man.

Rennora shook her head, lowering her eyes so he could not see her misery.

"Then return to your duties," Madam Tisza demanded, stepping out of the way.

Rennora whispered a most heartfelt thank you to them both as she slipped past, grateful for their timely interference, and dashed into the scullery. Alone at last, she stared at the forgotten parchment, still clutched in her fist. Tears fell unchecked until she could not stand the sight of the cursed thing for another second, so she flung it into the dying fire and viciously stirred the blaze back up! Her heart still felt like it had been torn mercilessly from her chest, but watching the pale parchment turn black and wither away to ash, then nothing, made her feel slightly better. She sobbed until she had no tears left, dried her eyes, and immersed herself in the dishes silently. For once, Rennora was delighted that no one paid her any heed. It saved her the trouble of having to invent something to explain her wretched state and risk falling apart again.

After she was relieved for the day, she made her solitary way back in the early evening as the sun

Broken Heart

descended in the sky. She halted on the path leading to the house, her mind growing as numb as her heart. She stood there for several minutes, wondering if it was even worth walking through the door, and not for the first time. She gazed at the thick forest behind the house's rear grounds, dark and daunting, yet inviting at the same time. Everyone had been forbidden to enter it by the ruling high lord himself many years ago. It was the favorite hunting grounds of an immense monster. Five people had been found dead in the boundary ditch after daring to trespass within it over the years, but once people had begun to maintain their distance in the past thirty-eight years, it had remained quiet, like it was waiting for a single person to dare another try. She wished that she was brave enough to flee into its mysterious depths to escape the world in which she was trapped, whatever the risk. It had to be a far better existence than her current life…

    Then suddenly, Rennora heard her name roared from within the house! She sighed heavily. She was in serious trouble again. It did not matter which task she was given or how well she completed it, it was never enough or always done wrong to Mistress LaZella. She stepped across the threshold into the central room, resigned to her fate. A much older woman with snowy, thin hair thundered up to her and dressed her down quite

Beastly Cycle

fiercely in her raspy voice! Rennora barely listened, hanging her head in dismay.

Mistress LaZella's words pierced through the girl's thoughts, "You should be quite grateful for my generous nature for taking you into my precious home, all those years ago, when no one else among the townsfolk would! Need I remind you that there are an awful *lot* of other poor, suffering souls in town who would kill for such a privilege, who would be far more thankful to me than you have been! Your constant negligent and careless attitude is making the scant money that I receive from the town counsel for my *generous* care of you barely worth the effort! Do tell me why it is that *you* alone cause me so much trouble, while Thevesta and Arissera, who are *also* orphans that reside here, have been such obedient pleasures for years, and how *dare* you bring shame to me and my home through *your* constant stupidity and selfishness!" Mistress LaZella persisted on and on in her tirade, frequently repeating herself, until she had yelled herself almost hoarse half an hour later. She then narrowed her eyes and snarled, "You had best think on what I said and fix your behavior *immediately*, or you *will* no longer have a home to return to, spinster or not…"

Rennora watched the woman's feet promptly storm out of view through her despair. *Tomorrow*, she promised herself. She would be free then to figure out what she had wrecked, or forgotten, and

Broken Heart

quickly correct it. One of the girls declared something about time to eat. Rennora muttered that she was not hungry, then quietly slipped past them, through the curtain, and into her shared room, before things could worsen for her. She eased open the faded shutters in the window and rested her head on her arms on the cool sill, letting the sweet night air embrace her, while the crickets serenaded each other. She was relieved that the day was finally spent. It had been one of the worst ones of her life! Her hopes of true love and a happy marriage had walked away with someone else forever… She could not understand what on earth she had done to drive Fistorik away permanently! Could it have been Arissera or Thevesta? She did not think so. He had rarely acknowledged the two other girls she resided with and informed her almost six months ago that it was her, not them, that he was courting.

    Tears welled up again. She was so lost, hurt, and confused that she did not know what to think anymore! She could hear the scraping of chairs against the stone floor. Supper was done. The others would tidy up, seat themselves around the fire, and chatter away until exhaustion drove them to their beds. She was willing to wager that they would have heard about Fistorik's chosen bride by now. The thought of it enlarged the hole in her chest until she could hardly breathe. Yet, she did have one thing that other girls who had had the same thing happen did not. She had heard about it from him directly, and not someone else. The notion took the edge off her pain, but did not deaden it. She soon heard the curtain shift behind her. She maintained her focus firmly outside.

"Are you alright?" gently inquired Arissera, the older girl who shared the room with her.

Rennora could not bring herself to dare to speak of it yet, so she said nothing.

"I heard what happened…" Arissera pressed.

Rennora's vision blurred. She wiped her eyes with her sleeve.

"Just remember that there's plenty of fish in the sea, as the saying goes. You'll catch a better man next time."

The girl then left Rennora to her thoughts.

"There may be other fish in the sea, but none are quite like he," Rennora whispered to the watchful stars above, her voice quivering a little. She gazed at the twinkling lights and took comfort in their quiet presence. She had done this many times over the years. When she was very small, she used to pretend they were her friends because she had none of her own. She could have used a real friend who truly listened and could help her with her pain, instead of only telling her to ignore her heartache and move on. She had a few friends, but they had their own troubles in life and rarely paid attention to hers, so she cast her burden to the

Broken Heart

emptiness of the night sky, wishing desperately that someone would hear her.

"I'm quite tired of giving my heart away only to have it slashed each time," she told her favorite star. "Either he doesn't return my affections, and I get laughed at by others, or when I find someone that can take me away from this living nightmare, he isn't what he pretends to be." She sighed heavily. "Or he simply walks away forever… I can't do this anymore. I'm going to grant love one last attempt. If it fails to be true for a good reason, then that's it. I'm through and will accept that I'll stand alone for the rest of my life. No more…"

She dried her face and cast her eyes down towards her arm still resting on the ledge when she noticed a large petal of some sort had landed on her hand. She picked it up gently, wondering where it had come from. She could not tell what color it was in the moonlight, but she was sure that it was not from the tiny garden in the land below her window. The shape and size were all wrong. It looked like a rose petal, but the closest ones that she knew of were at the manor where she served, and those were all red or dark pink. This one was far too pale. That, and it would have taken quite a massive gale to bring those rose petals to her, and her window was facing the wrong direction even then! Her gaze shifted to the forbidden forest beyond the cultivated plants. She had never seen any rose bushes there in

Beastly Cycle

any of the times that she had spent staring into its depths, trying to work through life. She set the petal on her personal box, readied herself for bed, climbed under the bed clothes, and examined it again. It was softer than any she had ever touched and brought a touch of warmth to her despair. She wished that she could behold the beauty of what flower it belonged to, just for a moment. She tucked it under her pillow and laid there with her back to the room, letting her mind empty so she would not dream, as Arissera crept in once more. Rennora's eyes slipped closed of their own accord. She soon drifted off....

She stood in a vast field of strange flowers. A figure wrapped in a long, forest green cloak stood a few yards away. She did not know who he was, but knew that he meant her no harm. Somehow... He raised a single, pale hand and beckoned her closer. She did not move. A wind suddenly whipped around them! She could have sworn that she heard a whispered plea within the fiercely moving air, desperately begging her to save him before it was too late!

Chapter 3
~ Beauty ~

Enough

    Rennora awoke early the next morning, tired, but calmer. As long as she did not think of *him*, she hoped that she could make it through the day. She lay on her bedding in the empty room for almost half an hour, trying not to contemplate the miserable hours ahead, before she finally forced herself up. As she dressed, she felt something brush across her bare foot. Her gaze dropped to the pale petal from last night, resting on the chilly floor in the dim light. She slipped it into her apron's pocket for later study, tip toed into the kitchen for a quiet bite to eat, and then headed outside to tame the weeds that she had been her downfall the day before.

    A couple of hours later brought the sun fully up and found her ripping up the last of the troublesome plants that were attempting to invade the precious vegetable patch. She gathered up the offenders along with some dead branches she had trimmed from one of the larger berry bushes. She then hauled them all to the mulch pile at the edge of the modest grounds, taking great care not to set so

Beastly Cycle

much as a single toe in the wide, deep ditch that bordered the trees, when she had the strange and unwelcomed feeling that she was being watched! Friend or foe, she did not know. All of a sudden, she heard a loud, deep growl from the foliage in front of her. Terrified, she stumbled backward! A twig snapped somewhere behind her! She whipped around in time to catch the edge of a worn, gray cloth, like a cloak or something, disappearing around the far corner of the house.

    She dashed to the opposite wall of the small structure, snatched up a large empty bucket, and fled to the well in the next field for safety from both! Once she was there, she braced herself against the rough edge of the well's large, stone exterior and calmed herself with great effort. As she drew the water for the waiting plants, she pondered things over. She was convinced that more had happened a moment ago than met the eyes. She really was not certain which had made her more nervous, the massive sounding animal that could have ripped her to shreds, or the persistent stranger that she was sure had been spying on her yet again, before the individual had vanished! She decided that she really did not want to meet either one. She had enough troubles in life as it was.

    She filled her bucket and dragged it off the wide ledge with a grunt. It took all of her efforts not to spill the sloshing water as she waddled her way

Enough

back toward the garden, one awkward step at a time. Suddenly, something hurtled her into the ground! The bucket flew out of her hands! It landed three or four feet away, splashing water in all directions. She gritted her teeth in fury. She did not even bother to gaze upward to see who the culprit was who had crashed into her. She breathed deeply to compose herself instead. She then retrieved her bucket calmly, doing her best to ignore Thevesta sauntering past the well, enjoying her handy work. Arissera had told Rennora over and over not to let the larger girl infuriate her. It only fueled and emboldened her tormentor. She headed back toward the well with her eyes on the ground to focus herself, when she heard a splash come from it. She glanced up, very apprehensive. Thevesta seemed particularly pleased with herself this time. Rennora then noticed the rope that connected to the other bucket for hauling water from deep within the well dangling freely! Her face fell. It had been sawed clean through. Thevesta caressed a large kitchen knife in her hand and chuckled as she meandered arrogantly toward the house.

  Furious, Rennora quietly stormed over to collect the spare bucket that she kept near the side of the house. She tied it to the remaining length of rope and refilled her large bucket once again. She almost hauled it to the plants, when something ripped it out of her hands, scrapping her knuckles in

Beastly Cycle

the process! She shook them in pain. They were raw and skinned in various places. She awkwardly torn off a strip from the bottom of her apron and wrapped them, then she spotted the well's rope had been sawed off completely from the handle! Thevesta stood near her, her arms folded across her chest, grinning. The bucket laid on its side by her feet.

"What will you do about it?" the larger girl challenged in her nasally voice as she shoved her.

Rennora glared venomously at her, but kept her silence, fighting to master control of herself. Her anger approached a boiling point. She knew that if she did not pull herself together, and quick, she might do something she would regret. Thevesta chuckled at Rennora's obvious dilemma. She then slammed Rennora into the rough ground. The slender girl skidded a short ways. She winced at the sight of her shredded sleeve and blood dripping down her arm. It took her a moment to sit up from the pain. Rennora kept her eyes on her wounds as she heard Thevesta step closer and closer to her, laughing all the while. She slipped her hand onto a nearby rock, just smaller than her fist, and clutched it for support, both physically and emotionally.

Thevesta then leaned over her. "Still the weakling as ever," she sneered with a grin.

Rennora glared into Thevesta's cold eyes. She saw the other girl raising her fist to strike. Her

Enough

vision flashed red! She swung her clenched fist at Thevesta's head! The girl collapsed into a heap beside Rennora, her eyes rolling back into her head.

Rennora stared in shock, unable to believe what she had just done! Her slate blue eyes drifted to the stone still in her hand. She gasped in horror and flung the vile thing away from her as far as she could! She rose to her feet, frantically scanning around her as her thoughts scrambled over each other for what to do! She then heard Mistress LaZella calling for *both* of them. She froze! Her heart plummeted. She knew that she would be in for a serious beating over this. Thevesta soon groaned and began to stir. Rennora gasped in relief! Thevesta staggered to her feet. She shook her head a couple of times to clear it.

Rennora almost said something, when she heard Thevesta viciously snarl, "You'll pay dearly for that…"

Rennora could only watch as Thevesta teetered back to the house, calling weakly for Mistress LaZella. She knew that things just went from bad to miles worse. She dropped to the ground, tears streaming down her cheeks in fear. How could she possibly mend this?! Apologizing would not do. It would just get thrown back in her teeth and intensify things further! Remaining silent would yield the same results for her…

Beastly Cycle

Suddenly, she heard Mistress's mortified scream pierce the air, "THAT *MURDERER*! ARISSERA! FETCH THE—"

Rennora did not linger to hear the rest. She tore off through the field and along the back of various people's scant lands, until she came to a half-hidden gate of his lordship's land. She hopped over the gate without breaking her stride, raced to her precious sanctuary, grabbed the lower branches, and scrambled midway up the sturdy tree. She was trapped! She had dared to lay a hand on Mistress LaZella's favorite! It did not matter that it was done in self-defense. In the older woman's eyes, Thevesta could do no wrong. Rennora knew that she would be beat with that hated switch until she had not only angry red welts on her legs and back, but bruises to the point she would barely be able to crawl away. She wanted to tell someone to protect her! Anyone! The trouble was who would believe her? The townsfolk would simply tell her how wonderfully sweet Mistress LaZella and Thevesta were and not to spread such awful lies. She had no one… She trembled at the thought of returning. Her eyes drifted to the forest far beyond his lordship's borders. It was dangerous in there with a monster on the prowl. She rested against the warm bark, her strength spent, and silently wept.

She shimmied down the tree hours later, a hopelessness still weighing heavily on her heart, and

Enough

dragged her feet as she left by the small gate, wondering where she could possibly go. She then recalled that the carriage was due to return any time to select the next lady. She headed toward the town square where the other onlookers were already gathering. She had never heard of the carriage taking volunteers. She decided that if she was not chosen, she would throw herself into it anyways and take her chances with the cursed prince.

    Rennora stepped onto the paved road surrounding the square when she spotted Mistress LaZella mingling amongst the growing crowd, happily chatting away without a care in the world. The girl halted immediately! Her heart pounded within her trembling body. She prayed that she would not be noticed by the older woman as she slowly stepped backwards. Suddenly, Mistress LaZella's sharp eyes darted to Rennora before she could take a single step further, as though she could sense the girl's thoughts! Mistress LaZella's hard eyes narrowed. She shifted toward Rennora. A guard then crossed in front of the older woman, accidentally bumping into her. He steadied her with an apology. Mistress LaZella spoke with a warm smile until her gaze returned to Rennora. The girl could see the malice staring back at her. Mistress LaZella continued talking pleasantly to the guard. Rennora was terrified that the woman would have the guard arrest her for what happened with

Beastly Cycle

Thevesta. Then suddenly, Mistress LaZella gestured right at her! The guard turned around. Rennora promptly fled down side roads and past houses, until she could not run another step!

    She gasped to catch her breath in a far field near the edge of the town. Her body shook from both fear and exhaustion. She felt fortunate that she had escaped. However, she recalled that she still had nowhere that she could call safe… The forest then caught her attention. She cautiously made her way to the edge of the ditch on its borders, her eyes intent on the lush foliage. She noticed an area in the underbrush that seemed thinner than the rest. She stood there, contemplating the sight before her, when a sudden wind whipped at her hair and clothing! She threw her arms up to protect her face! Once the gust had settled down, she lowered her arms and found herself staring into the trees framing the underbrush in front of her once again. She seriously debated what chance she would have of surviving in there. The thought of being torn apart terrified her, but the knowledge of what certainly awaited her if she stayed was worse still. Yet, the idea of living on her own in the forest, whatever the cost, brought her a feeling of peace…

    She shifted her weight to take a single step into the deep ditch, when all of a sudden, something fluttered out of the forest and drifted downward. She hesitated for a moment, watching its slow

Enough

progress, until it suddenly darted toward her and landed on her dress, just over her heart. She cautiously pulled it off. It looked like a large, pale blue flower petal, softer than anything she had ever touched, and slightly familiar. A younger man's concerned shout from somewhere behind her shattered the stillness! She stashed the petal into her hidden pocket, took a deep breath to steel herself, retreated several steps, then charged as hard as she could, and leapt the ditch!

Chapter 4
~ Beauty ~

Volunteer

Rennora did not quite make it to the top. She managed to grab a hold of a low branch and scrambled up the other side. Her foot slipped on the thick grass as she righted herself. She thrashed her way through the prickly bushes, ignoring the fading voice of Wescar, and stumbled over the rough stones on her bare feet as she wove her way through the forest, seeking to put as much distance behind her as possible. The trees, however, seemed like they had other ideas, blocking her first one way and then another, until she came across a large, dirt road that held some promise.

She paused to catch her breath along the edge, when the sound of hoof beats pulling something heavy trundled toward her. She dove behind the nearest bush and watched the black carriage pass her by. She wondered who the chosen lady was this time as she returned to the task of making her way through the forest to find shelter, while keeping the road in sight as a guide. Would the prince accept two girls at his threshold, or at least, allow her to

Volunteer

serve as the lady's maid until his chosen left, or the curse was broken? Being a servant would at least give Rennora a little time to prepare herself for life in the wilds. She knew that she would definitely require a good knife and oiled cloak as she gazed around for a moment to gain her bearings. She then tried to force her way between several taller bushes, with no other way around, hoping that she would be able to trade for the items when the time came. Somehow... She quickly realized that the foliage demanded her full attention, so she set her thoughts aside. She was almost through when she fell the rest of the way free and landed on her face in a vast clearing. She slowly rolled onto her back, exhausted from her trek. She then noticed something on the edge of her vision. She tilted her head back and spied what appeared to be a partial tower of sorts. She shifted onto her stomach to gain a better view. A small castle of crumbling, dark gray stone barely crested over the immense wall surrounding it.

  She dusted herself off and crossed the barren land for a closer look, but could only see two floors peering above the stone wall. There may have once been more to it long ago. However, time had withered it away. She followed the wall to the nearest corner. A road of gravel ran parallel to the next wall. She continued around until she came to a tall, unruly bush growing close to the wall. She

Beastly Cycle

began to skirt it, when suddenly, she heard the groaning of metal on metal from the other side. She froze! She heard footsteps slapping on what sounded like smooth stone, then halt. She quietly inched her way to where the dense bush hugged the wall. Then suddenly, she heard horses and wheels behind her! She glanced back. The carriage was coming! She shimmied between the bush and the wall until she was well hidden in its foliage. She wondered how she had gotten ahead of the carriage as it slowed a halt just on the other side of the bush.

A male voice warmly greeted, "Welcome, milady, to the home of his royal highness."

A few metallic clicks sounded. A couple of footsteps then crunched on the gravel.

"This cannot be right?!" a bossy female voice demanded. "Where is the rest?"

"I beg your pardon, mademoiselle?"

"Do not play ignorant with me! Where is the grand palace? This place is a complete ruin! There can not be more than eight rooms at most, with the rest in pieces, and half of it is going to fall off the cliff that it is perched near any second! I am not setting one foot in there!"

"I take it that you are refusing your only chance to aid the gentleman that lives there, milady?"

"Yes, if it means residing in that death trap!"

Volunteer

"Very well, milady. As you wish. Please, take this…"

"Why should I?"

"It is a simple gift of gratitude for accepting the master's invitation."

"Well… since he has gone to all this trouble. It would be rude of me to refuse such a generous and beautiful gift. What a lovely emerald pendant it is…"

Rennora heard a surprised gasp! Some gravel then crunched for a few seconds.

"Remove your hands from me at once!" the girl snarled.

"Pardon me, milady. You fainted for a moment."

"Where am I? What is this place?"

"Some old ruins that I thought might interest you while you stretched on your journey to Sennelton."

"Sennelton? Is that where I am headed? Things seem slightly hazy at the moment…"

"Yes, mademoiselle. It is a charming town where all the nobility often stay for a few weeks of rest after the excitements of exotic traveling and numerous balls with dear friends of the court."

"Yes… of course. Let us go then. No time to waste!"

Rennnora heard footsteps, some metallic clicks, more walking, and the snap of leather straps.

Beastly Cycle

The carriage then headed off down the road. She waited several minutes, but heard nothing more. She wriggled out from behind the bush and saw massive, closed iron gates before her. Beyond them was a stone paved road left to deteriorate, with land on either side that the wilds reclaimed in the years past, lined by stone statues of various shapes and the remains of immense pillars. It led to a half-crumbled castle that once must have been very grand to see. The shattered remnants of a village nestled to the right of it. Mountains stood in the distance behind it, but a tall, thick hedge on either side of the castle blocked her view of much else.

"So this is the home of the cursed prince," she muttered to herself. "Not much to gaze upon, but then, neither am I."

She rested a slender hand on each side of the gate. The thick iron felt solid beneath them. A huge rose outlined in metal, right down to the individual petals, spread across the upper halves of both gates caught her eye. She thought it was lovely, then she noticed something a bit strange about it. In the very center of the rose were two small figures, the silhouette of a slender man reaching his hand out on one side of where the two gates met, with a hawk-like bird flying away from him on the other. The design seemed slightly wrong to her. She would have had a woman facing the man and holding his hand instead of an animal fleeing him. As she

Volunteer

barely touched the man, both of the gates swung open. She gasped in surprise! The building before her now was not the ruins of a few minutes ago. It was aged and neglected, but whole! She could see towers, glass windows, and even the modest village was more intact than she had originally thought. The large building appeared to be four levels with a domed, glass structure of some kind on top. It was more massive than any manor she had seen in her life! She cautiously stepped forward. Unseen eyes felt like they were watching her from the castle. Suddenly, a breeze fluttered by her.

"Why are you here?" a younger man's pleasant, mid-ranged voice whispered from somewhere around her.

Rennora searched as the wind died down, but saw no one.

It then returned. "Why are you here?" the voice demanded again.

"Do you want the truth or a lie?" she muttered sarcastically.

"Truth," he answered.

Her eyes widened! She had not thought he had actually heard her! "I'm terribly sorry!" she hastily apologized! "I didn't mean to be disrespectful, your highness! The truth is that I fled into the forest and stumbled my way here."

"Why?"

Beastly Cycle

"To escape those who seek their version of justice."

"The local lord's justice?"

"No, not exactly. I lashed out against a favorite, and now they will make me pay severely."

"Surely the magistrate will hear both sides and rule fairly."

"Not likely. Thevesta and Mistress LaZella are well liked by most. No one has ever seen or believes the part of them that I endure daily. Mistress LaZella has them thinking I'm a monster that only lies. There would be no justice for me."

The voice fell silent for several minutes, leaving Rennora wondering if she would be turned away.

"If you enter, you'll have one week to leave as you choose," he explained. "Otherwise, you're here to stay until I release you."

"If you're not cruel to me, I can live with those conditions."

"Agreed then."

Suddenly, she gasped as the breeze turned into a massive, thick gale for a moment, then vanished completely! It felt like she had passed through a gigantic wall of cool water instead of air! She shivered as she inched forward, wondering if she had done right by herself. All of a sudden, she heard a metallic groan behind her! She whirled around in time to see the gates closing, until just a

Volunteer

sliver remained. She dearly hoped that the voice would keep his promise, if she decided to part…

    She continued the long march, giving her plenty of time to absorb many of the details of the building itself. It was more humble than noble, with sharp angles and snarling animal-like statue adornments. She halted in front of the rounded front steps. The entire place seemed to have the sense of waiting, mixed with a hint of lingering sadness. She gazed at the opened double doors. She did not feel proper using them, since she was only a scullery maid in rank. Most people she had come across were touchy about propriety, especially those of noble blood. She circled around the massive place and a large corner tower until she spied a very neglected garden of sorts up near a tall wall of hedges. It seemed large enough to feed an army! She spotted a well-worn road passing by a set of wide stairs which led to double doors in the wall that she was following. Pleased with her find, she headed toward the large, wooden doors, heavy and reinforced, with what appeared to be a fox carved on each face. She thought that it was a strange creature to choose for an adornment, but was not the oddest by far. She had once seen a nobleman that had a common brown mouse as part of his crest. The upper nobility never ceased to stir her questioning if they had any sense, or simply enjoyed the reactions their antics raised, good or bad. She searched for

Beastly Cycle

the rope to pull for the bell, but could not find one at all, so she raised her fist to knock. Both of the doors swung open before she could even touch either! She froze, wary.

"H-hello?" she cautiously stammered.

No answer. Rennora peered into a vast kitchen with a single blaze roaring in one of the numerous cavernous fireplaces. Delicious aromas wafted around her. Her stomach growled in anticipation. She wondered whether it was acceptable for her to help herself to the delicacies that were laid out. She then noticed an ornate candlestick of shining brass sitting on a polished, cherrywood pedestal by an open door at the far left end of the room. Beside its base was a light blue something that seemed very familiar to her. She picked it up. It was an incredibly soft flower petal, just like the others she had tucked away. She pulled the rest of them out to compare. They were exactly the same size and color as the new one! It felt to her like she was being secretly led, but the questions were where, by whom, and more importantly why. She noticed a flickering light out of the corner of her eye. It came from inside a room on the far right side within the darkness beyond the doorway beside her. She grabbed the candlestick, steeled herself, and stepped into the unknown. She could not see much past her meager light, so she passed through what seemed like an immense room, step by step, on the

Volunteer

polished stone beneath her bare feet. She came to an open pair of double doors on the other side of a very large fireplace with dying embers. She wondered where to go next, since the faint glow within the marble mantel was too dim to be the light that she had seen, when she noticed a bright dot of light flickering beyond the doors. Not wanting to linger in both her uneasiness and the darkness, she entered the next room and made her way to the center of an even grander room.

All of a sudden, a massive thunder clap overhead startled her! She did not recall any hints of a single cloud, let alone a fierce storm, before she had entered the castle. Yet, she could hear the pounding of heavy rain against the stones. She hoped that the roof was sound enough to keep the weather outside. She headed toward the far light again, when she had the feeling of eyes upon her once more. She froze, scanning around her. Odd shapes were scattered in the darkness. Lightening flashed through the clear windows lining an upper balcony. A dark, person-like shape, with pointed ears on top of his or her head, like an animal's, stood silently in front of the center window. Glowing eyes of yellow gazed back at her. Her heart stopped for a moment.

There he is... flashed in her mind.

She wondered at such a forceful thought! She then pulled her attention to the person above her, so

Beastly Cycle

she would not appear rude. She knew that she should say something. The tense silence hung heavy between them. She took a deep breath to steady herself.

"Pardon me, but are you the master or caretaker of this great place?" she asked the person, feeling like an imbecile for lack of a better greeting.

"I'm the current master," a mid-ranged voice of a younger man responded, bitter, but not unkind.

She recognized it as the same one from outside. "I'm sorry to intrude unannounced, but I didn't see anyone to assist me."

The figure said nothing. However, he continued to hold her gaze. She could not seem to tear her eyes away from his! The minutes ticked by. She soon realized that she was blatantly staring and gave herself a mental shake to snap herself out of it.

"Forgive my rudeness, please, milord," she blushed. "I don't know what's gotten into me."

"Pardon me as well," he replied. "The room beyond the hall you were headed towards contains food and drink that I hope you'll find to your satisfaction. Some dressings for your wounds will be sent shortly. When you are ready, the lights will guide you to your rooms during your stay."

"Thank you. May I ask what is the correct form of address I am to use for you, please, milord?"

Volunteer

"I have no title to claim" he responded, a hard edge to his voice.

"I'm terribly sorry, monsieur. I didn't mean to pry." She was not off to a very good beginning. "I'll just go then, if I may," she said, then headed toward the lit room, afraid that she would damage things beyond repair, if she lingered any longer.

Chapter 5
~ Beast ~

First Impressions

The creature watched the girl depart the entrance hall from the darkness of the upper balcony. He was not sure how he felt about the lord's daughter being replaced by a simple serving maid of some kind, from what he had seen through the magic mirror that lurked upstairs, and voluntarily, to his complete bewilderment! She had caught his attention from the first moment he had stumbled across her while on the hunt for his third attempt at locating a lady of any rank to break the spell. Her life was an unhappy one, from what he could gather from the silent images, but the man, who was within a few years of his age and was courting her at the time, had brought such warmth and happiness to her face, that he was loathe to tear them apart. He chose the merchant's daughter instead, despite his thunderous thought of *There she is...* when the servant's eyes seemed to meet his that very first time he gazed upon her.

He had watched over the girl as her happiness had turned cold a few days ago. He had tried to

First Impressions

bring even a partial smile to her face, no matter how fleeting, with his small gestures, without her knowing the source. He even risked exposure to protect her! Now she was here, sharing the same roof! He took a deep breath to calm his pounding heart as the hem of her skirt vanished through the doorway, his night vision serving him well. He left her to dine in peace while he paced the halls on quiet footfalls, pondering what her presence could possibly mean for them both…

Chapter 6
~ Beauty ~

Crystal Garden

    Rennora stepped into a large room with a merrily crackling fire, pleasant furnishings, and several various covered platters waiting on an ornate, wooden side table near the door. The same delightful smells that had been in the kitchen enveloped her. Her stomach rumbled as she sat in a large, well-padded chair near a small table before the blazing fire. She pulled the warm cover off the prepared plate beside her and ate without really tasting very much through her nervousness. She drank from the crystal glass of water, leaving the wine untouched, until she spied a single, deep red rose beside the dish. It matched the petal that always marked the chosen girl exactly… She felt like a barely tolerated intruder. She did force herself on his hospitality, taking the place of his desired lady, even if the other girl did reject the offer… She hoped that he would forgive and accept her company, with time. Her thoughts drifted as the coziness of the room washed over her. Before she realized it, her fork fell with a clatter onto her silver

Crystal Garden

plate, startling her awake! She neatened things up, then stretched, eager for a bed.

She collected a fresh candlestick and peered into the doorway to find a basin of warm water, several rolls of clean cloth strips, and a tiny glass cup of salve. She ripped her ruined sleeve off, carefully cleansed the dried blood streaks from her skin, applied the stinging salve, and wrapped it using the cloth strips. She applied a little salve to her skinned knuckles, but left them exposed to the air, since the wounds were minor. Once she was done, she noticed a trail of lit candelabra beginning beside her and leading through the nearest corridor doorway, across a multi-colored stone floor, up wide sweeping stairs, and along the upper balcony. She followed them nervously as they wove their way through the castle's second floor and entered a spacious room adorned in rich purples, delicate golds, and highly polished woods. The fabrics appeared slightly gaudy on the expensive furnishings to her. A vast wardrobe stood opened with several elaborate dresses laid out on a bench. They were clearly meant for a slightly larger lady of means. She felt very plain and scrawny in her worn, humble clothing. A faint scraping sounded on the floor behind her. She could feel someone's presence in the darkness beyond the doorway.

"I know I wasn't chosen," she admitted aloud. "I'm no noble lady, or even pleasant to look at. I

Beastly Cycle

thank you for not imprisoning me or sending me away. I hope that you don't come to regret my presence here."

She heard the shifting of feet for a moment, with a faint tapping on the stone, before the person fell silent again.

"You're more welcome here than you may ever know, not a burden nor unwanted, ever," the person softly replied, a gentleness and slight quiver to his voice.

Rennora stared into his yellow eyes shining back at her from the darkness! Her mind was blank, uncertain how to react, or what to say to such a response! He slowly blinked after a minute of returning her gaze and silently left her to her thoughts. Her legs quickly collapsed out from under her! Her eyes lingered on the empty doorway. She then spied a beautiful rose of pale blue resting on the threshold. Her heart skipped a beat! She inched toward it, picked it up with a shaking hand, then slowly closed the door. It was not possible! The flower did not exist outside of fictional stories, yet there it lay in her hands, as real and solid as she was! Where did he find it?! How could he possibly have known about the challenge she had set for her potential suitors, when she had first come of age, with the idea that only the one destined for her would ever be able to present her with it in some form?! She eased herself into the chair by the fire.

Crystal Garden

She stared at the rose, the firelight dancing on its soft petals, and drank in its strange, delicate fragrance. It had equal amounts of rose, sweeter honeysuckle, and heavy rains to enrich both florals. It smelled like heaven to her. She smiled to herself as her spirits lifted under the rose's influence, and then she nodded off.

Rennora was hauled roughly to the edge of town to stand trial for her crime against Thevesta. Mistress LaZella stood in sneering delight on a pedestal. The older woman delightedly condemned her repeatedly as Rennora was dragged, screaming, to the town square and chained into a forced kneel with her arms stretched out between two thick metal posts! Angry crowds with torches and pitch forks gathered around her. A single, pale blue petal then drifted across her vision…

Rennora awoke, gasping for air and dripping in cold sweat! Her mind continued reeling as her body trembled. A persistent knock on the door startled her out of the chair! She clung to it desperately for stability. Someone pounded insistently again!

"Mademoiselle?" she heard the person from before gently inquire from beyond the door.

She tried to swallow, but her throat was so terribly dry.

Beastly Cycle

"Y-yes?" she stammered with all the courage she could muster.

"Is everything alright?" he asked, quite concerned.

It took her a moment to pull herself together enough to respond. "Yes, monsieur," she replied with more confidence than she felt. "I'll be fine."

A heavy silence hung in the air. "Are you certain?" he sternly pressed.

"Yes," she stubbornly insisted.

"As you wish," he respectfully replied. "My servants have your breakfast and clothing. They're a little unusual, as you will see. The promise of no harm to you applies to them and to anyone else within these borders as well, so don't be frightened of them. They're ladies and are here to see to your every need. No one can cross the threshold of the chambers you claim without your permission, either limited or unconditional. Once you are finished here, feel free to go anywhere you wish, except the fourth floor. It contains my personal rooms, and I value my privacy very highly.

"You're required to dress and dine with me every evening. All other meals can be in the place of your choosing. The servants also have a bell for you to summon them from anywhere, should you require them. I keep to my rooms or the village, so you can wander anywhere else without fear. A more suitable room will be prepared for you before you retire this evening."

"What do you mean by unusual, monsieur?" she hesitantly asked. She received no response. "Hello?" she pressed.

Nothing.

"Are you still there, monsieur?" she half demanded as she crossed the room and threw the door open.

She peered out into the large corridor in both directions and discovered nothing but a covered tray with a small bell and a neatly folded bundle floating in the air close by. She slammed the door at the terrifying sight! She pressed her back against it as her heart raced! She figured the prince was cursed, but had never considered that the castle or the objects within it might have been as well! She heard a slight scraping on the floor and a gentle knock behind her. She was far too frightened to answer! A few people's footsteps then retreated down the corridor.

When Rennora felt that it was safe, she cautiously poked her head out and checked both ways. A large, round base of some kind adorned the empty area at one end, with many doors lining the walls as the vast hallway turned sharply out of sight. The corridor also contained a huge statue instead of a base, but was otherwise the same on the other end. There was no one in any direction. She glanced

Beastly Cycle

down. The tray and bundle rested beside the threshold on the floor. She watched them, but they simply laid there. She scanned again before she brought everything into the room. She ate the lovely meal and shifted her attention to the bundle, which turned out to be a simple dress with slippers to match, under clothes of a very fine weave, and fresh items to tend to her arm. She drew her own bath, wondering where the servants were. She carefully cleaned, rinsed off, redressed her arm, and clothed herself, feeling much better afterwards. She gathered her dirty laundry and set it outside the doorway, along with the tray of dishes. She then studied the half-forgotten bell. The stunning piece was so small that it easily fit into the palm of her hand, and it was made from a bright silver with delicate engravings of a sword and rose intertwined beneath a full moon. As she tucked it into a hidden pocket of her dress, she noticed that the rose that had fallen on the floor. She placed it in a crystal goblet of water on the small table by the chair and scattered her petals around it for safe keeping. She soon set off in no direction in particular at first. She opened doors along the corridor at random, finding personal apartments and bedchambers of all sizes. She then discovered a modest, single-story library, with two levels inside, around the corner from the stairs and similar to the one from his lordship's home.

Crystal Garden

She perused the entire room until she came across the historical section where she found a few shelves' worth of books missing there. Judging from the well-organized remaining ones and the empty shelves, she figured that the ones from about one hundred years ago to the present were missing. She thought it was rather strange for so many from a single area to be gone at once. She scanned around her, thinking that they might have been mislaid. A massive number of bound books were stacked on a large desk near a cold fireplace. She checked through them. Large, small, predator, prey, domestic, wild, exotic, different animals of all kinds were in each. She even found one on various varieties of wolves, which was one of her favorite animals.

She wondered why the obsession with creatures, as she examined one on the different types of foxes, when she noticed something half-hidden under one of the bookcases near the desk. After a few tries, she managed to drag out a very battered copy of her favorite fairy tale. To her horror, she found that someone had slaughtered it to pieces by ripping most of the pages out! Judging from the smudged and sooty fingerprints all over the remaining pages, she thought that they were probably burned as well! But why would anyone want to destroy from where the heroine's father became lost in the woods to the ending, and what

Beastly Cycle

caused the jagged slash marks on the inside cover? Her heart ached at the wretched state of it as she sat down in a nearby chair. She used her skirt to wipe it off the best she could. She held it tenderly with a melancholy sigh, uncertain if anything could be done to salvage it. She peered into the grate to see if anything survived, not knowing how long ago the vile act had been done. Nothing but fresh logs and cold stones remained. She scanned the room for other possibilities. Her eyes wandered to the empty stone wall above the marble mantel and the thick nails in it. It seemed to her that a large painting of some sort should be hanging there. She wondered what had happened to it…

    A firm knock at the door pulled her out of her musings. She slipped the damaged book onto the desk and answered the door to find a covered tray with a scroll waiting beside the threshold. She peered down the hallway in all directions. A very faint haze near the farther end vanished as she attempted to gain a better look. She shook her head, certain that her eyes were playing tricks on her, and brought the tray inside. She finished her meal in the silence, returned the tray to the hall, and rang her bell so the servants could retrieve the tray. The sound was more beautiful than any other bell that she had ever heard in her life. Its delicate, silvery tones seemed to carry no further than the room around her. She did not see how anyone else could

Crystal Garden

have possibly heard it. She then watched the tray from the comfort of the chair. Nothing happened for a while. Then, a haze slipped into view, scooped up the tray, and departed with it. She snuck over and peeked out into the hallway. The tray was visible through the haze's seemingly human shape and appeared like it was floating away! She headed down the hallway after it as it turned the corner, her curiosity afire. She rounded the corner herself and discovered several more doors at the end of the hall. Most of them were various bedchambers, storage, or linen closets. The last door led to a large tower with stairs that spiraled out of sight in both directions. She chose to head down to the tower's ground floor, where she noticed a simple wooden door near the bottom stairs. As she reached to open it, she heard a faint creak from behind her. She whirled around, but no one was there. She scanned up the stairs. Nothing. A thin line of dim light in the darkness under the stairs then caught her eye. She hesitated. She soon heard another creak, but in front of her this time.

    Rennora helped herself to one of the lit torches from the wall and moved in closer. She found a heavy, iron-enforced door tucked away in the wall. The handle was quite cold to the touch. With a lot of effort, she wrenched it open! A wild gale suddenly slammed into her, trying to hurtle her back inside! She threw her arms over her face, dropping

Beastly Cycle

her torch in the process! She leaned into the wind to steady herself. It felt like it was weakening. She slid her foot forward over what seemed like the threshold and planted her slippered foot firmly in the bare dirt beyond it. All of a sudden, the gale ceased, taking her balance with it! She stumbled forward several steps before she regained her footing.

She heaved a sigh of relief, wondering what in the world that was about. She then spied an interesting sight before her. Several feet into a well trimmed section of the grounds, a large low garden of various flowers sat with one side running near a tall thick hedge that stretched from near her to a high stone wall several yards away. A giant tangle of blood red rose bushes stood well beyond the far edge of the garden. Large, oddly shaped objects shimmered in the sunlight amongst the flowers. A warning hung heavy in the air around her as she took a single step toward them.

She almost fled back inside when she heard someone whisper, "Help!" from somewhere behind her. She slowly turned back to the garden.

"Hello?" she tentatively asked.

There was no response. She worked her way, step by step and wary, to the edge of the garden's mossy stone path from where she thought the voice had come. Several life-sized statues of glass or crystal people on stone pedestals stood frozen in

Crystal Garden

time. Each had its own ring of flowers around most of the base and a smaller statue of a different animal poised at its feet. The detail and care spent on each and every statue stole her breath away. There were no tool marks to be seen at all! Her eyes shifted to closely study the nearest statue. It was a girl that appeared to be a year or two younger than she. Her hair, eyes, and various parts of her flowing dress were unpolished, giving the impression of contrast to the other perfectly smooth surfaces, like her skin. At the girl's feet was a large bird of prey. Rennora guessed it to be a hawk or falcon of some kind by its curved beak and fierce looking talons. Its wings were spread wide, as though it was about to strike! She could not understand why the girl was glaring at the animal with such pure hatred! Rennora thought it seemed so graceful, noble, and a little melancholy, with a single gleaming tear frozen by its eye. Her gaze shifted to another pair of statues. This one was a man, a few years older than she, with a hard face and polished hair that was tied back at the nape of his thick neck. He was tall, muscular, and massive, like the snarling boar ready to charge at his feet. She could not tell if the animal had a tear or not, but the man's face had a look of sheer terror carved on it, for what seemed like such a brave fighter. She counted five men and six ladies, most with faces of panic, horror, or shock, and all so real, she half expected them to step off their pedestals. They had

Beastly Cycle

an air like they were waiting for something, good or bad.

Suddenly, a faint voice softly cried, "Help us!" overlapping a different one that whispered "Run far away while you still can, girl," with a snarl.

Startled, she scanned around her, but did not see a living soul near her at all! "Anyone there?" she demanded one more time as her heart pounded.

No answer again. She wondered who it could have been, since it did not sound like the master of the castle. She followed the garden's low planted edge the long way around, toward the far hedge wall, checking all around her as she went, trying to locate the source of the voices. She still saw no one, except the statues. She paused between the garden and the rose tangle. One of the girls on the very edge was holding something in her outstretched hand.

Rennora moved closer, until a different mysterious voice warned her, "Do not enter!"

She halted! The air fell silent once again. She inched forward and examined the glass hand before her. It was a small, leather-bound book! Crystal tears were frozen on both cheeks of the girl as she and the unpolished squirrel statue at her feet were staring, heart broken, at the roses. Rennora wondered how it had ended up in the statue's hand, and how it had survived so exposed to the elements. She tried to reach it, but it was just out of her grasp.

Crystal Garden

She was half tempted to step into the large garden, but felt that would be a disastrous idea, especially after the warning. Instead, she leaned as far as she dared. Her fingers just barely brushed the edge of the leather cover. She reached a tiny bit further and managed to flip the book out of the statue's hand and onto the low plant border at her feet. She scooped up her prize, quite pleased with herself. She began to open it when she heard a collective gasp, then a very tense silence. Enough was enough! She dashed inside and barricaded the door shut with her body.

Relieved that she was safe, she slid down it into a sitting position where she found her forgotten torch on the floor nearby. She promptly relit it and seated herself on the lowest stair, to be more comfortable. The book softly creaked open to reveal an elegant script written by a very skilled hand. She felt the lingering guilt and sorrow from the unknown writer as she devoured every word on the pages…

Honrik and I were overjoyed to finally bring an heir into this world and marked the occasion by planting the most beautiful deep red roses in our summer

Beastly Cycle

grounds where he was born. We ensured that our precious little Vindan had the finest of everything and was never left wanting. He grew into a beautiful boy, tall and strong, and loved by everyone, or so we thought.

  I suppose the first sign that all was not as it should be was the night of the royal dinner with the visiting dignitaries and their families. Vindan had a disagreement with one of the other boys over who received the better dessert. I am not sure how it was permitted to continue, but I was pulled from my own dining, much to my embarrassment at the time, to aid in sorting it out.

  By the time I arrived, Vindan had actually struck the boy! I had my son

Crystal Garden

placed in his room and the other boy returned to his parents. I permanently dismissed his nursemaid for being incapable of dealing with him again. I then had a discussion with Vindan to bring him to his senses. He was so outraged at everything that he ordered the other boy beaten and me executed within the hour! I was stunned! Before I could do anything, Amheer requested that he be permitted to handle the situation with the delicacy and tact that was needed. I was still in silent shock, so I mustered my dignity and left him to it. Soon, Vindan apologized to us both and retracted his orders.

    Discipline and love are two vital things that every child, even one of royal

Beastly Cycle

blood, need to function and flourish. I am ashamed to admit that I left the former to others incapable of giving him the firm structure that he needed, or Honrik, and myself to an extent, would overrule them on what seemed like minor things, yielding to our child's demands. Years of this passed. His majesty, my beloved Honrik, then fell ill and passed away when Vindan was twelve years of age. Amheer, Honrik's most trusted advisor, took charge of the throne, placing it in safekeeping, with himself and me as acting regents, until Vindan came of age. He also took charge of Vindan's upbringing, which we all needed. He tried to have me embrace that role much more actively, but I

Crystal Garden

refused, under the argument that I was still in mourning for my king.

I am ashamed to say that the truth of the matter was that I had not been able to cope with Vindan, and did not want to. Oh how we both would pay for my selfishness and negligence.

Then, there was no more. Several pages were torn out, and the remainder of the book was empty. Rennora considered hunting around the crystal garden for the missing pages. However, she quickly dismissed the idea. She had no desire to approach *that* place so soon! She skimmed over the entries once more. She wondered about the person who had greeted her yesterday. He seemed quite different than the prince that was described within the pages…

Chapter 7
~ Beauty ~

Dinner

    A knock at the door near Rennora startled her out of her thoughts. She paused to see if anyone beyond it would say something. She then slipped over to the handle and ripped the door open! An ornate candlestick was floating in front of a person shaped haze. She could feel her heart pounding in her chest at the strange sight! She watched in silence as the arm of the haze reached out of sight on the floor beyond the door frame and brought a small, ornate, polished brass sundial into view. She noticed the face of it was divided into twelve slices. The haze indicated a slice near an elegant five. It contained a war-like scene with trebuchets and charging horses. The haze then returned the dial, walked around her, headed up the spiraling stairs beside her for a ways, paused, and seemed to turn back around, like it was waiting for her. She pondered its actions for a couple of minutes.

    "Do you wish me to follow you?" she asked curiously.

Dinner

The haze took a couple more steps and halted again.

"I gather that's a yes."

She slipped the book into her large pocket and followed the haze up to the second landing, through a door into a closet of some kind, and through a second door into an ornate, wider hallway with fewer doors running along its length on one side and massive windows along the other side. Each set of double doors was carved with a different intricate pattern on its surface. They turned the first corner and halted just around a second that was several yards from the first. A vine of silvery leaves ran along the wide door frame there. A single, large rose, with silver edging adorned the center of the top above the pair of doors. A larger leaf was carved sideways across each of the center of the doors from the handle outwards to the frame. The view outside from the window across from the doors caught her breath in her throat. A small lake was surrounded by overgrown vegetation of all kinds. A massive weeping willow stood on a modest island in the center of the water. It was so beautiful, and yet, somber at the same time.

The haze knocked on one of the doors, returning Rennora's attention to it. The doors opened to a beautiful sitting room decorated in blue, green, and silver. A crackling blaze was in the white marble fireplace with a tall, well-padded, blue

Beastly Cycle

chair on either side. A small table stood near one of the chairs and held her blue rose in a shimmering, crystal vase, her petals scattered around it, and the silver bell. Double doors opened to a gorgeous bed chamber of the same colors. She stepped in and clamped her hands to her mouth in astonishment and delight! Two large bookcases of cherry wood with silver inlay were filled with hundreds upon hundreds of books, just waiting for her to devour, each on opposite ends of the sitting room. She did not understand how they could have possibly discovered her passion or her favorite color!

    A pair of hazes closed the doors and headed into the bedroom. She reluctantly left the books behind to follow them. The furniture within was a little less ornate than the previous room she had stayed in and even more beautiful to her. Leaves, vines, and roses were inlayed in silver on the polished cherry wood pieces. Green with a slight touch of blue fabric, sheer enough to see through, draped the tall frame and posts surrounding the generous bed. A gorgeous, silver embroidered coverlet of deep blue satin adorned the bed. A well-padded bench sat beneath a massive stain glass scene framed in deep cherry wood, depicting more twisting leaves, vines, and roses. She tore herself away from the glass and noticed the hazes waiting for her in an immense bathroom decorated in polished blue and white marble stonework. She

Dinner

realized, to her embarrassment, that she was a bit odorous and would probably be expected to dress far grander than she currently was for dinner each night, just like the visiting nobles would do at his lordship's home. She thought it was a bit of a silly custom, unless it was for a ball or special occasion, but she was a guest here of sorts and did not want to offend her generous host. However, she insisted on bathing herself. She did allow the hazes to dress her and style her hair for her. She adored the flowing, deep blue dress of velvet that caressed her every movement, with matching slippers that flopped a touch on her feet, until she inspected the results in the full-length mirror, which was famed in beautifully ornate silver and standing in the corner of the bed chamber. She quickly averted her eyes. She did not feel that she did such stunning clothing any justice.

  She forced her attention away from the foul glass, rescued the book from her soiled clothing, and stashed it safely in a large empty trunk at the foot of her bed. She then followed one of the hazes back down through the castle to an elegant dining room with a long table set for one between two sets of candles in tall holders and cavernous fireplaces at each end of the room. She seated herself at the prepared spot. More hazes entered with covered trays. Each one removed the cover and held the dish steady while she served herself. Once her plate was

Beastly Cycle

filled, she checked to see if her host was ready to begin. She could see the dark silhouette of a single tall chair at the other end of the table against the blazing fire behind it. However, she could not tell if he was there yet, so she respectfully waited, gazing expectantly at the dark chair. Several minutes passed by in silence. She was certain that she could feel his eyes intent on her. She opened her lips to politely test his presence, when his voice came from the far corner in the darkness and interrupted her before she could speak!

"Enjoy yourself, please," he urged. "You don't have to wait for me to take the first bite."

The sound of his voice startled her!

"My apologies for surprising you, mademoiselle," he calmly replied. "I'll leave you to enjoy your meal in peace."

"Wait!" she exclaimed. "Won't you join me?"

Nothing but silence in reply.

"Please," she politely pressed. Her heart fluttered at her nervousness. She knew that this was the beginning of her chance to free him, and she was *not* going to waste it!

Still no response.

"I promise I won't hurt you…" she added meekly, feeling a little desperate.

He chuckled mirthlessly at her words. She watched as something large and very hairy moved calmly in front of the fire. It then stepped

Dinner

completely into her candlelight, and the master straightened to his full height. She gasped horrified for a moment, then quickly clamped her mouth shut! A creature stood upright, like a regular man, a couple of inches taller than she. His slender torso and arms seemed human, but his legs were shaped like an animal's hind legs! He wore a simple belted tunic, a half-sleeved shirt, and short, knee-length pants. His face had a longish, narrow muzzle with a black nose at the end. Coppery orange fur covered his face and most of his neck, with white fur that ran from his lower lip down the front of his neck. Touches of white and black fur were mixed into the orange-ish red fur on his taller, pointed ears that stood on the top of his head. He had black fur that ran from his elbows to his clawed hands and from his knees to his clawed feet. A long bushy tail of copper fur, with several inches of white fur on the end, stuck out of the back of his pants. He appeared to her to be a human crossed with a fox!

"It would take an awful lot for you to hurt me, my dear mademoiselle," he stated with a glare.

She quickly realized that she was staring, but not at his unusual appearance. She could not tear her gaze from his gentle eyes. She saw intelligence mingling with sadness in their earthy brown depths. She shut her own and swallowed, trying to pull herself together. She had been half expecting some animal-like human, similar to the one in the fairy

Beastly Cycle

tale book, since she realized that the hazes were servants. The truly startling thing was that he did not appear at all like a fully grown man combined with a lion and a goat, like the sketches that she had seen! However, it did not make the creature towering over her any less frightening, or unsettling! She took a breath, opened her eyes, and gave him a small, shy smile. She was here now and determined to help him in any way she could. She swallowed against the rising fear.

"J-join me," she softly stammered.

"Are you certain that the sight of my hideous face won't ruin your precious appetite?" he challenged, a touch of bitterness in his undertones.

"I'll grow used to it," she replied, with her eyes fixed firmly on her dish.

"The real question is, do you honestly want to?"

She met his intense gaze, feeling her courage beginning to return, and answered with a determined, "Yes."

His face was unreadable. He lingered for two slow breaths, then left without a word. Rennora let out a loud gasp, not realizing that she had been holding her breath since she answered. She did not know what to think of the strange creature as she poked hesitantly at her food! She ate in the heavy silence, wondering if he believed her at all. She quickly decided that it did not matter in the slightest.

Dinner

She would simply prove her intentions to him. She soon finished, then waited for a haze to lead the way to her chambers, but everyone seemed to have vanished. She lit a smaller candelabrum off a side board and headed out into the dark castle to locate her rooms herself. She passed through room after room, until she had lost track of where she was and found herself in the grand entrance hall instead. As she climbed the top of the stairs leading to the balcony, she heard a faint, but steady thumping through one of the opened windows that captured her attention. She followed it through a long hallway, past the empty circular base, and down a spiraling staircase inside a large tower. She could vaguely hear it through the heavy door tucked under the bottom of the stairs. She hesitated in front of it for several minutes, wondering if she was going to have to fight through the winds again. She was still debating when the sound fell silent.

  As she turned to leave, a beautiful sound froze her where she was! She listened intently, trying to decipher what it was, but it was too muffled through the wooden door to hear clearly. She braced herself, eyes shut tight, and ripped the door open! Nothing happened… She peeked through one eye. A well-worn path began at the bottom of the wide stairs on the other side of the stone threshold and cut through the tall grass into the night. She could hear a faint tune of some kind drifting toward her, beckoning

Beastly Cycle

her onward. She took a calming breath and followed the path, despite her uneasiness at what potentially awaited her within the darkness. The sound grew steadily louder as she walked along the winding path, crossing a wide dirt road along the way. She came to a long low building of stone in an empty field that had been cleared down to bare earth. A well, with a large pool attached to it and surrounded by a low stone wall, was a couple of yards or so off to the side. Seated on the pool's wide edge was the beast, bathed in an immense light, like a huge fire's, and stripped to the waist with a leather apron over his white furred, well-muscled chest. Copper fur covered his upper arms, shoulders, and back. She quickly darted to the nearest building wall, out of sight, before he could spot her! The song ceased. She remained very still. The minutes dragged on with only the sound of her slow, controlled breathing in her ears.

    The most beautiful tune from what sounded like a flute of some kind then danced through the air. Its melancholy notes felt both bitter and sweet at the same time as they gently sang to her very heart, whispering a goodbye to what once was, and a hello to the end of what might have been. She slowly leaned against the wall behind her. She could actually feel the creature's heartache and pain while the music played on behind her. Eventually,

Dinner

the last lingering notes faded into the darkness as the song came to a gentle end.

Tears streamed down her cheeks, unchecked. Her heart ached for him. His sorrow and loneliness ran deep. Just like hers… She heard a crunch on the path in front of her. She gazed up to see a haze with another candle waiting for her a few feet up the path. She heard a whisper of an older man's voice from there, then the clanging and banging of a smithy started up behind her. She rose to her feet and carefully followed the haze, pausing to peer back at the building and the vacant pool beside it as they crested a small hill.

Chapter 8
~ Beast ~

Forge Reflections

    The creature paused on his current task and listened as the girl trekked back to the castle with her summoned escort. He wondered if he dared to hope that she would be the one to do what he could not. He sighed, raised the heavy hammer in his furry hand, and resumed striking on the white hot bar of iron in his metal tongs with a steady thudding. He wanted her to be the one to succeed so desperately that he could almost taste it! However, if she failed… He could not bear the thought of his prison being forced onto another, willing or not.

    Yet, she was different from the other three girls, four if he included the one that had wisely left without trying. Her gentle, stormy gray-blue eyes, like a shy flower, blind to its own beauty, pierced into his soul. Her pale skin, like moonlight, and the wealth of soft brown curls that shone red when the sunlight caressed them just so were all he could see when he closed his eyes ever since he first noticed her at her work, then watched her reading under the tree, a dreamy smile on her face as she caressed the

Forge Reflections

drawing of a blue rose adorning the top of the page. He could not understand how such an incredible, beautiful girl could burrow so deeply under his skin with only a single glance and stubbornly stay there! She had barely been here a full day! It felt like she was some kind of sorceress, and he was powerless to stop her from drawing him under her spell. The problem was that he was not sure if he honestly wanted her to cease…

    He pounded harder and harder, using his tool to work not only the metal, but his frustrations off as well. His hammer struck with more force each time. Sweat trickled on his skin beneath his fur. The metal yielded to his will, stretching thinner and thinner until it bent in half from his intense blows. He snarled fiercely and threw the ruined sword into the oil barrel near him. Liquid sizzled and smoke bellowed into the air, like a demon rising from a lake from one of the books that he used to read, matching his dark mood. He removed his leather apron and stepped out to the pool to cool off, in more ways than one. He scooped up his ocarina that he had left there and turned it over in his hands for a moment before he raised it to his lips. He sent a few notes floating into the night sky. He then let his clawed hands fall to his lap. His heart simply was not in it anymore. He did not want to be a monster, like Kilda had been to him. He wanted to be free, but without risk to the girl, or have the curse to die

Beastly Cycle

with him so no one else would have to suffer as he had. The second felt like the most likely option of the two. The first question was would the girl ever forgive him? The harder one was would he be able to let her go?

    A single tear trickled down his cheek as he began with a fresh bar of metal and a heavier heart. Only time would tell…

Chapter 9
~ Beauty ~

Royal Changes

Rennora woke to the soft glow of dying embers in the chilly morning hours. She was exhausted from tossing and turning so much during the night. All she could remember from her dreams was a burly man, richly dressed, pleading with her to save them all before he began screaming shrilly as he transformed before her eyes! He was several inches taller than he had begun, with white fur covering his entire body. His torso and arms had broadened. His fingers had shortened slightly and thickened. His legs were now curved like an animal's hind legs, ending in massive paws. Black stripes ran from the sides of his neck and top of his head toward his back. Two triangular ears sat on top of his cat-like head. A single lock of longer fur from the top fell in a curl on his forehead, and there was a large tuft of fur near the side of each of his cheeks. Several thick whiskers had sprouted on his cheeks. His pink, inverted triangular nose sat on his short muzzle with a thin line that connected it to his curved upper lip. The large, human-like cat creature

Beastly Cycle

then shifted one more time into a fully human stone statue that turned from gray rock to clear! It left her heart pounding!

Someone suddenly knocked at the outer door, startling her! She pulled herself together for a moment and answered it. She then stepped aside to let in a pair of hazes with a tray, but they simply stood there. She could hear a faint whisper of words coming from one of them.

"You may enter," she explained.

She ate, dressed with the help of the hazes, tucked her bell safely in a pocket, and wandered around, her mind on her dream. Her favorite story spoke of only the one creature. Where did the cat person come from then? Perhaps he was a figment of her overactive imagination. However, that did not feel right either. She continued her pondering as she explored. Most of the doors she opened led to bed chambers, lavish apartments, or empty rooms of various sizes. Some were ready, with a few quick adjustments, to receive visitors in a matter of minutes. As she explored further on the same level, she found rooms with thicker and thicker layers of dust and other signs of neglect. One set of chambers in particular caught her attention as she stood in the doorway, so she slipped in to investigate it further. It must have once been used to house the grandest of ladies, possibly even princesses. Its faded brocades and satins of turquoise and soft pinks with worn

Royal Changes

threads of gold bore a mute testimony of the breathtaking splendor that it once was. It felt so melancholy and lost to her that it broke her heart.

    She carefully sat down on a creaky, barely padded bench by a window and wiped some of the grime off so she could see out. On the ground below, a large courtyard of stone lay empty within the castle's exterior walls that framed three sides of it. A maze of neglected shrubbery beyond it threatened to consume the many paths that wove their way to what appeared to be a circular path wrapped around a dried-up fountain filled with half dead plants of some kind. A plethora of tiny colored dots studded the vegetation and land beyond it. The scene below felt even more agonizing than the room around her. She heaved a sigh and began to rise when something wedged between the pad and the wall caught her eye. It was mostly hidden by the tattered curtain. She pulled it out to discover a small, worn, dark leather-bound book. Curious, she opened it to find it was Prince Vindan's personal journal! Most of the entries showed that his attitude had not improved with age. However, the last several pages in particular drew her in…

December 21st - Another blasted

ball over with! I get so dreadfully weary

Beastly Cycle

of Mother's continuous efforts to marry me off to anyone of decent blood that breathes. Watching mademoiselle after mademoiselle practically throw herself at me, under the barely concealed guise of 'refinement', without a bit of intellect between her ears. I swear, if I hear another brainless giggle from a supposed 'vision of loveliness' or 'breathtaking beauty', I'll have her and her kin beheaded to spare the rest of the world from their collective stupidity! Mother's been moaning that I never grant any of them a true chance. Truth is that no one has been worth even my notice. Time to rest. I expect to be 'surprised' with another ball soon. And another, and

Royal Changes

another, until I grant my darling mother's wish of a royal wedding. Someone rescue me from my misery!

April 6th – Last night, it happened! I am expected to dance at least one dance with every eligible mademoiselle in attendance, as both Mother and Amheer remind me at the beginning of every ball. I had just finished with the final lady and was looking forward to resting both my feet and my smile for a few dances before I would be forced to favor a person, or persons to everyone's dismay, with my many charms for the rest of the evening, when Amheer informed me that there was a latecomer who required my

Beastly Cycle

attention. I concealed my irritation at the thought of yet another lady to entertain quite well. I then turned around. Before me stood a true ravishing beauty, her soft eyes down cast as she greeted me with a deep curtsy of such grace and ease, it surpassed all ladies I had met before.

    I was actually gaping at this visiting niece of some minor lord's for a moment before I remembered myself! I had not behaved so foolishly over a mademoiselle since I was a young boy on the verge of manhood! I quickly pulled myself together and led her onto the dance floor. I was astonished at how light she was on her feet! She followed

Royal Changes

my lead like I was guiding a gentle breeze! We said nothing at first, but then she blushed shyly at me. I knew it fell upon myself to break the silence hanging heavily between us. I braced myself for the loveliness before to me to be shattered by mindless chatter as I brought forth the charm. Imagine my surprise at not only was she able to keep up with my conversation with thoughtful and intelligent contributions, but her sharp wit had me at her mercy within minutes! For the first time in my life, I never wanted the dance to end, and I certainly did not want to let her go!

Beastly Cycle

September 18th – I never thought I could ever experience such happiness in my life! Courting Belnisa has been like living in a wondrous dream. Mother thinks that I could do better, but is content to say no more and promises to learn to love and embrace her as I do in time. Amheer, however, does not care for her in the slightest, though he works quite hard to conceal it from everyone. I know him too well to be fooled. He is simply put out with me for not choosing a particular lady that is a distant cousin of someone he knows that he favored for me. I am the one that has to live with the choice, not him. I will make it up to him after we wed.

Royal Changes

Oh, did I not tell you. Yesterday in the smaller rose garden, beneath the light of the full moon, I commanded her to marry me. Would you believe she promptly informed me that I could present my proposal better than that, and if I did not, she would depart the grounds immediately! She actually wanted me, a crown prince of the realm, to kneel before her and beg her humbly, using flowery words from my own heart!

I seriously considered walking away to find someone else that would be thrilled at my current method, until my eyes met hers. I could lose myself in their vast depths for hours on end... I realized then, in that moment, just how

Beastly Cycle

much I loved her, and that she was actually correct! So I kissed her cute nose, knelt right there in the dirt, and stumbled over even the simplest of words as I poured out my heart to her. To my relief and delight, she threw her arms around me, knocking us both down into the mud behind me, and agreed to be my bride! I can still see the look on Mother and her ladies-in-waiting's faces when they came rushing up to see what all the commotion was about, only to discover our finery ruined, and both of us laughing like a pair of mischievous children! She made us cleanse thoroughly, then congratulated us and welcomed Belnisa into the family.

Royal Changes

July 31st – To tell the truth, I do not remember much about the wedding, except that there had to have been over 500 people in attendance at least, which did nothing for my already delicate nerves, and I do not remember the exact details of the ceremony as Belnisa floated toward me, but one look from her melted both my fears and my knees. The moon was truly honey for us for the next month!

We then settled into both married life and ruling our boundaries. No one ever told me that having a wife and queen would be so blasted difficult! She is constantly questioning every little

Beastly Cycle

decree I issue and ruling I make! I keep informing her that she has <u>no</u> say in any of it, but she has been hunting through our private library to verify even that! She wishes to rule by my side as an equal! No one has ever even heard of such a thing as a dual throne! Mother has been pushing us for an heir to the throne, but that will have to wait until we can figure a way through our current mess of troubles. What did I get myself into?

August 6th – Belnisa and I spent many days working through our troubles and compromising on both our parts. It has been one of the hardest things I have

Royal Changes

ever had to do! It was worth it. There was finally peace in the lands once again, for a while. We held our first ball, since we were wed, to formally present ourselves to the world. All went well, or at least, I think it did. I remember greeting everyone, then dining, then dancing with my Belnisa and Mother. Amheer then insisted that I indulge some of the other ladies as a diplomatic gesture of goodwill. Things became hazy after that… I danced with several ladies, or so I have been told. Every time that I try to remember that night, all I bring to mind is a single lady's shifting face and the name that begins with Jess-something. What is strange is I cannot recall

Beastly Cycle

anything more specific about her. I could not say whether she was tall, short, thick, thin, fair, dark, nothing but a raspy voice that never seems to leave me.
Everything else only seems to elude me. It is like trying to hold water in your hands. The more I try, the more escapes me!

Belnisa is very worried about me right now. She keeps moaning that I am granting this far too much of my attention and not enough to her or the realm. A small part of me seems to whisper that she is correct, and I need to force it from my mind entirely, but the rest devoutly refuses without seeking some answers first. The entire mess is

Royal Changes

giving me an immense headache. I think I will go hunting tomorrow. The peace and stillness of the forest always clears my head and calms me.

August 12th – Something is wrong! I know it is, but I cannot quite seem to put it into words. How could courting such a lady of refinement and beauty feel so very right, and yet, very wrong at the same time? I am told I am already wed and have been so for the past two months. My journal confirmed it, but I just do not recall any of it! Perhaps Jesseva and her cousin, Amheer, were right. Maybe my mother and that Belnisa did keep me under an

Beastly Cycle

enchantment this entire time! Now that Jesseva resides with me in the summer castle, the tea she brings me every evening will rid me of their vile spell soon enough. I have even banished Belnisa from our bedchambers at Amheer's suggestion, for my own good! I should be relieved, but deep down, I have begun to feel hollow, alone, heartbroken, and slightly terrified. I only wish I knew why…

Rennora could barely make out the last two entries. It appeared that someone had sprinkled water, or possibly wept, over the pages. She took her time and carefully read every word…

August 17th – As Jesseva and I went for our daily stroll, I presented her

Royal Changes

with another trifle that Amheer selected on my behalf. I will have to raise my people's taxes again, but keeping a lady such as her is always very expensive, or so Amheer keeps assuring me. Jesseva has been hinting very strongly to me that her dearest wish is to be my new queen. I would have to do something about both the old queens first though. I did not wish to at first. I then vaguely remember gazing deeply into the immense depths of Jesseva's eyes, and all thoughts drifted away. She promised to be far more loyal to me than the other girl, whom Amheer spotted stealing away with the captain of my personal guards. This does not feel quite right to me, but Amheer's sworn to

Beastly Cycle

aid me in dealing with the girl properly, and with little embarrassment to the crown. Strangely, I cannot seem to recall her or the older woman's names anymore. I wonder what happened to the woman. I recently realized that I have not seen her in the castle in a long time... I am so delighted to have both Jesseva and Amheer to assist me in even the smallest of things. I can no longer imagine my life without them and do not wish to!

August 22nd – How sensible Jesseva and Amheer are! They have informed me that they have undeniable proof for me that the girl has been

Royal Changes

courting another man! I think I should be at least hurt by this information, but I feel nothing anymore! Is that not wonderful! Jesseva and Amheer have a plan. I will go 'hunting' tomorrow, as I do every few days, but I will not actually be hunting this time. Amheer, some very loyal guards that Jesseva has hand selected, and I will be lying in wait, hidden on the edge of a clearing where he knows the girl and man have been frequenting, until they make their appearance. We will then leap out! I do not exactly recall the rest, but I think I will be using a very sharp sword on someone. Her neck? Or was it her heart... Jesseva will remember, so I will

Beastly Cycle

be fine. Once the girl is done, I will be freed from my hazy prison at last! I think I will throw a ball in celebration. Jesseva often tells me how much I love those. She has even surprised me with a massive white and black striped cat, which she calls a 'tiger', to mark the occasion. Amheer tells me the white beasts are quite rare!

    Rennora considered the events with great care. It was quite strange to her how quickly the prince seemed to have changed. Just when he appeared to mend his ways and become a good man, he turned into a manipulated imbecile! She actually felt quite sorry for him as she closed the book and wandered toward the doors. She scanned around the room one last time, wondering how the book had ended up in there, and exactly to whom these chambers had once belonged…

Chapter 10
~ Beauty ~

Hearts Hint

Rennora slipped out into the hallway with the book in hand and over to a padded bench position under a long wall of tall windows overlooking the lands below. She noticed a quaint village of small, partially crumbling houses, which were half hidden in the tall dry grasses, within the massive stone wall's borders. It appeared so empty to her in the daylight. She was too used to the hustle and bustle of the town where she had come from. The vacant stalls of the market and the main thoroughfare wept with loneliness, but at least the blacksmith's shop, a fair distance away, was still in use. She could not tell if the fires were going from this angle, nor could she hear any sound of pounding from this high up. She wondered how often he worked there and what other tasks he spent his time on. She then spotted a small figure immerge from the smithy into the sunlight and head towards the village. A bright light flashed periodically from the person along the way. She had not seen anyone else other than the creature and hazes thus far. She figured that it had to be the creature, but she was too far away to be certain. The person then vanished behind some of the houses below. She scanned around her at the many doors along the hallway. She pondered which one could possibly take her to the lower floors and felt a little overwhelmed at the idea of searching all those doors, so she used her bell to summon some assistance instead. A haze rounded the corner and halted before her. She watched it do what looked like a deep curtsy, so she assumed it was a maid servant.

"Thank you for coming," Rennora addressed her. "Which door will take me to the lowest floor, please?"

The haze stretched her arm out and indicated a single door set in a curved wall at the far end of the hallway.

"Thank you. I take it that the master, or creature rather, is out on the grounds today?"

She heard a female whispering something, but could not make out any of the actual words. She thought for a few minutes after the sound had ceased. She then had an idea!

"Would you, by any chance, be open to a bit of an odd method of limited communicating, so you and the rest of the household can be better understood?"

More whispers.

Hearts Hint

Rennora shook her head. "Let me be honest. I can't understand your words at all." She pulled out a clean handkerchief. "I don't know about you, but I find it quite infuriating, so let's give this a try. Would you mind holding this for me, please? I assure you that it's quite clean." She handed over the lacey cloth.

She noticed the head tilt slightly as the servant granted her request.

"Now, when I ask a 'yes' or 'no' question, you'll use the cloth, or similar item, to show your response," Rennora explained. "If the answer is 'yes', then shake the cloth up and down. If the answer's 'no', shake it side to side. If the answer is 'you don't know' or are uncertain, move it down only and hold it for a couple of seconds. Understand?"

She watched the hovering handkerchief. A heavy sigh sounded from the haze, then the cloth flopped up and down for a moment. Delighted, she beamed radiantly!

"Wonderful! I figured that this would be better, and quicker, than having everyone write down their answers all the time. I can read and write, so we can use that for the more important and lengthy responses. Okay?"

Another sigh, and the cloth flopped unenthusiastically again.

Beastly Cycle

"It does feel a bit silly to be doing this, but it's better than nothing, and you can use the handkerchief to gain my attention in a hurry by waving it around wildly as well. Now, is that the creature down in the village?"

Yes.

"Do you think he would mind some company, by any chance?"

The cloth dropped down and stayed for a moment.

"You don't know… Thank you so much. Would you please explain the cloth response to the others for me?"

Yes, with a curtsy.

"Thank you again."

The haze attempted to return the handkerchief, but Rennora insisted that she keep it instead for future use. The haze curtsied again, then headed down the hall and vanished around the corner from where she had come. Rennora hoped that being able to better understand the servants, even slightly, would aid in improving things for everyone. She gazed out the window once more at the well-worn path that she must have followed to the smithy and noticed the periodic glints of light flashing again for several minutes more before they disappeared completely behind a few of the more neglected structures. She rose to her feet and slipped into the tower and down the stairs, hoping that her friendly

Hearts Hint

gesture would be taken in the correct manner. She noticed two doors at the bottom as she stood in the center of the round floor. One was in the middle of the wall, while the other was tucked under the stairs. Not sure which to take, she glanced between the two for a minute before she chose the exposed one. Her escapade from the first half hidden door was still fresh on her mind.

  She stepped into a very plain, narrow corridor with high windows, which she had not been in before, but appeared to be similar to some of the ones that were dedicated to her fellow servants' usage in his lordship's home. This thought brought her little reassurance. Many of the servants' passages were like labyrinths, if you did not know how to navigate them. She had become quite lost several times in that house when she first began. Feeling turned around and slightly flustered, she halted where she was within the castle corridor, pulled herself together, and strategized a bit. She counted five doors, including the one behind her. She figured that one of the others must lead her back to a familiar room on the ground floor. Which one was the trouble. The idea of using her bell again flitted through her mind for a moment, but she dismissed it. She did not wish to be too much trouble. It was a common complaint amongst the maids and manservants back in town.

Beastly Cycle

    She steadied herself and decided to tackle this mess exactly like she had at his lordship's house years ago. Pick one direction and stay with it, so she entered the first door on the left side. She stepped into a vast room with sunlight streaming through immense, grime crusted, cracked windows. Her slippered feet barely made a sound on the thick dust coating a light colored stone slabbed floor. She noticed a huge scene, or possibly multiple images of some kind, inlaid into the stone in the center, but she could not quite decipher any of them clearly. Above her, a few huge chandeliers hung low on their ropes and were wrapped in layers of light cloth to protect them from the dust when they were not required. A few others appeared to have been ripped viciously apart or crashed into the floor so hard that the stone beneath them had cracked! Her eyes shifted to a raised platform in the far corner of the room near a pair of double doors that stood open. Tears welled up as her heart broke at the sight of the shattered remains of several instruments, including a lute. She dropped to her knees beside the slashed strings and splintered wood, wondering what possible reason could anyone have had to do such a monstrous thing! Judging from the heavy dust on the various pieces, the deed had been done long ago. She heard a familiar tapping of the creature's footfalls approaching from behind. He came to a halt a couple of feet somewhere beside her. She attempted to politely acknowledge his presence, but her hurt robbed her of her voice at the moment.

"They informed me that you wish to speak with me?" he inquired, his curiosity evident in his calm tone.

She tried to explain, but still could not seem to speak past the lump in her throat. She sat in silence instead, wishing he had found her in better spirits, or in stronger control of herself.

"Have I offended you?" he asked, sounding like he already knew the answer, and it was not a favorable one.

She shook her head and hunted for another handkerchief within her pockets until a clean one slipped into her view. She blinked back tears of embarrassment at being found like this. She averted her face as she accepted the offer with a whispered thanks.

"Are you well, mademoiselle?" he carefully inquired.

She could hear the concern in his gentle voice. She was touched that he cared enough to ask. She dried her eyes and attempted to return the handkerchief, but he refused, requesting that she keep it. A shy smile spread across her lips as she tucked it away. She sighed and gestured at the mournful sight before her.

"I was on my way to keep you company, if you would have permitted me to do so, when I

Beastly Cycle

stumbled across this," she explained in a slightly shaky tone.

She watched him scan the wreckage surrounding them, noting the confusion on his furry face.

"I don't think that this is truly worthy of your tears," he hesitantly replied.

She shook her head. "Not the room, just the music that's been silenced forever."

He was still puzzled.

She continued, "I was on an errand to deliver clean linens to one of the upstairs maids in preparation for a large party about a year ago. On my way back to the kitchens, I heard this indescribably beautiful music coming from his lordship's supposed to be empty music room. It froze me instantly, and I had to find out who had me captive with each note that lingered on the air. I peeked into the room from the cracked door and watched this man at the lute. I could only see his side as his fingers danced across the strings, not simply playing the notes from memory, like all the others I've heard to put themselves on display, but actually pouring his heart into his hands and giving the instrument such an amazing voice in song that it had me spellbound and afraid to breathe, lest I shatter his concentration and silence the precious lute!

Hearts Hint

"Since that day, a sight such as this, especially of a lute, rips my heart in two, because I've had the honor of hearing the voice it could have had and now, it never will… Forgive me, monsieur. I'm only being silly again."

She shifted to her knees to rise when she noticed him offer his hand to assist. She gazed up at the unexpected gesture for a moment, then at his face. He refused to meet her eyes, but his demeanor told her that he fully expected to be ignored. She hesitantly placed her small, slender hand into his larger one. His gaze snapped toward her. She blushed as she stood with his aid.

"Thank you, kind monsieur," she whispered.

Stunned, he only nodded.

She dusted herself off, not sure what else to say in the awkward silence. She then dropped into a quick curtsy. "Forgive me monsieur, if I have offended you with my silliness."

He shook his head in response and indicated the entire room around them. "No apology necessary. This mess happened before my time."

That ensnared her attention! She gazed at him intently, now the perplexed one. "Before your time?" she questioned. "But I thought…" She bit off the rest of her assumption before it could cause any damage.

He chuckled halfheartedly for a moment. "That I have always been here," he finished for her.

Beastly Cycle

She nodded, thoroughly embarrassed.

"Stupid book," he snarled. "They all assume that. No dear mademoiselle, I am not the—" he began to declare, but cut himself off.

He tried to explain again. However, his mouth refused to even open. He snarled viscously in frustration and stormed a couple of paces away from her. She could see his deep breaths as he maintained his back toward her. Concerned, Rennora took a hesitant step toward him.

"P-pardon me," she stammered. "Are you alright, monsieur?"

He gestured for her to stay where she was and wait. She obeyed, wondering what the trouble was. He took one more calming breath before he turned to face her again. He bowed deeply.

"Forgive me, belle mademoiselle," the creature apologized in a sincere whisper. He cleared his throat and spoke more clearly. "As you have seen, there are many answers that you must uncover for yourself. I am unable to aid you, no matter how strong my desire may be otherwise." He straightened. "Is there anything else that you require of me?"

She could see the half-concealed infuriation and pain in his face. Her own frustration at causing it began to mount. She huffed for a moment and dropped her eyes in an attempt to master control of herself again. He did a small nod of his head in response and turned to leave.

She threw her hand out and squeaked at his retreating back, "Wait! That wasn't directed at you!"

He promptly halted, but failed to face her.

She explained, "I'm mad at myself, not you. I simply wanted to get to know you better, and all I've done is add to your misery."

"My misery," he stated calmly and with a half turn toward her, "is of my own doing. I unknowingly gave my heart to one who had none. You had nothing to do with that, nor increased my misery. If that changes, you'll be promptly informed."

She could not help but sigh, "You hurt too…"

Startled, he fully turned and stepped closer.

She nodded, confirming that he had heard correctly. "I loved someone that I thought loved me in return, but a couple of months ago he explained that he desired only my friendship and recently gave his heart to another. They're to be wed soon…"

The silence hung heavily in the air between them for several minutes as he studied her.

"I'm sorry, belle mademoiselle," he replied.

She teared up a bit as she shook her head and responded with a slight quiver to her higher voice, "Not your fault either. Don't worry about me, though. I'll muddle through somehow." She

Beastly Cycle

heaved a resigned sigh. "I always seem to… His finding happiness so quickly has me wondering if he ever honestly cared for me in the first place…"

"He would be a fool if he didn't," the creature insisted.

She smiled a little at his kind words. "I believe I could say the same for you," she stated.

His brown eyes hardened slightly as he shook his head. "You may not agree with that sentiment as you continue your hunt for answers." His face then softened. "Please bear in mind that I act not for myself, whatever you discover. I'll leave you to your thoughts, mademoiselle, and join you at dinner, if you'll still have me…"

He bowed once more.

"Of course you're still welcome to dinner," she replied to his fading footsteps.

She stood there in the empty room, wondering what in the world he meant by all that. Could there possibly have been more than one person that turned into a partial animal? If so, what had happened to the rest of the creatures? And what had he meant by 'he was not acting for himself'? Was there some other person or force that was driving him? Was he more of a prisoner than her favorite tale had led her to believe?

She gazed at the forgotten book still clasped in her hand. She wondered whether she should find the current creature and press him for more

Hearts Hint

information, but quickly dismissed the notion. She felt that he had probably had enough of her for one day. As she walked toward the opened double doors near the platform, she figured that this evening's meal would most likely be a silent affair.

Chapter 11
~ Beast ~

Blasted Curse

The creature maintained his composure just long enough to dart out of the ballroom, through the servant's passage, and out the lone door along the outer wall without damaging any of the doors in his mounting rage and frustration at himself and the curse he was under. He charged down the wide dirt road, returned to his small field of thick, wooden poles behind the village, and snatched up his newly made sword that he had been testing before he was summoned. He hacked and slashed at a tall log half buried vertically in the ground harder and harder with each stroke, not caring whether the blade could handle the additional power. He continued to allow his emotions to strengthen his blows until a particularly fierce swing bit deep into the battered wood. He grabbed the weapon with both hands and heaved with all his might, but to no avail. It was stuck fast! His patience spent, he slammed his claws across the offending log, ripping off the weakened top portion, and sent it flying a fair distance away to crash into the earth!

Blasted Curse

He flopped down exhausted, numb within, and dripping with sweat. As he pulled off his tunic to aid in cooling down, his gaze fell on his black furred forearms. He cursed the blasted spell on him and the day that he had heeded the summons of Kilda's rose petal. He loathed the terms of the curse, every rotten word that he had pieced together almost four years ago, exactly like the girl inside was doing now. However, he had no intention of even hinting at the locations of the remaining books or scrolls, unlike Kilda who had subtly guided him to each of them so eagerly.

He wanted to break the curse, but on his own terms, and using that missing second part of the poem he had stumbled across not long after he had become cursed. The other girls he had summoned to aid him in this had rejected him easily enough, despite his polite, but somewhat distant companionship that he had offered them. Two others had read that infernal book as well, but it had made no difference. They had still fled at the sight of him. He wondered what made this current girl so different from the others. Why was she so stubborn, so determined to free him? Love? No one could possibly love a monster, no matter how charming the person or human the heart. Pity? Possibly, but she did not strike him as one who sought to demean or belittle others. Her unexpected tears over that lute and the embarrassment afterwards had shown

Beastly Cycle

him a small piece of her mind and the beauty within her heart. He stretched out on the ground with his hands behind his head and sighed. She seemed to think that she was being silly. She could not have been more wrong. Her sweetness and love of not just any music, but the kind that sang to her soul had touched him. He was genuinely surprised to hear that any man had held her heart and still set her free! Well, if he was honest, a part of him did a little leap of pleasure inside his chest at the declaration that she was unattached…

His scattered thoughts were suddenly interrupted by a shadow creeping over his face. He shifted his gaze over to his personal manservant standing quietly nearby.

"Pardon the intrusion, Lord Alleron," the servant said with a respectful bow. "Luncheon is ready. Where would you care to dine today?"

"I've told you many times, Kestin, that there's no need to call a simple blacksmith 'lord'," the creature explained with slight exasperation. "My name alone is fine, or just 'monsieur' will do, if you insist on any formal address of me."

"Forgive me," Kestin replied with another bow, "but anything except 'lord' would be disrespectful to you. The servants and I have cared for all the beasts of various ranks over the years, and we agree that you have earned the honor, humble though you feel your position in life to be."

Blasted Curse

Alleron shook his head at the steward's stubbornness, rose to his feet, and retrieved his tunic and sword that had been unknowingly released when he had torn the pole in two.

"Would you mind returning this to the shop for me, please?" he asked Kestin as he handed over the sword. "I'll examine it tomorrow and fix it then, if needed. As for my meal, by the pool will be fine."

"Very good, milord. How many for this evening?"

Alleron sighed, a little sadden at the thought of facing her after what he had eluded to earlier.

"Set the table for only her," he instructed. "I'll be there as well, but I doubt that she'll have a desire to linger in my company for very long, so have a meal sent to the upper garden this time, once I leave."

"I think you are doing her ladyship and yourself great injustice. Speak your mind, tell her what you can, grant her a full chance, and give things time, milord. Oh, and never forget who you really are. She needs to continue seeing that. Not what you fear you are becoming."

Kestin bowed once more and left. Alleron stood there with his thoughts for company as he gazed at his furry hand and wondered at the sudden change in the servant's reference of his guest from simple commoner to one of nobility. Perhaps she too had earned the servants' respect in a way that

Beastly Cycle

the other girls had not, but how and why were the questions.

Chapter 12
~ Beauty ~

Servants and Images

Rennora found herself in another immense room with a balcony that ran along one side, opposite a pair of huge, ornate, double doors. Grand sweeping stairs connected the balcony to the marble floor one which she stood. She noticed many tall windows that lined the balcony as she moved to the foot of the stairs. She wondered why the view above her looked vaguely familiar, and then it hit her! She realized that this was where she first laid eyes on the creature! She gazed around her, amazed at how different it looked with bright daylight streaming in, caressing everything it touched in its gentle light. She noticed many chandeliers and tall candle stands, but very sparse furnishings.

She meandered to the center of the room, when she spied something under her feet. A huge image was embedded in the floor's center between the massive double doors and the bottom of the grand stairs. She had a difficult time trying to make out what it was, so she climbed the stairs until she reached the balcony. Below her laid a massive

Beastly Cycle

circle. A faceless man of crystal, with a ring of red roses around his feet, stood in one half of the circle. A woman in a simple brown dress stood in the other half on a small mound of grass, which had a partial ring of water around the base. A tall, slim weeping willow grew beside the woman in such a way that the woman almost blended into the tree's bark. The man held a single, half wilted rose in his hand by his side. Both figures were facing each other, but there was a thick band of an ominous, black, cloud-like haze that divided the circle right down the center, like it was blocking the pair from ever reaching each other. There were some strange symbols that formed a ring around the outside edge of the circle. She did not recognize them at all. The positions of the people's faces made her sad for some reason. The woman's featureless face was aimed straight toward the man with a single tear on her cheek. She seemed heartbroken as she reached for him, but slightly hopeful. The man seemed to be avoiding her gaze, his face was pointing in the direction of her feet instead, sorrowful and remorseful, with a tear on his own cheek, like he desperately wanted something from her, but had no right to ask for it.

  Rennora noticed a movement in the corner of her eye, breaking her reflections and startling her a bit. She turned and saw a haze with a handkerchief and a note on a silver tray. The haze curtsied and held the tray out to her. She thanked her and read

Servants and Images

the folded note asking her where she would like luncheon. She thought for a moment as she gazed around her, her eyes falling on the warm, inviting sunlight streaming in from the windows near her.

"A nice place outside would be lovely, please," she eagerly replied. "Oh, and would you put this in my chambers for me, please?" She handed over the book.

The haze curtsied again and left her to her thoughts. She recalled the fox creature on the night she met him and wondered if the man in the circle was what he looked like before the curse. After a while of study, she decided against it. The creature's body was too slim to be the man in the floor, nor did he have that baggy skin appearance of one that had allowed his once very muscular body to go to nothingness. She compared the man to what she could remember of the crystal statues, considering the possibility that it could be one of them. She sighed, flustered. She could not know for certain unless she visited the garden again. She peered around the room hoping to find a better way to reach the garden, without going through the tower door, when she noticed a girl shaped haze with a handkerchief approaching her.

"I take it that the meal is ready?" she politely asked the servant.

Yes.

Beastly Cycle

"One quick question, if you would." She indicated the images in the floor. "Who are they, please?"

No response.

"You don't know who they are then."

No response again.

"Then you do know who they are."

Still no response.

"Let me guess, you can't tell me, and I have to figure it out for myself."

Yes.

"Lovely… Lead on then, if you please."

Rennora followed the haze back through the ballroom, dining hall, kitchen, a large storage room beyond that, and into a tower with winding stairs. She froze in the middle of the room while the haze continued on through a familiar door under the stone stairs.

"Wait!" Rennora frantically called, but was completely ignored.

She did not want to fall too far behind and risk getting lost, but her memory of the wall of wind sent her heart racing in fright! She stood, hesitating for several minutes, until she finally accepted that she had no other options before her. She closed her eyes, took a deep breath, and tore the door open! To her surprise, nothing happened. No invisible wall, nothing but sunlight gleaming on the unruly grounds. She headed out, feeling rather foolish for

Servants and Images

hesitating. She spotted the haze waiting for her beside the crystal garden. Once she had caught up, the haze grumbled something at her and took off again. Rennora tried to speak to the haze as they made their way around the garden, then between the massive tangle of roses and garden to the hedge beyond, but the servant refused to even acknowledge her. They halted at the hedge. The haze searched for something amongst the dense foliage for several minutes before she pushed some particularly long branches aside, revealing an iron gate underneath. The haze guided her through the neglected gate, across the overgrown field beside the kitchen garden, and to the village that Rennora had seen earlier. They skirted around most of the various houses and came to a halt in front of a larger, long, stone building with a heavy metal door that faced the castle behind them. The haze draped the handkerchief over her hand and pulled it snug so Rennora could see the shape of her hand within.

"Why did you bring me here?" Rennora inquired as a feeling of apprehension filled the pit of her stomach.

The haze pointed at the old rusty lock on the door.

"You want me to go in there?" Rennora's apprehension turned to dread, like she was being demanded to do something *really* wrong.

Beastly Cycle

The haze pointed insistently at the door. Rennora could see how badly neglected the large padlock was from where she stood. One good strike with a sturdy rock or such would probably be enough to break it free of the metal loop. She did not want to obey in the slightest, but she was rather curious about why she was being told to do this, and what was inside. She stood in silent debate with herself, when the haze took a huffy breath and stomped toward her.

Suddenly, a female voice roared loudly and clearly, "WHAT IN THE WORLD DO YOU THINK YOU ARE DOING?!" from behind her.

Rennora leapt at the sound and noticed a more voluptuous, womanly haze that was slightly shorter than she, was storming up to them! She guessed that the new haze *had* to be the head housekeeper, from her demeanor and the continuous shouting, as she halted by the first haze. Rennora could only catch the odd word from both of them, despite their raised voices. A male voice suddenly snapped at the pair from behind her! She turned and stepped to the side when she saw the creature and another haze, a man by the look of the silhouette, approaching them in a rush. The creature stood protectively half in front of her, while the man haze joined the others.

"Are you alright, belle mademoiselle?" the creature demanded of her.

Servants and Images

"Fine, but a little confused at the moment," Rennora explained. "I asked for luncheon outside in a nice place and was led here instead."

They watched the hazes continue the heated argument, making Rennora feel more awkward by the moment, until they heard the first haze scream in a raspy voice at the others, "I AM SICK TO DEATH OF BEING TRAPPED HERE BECAUSE OF *THAT* DEMON!"

Shocked and dismayed, Rennora placed her fingers gently on the creature's upper arm to comfort him.

"HOW *DARE* YOU CALL MILORD A DEMON WHEN *YOU'RE* THE ONE THAT GOT US INTO THIS MESS IN THE FIRST PLACE!" the other woman bellowed in return! She snatched up the girl's arm and dragged her back toward the castle, still berating her along the way.

Rennora made out her snarling, "…back to the scullery…" and "…not see the light of day…" as they passed by.

As the servants headed inside, Rennora began to say something to the creature, but she noticed him gazing down at her hand, which was still resting on his arm in confusion and slight surprise. She let it drop and blushed. The remaining haze cleared his throat, gaining their attention. He said something, then waited as both of the males peered at Rennora, expectantly. She figured that he asked her a question.

"Forgive me, monsieur," she responded, "but I can only understand a few scattered words. I hear anything that is screamed clearly, but I personally don't care to be shouted at all the time, if you don't mind."

She could have sworn that the creature had smiled at her for a brief moment.

He then faced her and indicated the haze near him. "This is Kestin, who is steward of the household. He apologizes for Jes, the servant's actions and wishes to know if you were harmed in any way."

Rennora shook her head. "No, but if I may, what's in there, please?" as she gestured toward the nearby stone building.

"That's part of our armory, belle mademoiselle," the creature explained.

"Any thoughts on why she would want me to go in there?"

"None that I can think of, unless you feel yourself in some kind of danger."

"I'm far safer here than I was where I lived," she commented, a little melancholy.

Kestin addressed her, but all she caught was the word 'luncheon'. Before she could further inquire, the creature responded, "In light of what just happened, perhaps it would be better if you join

Servants and Images

me for this meal as well, or at least, remain within my sight and fairly close reach for your own safety. Would that be alright with you?"

She smiled with relief. "Yes, please!"

The creature was a little startled at her quick acceptance. Kestin politely bowed and promptly left. The creature led her through the village at an easy pace, past tall, rough looking posts, and on a winding path through an overgrown field. They emerged onto the bare clearing surrounding the blacksmith shop. A single cloth covered platter sat on the low stone wall of the pool. The creature invited her to sit anywhere she liked. However, he remained standing himself. Their wait was not long before a haze brought a second meal, set it down beside the first, bowed to them both, and retreated back to the castle. The creature stayed where he was and waited still.

"Please be seated," she invited with a friendly smile as she gestured toward an empty space on the other side of the trays.

He took a deep breath and obeyed, seemingly a little nervous. They ate their delicious food in silence. Rennora finished first and set her tray with the empty dishes on the other side of her, away from the creature. He finished a few minutes later and hesitated with the tray in his hand as he noticed where Rennora's was placed. He slowly set his on his other side and watched her carefully. She wondered what exactly he was expecting her to do. The silence soon became awkward.

"It's a nice place," she stated. "I can see why you like to spend time here."

He chuckled. "I suppose. Mostly, the forge keeps my skills honed, and me too busy to dwell on my unpleasantness."

"Oh." She thought back to previous conversations before she politely inquired, "Then you are a tradesman? A blacksmith, I would believe?"

He tried to say something, but his mouth refused to open. He calmed himself down and tried again. "That's for you to decide. Somethings I already knew, while others, I learned after…"

"I see… And your family? Where are they from?"

His mouth froze again.

"Do you have any brothers or sisters?"

He was unable to answer still. She admired how he was taking the questions in stride. She thought things over for a minute before she continued, "Are you able to tell me anything about your life before you came here, by any chance?"

He sighed, resigned to his plight, and shook his head.

She changed tactics. "How long have you been here?"

"Too long is all I can say."

Servants and Images

At least he's speaking again, she thought. "What was the previous beast like?" she politely inquired aloud.

Rage, pain, and sadness flashed across his face as he clenched his fists for a moment. She was curious if the confused prince succeeded in his plan, when the creature rose to his feet, headed toward the village, and then halted. It took her a moment to realize that he was waiting for her. She quickly dashed over to join him. He led her back to the crystal garden on the other side of the hedge. He halted near one of the low planted edges. He struggled to speak, then pondered in silence for several minutes.

"She was what I will never be," he explained, cryptically. "She is what I shall be, if I fail." He gazed directly into Rennora's gray-blue eyes. "I *refuse* to pass on my prison like—" He fell into a fuming silence, shifting his focus directly into the garden.

She followed his gaze to the statue of the girl with the hawk. It then dawned on her precisely what he was hinting at!

Chapter 13
~ Beast ~

Mastering Frustrations

Alleron took several slow, deep breaths while he discreetly watched a stunned astonishment spread across the girl's face as her eyes shifted back and forth between him and Kilda's frozen form. He had guessed correctly that she did not know about the cycle of the curse, passing from one person to the next.

"Y-you mean," she ventured as she indicated the remaining statues.

He said nothing.

She whispered with sorrow, "So many…" She then asked in a calmer tone, "Which one is the original prince?"

"There's only one prince, and he's not here."

He noticed her puzzlement.

"You mean he left all of you here to suffer!" she exclaimed, outraged.

He tried to explain further, but he felt like his jaw was sealing itself shut and his tongue had gained ten pounds, both refusing to move at his command. He breathed slowly again to master

Mastering Frustrations

himself. He pondered a way around the curse's limitations to give her even a tiny inkling, when he spied her mulling things over as well.

"No," she said after a while. "That wouldn't fit at all…"

Alleron waited for her to finish her thought, hopeful. He saw that she was lost within her musings.

"What do you mean, belle mademoiselle?" he inquired, encouraging her to continue.

"Hmm?" she said, coming out of it. "If the curse trapped all these poor people, before they had a chance to leave, I assume," as she gestured at the crystal figures, "then it stands to reason that the prince that began this curse is still here. Where is the question."

"If I may," he offered, startled at his own desire to continue the conversation. "If it were me, I would hide his statue well, because he would be the first thing any beast would hunt down to shatter to a powder upon discovering his or her predicament after the cur—" His words seized in his throat.

He struggled to get past the curse's bind on his mouth when she raised her hand and assured him, "I believe I understand what you're fighting so hard to explain."

She gazed into his eyes, heartbreak reflected in her own. "The rage in your heart at the sight of your new skin must have been truly terrible."

Beastly Cycle

"You have no idea." His gaze returned to the hopeless garden before him as he wrestled back the pain, terror, and fury from the memories of that nightmare.

Her soft voice broke through his thoughts. "I won't rest until you're free," she sincerely promised in a whisper.

He faced her. "Perhaps it would be better if you ran while you still could instead," he suggested in an even tone.

Her face showed plainly her thoughts of wondering if he was serious or in jest. He turned his back on the garden, rather sickened by the sight of it now, and waited for her to break the silence, fully expecting her to dismiss him. To his bewilderment, she shyly asked him to show her the rest of the grounds upon noticing his discomfort. He guided her across the field near them, towards the rear of the castle, at a leisurely pace.

Chapter 14
~ Beauty ~

Getting Better Aquainted

Rennora did not know what to make of the tall creature keeping pace beside her. At times it seemed like he desperately desired her company, while at others, he was half sending her on her way and washing his hands of her! She hoped that he was not toying with her for his own pleasure. She peeked at him as they skirted the border to a huge garden of half wilted plants that reached well above her head, but not so high that it hid the upper floors of the castle behind it. He did not strike her as a malicious person that would take delight in such things. At least she genuinely hoped not. Mistress LaZella and Thevesta, however, were entirely different matters completely. She sighed dejectedly at the thought of those two when, suddenly, she bumped into someone in front of her! She stumbled back a step. The creature steadied her for a moment. She apologized for not paying better attention to where she was walking, then their eyes met. She could feel the years of hurt lingering in her heart from the memories. She fought it down and hoped that it was not showing on her face. Her troubles were hers alone. She soon noticed a concerned look in his warm, brown eyes.

"Are you well, belle mademoiselle?" he inquired.

She nodded and dried her eyes on her clean handkerchief. He waited.

"It's nothing," she assured him.

"You seem rather distressed over this nothing," he observed. "I think you'll find that I'm a good listener."

She managed a smile at his gentle face. She paused to mull things over and collect her thoughts, turned her back to the castle, and stepped forward, not really paying much attention to her surroundings. The creature quickly snatched her arm, hauling her back a few steps.

"I strongly recommend not going that way, belle mademoiselle," he insisted.

She gazed at him, confused, until he released her and pointed just past her as an explanation. Two hundred yards beyond the open field where they stood was a massive, gaping chasm that had to have been at least eight miles across, so long that she could not see either end of it, and with a sheer drop off! She stumbled back, terrified of getting any closer to it!

Getting Better Aquainted

"Nothing to fear," he assured her. "Just keep your distance and be mindful of where you are, if you travel along back here."

"Quite a natural barrier!" she exclaimed.

"I wouldn't exactly call it natural."

"What do you mean?"

"Castle and land," he blurted out. "The cur—"

She finished his thought, to his obvious relief, "The curse affected those as well." She then fell silent for a while as she scanned around them, taking in everything in a new light. She inquired, "So the castle hasn't always been in such a state?"

The creature smiled politely. She studied the structure's angles, curves, and carvings before her.

"I wonder what it was like before the curse," she commented.

"Not sure," he answered. He then cleared his throat. "Different outs—" He cleared his throat again. "For each—"

She noticed that his mouth had frozen shut on him again. She carefully pondered over his hints.

"So the castle is different on the outside, correct?" she puzzled.

He gestured for her to continue.

"Different for each…" She then wondered what in the world he could mean? She gazed at the building again. "Once the curse hit, it changed the prince, the castle, and the land," she thought aloud. "It then changed the next person. Wait! Do you mean that the castle's exterior changes with each person the curse changes?!"

He beamed.

She examined it again. "I like the winged statues along the top," she offered after a long pause.

"You don't have to be polite about it," he explained. "I detest the place, every stone and mortar of it."

"Will the curse allow you to leave the boundaries of the land?"

He scoffed, "That doesn't mean that the good people outside will permit me to keep to any part of the forest in peace."

She began to say something when she realized something else. "So you can leave any time you wish, correct?"

"Yes, if I have a strong desire to die."

"Have you ever done it, even for an hour or so?"

"A few times, but I've always kept to the relative safety of the trees and brush."

"Did you ever go near any of the towns or villages that bordered the woodlands?"

"I have, but found it far too dangerous to linger."

"When was the last time, and where did you go?" she pressed with a strong suspicion that she already knew the answer.

Getting Better Aquainted

He gazed at the ground with a guilty look on his furry face.

"So it *was* you that day!" she exclaimed! "I hope you realize that your snarl scared the life out of me! What were you thinking?!"

"I assure you that that wasn't my intent in the slightest, belle mademoiselle. It was aimed at that *thing* that was concealed around the corner, watching you. I sped it on its way with a warning is all. Pardon the liberty I took, but I didn't like the feel of it. It seemed like it was harboring dishonorable intentions towards you."

"The person did frighten me quite a bit. Did you see his or her face, by any chance?"

"I'm sorry, but no. However, I know its scent quite well."

"That's something. Thank you for frightening it off, whoever it was. That's the second time that it's spied on me that I know of. I really wish the person would stop."

"I would recommend keeping a dagger, or even two, on your person every waking moment and within easy reach as you slumber. That way, if it tries something, you have ways of defending yourself."

"You don't happen to have a few spares laying around, do you?"

"Actually, I do. Come with me."

"Oh!" she exclaimed, startled. "Uh, alright."

Beastly Cycle

They returned to the smithy, and the creature headed in. Rennora lingered in the huge, open, main double doorway of the rectangular building. Before her was a large anvil strapped tightly down to a solid stone pedestal beneath it. Tools neatly arranged on metal racks flanked it on one side, with a long stone basin of liquid that could easily hold large, completed pieces on the other. A massive forge with a huge opening beneath an equally impressive chimney stood beyond the anvil, looking like a great, hungry mouth with a fiery appetite. A generous stone box stood on one side of the forge with both wood and coal ready and waiting. Behind the fuel was a huge bellows attached to the forge that she assumed was operated by the pull hanging within easy reach near the anvil. There was empty space between the work area and the shorter, left wall. On the right of the forge were a couple of benches, a few tables, and some stone wheels with a seat attached to a few of them. She could see several shelves containing various wooden boxes behind them and along the long back wall that ran the length of the shop. On the shorter right wall was a large door that stood open into another room. The creature emerged from it with four blades in his clawed hands, so she figured that it must be a storage room of some sort.

Getting Better Aquainted

"I've passed by a few blacksmith's shops many times, but I've never actually been in one before," she commented.

He glanced around him. "This place is a little larger than most. I did some rearranging to it over time."

"Did you not approve of the previous blacksmith's layout?"

He explained, "The flow of it didn't fit how I work."

"Oh."

"Each smith has his own way of doing things and sets up his shop accordingly."

"Was the old blacksmith alright with the changes that you made?"

"I found it abandoned. They told me that the blacksmith had died of despair years ago, so I could do as I wished with it."

"I see…" She did not know what else to say to such a heartbreaking event, so she wandered around the room until she came to a pair of doors in the opposite side wall. "What's in there?" she inquired.

He looked over. "The right door is my fuel, and the left is where I store my raw metals." He presented his finds to her. "Would any of these suit you?" he asked.

She crossed the shop and examined each well-made piece in turn. The first felt too large and

Beastly Cycle

unwieldy for her use. The next one was slightly smaller, but still too big for her. The next one was a better size. However, it seemed too difficult for her to hide easily. The last was small, delicate, and sturdy. She could easily conceal the entire weapon in her hand from her fingertips to her wrist, and it was sharp enough that it could cause plenty of pain to allow her to escape. She noticed a small mark on the blade, near the base where it met the crosspiece. It appeared to be an elaborate letter 'A' with a few squared off scribbles attached to it.

"What's that?" she inquired.

He peered closely at it. "Smith's personal mark," he explained. "Is that the one you would like? I have others, if you wish."

"That's alright. I do like this one." She bit at her lower lip in distress for a moment before she hesitantly continued, "How much are you asking? I must tell you that I have no money. Any I was paid from his lordship goes to Mistress LaZella for room and food every week, but I can work your price off! I could wash dishes, clean, help with the gardens and grounds, or polish and fetch things around here."

He shook his head with a gentle grin. "Worry not, belle mademoiselle. No charge. It's nice to know that all the work that's gone into the piece will be put to good use by someone. Otherwise, it just sits around, waiting to be dusted and polished."

Getting Better Aquainted

"Oh. Thank you."

He considered the one she held for a moment. "I think a second one of a slightly different size for you to wear hidden at your side while you keep the one in your hand in a more secret place, but still within easy reach should you need it, would be an excellent idea. Let me put these back and have another look."

He vanished into the side room. She could hear him shifting things around as he searched. She wondered what else was in there, inched her way over, and peered into the doorway. Thousands of completed pieces lined tall shelves and metal racks along three of the walls within the long room, and ranged from tools to pots to spare parts for wagons or carriages to weapons of all sorts to anything in between and more. She stepped inside. He was busy sifting through a couple of shelves to notice her. She waited in silence until she spotted something interesting on some of the kitchen knives closest to her. The smith's mark near the handle was different from the dagger she had. It was rather blocky and had the letters 'G' and 'r' with what appeared to be a bunch of other letters jumbled together between them.

"I see you found the previous smith's work," she heard over her shoulder suddenly.

She jumped back with a gasp!

~ *149* ~

Beastly Cycle

"I'm sorry," the creature quickly apologized as he stood beside her. "I didn't mean to startle you."

She had not heard him walking toward her. "I'm the one that should be apologizing!" she insisted. "I entered without your permission."

"If I didn't want people in here, I would have locked the door. Simple as that. Feel free to search around as you like. All I ask is that you take nothing that isn't freely given to you. If you see something of interest to you, simply speak up." He smiled at her as he took some other daggers back into the main room.

She closely examined many of the items and noticed that only some of the knives and weapons had the 'A' smith's stamp. The rest of the items in the room bore the 'G' stamp. As she watched the creature return for more, a thought occurred to her. She peered down at the well-balanced weapon in her hand. It lacked the adornment that she had seen in passing on some of the town's local nobility's weaponry, but had a kind of simple elegance to it that appealed to her. She gazed up to say something, when she noticed the creature was missing. She found him in the main forge arranging his selection of weapons for her on a table near the stone wheels. She joined him.

"Here you are." He indicated the daggers. "I selected the best the stock has to offer for you."

Getting Better Aquainted

She walked along the table, examining each one in turn. "They are all very fine," she observed. "You did a wonderful job on them." She beamed warmly at him.

"What makes you say I forged them?" he asked, curious.

She pointed at the 'A' stamp. "That's your mark, is it not?"

He nodded. She shyly continued, "My name's Rennora… What's yours?"

He sighed in dismay. "That's something else you'll have to find out for yourself. That or give me a name of your choosing."

"I would rather use your actual name instead of making one up. It wouldn't feel right otherwise."

"Fair enough. What will you call me until then?"

"I honestly don't know. 'The master' seems so formal."

"And what of 'the creature'?"

She shook her head. "I honestly don't like using that one either."

"It's far better than many other names I've been called. 'Monster' being the kindest."

"And completely undeserved," she snarled. She noticed him staring at her, stunned! She gazed around to see if someone or something else had merited his strange reaction, confused herself, then cautiously asked, "Are you alright?"

~ 151 ~

Beastly Cycle

Before he could answer, they heard someone clear his throat from the main doorway. Two hazes stood there, waiting. The taller one said something in a familiar male voice to them.

"Time to dress," the creature explained. "Minna will see you to your room."

The shorter haze curtsied.

"Looks like we'll have to continue this upon the morrow, if you wish," he commented. He bowed to her. "Till dinner then."

"I'm looking forward to it," she replied sincerely as she curtsied in return.

She then followed the maid haze toward the castle, while the creature and other haze remained behind. She gazed back as they reached the edge of the village and caught the creature watching her with a conflicted look on his face, part wistful, part determination, and mostly confusion. She smiled warmly and continued on into the castle, wondering at the thoughts behind his gaze.

Chapter 15
~ Beauty ~

Rennora's Hurt

Rennora followed Minna back to the entrance hall while the servant hummed a familiar tune. She recognized it as the same one that the creature was playing that night as she wondered how often he played and marveled at how truly stunning his talent was. They entered a grand room on the far side of the hall with a few very intricate tapestries along the smooth stone walls, two doors on each side wall, a large rounded corner on the far left with a single door in it, and a huge tapestry at the end. The maid guided her toward the single door in a rounded corner without pausing. Rennora glanced into the first opened door on the left as they passed and noticed a stylish sitting room elegantly adorned in its simplicity. As they began to pass the second door on the same side, the interior of it caught her attention. She could not resist halting the servant and stepped into the large room with an empty fireplace framed in a white marble mantel and pleasant furnishings in rich reds and golds. She noticed an ornate wooden side table of oak near the

Beastly Cycle

door, a large, well-padded chair of red with gold trim that faced the fireplace, and a smaller table of matching oak beside the chair that seemed strangely familiar to her. She meandered over to the chair and rested her hand on its back, when it dawned on her! She did not know what to think as she stood in the room where she had dined and patched up her arm after meeting the creature on that mysteriously stormy first night. She could hardly believe that she had been there just three days! Her arrival felt like another lifetime ago… She gazed around her, her thoughts miles away, when she noticed something mostly hidden under a smaller chair in the corner. She kneeled down and fished out what turned out to be another plain book. This one was clad in a lighter colored leather. She settled herself in to read it when Minna suddenly cleared her throat.

Rennora thought for a minute before she responded, "I'm going to be late if I linger any longer, aren't I?"

Yes.

She promptly rose to her feet with the book and dagger in hand. "Forgive me, please. Shall we?"

She quietly followed through the door in the rounded corner of the previous room, up the spiraling stairs in the tower, through the massive corridor, and into her personal rooms. She headed over to one of the bookcases in her sitting room,

Rennora's Hurt

shifted things around, and placed all the books that she had found thus far on a single shelf in the order that she had discovered them. She barely had time to wonder what the new book would impart, when she heard a knock at her door. She let in the two maid hazes, placed the weapon on her chest, and allowed them to bathe and dress her. As she sat there patiently, while one attended to her hair and the other gathered her dirty clothing, she felt a little foolish allowing others to do what she was perfectly capable of doing herself as though she was a very large and helpless doll. However, she knew that they had a position in which they took pride, so she did as they requested. Once her hair was finished, she thanked them with a friendly smile.

  She spied the full-length mirror and gazed down at the lovely light purple dress of a finely woven fabric, with a delicate dark purple stitching along the neckline and skirt hem, and matching slippers that the maids had chosen for her. She wondered if she dared to peer at her reflection this time to see how everything had come together, but quickly decided against it. She knew that she was so ordinary that no amount of work on the maids' parts could beautify her at all. She wished that she was even slightly prettier. She sighed heavily, a little melancholy at the thought.

Beastly Cycle

Rennora then noticed one of the maids waiting by the door, while the other had already departed with her clothing.

"Is it time to go down yet?" she asked.

Yes.

"Thank you. Would you guide me there, please?"

The maid curtsied, stepped into the hallway, and waited for her. She followed all the way back to the first room with the tapestries and was motioned to wait in a huge gallery. She seated herself carefully on one of the padded chairs facing the doorway that she had entered and admired the paintings coating all of the walls to pass the time. She then heard some faint clicking on the stone stairs beyond the tapestry room. She followed the sound to the entrance hall's doorway and saw the creature as he came down the stairs, dressed nicely, but with no shoes still, and appearing like he had attempted to neaten his fur, but had given up. She greeted him with a polite curtsy. He bowed, then hesitantly joined her. They wandered slowly back into the gallery. He seemed a little nervous, standing there beside her with his hands clasped behind his back.

"The paintings are lovely," she commented. "Do you know who the people are?"

He scanned around them and admitted, "I honestly don't know. Past nobility perhaps."

Rennora's Hurt

"Oh…" She was slightly disappointed in his response. She quickly thought for a new topic to maintain the conversation.

"I would imagine a historian or two of the court would have notes of some kind on them," he politely offered. "The library on the top floor would be the best place to search. That's where the royalty house their private collection of books. Let me or Kestin know when you're ready, and either one of us will be delighted to let you in there."

"Thank you. I will." She paused for a moment, then asked, "Exactly how many libraries does this place have?"

"Four, one on each floor."

Her eyes widen with amazement! "So many! The royal family must have adored their books! Or is that your presence that's created the rooms?"

The creature shook his head. "Outside only."

"Do you like to read by any chance?"

He smiled warmly. "I do know how to read and write beyond my own name," he teased. "Very few books capture my interest, and I must confess that it is not my passion, like it seems to be yours."

"How do you know about that?"

He studied her, silently debating. "Let's discuss it more after dinner, before I answer that particular question."

Beastly Cycle

She wondered why he was being so guarded and mysterious, when a tall manservant haze stepped into the doorway and declared something.

"Kestin says that dinner is served when we are ready," the creature explained.

They promptly followed him into the dining hall. A different manservant haze assisted her with her chair this time. She wondered why they had so many small nibbles of food, when she noticed the creature eating neatly with his slightly trembling hands. She realized that it must be very awkward for him to use such small and slender things as a fork and knife, so she set down her own and carefully ate in silence with her fingers as well. She noted that as they ate, his hands ceased shaking, and he seemed to relax slightly by the time the dessert course came. She was delighted that he was eating with her this time, instead of only watching, but she could bear the quiet no more.

"Tell me, what other things do you enjoy?"

"To be honest, I've kept myself so immersed in my smithing, that I've had little time for anything else," he admitted.

She nodded. "And your music? What was that lovely instrument, and how long have you been playing?"

He blushed briefly. "You remembered that. It's called an ocarina, or a kind of flute, if you will. I've been playing a long time, but mostly to please

Rennora's Hurt

myself. I'm amazed that I can manage it at all with these paws, or fingers, or whatever you would call them. It took some adjusting, and quite a bit of practice, at first. And you? Do you play anything back at your home?"

Her face fell in dismay. Her eyes dropped to her plate. "I have no home. It's just a place where I live. No more than that…"

She felt his gentle eyes upon her, but she refused to meet them.

"I'm sorry," he said. "I had hoped that the images I had seen were wrong, or I had misunderstood them somehow, since I can't hear any sounds that are happening within them."

Her head snapped up. She tried to speak, but her emotions had her choked up. She blew her nose into her napkin, apologized, took a drink of the clear, cool water, and began again. "What images?" she softly demanded. "How, why, and how long have you been watching me?"

He studied her for a moment. "You of all people deserve the truth."

She followed the creature's example, carefully cleaned her fingers in a water bowl with rose petals floating in it, and dried her hands with a fresh napkin, wondering what the answer to all her questions would be. The creature rose, waved the manservant back, and assisted Rennora with her chair himself. He then shifted his feet, like he was terribly nervous again, and began to hold his hand out toward her, but quickly changed his mind, and clasped both his hands behind his back.

"Come with me," he said as he accepted a lit candlestick from another servant who had just entered. She accepted one as well and followed him into the growing darkness.

As they made their way to the upper floors, the creature politely inquired, "How is the blade I gave you working so far?"

"I haven't had time to test it yet, or seen to a sheath that I could strap to me somehow, since I'm not exactly certain on how to make one," she shyly admitted. She then debated on whether or not to tell him the truth. After a while of awkward silence, she decided that being honest was best. "I think there's something you should know…"

He halted them on the last landing in the tower and waited for her to continue.

She gazed at the floor in embarrassment. "I don't exactly know how to wield a weapon of any kind properly, nor do I know how to actually fight."

"I see," he commented. "Have you had the opportunity to learn or use any weapons?"

She shook her head.

He carefully continued, "Have you had a need to fight?"

She sighed, knowing how unladylike her next response was going to reveal her to be, possibly ruining any good opinion he may have had of her. "Plenty, unfortunately, but I usually back down because I've been urged to, or I run to avoid or tend to my scrapes and wounds…"

She finally brought herself to meet his brown eyes hesitantly. She was astonished to see the concern and hurt for her in them!

"Meet me at the forge tomorrow morning, after you're ready and have eaten. I will assist you in those matters, if you wish," he offered. "If you aren't there by luncheon, then I will assume that you would rather not, or are fine as you are, and will see you at dinner that evening.

She nodded as she humbly whispered, "Thank you."

She entered the door he held open for her, then resumed trailing slightly behind him. She was truly touched that he wanted to aid her in learning to defend herself. She was grateful, but began to wonder if he had a hidden reason for the gesture… Surely, he knew that teaching her to honestly fight would allow her to protect herself against those seeking to harm her… including him, if needed. She watched him striding confidently and prayed fervently that it would never come to that. She wondered at her reluctance to hurt him, even in the idea of self-defense, when it hit her! He held open another door for her and muttered an apology about a mess, when their eyes met, and she realized that

Beastly Cycle

she genuinely cared about the fox-man before her. She stood there gazing warmly at him. A bright blush rose to her cheeks as she realized what she was doing and saw a startled, but hopeful look in his eyes. She hastily darted through the doorway and off to the side to calm her pounding heart! She had not been this flustered since Fistorik first asked her permission to court her! She watched the creature use his candlestick to light candelabra of various sizes within the massive room, sneaking glances her way as he worked, and wondered at his growing power to unsettle her heart and weaken her knees.

As she took a minute to compose herself, she gazed around the spacious room. The side wall to her right had floor to ceiling windows of dusty glass sections, framed in metal and double glass doors in the center, with one of them half torn off its hinges, and what appeared to be a balcony of some kind beyond them. A single flowering bush stood in a large clay pot within the darkness outside. The opposite wall across from her had two more sets of double doors that were elaborately carved over their entire surfaces. There was a fireplace with a dingy mantel on the left wall and a single, ornately carved door on either side of the mantel. A large pile of shattered wood, shredded cloth, and other unknown items occupied the far corner of the room. Another sizeable pile of something, hidden beneath a massive cloth, lay beside her, leaving the floor of

Rennora's Hurt

the room clear and clean. In the center of the room stood a tall object covered entirely by a thick fabric of dark purple velvet. Whatever it was must have been a fairly recent addition, because it was missing the heavy dust that coated the piles, broken door, and even the mantel. The creature stood beside it and beckoned her to stand before it. Once she was in position, he ripped off the cloth! In front of her was a mirror that towered over her at around seven and a half feet. It was four feet across, including its wide, smooth stone frame of gray, with faint white flecks and slightly darker gray veining throughout. Intricate scrollwork covered the rounded top of the frame. A thick strip of blank stone ran below it along the entire bottom portion of the frame, and the sides. The glass was some of the clearest she had ever seen, with the purest silver coating the back of it.

    She then noticed her own reflection. The dress was beautiful in its humble elegance, with its straight sleeves, squared neckline, and form fitting bodice that tied at her sides and fell into a fuller skirt at her hips, just brushing the floor. Her hair was pulled back with a gorgeous comb of sparkling crystal and pearls, while part of it fell into natural, soft curls that lay across her shoulder. Her eyes teared up. Her heart ached. She had to look away, so she dropped her gaze to the floor. While the maids' efforts were to be commended, and the items were radiant, it was just another reminder that she would never be beautiful to anyone, not even to herself. If she had even just a little more beauty, or intelligence, or something, perhaps she would have been able to remain at Fistorik's side, instead of standing there cursing her very existence.

She said nothing, wondering why the creature greatly desired to show her the foul thing, when she saw movement in the mirror. She could not help but peer into the lower portion of it and watch as the creature's bare feet moved into view a couple of feet behind her.

"Are you well, belle mademoiselle?" he asked, concerned.

"Why are you showing me this?" she demanded softly, her voice shaking with her pain as she gazed into his reflection's face, tears falling unchecked down her pale cheeks.

He moved closer, placed his hand on the blank side frame, and stood there next to her side, gazing intently into her reflection. "This is why…" he simply stated.

Strange symbols of silver then suddenly appeared along the sides and top of the frame! They flared up until she could hardly stand to gaze at their brightness! The images on the mirror swirled into a thick fog of dimming colors before vanishing into an inky black darkness. Rennora stumbled back a

Rennora's Hurt

step, shocked and frightened at the sight! She peered at the creature, quite perplexed.

"Just watch," he gently urged, assuring her with his calm and steady tone.

The blackness shifted into a haze of images that quickly cleared. She stepped forward in awe. Within the glass, she saw the central square of her town! She watched the people going about their day, Conadora's father bartering with a fellow merchant, while his daughter was happily talking with friends, the lost look still hovering within the edges of her green eyes.

Rennora pointed at the silent images. "H-how is this possible?" she whispered.

The creature chuckled at her caution. "No need to lower your voice. They can't hear us any more than we can hear them. I'm guessing that the mirror is enchanted only to show images and scenes of the present. It can't convey any sounds, however. You only need to think of the place or person in your mind, your desire to see it in your heart, and place your hand on the stone. It doesn't matter whether or not you've actually been there or met the individual, the mirror will still show you the place or person."

He dropped his hand to his side to prove his point. The bustling images remained as they were, like the most lifelike and exquisite painting, but they were moving! She reached out her hand and barely

Beastly Cycle

brushed the warm surface with her fingertips. Suddenly, the mirror fell black and returned to its original state as an ordinary looking glass! She quickly jerked her hand back!

The creature explained, "And that's how you halt the enchantment. That, or everyone leaves the room."

She thought for a moment and realized something. "This is how you've been choosing your ladies."

He nodded.

"And what of the petal?"

"I simply have to place any one onto the person's image, focus on how it's to be delivered, and set it free. I usually use the bush on the balcony over there."

"And how long have you been watching me?"

He heaved a heavy sigh and shyly admitted, "I first saw you in your kingdom of suds and dishes about three months ago."

She nodded sagely. "That's one way of putting it."

He quickly continued, his confidence slowly rising, "I watched you return to that house each evening and the pain of dealing with those two people, before I would end the enchantment to preserve your privacy every time. I saw you often under the tree with a book in hand. You assisted that father to carry his daughter home and keep her

Rennora's Hurt

company until the healer arrived. I saw your heart in your eyes as you gazed at that foolish undeserving fellow, then watched as that unsavory boy pursued you back to his lordship's house. Who was he?"

"The son of a lord who once courted me and wishes to wed me," she coldly stated. "He's quite persistent about it. I have no desire to be his wife, ever, as I continuously have to remind him. He's not the kind of man that I want as my husband for a variety of reasons, lying to me being one of the highest. I may have to seek a new life in another town, as far away as I can manage, in order for him to finally understand that 'no' means no."

"Wise lady. When you leave here, I'll do all within my power to aid you in that. I watched that woman dress you down fiercely, and your tears that night…"

"You sent all those petals, didn't you?"

His gaze became concerned and gentle. "I just wanted you to know that you weren't alone and to bring a smile, no matter how small, to your lovely face. Then I saw that cloaked *filth*," he snarled, "waiting for you the next morning, so I charged from the castle and drew as close as I dared to drive it off before it could lay a single, unworthy finger on your person. I lingered to ensure that it wouldn't return and that you were safe. I began to return when I heard someone scream something about

Beastly Cycle

murder! As I turned around, I saw you fleeing for your life! It pierced my soul that I couldn't follow, so I rushed back here in time to see you alive and in one piece in the mirror, but standing at the boundary between the town and the lands surrounding this castle. You were panicked, desperate, and your thoughts seemed torn! You needed a friend. Then after you received the petal, I could only stand here, frozen with my heart pounding in my ears, as you leapt the ditch with your unwelcomed suitor frantically trying to halt you! Now," he stepped away from the mirror and her. "It's your turn to use it if you wish."

  She placed her hands on either side of the frame. She then froze! She had no idea where or who she wanted to see at all! She pondered for a bit. She soon remembered the few people that had been kind to her… She carefully focused herself. Mistress Tisza and Groundskeeper Quorrick were on the other side of the central square and talking very animatedly with a couple of the town guards. Both were clearly upset about something.

  "If I may inquire, who are they?" the creature politely asked.

  Rennora had forgotten that he was still nearby. She explained about both of them and their kindness to her. She then moved on to dear Arissera who was, oddly enough, with Wescar and also talking with some other guards. She wondered what they

Rennora's Hurt

were saying, or why they seemed so terribly worried. It tugged at her heart to see her three friends, not counting Wescar, so troubled, whatever they thought of her now. She soon watched Mistress LaZella and Thevesta slip over and join the conversation. It was not long before all four people were screaming heatedly at each other! She informed the creature of whom they were as well and reached up to put an end to the images when she spied Fistorik watching in the background. She placed her hand back on the frame, and it shifted to his person alone. He appeared distressed as well. Rennora drank in his handsome face until his beloved came to his side from somewhere out of sight. She spoke to him. He responded. She then gently assured him of something. He beamed down at her, kissed her hand, placed it on his arm, and they went on their way together, arm in arm. Rennora half smacked the mirror to put an end to the tormenting sights! She stood there, her eyes staring into her own reflection's tears. As she turned to leave, she caught the sight of the creature. He stood in silence, worried, for several agonizing minutes.

    He then got down on one knee, with his fist on his chest and his other hand on the floor, and pleaded with her, "Please forgive me, belle mademoiselle, for both spying on you and your life, and not understanding what I was seeing, or I would

Beastly Cycle

have come to your aid far sooner, no matter the personal cost to me. I assure you that whatever happens here, I will come to your aid should you need it. Use your bell to summon me, and I will come without hesitation."

  She hesitantly nodded, then turned back to the mirror and the heartbroken person in it. Tears were streaming down her cheeks. "I can't stand you," she snarled to it under her breath and fled toward the door until a hand caught her.

  She begged the creature to let her go, trying to release his firm hold, but she did not have the strength anymore, so she collapsed to the floor, sobbing. He sat down beside her, collected her into his arms, and just held her tenderly while she cried herself out, clinging desperately to his tunic.

Chapter 16
~ Beast ~

Alleron's Heart

Alleron's heart ached for her pain. Rennora was such a gentle soul. She did not deserve the nightmare that was her life! He held her as long as she needed it and released her when she sat upright, her hands still on his chest. She refused to meet his gaze, but he could understand her embarrassment. He remained where he was, hesitant to break the silence quite yet. She then peered at his chest, gasped in horror, and blushed deeply. She covered one hand with the end of her sleeve and proceeded to wipe at the damp spots on his good tunic, which was now slightly wrinkled.

"I am so terribly sorry about that!" she softly apologized, looking absolutely mortified.

He placed his hand over hers on his chest, with a prayer that she could not feel his racing heart underneath, halting her efforts.

He gently assured her, "It'll dry, I promise, and besides," he leaned down slightly so he could better meet her amazing, slate blue eyes, "I was going to bathe later. You simply saved me the trouble."

She let out a slight chuckle. His heart almost leapt out of his chest at the beautiful sound and her warm, lingering touch. He removed his hand, and she did the same with hers. He was delighted to see her emerging from her gloom and beginning to cheer up. It was torturous to him to see her so hurt. He had the overwhelming urge to rip those that had brought her such pain into very minute pieces.

"Are you any better, belle mademoiselle?" he carefully asked her.

She nodded and whispered a thank you.

"Good. May I ask you what those words you muttered were about?"

She shook her head dismissively. "I'm being silly again. Pay me no mind."

He rose to his feet and assisted her to hers before he continued, "If I didn't know any better, I would have to say that you were saying that to yourself and not to those people back in your town… Am I correct?"

She refused to meet his eyes, but he could see that she was very ashamed. Whether it was because she had said them aloud, or because she had been caught by his excellent hearing, he did not know. He wanted so much for her to think better of herself. She had so much to give, and her shy beauty left him breathless. He wanted to aid her in realizing this. He scanned around them, seeking anything that would assist them, when he recalled the mirror.

"Come with me," he urged her as he held her hand and guided her reluctantly back in front of it. He hurt to see her refusing once again to gaze upon herself. "Tell me what you see…" She promptly turned to walk away, but he kept hold of her slender hand. "Please," he pleaded tenderly.

She shakily answered, "I beg you not to do this to me… please."

"Why is that?"

"Because I already know that I'm hideous, inside and out!" she snapped, tears trickling. "You have no need to reaffirm that!"

"Is there nothing at all that you like, even a tiny bit, about yourself? Anything at all?" he begged with all his heart.

She stubbornly shook her head, refusing to meet his eyes.

"Please, look just once more before you fully set yourself against it."

Her eyes made their way up the mirror, inch by inch, until she was fully gazing into it. He watched and prayed that she could open her heart to just one thing.

After several long minutes of examining herself, she replied, "M-my hair, I suppose."

He was relieved! "What about it?"

"The color's nice…"

Beastly Cycle

"And?"

"I like my curls."

He beamed lovingly at her. He then took a step closer and whispered gently into her shell-like ear, "Now, my dearest Rennora, let me tell you what I see. I see a lady of such grace and beauty that it has almost every man that crosses her path spellbound, and those who don't see that are blind. I see hair as brown as a chestnut tree and soft as down. I see eyes like a stormy sky that shine brighter than the sun and twinkle with stars at times. I see skin as soft as silk and pale as cream. I see a lady that has been through things that would crush others, and yet, can still manage a sweet smile that makes hearts skip a beat, or three. So unselfish that she puts others' needs, desires, and pain before her own, leading to negligence of herself quite often. I see such a wondrous and incredible lady, that it makes me ache inside for her…"

Her face snapped toward him, eyes wide and unbelieving at what he was declaring! He felt his heart pounding again. He was amazed at his own words and spine of steel at giving voice to them, but he meant every single one of them. As he stood there gazing at her loveliness and wonder at his sincerity, he desperately wanted to caress her face and finish pouring his heart with a simple *I love you*. But somehow, he could not bring himself to do it. His nerves were deserting him, and if by some strange miracle, she returned his love… His heart plummeted to his feet at the thought of her being the next beast and hating him for the rest of her life because of it. He knew what he had to do… He retreated a few steps, bowed to her, produced his own small bell that he carried in a hidden pouch, and summoned Kestin to personally escort her back to her apartments. Alleron calmly, softly bid her pleasant dreams, but she said nothing. She seemed to still be reeling as she hesitantly followed in silence. He watched the door slowly close behind her, feeling like it had just slammed on his last opportunity to be human again with her…

"Good," he said aloud. "I won't do it at someone else's freedom."

He began to cover the mirror back up, when he noticed himself. "Especially *hers*," he snarled at his reflection and saw the resolve tighten in his own heartbroken eyes before they vanished under the fabric.

Chapter 17
~ Beauty ~

Peace and Understanding

Rennora humbly accepted a spare lit candlestick from the haze and simply stood there with her back to the closed door. With some urging, she followed the servant through the darkness, her mind in chaos, and her heart still racing as she dragged her feet along the way. She desperately needed some time to sort through what had just happened, and she needed it *now*, in a place of her own choosing, *not* the room she had been given, which did not feel like a sanctuary to her! She wished for a tree to rest against or even a quiet room nearby. Shortly after they turned a corner, she noticed a pair of double doors. One looked like it had been half ripped off, but the other was still intact and partially opened. She was grateful beyond words for the sight. She waited until the haze passed it, then noiselessly slipped inside a massive room bathed in darkness. She followed the wall beside the undamaged door for a couple of feet until she was sure her light could not be seen from the corridor any more. She then leaned against the

Peace and Understanding

wall and slid down it into a sitting position. She quietly set down her candlestick, hugged her knees, and buried her face in the soft fabric of her dress.

She heard a man calling her frantically, but she ignored him. Her head then snapped up at the sound of the creature's voice joining the first! She could hear the worry heavily laced into his tone…

"What do you mean she vanished?!" he heatedly demanded of the other person. "Where were you when you lost sight of her?"

She heard a long, mumbled response.

The creature then spoke again, somewhat calmer, "Search the floor below and her rooms. She may have taken a different way there. I'll begin here. I would know her scent anywhere now. I should be able to track her easily enough. I'll quickly summon you or her maids if needed."

She heard more mumbling.

"I hope that you're right, Kestin. I would never forgive myself if something happened to her. Is Jes still bound to the kitchens?" He paused. "Good, keep her there. I don't need her to add her special charm to this mess I've made. What?"

More mumbling.

He sighed heavily. "I'll explain tomorrow. We need to see to Rennora's safety first. Go!"

She heard their footsteps fading away. She closed her eyes, leaned her head back on the cool stone wall behind her, and took slow, deep breaths.

Beastly Cycle

No one had *ever* told her such things about herself, or in a manner like that! True, Fistorik and Wescar had told her how pretty she was and how much he had cared for her when each was courting her in turn, but nothing like this! She had felt the creature's very soul, as well as his heart, in his words… She wondered if the creature had meant to declare his heart to her, or if he was only trying to help her, and she was simply confusing his intent. Most of her wanted to believe that he was offering his entire heart to her, while a very small part did not want to risk being hurt again. She did not know what to think of his halting her from running away when she was upset. It was certainly a first for her! The others had simply let her go. Fistorik would usually find her after a couple of hours of her calming down in hiding. Wescar would wait until the next day and walk with her from the house to his lordship's house. He had never been able to find her since the first time she hid on him, so he had given up trying long ago. She sighed heavily. The three of them were so different in so many ways and similar in others. She continued to mull things over, still quite mixed up, but feeling a bit calmer now.

   She then heard soft footsteps and the clicking of claws on the stone floor beyond the door. She watched a light spill onto the floor in front of the doorway and grow brighter as the footsteps drew

Peace and Understanding

closer. She listened as the person halted just outside the doorway.

"Are you alright, belle mademoiselle?" the creature carefully asked her, remaining in the hall.

"Yes, thank you," she hesitantly answered, not certain if she was quite ready to face him yet.

"Are you hurt at all?"

"I simply needed a little peace for a while," she shyly admitted. "I'm terribly sorry for frightening all of you like that with my selfishness."

"Everyone needs some time to themselves now and then for various reasons," he gently assured her. "Should you need it again, say something, and you shall have it immediately in the place of your choosing and for as long as you desire."

"Thank you for being so kind and understanding."

"Are you ready to leave the ballroom, or do you need longer?"

"Ballroom?"

"Yes. You're in the royal's private ballroom that they apparently used for more exclusive parties and privileged guests."

"Oh…" She gazed around at the few blurred shapes that she could see against the dim light of the bare windows. "I see… Give me a moment, please."

As she began to rise, she noticed a rectangular object coated in a thin layer of dust near the corner

Beastly Cycle

beside her. She brushed it off to discover another book. She wondered how it came to be there as she scooped both it and her light up. She then slowly walked over to the doorway to stand before the creature, slightly nervous, embarrassed, and confused.

"Would you prefer me or someone else to guide you back?" he carefully inquired.

She stood in silence, not sure how to answer. He had done nothing wrong, but she did not know if she desired his company or not.

"How many have you found?" he politely asked, indicating the volume in her hand.

"Four so far."

He nodded. "So you're about halfway through their tale."

The creature then stood there in silence as though he was waiting for her to reply, but she said nothing more in the growing awkwardness. After a while, he stepped to the side within the corridor to let her pass. She hesitantly remained where she was. He clasped his hands behind his back, smiling gently at her. Soon, they heard a door slam shut somewhere from behind him. Quick footsteps followed as a tall manservant haze came rushing up to them. She could hear him breathing heavily after he halted near them. The haze promptly said something to the creature.

Peace and Understanding

"Kestin wishes you to know that he is glad to see you're safe and wonders if he has done anything to offend you."

Rennora assured him, "You've done nothing wrong, I promise." She shuffled her feet for a moment, not really wanting to explain herself further.

"You must be tired, and it's getting quite late," the creature offered. "Why don't we both walk you back."

She nodded, grateful to be allowed her silence. Kestin said something else to the creature, but he shook his head, refusing to respond in return. Without another word, Kestin took the lead, with Rennora in the middle, and the creature trailing behind. They made their way through a massive hall, to the tower, down the stairs to the next floor, and on to her rooms' double doors. Kestin said something to her.

"Kestin wishes you a restful slumber," the creature politely explained.

"Thank you," she replied. "Pleasant dreams to you as well."

Kestin bowed respectfully and left them. The creature shuffled his feet nervously for a minute.

"Well then," he ventured. "I suppose that I'll wish you pleasant reading."

"Thank you, and pleasant dreams to you as well," she softly answered.

Beastly Cycle

She readied herself for bed without ringing for her maids and began to climb under the covers, physically and emotionally exhausted, when she remembered the two new books that she had found. She collected them and began to read, wondering what was going to happen next. The first of the two books took her a bit to figure out who the author was. She found it cute that Princess Belnisa's personal maid was sweet on the steward of the castle. She skimmed through most of the book, which mostly contained ordinary, day-to-day life, until she came to the last set of entries.

> *August 10th – My heart is breaking for my poor mistress... She is becoming increasingly distressed over her husband lately. The prince has been acting very strangely since their ball. He has been spending less time with her and more time closed away in his advisor's company. That is not too unusual of itself. Even crown princes still need to learn the laws and ways of their kingdom. Who better to help teach them but the King's own trusted*

Peace and Understanding

advisor. What has my mistress, and me as well, greatly worried is that his niece is often invited to join them on their councils! It is to the point now that his highness even meets with only her!

His mother, her majesty, has assured my mistress that he will grow bored of the other woman soon enough. The princess knows as well as anyone that he should not be alone with her in the first place! Surely the prince knows this too! I understand from the other servants that he has never strayed with a lady before, so my mistress's question is why is he doing it now? She does not think that it will end any time soon, so she is determined to put a stop to it as delicately and discreetly as she can. The trouble is that every time she tries to talk some sense into him when they

Beastly Cycle

are finally alone, he gets a strange look in his eyes. I have seen it myself! It is like his mind is thousands of miles away, and there is a slight dullness to his eyes.

She does not know what else to do right now! She figures that patience and endurance are going to be key to finding out what is happening with him and fixing it. She has even asked me to discreetly watch and listen. I have to admit that I would dearly love to see his highness return to himself and both him and my mistress blissful once more.

August 13th – You will never believe what happened two days ago! I was summoned urgently to my mistress's side to aid her in moving her things into a spare room on a lower

Peace and Understanding

floor on the other side of the castle, as far from her husband as possible and by his own demand! I have spent the last two days tending to the princess every waking hour, listening to her heartbroken sobs and helpless accusations against two highly placed people, and preparing a calming drink each night to aid her getting some semblance of rest.

I am terribly exhausted from the constant care, but I cannot fail my mistress in my duties. She needs me now more than ever! I did notice that the advisor's niece's personal maid has taken over preparing his highness's nightly drink and refused to let anyone else go near it ever since the princess was thrown out of her husband's bed chambers... The girl even washed the dishes it creates herself! Most

Beastly Cycle

servants, especially ones in our position with noble charges, think dish washing is well beneath us! The kitchen scullery maids are in an outrage at the insult, thinking that she believes that they are not capable of doing a thorough cleaning of the items! What in the world is she thinking!

Forgive the short entry, my mistress beckons again. I must go. Heaven aid us through this mess...

August 17th – Help me! I fear for both my mistress and her majesty's very lives! I had noticed over the past week, the glares and sneers that his highness's favored lady had been giving both of them when she thought that no one was looking have suddenly changed into a knowing smirk today! I promptly informed both ladies of my

Peace and Understanding

observations, frightened by the punishment that such a thing could bring down upon my head. Happily, they heeded my suspicions, and now, each keep a well trusted guard close and discreetly with her at all times. I wish that my mistress had not chosen someone so highly placed within the royal family's personal guards, but I have seen for myself that he can be trusted with her safety and will keep his hands to himself in her time of agony.

August 21st – I cannot believe it is actually happening! His royal highness has completely lost what sense that he had! I was walking by the rose garden behind the castle on my way to collect some blooms, to assist in lifting my mistress's spirits,

Beastly Cycle

when I heard voices on the other side of the hedge. I was going to ignore them, like a good servant, when I recognized his highness's favorite as she said something about undeniable proof and the princess. I halted, quietly parted some of the foliage, and listened closer. You will never believe what I heard! That hag was talking his highness into believing that his wife had been unfaithful to him with one of his close guards, his mother was aiding in hiding it, and he needed to make an example of them both by disposing of them for all to see, and as quickly as possible!

I quietly slipped back into the castle after that. It took everything in me not to break out in a run and scream at the closest guard what I had heard! However, I kept myself in

Peace and Understanding

check. With the thick air of suspicion lying on the castle lately, I could not bring myself to trust any of them. I found both my mistress and her mother-in-law in her majesty's sitting room. I whispered my information and urged them to leave at once! Her majesty was so calm and unruffled. Thankfully, she has a close trusted friend that can break the mysterious hold on his highness, finally freeing us all of this terrible curse that is hanging over us. All we wait for is the afternoon's peace to make our way to the forests beyond the boundaries of the royal lands.

So farewell, my dear friend. This will be my last entry. If things turn out well for us, the monsters will be discovered and punished, and the royal couple will be reunited in marital bliss.

Beastly Cycle

I will write again in a new book, for this one will be burned first chance I have. Wish us well and safe journey.

Rennora wanted more information, but realized that the maid had risked so much to put down what she had. Even just hinting at an accusation at the prince's favorite could have seen her and the princess killed! She wondered if the three ladies made it to safety in time… She laid back onto the soft pillows and drifted off, pondering what she would have done had she been in the maid's shoes…

Rennora woke up trembling with soft screams hours later, half tangled in her bedding! A tall mirror in a darkened room still danced across her mind. She could see images of evil enchantresses and advisors, a man turning into a tiger, and a woman imprisoned within a lone tree, surrounded by water and grievously injured people, all begging for their lives to be saved shifting on its polished surface! Then suddenly, Rennora practically leapt out of her skin as someone banged loudly on her outer door!

"Are you alright?" the creature fiercely demanded through the closed doors. "I heard you crying out!"

Peace and Understanding

She was so shaken up this time that she could not seem to bring herself to answer. She rose to her feet and stumbled to the bed chamber's doorway where she braced herself against it. She then heard the creature bang even harder!

"*ANSWER ME NOW, OR THESE DOORS ARE COMING DOWN!*" he heatedly roared.

"Please don't…" she sobbed in a whisper, doubting that he could hear her.

She was surprised when he responded in a strained voice, as though he was trying desperately to master himself and having trouble doing so, "Then please, tell me what's troubling you so. I beg of you…"

She moved to the outer doors, leaned her head on the cool stone of the wall beside it, and dried her teary eyes. "As you may have already guessed, I'm plagued by nightmares," she explained in a shaky voice. "It's been happening on and off for years now."

"I see…" he gently commented.

"Most times, all it takes to rid myself of them for the rest of the night is for me to fully awaken, then return to sleep."

"Then perhaps it would be best if I left you in peace."

Panicked at the thought of being left alone right now, she threw one of the doors open to find a startled look on the creature's face! "Please stay,"

Beastly Cycle

she softly pleaded, tears beginning to well up in her eyes again.

"I-if that is your wish," he finally managed to stammer.

She nodded frantically. She then leaned her back against her room's wall again and slid down into a sitting position. She whispered a sad thank you to him after a while in the tense silence. He nodded once and stood there, waiting for her to continue.

"I don't know if it's this place or something else," she quietly began, "but for some reason, my dreams are becoming far worse lately."

The creature sat down in the corridor next to her open door and facing her.

"It's this place," he gently assured her. "I had the same—" He cut himself off. He tried again. "In the first few days anyways. I think that all that had happened here in the past, all the fears and other feelings as well, have embedded themselves into the stones. Newcomers to the lands tend to feel it unknowingly, if they linger long enough. It affects their dreams while their minds are at rest." He gazed into her interested face for a couple of moments before he shifted his attention into the darkened corridor. "That's my thoughts on it. They're a little foolish, I know."

She smiled hesitantly at him. "Actually, they made good sense to me."

Peace and Understanding

She rubbed her arms, feeling slightly chilly. The creature scanned around them for several minutes. He then paused, thought, then pulled off his tunic and silently offered it to her as he sat there in his shirt and pants. She shyly accepted it with a whispered thank you. As she slipped it on, she noticed how warm it was from the creature's body heat. It smelled rather nice as well. She fought back a blush at the thought, thankful that the creature could not see into her mind at all.

"You look like you're feeling a little better now," the creature noted.

Rennora smiled a bit more at him, then she wiped at her weary eyes.

"Is there anything else that you require, belle mademoiselle?" he inquired.

She stifled a yawn before replying, "Wishful thinking on my part."

"Pray tell," he gently urged.

"I was just thinking that a nice steady rain would be heavenly right about now." She then felt slightly ludicrous for giving voice to her thought.

He was a little intrigued at her answer. "Rain? Why rain?"

"I've always found the sound and feel of it so calming," she explained as she blushed in embarrassment. "I love how it drowns out the sounds of the world, drives most people indoors,

Beastly Cycle

and cleanses everything it touches, leaving the air so sweet and everything brighter when it's finished."

The creature sat in deep thought for a while. She felt her eyelids growing heavy. She eased onto the floor, facing the doorway, before she had realized what she had done, and rested her head on her bent arm.

"I've never done this deliberately before…" he muttered, his voice betraying his uncertainty.

She watched him close his eyes and take a deep breath. Then her eyes closed of their own accord. Just as she was beginning to slip off into a light sleep, she heard the first patters of rain on the stones outside. The creature gasped for air after a couple of minutes of silence. She heard him steady his panting and sigh, content. She smiled warmly at the weather's sweet sounds and drifted into a deeper slumber.

Chapter 18
~ Beauty ~

Pleasant Surprises

Rennora slowly awoke in the morning to the pleasant sunlight caressing her from the tall hallway windows, half blinding her in the process. She sat up and stretched to relieve her stiffness, strangely happy. She pleasantly gazed out the doorway through the windows. The air seemed so crisp and clean outside. The day already held quite a bit of promise to her. She arranged the blanket that had slipped off of her, to better cover her lap, when she realized that it had not been there when she had fallen asleep last night! She heard a small snore from close by that startled her! She then noticed the creature, propped up against the wall just outside of her door. He looked so peaceful and content as he slumbered on, with his arms folded across his chest and his legs stretched out into the hall. She had never seen him so at ease. She wondered at it until a truly horrible idea hit her! She took quick stock of herself and found everything as it should be. She was touched that he had simply kept watch over her for the rest of the night. She carefully draped the

Beastly Cycle

blanket over him, then slowly removed his tunic, and set it beside him. She smiled shyly at the sight of him for a moment. She quietly headed into her bed chamber to ready herself for the day. She rang her bell as she wrapped a sleeveless robe around herself to stay warm and waited in the continued peace.

    All of a sudden, she began to worry about the servants disturbing the creature as they entered, so she returned to her sitting room in order to ask the maids to let him be, when she noticed that he had already left! She peered down both ways of the corridor, but saw no one. She glanced at the spot where he slept. He must have taken the blanket with him. However, he had forgotten his tunic. She scooped it up and tucked it into the bottom corner of her chest for safe keeping until she could return it to him later. It probably would be easier to hand it over to one of the servants, but she really wished to do it herself. It would give her an opportunity to thank him personally for his company.

    Suddenly, she heard a knock at her outer door. A girl dressed in a soft blue was waiting there with her meal while a second stood patiently behind her. Rennora thanked them as she set the tray down on the small table near the padded chair and stoked the dying fire. She sat down to eat while both maids entered her bed chamber to prepare everything for her. She noticed something different about the

Pleasant Surprises

servants as they worked, but could not figure out what it was. She finished quickly and joined her first maid in her bed chamber. Rennora took one glance at the fuller dress that had been chosen and politely requested either one which would allow her to move more easily, or shirt and pants instead. The maid stood there and thought deeply. Rennora spied a thick lock of black hair that had slipped out of the maid's head covering and laid on her shoulder. She thought it pretty against the dress fabric. She watched the maid sort through the armoire and pull out a simple dress of brown that would allow her full use of her legs. She approved the new choice and allowed herself to be dressed.

 A second maid, dressed in blue as well, then accompanied the first in fixing the guest's hair. Rennora requested that it be off of her neck so that she would remain cooler for the next several hours, figuring that she could possibly overheat with how active she was about to be. She startled at the first maid gasping in shock at the very idea!

 "If that is what the lady wishes, that is what we do, Minna," the second maid whispered to the first. "It is not our shame to have her walking around with hair like a married woman when she is unwed."

 "But her shame *is* our shame!" Minna softly exclaimed. "We are the ones that dress her! Maybe we can pretend that we did not hear her and quickly think of something better that will keep her cool and maintain her dignity at the same time. Perhaps just half braided up, with some loose curls along the back of her neck?"

"You are just as bad as she is!" the second maid snapped just as quietly! "Fine, do what you will! I want no part of this."

Rennora watched in the mirror without moving her head, as the second maid gathered the dirty clothing and left in a snit. She inspected her hair and thanked the remaining maid, well pleased with the compromise. Minna curtsied and left, quietly closing the door behind her. Rennora gazed at the door, wondering if even the manservants wore such a light blue, when she realized that she could actually see and hear the servants now! She froze, shocked and perplexed for several minutes. As her mind began to accept the changes, she relaxed a bit and pondered things carefully. They were still a bit hazy, so she could not make out their faces, but they were definitely clearer than yesterday. She was delighted at the thought of being able to communicate with them better, but wondered if she should let everyone know about it quite yet. She soon decided that she would keep quiet about her discovery until after dinner. She hoped that she could use the advantage to assist her in gaining a better understanding of everyone discreetly until then. She slipped out into the hall, closed her door,

Pleasant Surprises

and wound her way through the castle and into the entrance hall. She paused, wondering which way to go this time, as she watched the servants chatting while they cleaned. Her eyes then fell on the front doorway. She decided to head out that way to aid her in learning her way around.

She halted just outside at the strange sight before her. Tiny specks of green dotted the dry grass surrounding the bases of the crumbling pillars. She examined the nearest one to discover budding leaves that she was quite certain were not there when she had arrived! The sight of the new growth brought a gentle smile to her lips as she slowly wandered along the main road to the front gate. She then noticed that the tiny figures in the center of the gate's rose had changed! The hawk was replaced with a slender lady of grace reaching for the man. The man was still reaching for her, but there was a fox seated behind him. There was also a pair of watchful eyes as well, one over each figure. The eyes and fox seemed like they were waiting for something…

She fingered the barely opened gate, wondering if the creature changed it to reflect his heart, or if the curse did it to show what was currently happening within the borders. Too many questions, not enough answers.

"I'll get this figured out," she promised the figures as she rubbed her arm.

Beastly Cycle

She then quickly headed over to the village. She found the creature pacing around the pool with his hands clasped behind his back and looking a bit nervous. She smiled warmly as she approached. He just stared at her, stunned. She checked around her, but saw no one else.

"Is everything alright?" she inquired, slightly concerned.

He shook his head for a second. He then bowed respectfully as he replied, "Forgive me, belle mademoiselle. I wasn't certain that you would come. Very few ladies are interested in combat or weaponry. I'm delighted that you did though." He smiled warmly at her. "Shall we begin?" He directed her attention to the edge of the pool and the array of weapons waiting there. "I meant to ask you yesterday if there was any particular weapon that you would like to learn the basics of, other than the dagger."

She peered over the various swords and daggers, feeling overwhelmed at the thought of having to choose from the many types that she had seen in the smithy's storage room. She took a breath to steady herself.

"This will be fine, thank you," she hesitantly stated.

"If you feel that these aren't working for you, we can try some of the others until we find what will best suit you and your style."

Pleasant Surprises

She agreed, feeling more confident at his offer.

"Which would you like to try first?" he politely inquired.

"Umm," she muttered as she scanned the weapons. None of them really stood out to her. "I'm not sure what I'm supposed to be looking for," she admitted. "Whichever one you choose will be fine with me."

He nodded, thought for a minute, then picked up one of the shorter swords by the hilt, held it point down, and offered it to her. She grabbed a hold of the handle to take it, but he did not let go just yet. She was a little puzzled as to his intent.

"Always say 'thank you'," he explained. "It lets the giver know that you have a firm hold of the weapon, so neither of you becomes accidentally wounded by it slipping out of your hand."

She thanked him this time. He released it and quickly stepped back. The sword was heavier than it appeared! The unexpected weight caused the point to dip at first as she struggled to hold it single handed comfortably. She then tried to hold it with two hands, but could not quite position her hands comfortably.

"Like this," the creature stated as he showed her using a second sword.

She studied his grip carefully and fixed hers to her delight! He then moved onto a basic thrust. She felt quite foolish as she stabbed at a thick pole

Beastly Cycle

wrapped in heavy rope with her feet set slightly wider than her hip width, but she forced the feeling aside. This was very important to her, and she was not about to allow her thoughts to hinder her in any way. They continued by adding an overhead swing. Once she was reasonably comfortable with both, he taught her to block both, and she practiced on him, slowly picking up speed as they went. He corrected her here and there. They continued on the drills and adding new skills until luncheon arrived. They then halted to rest and eat their fill.

Curious, she asked, "How do you think I'm fairing?"

He quickly swallowed his bite before he answered, "Quite well, actually. Just remember the little things I explained, like your grip and footwork, as you practice, until they're engraved so deeply into both your body and memory that you can do each correctly without thought every time."

"How long will that take?"

"Months, possibly years, if you're dedicated to mastery of this. Many things in life can't be learned in a single day."

"True." She rose to her feet with a resigned sigh. "I guess I should better return to it, if I want to reach that level."

He chuckled merrily at her.

"And *what* exactly is so amusing?" she playfully demanded.

Pleasant Surprises

"Forgive me, fair Rennora, but you are one strange lady. You find enjoyment and passion in things that most other ladies turn their noses up at."

"So people keep berating me for… All I can say is that I am me, no more, no less, oddities and all."

He rose to his feet, slowly leaned toward her, looked her straight in the eye with a soft gleam in his own, and breathed, "That wasn't intended as an insult in the slightest."

Her eyes widened in surprise!

He then indicated the waiting pole with a mischievous smirk. "Shall we?"

She once again did not know how to react to such a remark! She took a minute to quickly calm her pounding heart before she joined him, determined not to allow him to unsettle her again for the remainder of the lessons. They practiced for another hour, then shifted to basic weaponless attacks and defenses before she called a halt to the session. She was becoming sore and quite exhausted.

"Wise idea," the creature cheerfully observed. "We'll call it done for today and continue tomorrow's skills by including your daggers, if you desire."

"Yes, please," she quickly replied.

"Until dinner then." He bowed and retrieved both swords. She seated herself on the edge of the pool and dipped her hands in the cool water. She then dried them on the bottom of her skirt as the creature returned to find her still there.

"Thank you for the lessons," she stated with a warm smile.

"My pleasure entirely," he assured her with a return smile as he pulled out a small bell of brass with green enamel inlay.

She saw him ring it, but did not hear a tinkling that she knew should be coming from it.

"I think your bell might be broken," she pointed out.

He examined it briefly before he rang it again with no sound.

"I take it that you can't hear that?" he inquired, very curious.

"Yes," she stated, perplexed. "I can see it ringing, but nothing is coming from it."

"Intriguing…"

They both fell into a contemplative silence, when she soon noticed a tall manservant coming toward them. He had darker, slightly yellow-ish skin, dark hair and eyes, and was dressed neatly in dark green, which reminded her of the trees in the forest.

"Kestin here will guide you wherever you wish," the creature explained.

Pleasant Surprises

She watched the steward bow as he warmly whispered in a pleasant, mid-range voice, "With pleasure, milord."

The creature shook his head at the servant and departed with another bow to her. Kestin gazed at her politely and expectantly. She would not mind a lovely place to rest for a bit. She gazed around them and spied the forest beyond the boundary walls. It gave her the perfect idea!

"Are there any trees within the walls?" she politely inquired. "If not, the garden behind the castle will do fine. Please."

She watched him pondering her request in silence for several minutes. His gaze then shifted to her face as he studied her, his expression on his square face like he was debating something quite seriously.

He then declared in a whisper, "I suppose you stand a better chance than the others," as he pulled out a clean handkerchief, draped it over his hand, and motioned for her to follow him.

As she followed Kestin, she could feel the creature's eyes watching her. She paused and turned to return his gaze, but found that he had already vanished. She shifted her attention back to the servant and her aching body, eager for a rest.

Chapter 19
~ Beauty ~

Lesson and Clues

Rennora and Kestin strolled past the overgrown garden to the far side of the building. She was beginning to lose patience when he brought her to a halt on the other side of the tower. She spotted a crumbling, stone church next to an old cemetery and surrounded by a very low stone wall several yards away. The grounds around it were neatly kept, which had her wondering why when the rest of the lands had been neglected so terribly. She did not think it a very pleasing place to rest and was about to question his choice, when he directed her attention to a different part of the grounds. Near the front tower was a long, low building that had completely fallen to ruin. She could see another wall of hedges that ran from the tower, behind the ruins, and continued behind the lake that she had seen earlier, with the willow standing on a grassy island in the center. The sight of its solitary stance, seeming so forlorn, captivated her. She thanked Kestin and worked her way through the tall grasses toward it. She then sat by the lake's shore, arranged

Lesson and Clues

her skirt neatly around her, removed her shoes, and dipped her toes into the cool, calming water. She closed her eyes, savoring the sensations around her. She soon began to feel refreshed and rejuvenated in the warm sunlight. A gentle breeze blew. She watched the lowest branches of the tree dancing in the wind until it grew stronger and swept them aside, exposing the rough, but graceful trunk beneath. She spied what appeared to be a small, smoother, oval-ish section part way up the trunk, and a tiny red dot on the ground directly below it, before the branches fell back into place, concealing it once more.

There was something strange about the trunk. She wanted to study it a bit closer, so she rose and followed the edge around, seeking some way across. Along the backside, the land narrowed between the immense stone boundary wall and the lake, to the point that there was barely room for one person to pass comfortably before it widened where the hedges met the stone wall, forming a corner. There she found two posts standing in the ground, hidden from the lake's front view by the tree. She thought them odd, until she gazed across the water at the island's shore. There she discovered the crumbling remnants of a small wooden bridge clinging desperately to the land.

"Just my luck," she muttered, irritated.

Beastly Cycle

She continued the rest of the way around, but did not see any way across still. She searched the terrain until she located a long stick almost her height. She used it to prod at the lake bottom within reach. Unfortunately, it was too deep to wade across either. She sighed heavily, her mind spent, and resolved to tackle the problem another day. She then spotted a servant girl, whom she did not recognize as one of hers, working her way through the tall grass and waving a small cloth frantically at her. The girl was about her height, dressed in drab gray with a plain cap, and had a sour expression on her face that reminded Rennora of some of the other servant girls back in the town who believed that life owed them a much higher rank than they were, adored grumbling constantly about it, but were unwilling to work hard to change things. She waited until the maid stood before her and gave her a moment to catch her breath.

"I take it that I'm needed?" Rennora politely asked.

"Yes, you stupid hag," the maid whispered in a raspy voice and demeaning tone as she moved the fabric up and down.

Rennora was surprised by the venom in the other's answer, but did her best not to react. She definitely did not wish to reveal her secret to this person.

Lesson and Clues

"Lead on, if you please," she calmly stated instead.

"You had better keep up this time," the servant sneered.

Rennora followed her at her own pace despite the remark. She refused to let the servant take full control like that other one had tried. They went through a tower door and wound their way through the first floor then under the balcony in the entrance hall. Rennora noticed that their path tended to avoid the other servants who were hard at work. She pondered at the maid's reasoning for this, since she was certain there were more direct ways to reach their destination, when they passed through the empty dining hall and into the damaged ballroom. She paused in the doorway as a thought struck her. She studied the maid who was standing by the shattered instruments, tapping her foot impatiently, and wondered if this girl was the same servant that tried to lead her into the armory…

Rennora hoped that she was mistaken as she scanned around for who had summoned her. She did not see anyone else there, so she wandered over to one of the immense windows that stood behind the low, raised dais and debris and gazed out over the grounds as she waited patiently. She then noticed a movement out of the corner of her eye. The maid was waving the cloth at her again.

"Yes?" Rennora asked.

Beastly Cycle

The servant pulled the cloth over her hand and pointed at the damaged instruments.

"What is it?" Rennora inquired as she came around to where the girl was pointing.

The girl sighed impatiently, then pointed more insistently near the bottom of the pile. "Just look there, imbecile, so we can get on with this," she snarled.

Rennora stood where she was, figuring that the maid was trying to speed up her efforts to break the curse. She was not certain what she thought of that. She did want to assist, but she did not wish to place herself at this girl's mercy in the process. She decided that she would go along with the servant for now, but be sure to quickly keep the creature and Kestin informed of what was happening, to be safe. She examined the pile and discovered a little corner of a cream colored something within the remaining curved body of a lute. She pulled out a scroll of heavy parchment coated in wood chips and dust. She carefully brushed it off and began to read, when she noticed the maid attempting to gain her attention again.

"Is this what you brought me here for?" she hesitantly inquired of the girl.

"I would not be here otherwise," the servant snapped, waving the fabric up and down.

"I take it that you wish to aid me in locating the rest. Correct?"

Lesson and Clues

"Anything to leave this nightmare!" as the cloth declared yes.

She watched the girl head toward a discreet door along the side wall and halt with the door in hand. Rennora thought the servant was glaring at her, but it was hard to tell from her hazy features.

"Why don't you wait for me on the other side, and I'll join you momentarily," she firmly stated after a tense couple of minutes.

The servant darted through in a snit, slamming the door behind her! Rennora wanted a moment to herself to think this through, when the creature stepped into the ballroom from the entrance hall. His surprised face told her that he had not expected to find her there. However, she was elated to see him!

"I'm glad you're here," she stated with a grin as she rose to her feet. She quickly joined him and informed him in a whisper what was happening. "Should I let her continue, or dismiss her and continue the hunt on my own?" she nervously asked. "I'm worried that she'll attempt to lead me to something sinister, but I would really like to help everyone as soon as possible."

He studied her in silence for several minutes before speaking his thoughts. "You're absolutely determined to aid us in this mess…"

She gazed straight into his questioning brown eyes and declared stubbornly, "Yes."

Beastly Cycle

"Then so be it," he replied with a resigned sigh. "I'll be watching from a distance, far enough not to be seen, but near enough to step in should you need it. Something you can do is insist on keeping to the main corridors and towers where you can easily be seen. Don't let her secret you off down the servant's passages, the fourth level, or places where you know you aren't supposed to be. Oh, one more thing." He pulled out a flattened leather tube with two long straps attached, one along the top and the other near the bottom, and shyly handed it to her. "This is for your dagger."

She thanked him graciously, astounded that he had taken the time to create a sheath for her! She turned the sturdy piece over in her hands. The craftsmanship was very good. She noticed that he had even stamped a tiny rose near the bottom tip and attempted to color its delicate petal lines blue. She blushed in delight at him. He awkwardly shuffled his feet with a foolish grin. She then recalled the waiting servant…

"Would you mind having one of my maids take both of these to my rooms, please?" she requested as she handed the sheath and the scroll over. "I have no place on my person to put them currently. After that, I'll meet you at the next location."

Lesson and Clues

He bowed to her and slipped out of sight. She crossed the room and pounded on the hidden door. The servant threw it open with a huffy sigh.

"Took you long enough," she sniped as she motioned Rennora to follow her with the cloth over her hand.

Rennora determinedly shook her head. "Let's use the main rooms and passages. I'm tired of the dismal servant's corridors," she firmly insisted.

The girl promptly slammed the door in her face with a snarl of "Fine!"

"If that's how you wish things." Rennora calmly headed back toward the entrance hall. Suddenly, she heard hurried footsteps behind her. She watched the servant rushing up to her, very surly. "I take it that you've changed your mind then," she observed.

"What choice do I have, you selfish hag?!" the girl snapped venomously as she answered 'yes' with the cloth.

"By your leave then," Rennora simply stated, allowing the servant to resume the lead.

The girl followed her up the balcony stairs at an easy pace, sincerely looking forward to the time when she would reveal her current secret. She then heard a shocked gasp from the balcony! She spied her personal maid with her arms full, gazing at them in horror!

Beastly Cycle

"What on earth do you think you are doing with milady, Jes?!" she sternly demanded, confirming Rennora's suspicions.

"Silence, Stelna, and do not dare say a word to anyone!" the servant snarled back at her.

"Just try to stop me first! Where are you taking her?"

"None of your concern!"

"Wrong! I am coming with you!"

"Do not dare!"

Rennora could not take the bickering any more. "Is there a problem?" she calmly and politely inquired. "I thought you were guiding me to the next book."

"You are doing WHAT?!" Stelna shrieked at Jes. "The last time you did that, we all were nearly killed by the next beast!"

Jes stepped closer to the maid and dared through gritted teeth, "I am done waiting for this fool to figure things out! No one is going to stop me from ending this one way or another…"

"I am still accompanying you," Stelna snarled in return.

Both girls fiercely stood eye to eye, refusing to back down! Rennora was thinking quickly on how to end this without giving herself away, when she noticed the creature coming toward them from the second floor. She discreetly motioned for him to let them be.

Lesson and Clues

"Fine!" Jes finally snapped and pushed past the maid to one of the second set of stairs that lead to the next floor. "Have it your way!"

"I intend to," Stelna stubbornly retorted. She curtsied respectfully to Rennora. "I truly wish that you could understand us. What must you think of us so far?!"

Rennora smiled warmly at her maid and continued onward with Stelna now at her side. She was honestly pleased for the additional person. It would certainly make it harder for Jes to cause trouble now! She then wondered if Jes had intended for her to kill the creature when she had taken her to the armory earlier. Considering that whatever her plan was then had been a failure, the servant seemed quite determined that this would not.

The small party rounded the corner, past a large statue in the middle of the spacious floor and toward the shorter wall with just two doors, ignoring the other, longer side with several doors lining it. Rennora paused at the statue to admire it while Stelna handed off her load to another servant, when she saw a small flash of orange retreat further behind it. She took one last glance at the figure's detailed helmet before meandering back to the waiting servants, hoping that they had missed the brief glimpse of the creature. Jes already had the nearest door opened and was motioning both of them in with a cloth over her hand. Stelna gently

Beastly Cycle

halted Rennora with a cloth covered hand and had her wait there. She poked her head into the room, scanned around carefully, then allowed her mistress to enter. The maid was half a step behind. Jes glared at them both and entered as well. Rennora asked for and was given a lit candelabrum to better examine the dim chambers. The generous space was a little barren along the walls with evidence that many paintings had been hanging along its lengths at one time. Four now stood their lonely sentry with another one lying face down on the floor and a sixth resting in the cold fireplace. A single bench remained whole near the doorway while the others had been shattered and piled haphazardly into a corner under the only wall sconce in the room. Two thick, metal chains hung from the ceiling had her wondering if they were once connected to chandeliers. The two servants stood to one side as Rennora scanned briefly for the next volume. She noticed Jes try to step forward, but Stelna promptly yanked her back!

"Let her find it on her own," her maid sternly insisted.

"She had better not be all day about it," Jes grumbled as she shifted in her place.

"I have every confidence in milady," Stelna calmly stated as she beamed with pride. "Patience."

Rennora was touched by her maid's loyalty and prayed that she would not let the trapped people

Lesson and Clues

of the curse down as she righted the fallen painting of a noblewoman of some kind. The lady seemed to preen on the canvas with a superior smirk dancing on her thin lips. Rennora leaned it against the wall so that it could be viewed once more. She moved toward the one in the fireplace as she took her time searching the room. She then carefully slid the ruined piece out. The painting was partially burned and torn in several places. It had a tall man on it, about early twenties, with dark hair, dreadful taste in clothing, a bit pompous, by what she could see of his stance, and potentially a member of the royal family, judging from the fur lined cloak draped artfully at his feet, a nobleman at least.

    Rennora found his choice in having a vicious snarling boar painted just behind him in the background near his legs, a little odd. At the bottom of the intricate wooden frame, she spied a small brass plaque with the name 'Lord Dunfelkar of Sennelton' engraved in scrolling letters. He looked familiar to her, especially the neat hair, but she could not think of why…

    "Would it be alright if I move this one to my room for closer study, please?" she respectfully asked. "I'll return it once I'm finished."

    Stelna silenced Jes and responded, "Of course, milady," as she waved a handkerchief.

    As Rennora set the painting gently beside her, she noticed a small, reddish leather-bound book

Beastly Cycle

leaning along the wall, half hidden by the mantel's thick frame. She ignored its presence for now and gazed around the room to see if there were any other items of interest to her. When nothing presented itself, she retrieved the book.

"I'm ready to return to my rooms, please," she declared, eager to continue her reading.

Stelna collected the painting as the others exited to the corridor. Jes headed toward the left and deeper into the hallway. However, her maid lugged her load toward the tower door nearby. Rennora glanced between both girls. She did want to continue searching with Jes, but her energy was spent.

She addressed Jes first, "Thank you for your guidance, but I believe I'll rest until dinner." She then turned to Stelna. "Please continue."

Her maid awkwardly curtsied with an approving smile. Both girls turned toward the door when they heard the servant snarl, "Oh no you *do not!*" from behind them!

Rennora turned around just as Jes snatched her arm.

Shocked and fearful, Rennora tried to pry the other girl's firm hold off as she fiercely demanded, "*Let go!*"

"Not this time, my pampered, little princess!" Jes sneered back as she raised the back of her hand to strike her.

Lesson and Clues

Rennora had a moment's flashback to Thevesta's incident! Suddenly, she dropped down, braced herself on one hand, and swept her leg around, knocking the servant's legs out from under her and freeing her grasp! She fled to the tower, threw the door open, rushed up the stairs to the next landing, flung the door open, slammed it shut behind her, and barricaded it with her body! She then slowly slid into a sitting position, trembling. All of a sudden, she jumped at the sound of a creaking to her right! The creature stood there with Stelna in tow. Her maid started forward, terribly worried, but he promptly halted her.

He cautiously approached Rennora, then paused a few yards away. He motioned Stelna forward and directed her to the first double doors closest to the corner and across from Rennora without a word. Once the maid had vanished into the chambers with the damaged painting, the creature closed in until he was a couple of feet away and slowly sat down along the wall. He said nothing at first, allowing her some peace to pull herself together.

He then broke the silence. "Are you alright?" he carefully inquired.

She heaved a resigned sigh. She then responded, "A little. You can tell me my punishment now… I'm ready and won't fight you on it."

Beastly Cycle

He was genuinely confused. "What have you done wrong today?"

"I struck one of your people!" she reminded him, stunned at his question.

He nodded sagely. "True. However, you've seemed to already have forgotten that Jes was about to strike you first. You were defending yourself from her. There's a subtle, but profound difference between the two actions. Others, including myself, were present at the entire scene, so there's no mistaking her intent. Jes will be the one to be punished, while you are not."

She felt numb! She knew that she should have been relieved, but she was more astounded and confused than anything. "And if I had struck first?" she hesitantly asked, curious.

"Then it would have been the other way around."

She did not know what to think of justice that applied to all evenly, instead of just a single person, but not others.

"I hope that you're not deliberately going to cause or seek out trouble now," he teased.

It took her a minute to process his words and understand as he meant them.

"Don't worry on that score," she firmly assured him. "I'm not that kind of person. However, I will warn you that trouble tends to enjoy my company from time to time."

Lesson and Clues

He sympathetically nodded. "Trouble tends to like me as well, since I arrived here."

"Once you're able to, you'll have to regale me with the full tale some time."

"Agreed. However, only if you can still stand the sight of me by then."

"I don't think that will be a problem," she replied with a friendly smile.

She was feeling more at ease about things now, so she shifted to rise. The creature leapt to his feet and assisted her to hers. She thanked him shyly for his company. He assured her that it was his pleasure entirely with an awkward grin. He walked her to the double doors of her rooms and the waiting Stelna beyond.

"I hope that you find your reading enlightening," he said politely. "Until this evening then."

He then bowed and left her to it.

Chapter 20
~ Beast ~

Privacy

Alleron paused just inside the tower door to ensure that Rennora had safely closed hers. Satisfied, he headed upstairs to the fourth floor, lost in thought. He was saddened that she had never seen justice when she was in the right, back in town. He had no doubts that she would have actually accepted whichever punishment that would have been thrown at her without complaint, no matter how unfair she honestly thought it, and because she did not know otherwise. His sorrow shifted to anger at the notion of the people in her life treating her so poorly. He opened the door on the last landing. She should be treasured and delighted with life! Encouraged instead of torn down. Smiles instead of bruises and tears. Listened to instead of cast aside or ignored. Loved dearly…

He passed through the corridor beyond, into the royal's family apartment, and paused at the solitary mirror, cover and standing in the center of the common room. He grasped the cloth at first for a minute, but then released it and scooped up his

Privacy

ocarina from off the mantel where he had last left it, instead. He was determined to give her the privacy to read in peace. He ripped open one of the ornate, solitary doors beside the fireplace and entered a lavish sitting room. He reached up deep into a bookcase that stood across what would have been a corner of the room, and triggered the lever hidden there. It swung forward, revealing the secret stairs in the final section of the tower. He half smiled at the idea of what Rennora would have thought of such a thing as he carefully closed the hidden door behind him and mounted the stairs. He just knew that she would adore it! That was, if he ever allowed her the privilege of viewing both it and the wonders behind it.

    He halted at the top with his hand on the outer door's handle. Part of him would have loved for her to pass through the door before him. The rest of him desired to keep his second sanctuary on the rooftop, where he actually resided, to himself for a bit longer, especially since he opened the first, his forge, to her. The idea of letting another into his last precious space felt like he would be allowing her free reign of not only his heart, but his soul as well. He did not believe that he was quite ready for that final step… yet.

Chapter 21
~ Beauty ~

The Tale Continues

Rennora noticed the painting had been propped up to one side against the wall of her sitting room as she turned around. She thought about examining it further. Her eyes then shifted to the waiting volumes. She decided to read first, then worry about the painting afterwards. She discovered that her maid had already added the new tomes to the old. She grabbed the last one that she found the previous day and settled into a cozy chair by the burning fire. She sighed in contentment and eagerly cracked it opened, when she noticed Stelna emerging from her bed chambers. She acknowledged her maid's curtsy with a polite nod. A thought then struck her!

"Pardon me, but would you happen to know the creature's actual name by any chance?" she asked.

Stelna turned her back to her mistress for a while, seeming a bit distressed. Rennora began to wonder if she would ever get an answer. Soon, Stelna faced her again.

The Tale Continues

The maid shook a cloth 'no' as she answered miserably, "I wish I could, milady. Nothing would give milord greater pleasure than to hear his name from your own lips, but I can neither speak nor write it in your presence."

Stelna slowly meandered to the bookcase and proceeded to straighten the various books and scrolls lining each shelf, peering over her shoulder at the curious Rennora occasionally, until everything was pristine. She gazed directly at Rennora for a couple of awkward minutes, curtsied again, and darted from the rooms with an anguished sniffle. Rennora stared at the closed outer doors, wondering if Stelna was being sincere, or possibly had something else in mind entirely. She hoped that it was not the later. She genuinely liked her maid. She shifted her attention back to the dark leather-bound book in her hands. It was another account from Prince Vindan himself. She found the second entry harder to read than the first because it was becoming much sloppier as she went, so she reread both again.

August 25th – We did it! We brought that lying woman back in chains! The people have heard of her

Beastly Cycle

deceit and are calling for her head now! A part of me wishes it had not come to this, but Jesseva assures me that I will feel better after the deed has been done in three months' time. She wanted the woman's head immediately, while Amheer remained silent on the matter, looking uncertain of himself. However, I <u>had</u> to wait for my Council of Lords' approval and could not bring myself to do it any sooner. She is still quite upset at me, but she just does not understand how these things are done like I do. I think…

The Tale Continues

October 18th – I did as she said. I held a ball in the largest ballroom to announce Jesseva as my new bride. Amheer refused to attend, strangely enough. Then, just before I could tell the people attending, two heavily cloaked persons pushed their way forward. I did not know how they had gotten in unnoticed, nor did I care at the time. Both the cloaks were well made, but frayed at the edges. The shorter one raised a thin, wrinkled hand, pointed at me, and demanded

Beastly Cycle

to know my heart over my first wife, whom I had completely forgotten about, in a strong, elderly woman's voice. I recall feeling truly mortified at what I had done and enraged at everything that had happened, but also mystified at how everything had managed to happen in the first place, all in the space of a single second. That woman at my side then touched my hand and sang a couple of words softly into my ear. Everything melted into a sea of calm and contentment after that.

The Tale Continues

I spent many days after my imprisonment took hold wishing I had taken a sword and run Jesseva through in that moment...

As it was at the time, I unknowingly obeyed her. I refused to answer the old woman and insisted that my heart belonged only to my new beloved.

Rennora solemnly returned the book to the shelf and collected one of the two scrolls lying there. She was pleased that the prince was sounding slightly more like himself, but was heartbroken at his plight. She did not know what to think about his confirmation of his being enchanted and controlled

Beastly Cycle

by Jesseva. Her heart ached for him as she started in on the scroll which was written in a very elegant hand.

I place my words as a continued record of his highness, Crown Prince Vindan's words and events, since he is currently unable to record them himself temporarily.

On the night of the ball, I, along with my apprentice, demanded of him the reason why he tried to murder and now planned on executing his first wife, even though he knew she was innocent. I then demanded to know his plans for his next choice that stood at his side, if she should begin to bore or displease him. Would she be flung aside, like so much filth, without another thought? Would he continue on as such until he had ruined or

The Tale Continues

killed all the ladies in his kingdom? What then?

As we awaited answers, the people were wisely taking their leave in silence. Once the room emptied down to a small handful of us, I challenged him with one final question that I hoped would pierce his heart and aid in breaking that demon's hold on him.

Was he such a selfish coward that he could not give himself fully each day to and love just one and the same woman, banishing even thoughts of any others forever?

Rennora thought over the woman's words, hoping that she had been successful in freeing the prince's mind before he turned into a beast. She then noticed a single line of tiny words hidden at the

Beastly Cycle

very bottom of the scroll. She tilted it closer to the fire, so she could make them out.

Imprison another, and your cold heart turns to stone.

They did not make much sense to her as she traded the scrolls. The second one turned out to be just a long list of names. She set it aside, figuring that she had grabbed it by mistake in one of her searches and dove into the last, lighter leather-bound volume. Prince Vindan had taken the tale back up again as he cursed the loss of his previous journal.

There is no point in repeating myself thus far. The woman's words did more than just sting, they lit an inferno within me. I began to defend Jesseva from the filthy accusations, when I discovered that she had fled from the room along

The Tale Continues

with any other guests that had lingered to my shock! I should have been torn by her desertion, but it only served to further fuel my rage instead. I roared at the pair before me that NO ONE dares to call me a coward!

How foolish and blind I was...

I then commanded my faithful guards that remained to seize the intruders. All of a sudden, a strong gale blew through the ballroom,

Beastly Cycle

sweeping the guards off their feet and ripping the cloak off the woman without moving the three of us even an inch! The woman was withered with age, but stunning, with hair like moonlight and sharp eyes that captured everything around her. The second person remained a cloaked mystery.

  The old woman pleaded with me to mend my ways and my heart forever. I stupidly laughed at her words and refused, Jesseva's hold still firm on me as thoughts of

The Tale Continues

pleasing her alone filled my empty head.

The old woman then declared herself to be a sorceress and indicated the person at her side to be her skilled apprentice. The second person threw her cloak off and straightened to her full height as my very own mother, the Queen, stood before me.

Rennora almost dropped the volume in shock! The prince's own mother was a sorceress as well! She scanned the other pages to see what happened next, but all she could find was another tiny line of writing on the side edge of the last page in the same elegant hand of what she now knew to be the sorceress. It read:

Beastly Cycle

Four tries must honestly attempt, if your prison you choose to keep instead.

More confusion. Rennora had to locate the rest of the tale! She simply had to know the Queen's part in it, and what happened to Jesseva and Belnisa! She figured that there had to be more to those mysterious lines and was confident that once she found them, they would actually make sense!

She closed her eyes out of exasperation and sought to calm the turmoil within herself. She took some long, deep breaths, which turned into several regular, steady ones as she drifted off with barely another thought…

Rennora awoke to a persistent knocking at her outer doors an hour later. She stretched for a moment, then answered it, still rather groggy. Minna and Stelna were ready to tend to her needs for the evening. She stepped aside to allow them past. They curtsied in response and headed directly into her bed chamber. She shook her head in exasperation at the pair, knowing full well that she was going to be beautified again, whether she approved of it or not. Perhaps this time, she could convince them to lessen the jewels or more intricate

The Tale Continues

pieces to a more comfortable level for her. It was worth a try at least.

She wandered over to the bookcase containing the prince's tale and ran her hand along the volumes until it came to rest on the list. She thought over the past few days, but did not recall ever picking up two scrolls. She thought over each portion of the tale and the location she had discovered it within. She then held the scroll, now absolutely certain that she was not the one who found it nor placed it on the shelf. She remembered Stelna's strange actions earlier and wondered if she had snuck it there. Rennora decided to at least scan it, since she had some time to wait before her maids were ready to bath and dress her.

The first name was Prince Vindan's, written neatly, but not as elegant as the sorceress's. Next came two ladies' names. Then a man's. Five ladies after that. Four men and so on, alternating between sets of women and men, until she saw the last set of four ladies at the bottom with her own name last and Conadora, the merchant's daughter, just above it. It had to have been a list of every person that had ever lingered at the castle from the beginning of the curse to now! She then noticed that some of the names had a dash with an animal next to them. She became excited as she noted that each person had a different animal, beginning with 'White Tiger' by Prince Vindan's!

Beastly Cycle

She scrambled around her to locate ink and parchment, when her maids heard her commotion. Minna poked her head through the doorway to check on her. Rennora immediately pleaded with her for the needed items. The maid darted back inside for a moment and returned bearing everything in her arms. Rennora relieved her of her load, delighted, and used the shelf as a writing table. She copied only the singled out names with their matching animals. Her heart pounding, she examined each of the thirteen people to ensure that she had everything correct, when one name caught her attention.

Dunfelkar – Boar

She recognized it after a second! She dropped to her knees before the damaged painting and ran her fingers across the engraved name plate. The spelling, the animal in the background. It could not possibly be just a coincidence! She spied a movement near her. She gazed up, elated at Stelna waiting to escort her. Her maid blinked several times with a knowing smile, curtsied respectfully, and stepped to the side. Rennora wondered what she wanted for half a second in her excitement. She then recalled her dining plans…

The Tale Continues

"I take it that everything's ready for me?" she inquired, politely.

Stelna curtsied again. Rennora rose, a bit disappointed with having to set her newest discovery aside for later. She joined her maid in her bed chambers with the copied list still in hand.

"Thank you," she said. "I'll be there in a moment."

Stelna entered her bathing chamber without a word. Rennora searched around her for a safe place to hide her precious treasure. She then remembered the creature's tunic within her chest. She decided that there would be as good a hiding place as any for now. She scanned the list again for future pondering as she opened the chest, when the last two names froze her in her tracks! The first of them was 'Soramilda' with 'Hawk' next to it. The one after it made her heart skip a beat! She fought to draw breath again as each letter of the gentleman's name burned itself into her memory. Suddenly, she heard her maids' voices echoing loudly behind the closed bathing chamber door. The cheerful sounds brought her back to her senses. She carefully rolled up the parchment tightly and buried it within the creature's tunic. She skipped to the door, most eager to be finished. She fought back a mischievous grin as she grasped the handle. The evening meal was going to be a most interesting affair in so many ways. Pleasant ones, she hoped.

Beastly Cycle

A while later, she entered into the massive dressing chamber that was connected to her bed chambers, clean and dressed in a thick robe. Three dresses of charm and grace were draped over a wide bench, awaiting her selection. One was a delicate pink. The next a soft orange. The last a deep green. She liked each slightly, but could not picture herself in any of them with pleasure. She wanted to look extra lovely for what she had in mind. She gazed around her at the rainbow of other garments lining the open chests and shelving, feeling more indecisive than ever.

"Which do you think the creature would like best?" she asked her maids.

"Simple," Minna stated in a normal volume, without hesitation.

She searched briefly amongst the other dresses in the room and presented a fitted green-blue one with long sleeves and an intricate combination of beading and embroidery on the bodice.

"Then that's what I'll wear, if you please," Rennora declared enthusiastically and allowed the ladies to go to work on her.

Once she was attired, she politely made her request concerning her hair as they seated her. She then examined the completed results in the full-length mirror. She was actually beaming at what she saw this time. She twirled around and then halted, facing her maids, who were delighted with

The Tale Continues

her reaction. Minna and Stelna began the cleanup while chatting merrily with each other. As Rennora watched them clearly, all sign of haze vanished completely, she realized that she needed to tell them the truth, and now, before they heard it from someone else and she lost their trust completely. She halted them in their tasks.

"I have something I really need to share with you both before you leave," she said, shuffling her feet nervously and hoping that they would not hate her for it. "I, um… I'm able to hear and see you both now."

She kept her gaze firmly fixed on the bottom hem of her skirt in the tense silence.

"When did you first notice it?" Minna inquired.

"This morning at breakfast. The haze was gone completely when I awoke just now, and you're no longer whispering when you speak."

After a while, Rennora could not stand the awkward silence in the room. She hesitantly peered up. The maids were gazing at her with blank faces.

"Why did you not say something sooner?" Stelna asked, slightly hurt. "Do you not trust us?"

"I wanted to gain a better feel of what was actually going on for myself," Rennora admitted, partly ashamed of herself. "Jes is the only one that I don't trust. Oh! I thank you, Stelna, for your loyalty earlier."

Beastly Cycle

"You heard the squabble?!" The maid was mortified.

"Yes, that and today have revealed much that I needed to know about the situation." Rennora curtsied low. "I'm truly sorry for deceiving the two of you. I'm planning on telling Kestin and the creature tonight. I have no desire to hurt them either."

"Would you excuse us for a moment, please?" Minna politely inquired.

Rennora nodded. The maids withdrew into the sitting room. She rose to her feet and waited nervously in her bed chamber. After several agonizing minutes, they returned. Suddenly, both maids curtsied before her so deeply that they were practically sitting on the floor! Rennora was startled and a little confused! She was sure that she had lost their trust completely!

"Rise please!" she urged them. "I-I don't understand. Why?"

"Each person that remains here is gradually able to see and hear us," Minna explained as both maids stood up. "For a select few, like yourself, it does not take very long. For most others, it is usually around the seventh or eighth day, and they do not bother trying to find a way for us to be heard before then, milady. We were hoping that you would be one of the earlier ones. We also wish that

The Tale Continues

you had made it known sooner, to us especially, but are thankful that you told us at all."

"I take it that few do."

"Even fewer. It normally does not take us more than a day and a half to realize that the person can. You and his lordship are a rare breed, milady."

Rennora blushed at the compliment, feeling much better now that she had spoken up. She refused both of her maids' offers of guidance, confident that she could find her way around this time. She headed into the corridor, downstairs through the tower, and out onto the second floor. She was delighted to see the statue that the creature had hid behind before her and the stairs beyond that, which led to the ground floor's balcony. She leisurely descended to the balcony, when she heard soft footfalls and the tapping of claws on stone from behind her. She halted part way down the last set of stairs. She gazed back to see the creature coming toward her. His eyes fell on her standing there. He slowed to a halt on the same step as she. He tried to speak to her, but could only stand there, staring instead.

She asked, "What do you think?" as she nervously shifted her feet and clasped her hands behind her.

He opened and closed his mouth several times, resembling a fish out of water to her, before he

Beastly Cycle

settled on foolishly grinning in silence. She lowered her eyes demurely.

"The maids wanted to add more to what you see, but I asked them not to," she explained, hoping to get him to say something as she glanced upward at him.

He closed his eyes for a second.

He then responded, finally finding his voice, "You were right to do so." He leaned closer and softly added, "Don't ever let others or yourself hide your perfection."

She stared at him in shock, not knowing how to respond, as he took a step back! She then blushed to her hairline as his eyes told her that he meant every word of it. He continued past her to the bottom, then around to the back of the stairs, vanishing from sight. Her knees buckled out from under her. She flopped down onto the step above her, her heart racing and mind reeling!

She wished that he would stop finding new ways to catch her off guard and make her weak, but she also took great delight in it at the same time. She shook her head at his antics. Perhaps he could give her just enough warning next time, so she could safely seat herself before she accidentally collapsed in a heap! She doubted that he would give her such an opportunity. She figured that he probably took a lot of pleasure in unnerving her.

The Tale Continues

Rennora steadied herself before she rose to her feet and descended. She paused at the last two steps and leaned over the railing, but he was nowhere in sight. She straightened back up, wondering where he went, when her eyes fell on the entrance hall's inlaid floor. A thought occurred to her as she studied the people. Could the depiction be of the prince and his bride? It made sense to her, given her recent readings. She wondered what the purpose of the roses for the man, the willow for the woman, and the black smoke that divided them was. Perhaps the darkness represented the curse? She dismissed that notion. The curse only affected the prince. It could represent a person possibly. If so, then who? The sorceress? Possibly, but she was trying to aid the royal couple, not force them apart like the smoke. Jesseva or her uncle? That thought had some distinct possibilities that she felt required further exploring. So what were the roses and the willow? She felt that they were definitely important somehow and worth the attention.

All of a sudden, she heard the soft music of an ocarina coming from under the balcony. She set aside her musings and followed the sweet sound to a partially opened door in the half level under the balcony and to the right. She carefully cracked it further open as quietly as possible. She slipped halfway through it, leaned against the frame's edge, and rested her head against it. She savored the

Beastly Cycle

creature's song as he set his heart free into a mossy courtyard of stone, warmly lit by numerous torches evenly spaced along the three walls of the castle that formed a 'U' around it. He had his back to her at first. Then, as his notes shifted from mysterious and questioning to hopeful, with a desire for love and warmth from a bitter, cold life, he half turned toward her. The song rose to a crescendo of dancing forever in a life of bliss and working through the tough times together, caressing her heart and sweeping it along with the music into the night sky above. He then halted, allowing the last note to linger a moment and fade before he softly played slower of wishfulness and ended with a wistful hope that it could happen, even for someone like him…

    She stood there, still frozen and captivated in the thickening silence. She blinked back a few tears that threatened to spill, her heart overflowing. She did not know how she understood his meaning, considering that he never sang a word while he played, but it was as clear to her as if he had. He had such beauty and love within him that she could not understand how in the world anyone could dare to call him a monster! She watched him raise the instrument to his lips and wished that she could play one as well, so that her music could weave together with his in a single melody that would embrace his heart forever.

The Tale Continues

She then blushed at such a thought, embarrassed! He nodded in her direction as his next tune was a merry jig that she recognized. She laughed in delight, stepped fully into the courtyard as she closed the door behind her, and clapped along to the beat, further encouraging him. Suddenly, she heard others joining in! She saw that she was not the only one that was drawn to the enchantment of his playing. Kestin and Minna were standing near an adjacent door to her. An older woman was just beyond them. An older man leaned on a long handled tool at a smaller tower at the far end of the wall, near the dried forest-like garden of plants that stretched between him and the small tower on the other side. Several other servants lined the other wall across from Kestin.

Then, to everyone's surprise, Kestin pulled a reluctant Minna away from the wall and began to dance with her! Glee and laughter rose up from all corners at the smiling pair. It was not long before others embraced the fun, either as couples or individually. The creature continued the music for the impromptu dance for another six songs. He then halted, out of breath, but well pleased with the applause as he awkwardly rubbed the back of his furry neck. Everyone began to return to their tasks, disappointed, when all of a sudden, a few clear notes sounded from a stringed instrument. Everyone shuffled to the side, revealing Stelna holding

Beastly Cycle

something like a slender lute resting between her shoulder and her chin in one hand, and a small, flat version of a bow weapon in the other.

She grinned mischievously as she placed the wide bow strings across the strings on the body of the instrument for a second, then launched into a lively tune! She appeared to be sawing at it from various angles, but the music from the strange thing was wonderful! Everyone cheered enthusiastically for the new musician and the dancers resumed. Rennora could not be more delighted for them! She tapped her foot and resumed clapping in time with the music. The creature slipped up beside her along the wall, empty handed. He explained that what Stelna was playing was called a violin, similar to a vielle, and was a gift to her from a well-traveled cousin long before he had arrived. The next tune was much slower as the pairs lined up with ladies in one line and gentlemen in another facing them. The creature then stepped in front of her and shyly offered his hand.

"W-would you care to join the dance?" he asked hesitantly.

"Oh! Normally I would love to, but I'm afraid that I don't know any of the steps to this particular one," she replied. "I've seen it once at someone's wedding that I was assisting with, but that's as close as I've come."

The Tale Continues

He was disappointed. "I could teach you if you would like," he offered. "It tends to be a favorite around here."

"I would like that very much." She blushed, truly overjoyed!

They watched the remainder of the dance in joyful silence. Then suddenly, Rennora's stomach pointedly reminded her that she had not eaten yet. She peered up at the creature, wondering how to tactfully bring it up without being rude. Her stomach grumbled again. One of his ears twitched in her direction. He reached behind him, opened the door, and beckoned her to enter. They returned to the peace of the entrance hall beneath the balcony and closed the door behind them.

The creature humbly apologized, "I'm terribly sorry for delaying your meal for so long. I hope that you can find it in your heart to forgive me."

"Actually, I found the dancing and music to be quite delightful!" Rennora explained with a glowing smile. "I haven't had such fun since the last time Madam Tisza allowed me to watch a few minutes of his lordship's ball a year or so ago! Does the castle enjoy such merriment on a regular basis?"

He shook his head as he pulled out his bell and rang it with soft, golden tones. "Not very often. Generally when we have no guests, some of the servants play so the rest can enjoy themselves for a while."

Beastly Cycle

"Do you play for them as well?"

"Occasionally. I mostly prefer to watch and listen from the fourth level balcony."

"I see." She then fell into a contemplative silence as she tried to work up some bravery. After a while, she softly admitted, "That song you played before was very beautiful… Alleron."

She watched as he stiffened with a wide-eyed stare at the stone floor between them. She began to wonder if saying his name was such a good idea, or perhaps it was not his to begin with. However, it had been the last name on her list and had the word 'Fox' next to it. Suddenly, Kestin entered from a door perpendicular to theirs and still under the balcony. He began to say something, when the creature quickly silenced him with a raise of his hand. The creature then changed it to a single finger, indicating for the steward to wait. He turned his head slightly toward Rennora and muttered something that she did not quite catch.

"I'm sorry," she said, worried that she had offended him instead.

The creature whispered softly, "Say it again."

"Your music—" she replied until he cut her off.

"That last part… please," he begged as he hungrily watched her face.

She smiled shyly and gently obliged him. "Alleron."

The Tale Continues

The creature closed his brown eyes and breathed in deeply as he faced the ceiling. He sighed aloud and met her gray-blue ones with a massive grin on his furry face.

"I had given up long ago on any lady that lingered here ever calling me by name," he admitted. He then gently took her hand in his larger one as he tenderly whispered to her, "I'm glad it was you…"

Alleron led her into the dining hall, past a beaming and teary eyed Kestin.

Chapter 22
~ Beast ~

More Human

Alleron took his place at the long table and waited until Kestin assisted Rennora with her chair before he seated himself. He wore a silly grin on his face, but he no longer cared. She actually called him by his name in that beautiful, soft voice of hers! His heart was pounding as he treasured both the memory and his belle mademoiselle across from him. It was wondrous for her to use it! Freeing to him somehow. He was no longer a nameless beast like the rest. He felt a little more himself and slightly more human.

He snuck a glance at her as they waited for their meals. He desperately wanted to pull her close and hear her lovingly whisper it into his ear. However, his reflection in the polished goblet in his clawed hand, within the brightly lit room, sent his celebratory thoughts plummeting. He recalled his plans with a heavy heart as he peered over at his fourth lady to keep him company at the castle. He cursed himself for allowing her to catch him off his guard like that! He hated the curse for forcing him

More Human

to give her an honest chance at breaking it, instead of allowing him to lock himself away in his garden until she left him to his lonely fate, for the benefit of all. He found himself now wishing that she had never found his actual name. His heart sat like a boulder into his stomach…

    He then heard her gently say it again, trying to draw him from his morbid thoughts. His heart lightened slightly within his chest. He refused to meet her lovely, stormy gray-blue eyes for a moment. He debated what to do about it. She hesitantly called him again. He could not help gazing into her worried face. His troubles compounded briefly as he forced a smile at her and promised her that he was fine. He delighted in her return smile, thinking that she was worth the long wait. He decided to save his heavy musings for later, after they had parted company for the night, and savor what time he had at her side while he could. His smile then shifted into a genuine one.

Chapter 23
~ Beauty ~

Shared Dreams

Rennora was not certain that she believed Alleron when he assured her that he was fine. He seemed so pleased when they first sat down. Yet, by the time their food had arrived, his face was clouded over with heavy dismay and soon tinged with either heartache or anger. She hoped that it was nothing to fret over, like he had explained. However, the lingering touches of it in his handsome brown eyes left her thinking that his heart was still quite laden with sorrow. She could not bear to see him like that. They ate through the first and second courses in a tense silence. It definitely was not the scene that she had envisioned earlier. She mulled over how to make things pleasant once again while they awaited dessert. Then she had it!

She tentatively inquired, "What are some of the things that you've been working on in the smithy?"

Alleron's blank face shifted to a friendly expression. He cheerfully explained about two hand and a half swords that he was creating, which could

Shared Dreams

be wielded as individual swords at the same time by one person, or hooked together so they formed a single, two handed blade. He was still working out how to secure them together enough that they would not come apart easily when in use, but not so well that they would never come apart. He thought that using a thirty-inch twisting blade for one, with a twenty-inch straight blade for the other, instead of two blades of the same size and shape, might aid in linking them together better. She listened politely, delighted at seeing his passion for the piece! He finished the last detail of a possible solution to the joining just as a stunning plate of cake drizzled in a mouthwatering sauce was placed before her and a small fruit pie before him. She watched him savor his, then he waited patiently until she swallowed her last delectable bite.

"Stunning!" she declared, beaming.

"Mistress Cavina will be pleased to hear that," Alleron replied. "Did you find your rest by the lake earlier today just as enjoyable?"

She gazed at him, surprised and a little mistrustful.

"I was very curious to know what kind of haven you would find here so I asked," he explained apologetically when she failed to speak.

"You could have asked me instead…" she responded, hurt.

Beastly Cycle

"I wasn't certain if you would welcome such an intrusion. Forgive me, please. Tell me, why that particular place?"

"I find trees, greenery, flowers, flowing waters, and such very peaceful and pleasant for the heart. And you? Is working in the smithy where you find your peace?"

He sat silent for a while. He then responded, "It's a great place to work off frustrations or troubles, but I have a different place that I can find rest in solitude when I need to."

"Such a thing is precious," she stated. She then timidly offered, "Perhaps one day, you could join me by the lake if you wish."

"I would like that very much…"

She blushed as Kestin returned to clear their places. The sight of the bustling servant reminded her of the heavy task still before her. She patiently waited until he had completed his task and was in the process of refreshing their water goblets before she hesitantly halted him. She nervously informed him of the truth about her new ability with the servants, including him. She then silently prayed that both men would take her admission reasonably well. Alleron said nothing. The steward raised a single eyebrow at her for a moment.

Kestin then smiled as he respectfully replied, "I am glad to hear it. Thank you for informing me,

Shared Dreams

milady. Would you like the others to know it as well, or shall I remain silent?"

"It would be better for them all to know as well, please. The handkerchief waving is a little awkward at times."

"It shall be done, milady," he assured her with a bow.

She could feel the late hour as she stifled a yawn, not wanting to appear rude. Alleron smiled gently and assisted her with her chair. She quietly thanked him. He hesitantly offered a lit candle and to walk her to her rooms as he lit one for himself. She graciously accepted both. They wandered leisurely under the balcony and into the entrance hall. Their combined light fell onto the massive image in the floor as they headed toward the grand stairs.

She paused him with a soft touch on his arm and inquired, indicating the floor, "Do you know the meaning of this, or are you unable to explain it either?"

He gazed at it with a heavy sigh. "I wish I didn't. You should know most of the tale by now as well…"

"True, but what are the darkness, the roses, and the tree then? I've seen nothing about them that I know of."

"All I can say is the darkness you've already met. The roses aren't a 'who'. I don't know anything about the willow though. Shall we continue on?"

"Of course," she finally replied, tearing her eyes reluctantly away from the image.

They enjoyed some friendly discussion about this and that as they wound their way through the quiet of the castle to Rennora's chamber doors. She lingered just inside her doorway, relishing his company as they laughed together at a jest of his. She then gently touched his forearm and bade him a fond good night. He smiled awkwardly. He wished her pleasant dreams in return as he stepped back. She saw a genuine happiness filling his gentle brown eyes as she slowly closed her door.

Rennora giggled ecstatically. Such a perfect end to the day! She danced across the sitting room and paused near the crackling fire. She was so elated that she felt wide awake again! She glanced over at the shelves, wondering if a few minutes of reading would aid in calming her so she could actually rest, when she noticed something odd about the tale's volumes. She counted them carefully and discovered that there was only one scroll. She examined it. It was the sorceress's part alone! The full list was missing!

She searched around the shelves frantically, but could not find it anywhere! She flopped into the chair, wondering what could have possibly happened to it. A horrid thought then occurred to

Shared Dreams

her that sent her heart plummeting to her feet. She darted into her bed chamber, panic stricken! Ignoring the concerned questions from Minna and Stelna, she dove into the chest at the foot of her bed! She discovered her own list was still there, safely tucked within Alleron's tunic. She let out a relieved sigh. She then asked both her waiting maids if either had seen the missing scroll as she secured the chest closed and seated herself on a padded bench. Minna shook her head while she undid and brushed Rennora's hair out. Stelna slipped into the wardrobe chamber without a word and returned with a clean, long chemise for Rennora to change into. She then braided Rennora's soft, curly hair to keep it neat for the night. As her maid worked, Rennora wondered if she had taken it, since she was avoiding the question, and why. Minna draped a warm, sleeveless robe over the chest, just in case it would be needed later. Stelna stepped back and asked if there was anything else that she required. Rennora assured them that she would be fine and politely smiled, letting her suspicions go for now. She still had her copy to work from at least. Both maids curtsied and quietly left with the used clothing. Rennora pulled out the scroll and began the heady task of memorizing it, beginning with the animal side of it. She climbed into bed, recited the order of them five times to herself, blew out the candle beside her, and soon fell asleep.

Beastly Cycle

Thirteen dark, people-like shapes stood several yards in front of her within the empty space, surrounded in a massive, pale, rolling fog. One on the far left end of the line drifted closer and halted before her. It shifted into a handsome man that was slightly blurry, well dressed in very rumpled and worn clothing of the finest cuts and standing tall, but his sad eyes spoke of a heavy burden within. He then clutched at his head suddenly and grunted in pain as he blurred completely and quickly transformed. He straightened in full focus, looking every inch a white and black striped cat beast man. A ring of blood red roses encircled his feet. He reminded her of the white tiger that she had seen amongst the books.

"Help us," the tiger man humbly begged before the flowers vanished in a wave of mist, and he returned to his place.

The next shadow remained where it was. The third glided forward, taking its place in front of her, and promptly changed. It revealed a tall, barrel-chested nobleman that appeared every inch a hunter, or a fighter, dressed in a heavy tunic and pants, with dark hair that tugged at the edges of her memories. His face reminded her of Wescar, especially around his eyes. He seemed like he was ready to tear her apart in frustration before he

Shared Dreams

transformed as well. His clothing had grown to accommodate his new size.

The larger boar man suddenly snarled his demand at her to be released! He then returned to his place in line. The fourth one lingered where it was. The fifth one solemnly glided halfway to her, then halted. It turned toward the right end of the line and shimmered briefly in a mirage of cream and dark brown colors, with a man's cry of agony and loss. It simply hovered there, then soon returned to its place without another sound. The sixth and seventh shadows did not move from their positions. The eighth one did the same as the fifth, with a couple of browns dancing on it as a girl shrieked instead.

The ninth came fully before her and shifted into a stately man, five or six years older than she, with a soft, gentle face. His clothing was neither rich nor poor, but something in between. Without warning, he roared so loudly that it made her jump as he clawed at his head! He soon straightened as well, and gazed at her through misery filled, golden eyes. Long, golden hair with touches of white and gray surrounded his long face, which hid both his ears and neck, and several thick whiskers had sprouted on his cheeks. Shorter, golden fur covered his body. His torso and arms were as broad as the tiger man's, with thicker, slightly stouter fingers. His legs curved and his feet had become massive

Beastly Cycle

cat-like paws. A slender line connected his curved upper lip to just below his dark gray, inverted triangular nose on his short muzzle.

"They both are hidden in plain sight," the lion man gently rumbled. "Find them..."

The tenth shadow remained still, but the eleventh one was a swirl of a warm brown, with a slight hint of light tan, that she could not make out who or what it was at all. The twelfth stayed where it was as well. The thirteenth and final shadow slowly came before her. She could feel the heavy sorrow emanating from it. It shifted into a man, a year or two older than she, with light brown hair, slightly taller, and simply dressed. However, he failed to come into focus completely, like the others, before he shifted into the coppery orange, fox man she recognized as Alleron, which then came into full focus. A single tear trickled down his furry cheek.

"Leave us while there's still time," he pleaded with her, his voice shaking. "I will help you with a fresh start in a new town of your choosing. Just leave this to me and never return."

He refused to meet her eyes as his tears flowed freely. Her heart felt like stone in her chest.

"You can't fix this alone! Let me continue," she begged, reaching toward him. "I know I can do it!" Tears streamed down her face as well, as she reached for him and whispered, "Please..."

Chapter 24
~ Beast ~

Different Direction

    Alleron peered down the line of shadows to his right amongst the swirling fog surrounding them. He could feel their combined sorrow, misery, worry, and rage, along with his own agony. He glanced down at himself and almost panicked! He too was coated in a hazy shadow! He scanned around, searching for a way out. His heart sank as he noticed his belle mademoiselle standing several yards from them. He tried to howl for her to flee for her life! However, he could only stand frozen in silence along with the rest. He took a deep breath to master himself, wondering what was happening, when the first shadow moved to stand before her and shed his concealing shadow, revealing Prince Vindan, who then transformed into a white tiger man beast. His heart plummeted even further. He had had this same dream years ago, and even stood in his beloved's place as one by one, each of the prior beasts had fully revealed themselves and spoke to him. He could clearly hear the prince's remorseful plea from where he was.

Beastly Cycle

Alleron watched him return and waited for the sapphire blue, swallow lady that he knew was next to present herself. However, the shadow just stood there, unmoving and silent. The boar man went forward, yet the badger lady, still concealed, remained as she was as well. Alleron wondered what was going on, when the fifth shadow stepped forward. It then halted about half way between the line and Rennora. It slowly faced him instead. The shadow shimmered, then revealed a slender, tradesman of some kind, judging from his clothing. He gave a sudden cry of agony and loss just before he transformed into his beast form! Long, cream and dark brown banded quills sprouted from all over his back and head. Round ears sat higher on his head. Shorter, cream colored hairs covered his face, front of his neck, and down into his tunic. A small, round, dark gray nose sat on the end of his short, narrow, light brown muzzle. Very short, light brown hairs covered his human legs, which ended in small paws instead of human feet, and arms. Short, white claws were attached to each of his toes and human fingers. Two shorter quills laid diagonally flat on his forehead, giving the impression of a lock of straight hair.

"Don't lose faith in yourself, or others, especially not her," the hedgehog man quietly urged.

Different Direction

He then shifted into haze and returned to his place in line. The squirrel lady and the rabbit, or possibly a hare, man remained as they were. The next shadow stopped short and faced him as well. A beautiful, smaller girl, a year or two older than he, dressed in a flowing gown of dark gray shifted with a shriek. A pair of large wings sprouted from her back, covered in a thin brown skin between sturdy, long, finger-like ribbing. She quietly folded them neatly behind her. Large, rounded ears sat on top of her head. A soft, lighter brown fur covered her body, except for her arms and human legs. Her small, furry, brown face had a small, oval nose with large nostrils. A long, thin, brown tail flicked behind her. Her wide, bare feet splayed her long toes, exposing the fine webbing between them.

"Find her part of the tale, though her voice has never been heard," the bat lady gently insisted. "She weeps with each passing year, her tears pooling around her feet for all to see."

She quickly returned to the line. The lion man revealed himself and spoke to Rennora, while the salamander lady stayed still. The next shadow then stood part of the way and shifted into a man, just a year or two older than him and richly dressed, before he transformed as well, giving only a grimace to show his pain. Sleek, longer, darker brown fur covered his long body, with a light tan fur from his short muzzle, down the front of his neck,

Beastly Cycle

and onto his chest. His arms and curved legs had shortened slightly, while his neck had lengthened a couple of inches and thickened. His hands and feet had flattened and widened slightly with webbing between his fingers and toes, which ended in very short, cream colored claws. His ears were very small, round, and a dark brown. A black, diamond shaped nose sat on the end of his muzzle. Long, cream colored whiskers sprouted from his cheeks.

"She alone holds the final key to this mess," the otter man persisted firmly. "Do not ever give in to the darkness's desires!"

Kilda stayed in line beside him. He could feel the hawk girl's hatred and tremendous fear. Then came his turn as he felt the freedom to move return. Dragging his feet, he took his place before the breathtaking beauty standing alone. His heart skipped a beat as his eyes met her slate blue ones, so full of confusion and anguish. He wanted so much to end all of this and embrace her. He felt his shadow falling away. He stood there, fully human once more, before he quickly passed through that hated transformation again! He took a steadying breath and delivered his own warning from his heart, with a trembling voice full of his own love, concern, and fear for her, his tears falling freely as a result. He fully expected to return to the line in silence, when she pleaded with him to let her aid him. His heart shattered at the tears streaming

Different Direction

down her heartbroken face as she reached for him with a final "Please..."

Alleron woke up shredding the blanket that covered him and shouting, "Save yourself!"

He gazed at the darkened, unfamiliar shapes around him, his claws ready to slash again, listening intently for any signs of danger! After several minutes, he finally realized where he was... He held his furry head in his hands as he sat on his bedding on the floor to calm his racing heart, and sobbed uncontrollably for a couple of minutes. He then clamored out of the glass room and into the crisp, pre-dawn air, not caring about his messy appearance, as he dried his face with his sleeve. The darkness outside weighed heavily on him, like his dream. A lone snowflake drifted across his vision, then melted instantly as it touched the castle stones. He entered the southeast tower and headed down to the royal apartments. He halted before the covered mirror and debated whether or not to briefly peek at Rennora to ensure that she was slumbering peacefully. However, such an act would violate her privacy and trust. He headed into the hallway instead, descended into the northeast tower, paused at the third floor door, closed his eyes, and listened carefully for a while. He heard nothing out of the ordinary with his sharp ears, like her crying out or sounds of distress, so he retreated to the fourth floor

Beastly Cycle

corridor and slid into a sitting position with the closed door to his back. He propped his arm on his raised knee, lightly running one claw of his other hand in random shapes on the stone floor, as his thoughts brought him back to the mystifying dream.

He wondered at some of the beasts' warnings, why they were different this time, and why not all of them revealed themselves to her, like they had to him. If his information and count were correct, then his heart's delight just had the two remaining parts to find, the queen's lament and Vindan's final words. The words spoken toward Alleron by the bat lady, the lion man, and especially the otter man echoed in his mind. He had been given the same exact three warnings over three years ago when he had read the eighth part and made up his mind to free Kilda. Yet, something about how those three people had gazed directly at him, with a stern look in their eyes, before they had returned to their place in line made him think that perhaps their words were meant for him instead of her. Maybe, just maybe, he had one more part to play in breaking the curse beyond accepting a genuine declaration of love and a kiss on the muzzle by moonlight on a warm night. But what?

Chapter 25
~ Beauty ~

Dagger Lessons

Rennora bolted upright, gasping, "Don't give up!" into the darkness.

She hugged her knees, shaking slightly and weeping, as she peered at the hazy shadows around her, slowly coming to her senses. She slid to the edge of the bed and steadied both her breathing and her quivering. She soon dried her tears as she rose to her feet. She donned the robe to ward off the chilly night air, cautiously wandered into the sitting room, and stared morosely into the warmth of glowing coals. The beasts' warnings were still flooding her mind. She mulled through each one to attempt to make any sense of them, but the details seemed to be slipping away from her, like she was trying to hold onto water with her bare hands. She lit a thin stick using the hot coals, then a nearby candle with a slight smirk at her last thought. Fortunately, she knew how to tightly cup her hands together to secure the water. Perhaps if she thought through her dream carefully, like her hands, she

Beastly Cycle

could keep whatever she could of it and work with that to start.

She stepped out into the empty, massive corridor with the candle in hand. The sky through the windows showed that it was still a couple of hours before dawn. She had possibly one more hour of peace before the servants would quietly begin their tasks. Her bare feet softly slapped against the cool stones as she slowly paced up and down the entire length of the hallway to aid in her thinking. She set aside the tiger man's and the boar man's pleads for freedom, since that was already her intent. She pondered the lion man's, but could not quite recall his exact words.

As she reached the corner near her rooms, she heard a heavy door creaking open from the other end of the hallway behind her around the opposite corner! She froze, not wishing to be caught in the hallway, but also not wanting to be interrupted, or worse, lose her musing through distractions of the servants! Her eyes fell onto the tower door in the rounded wall. Perfect! She darted inside and carefully shut the door behind her. She moved to sit on the nearest step, when she heard footsteps from further below! She quietly slipped up the stairs to the last landing. To her relief, she heard the door on the third floor open and close heavily. She sat up against the forbidden fourth floor door so that she could have some peace for awhile, unseen from the

Dagger Lessons

stairs. It took her a minute to recollect where she was as she softly counted off the list of beasts to herself. The lion man's words felt vital. She focused intently, but still could not remember after several minutes. Determined not to give up, she muttered to herself as she mentally walked one step at a time through his portion of the dream.

Suddenly, she felt the door behind her back shift slightly a few times. She dismissed it, so she could maintain the task at hand. She then remembered that the lion man had mentioned something about someone being hidden! She chuckled in delight! All of a sudden, she heard a gentle knock behind her. She scrambled to her feet with her candle in hand and darted to the side! The door inched open to reveal Alleron with his shirt untucked, pants rumpled, and fur sticking out all over the place at odd angles. She snatched her robe closed and curtsied, embarrassed at being caught so disheveled and in her night things!

"I'm terribly sorry for disturbing your rest," she apologized. "I awoke with a lot on my mind and went wandering to help me think. I assure you that I would never have entered this door without your permission. I didn't think I was very loud though. I'm so sorry about that as well."

She turned to leave, hoping that he was not too angry with her for being so rudely awakened, when he quickly halted her.

Beastly Cycle

"I've been awake for a while now, sitting here trying to think things through as well, when I heard you on the other side," he explained. "What brought you up here?"

"I wasn't ready to be waited on or talk to others yet, so I hid here."

"Sensible idea," he agreed.

He then shuffled his feet, looking slightly awkward for a minute. "The servants will tend to this level soon. I, uh, h-have a place here that's quiet and can assure you that you won't be disturbed until you're ready. It's the royal family's apartments. You're welcome to use it this time, if you wish…"

She positively beamed at him! "Thank you! That would be lovely!" Her face then fell slightly as a fear that she was forcing her company on him again struck. "A-are you sure you want me in your personal rooms?" she hesitantly asked.

He gazed deeply into her eyes, with a warm smile on his lips, as he held out his hand to her. "I wouldn't have offered it to you otherwise."

She blushed as she accepted it. He began to guide her in when he halted, peering behind her with a questioning look on his face. She turned to see Stelna staring at them, hand in hand. The maid dropped into a deep curtsy at the top of the stairs.

"Forgive the intrusion, milord and milady!" she apologized. "You were gone, milady, and left

Dagger Lessons

your bell behind. We became terribly worried." She returned the silver bell to her mistress. "Is there anything you require while I am here?"

"A little peace to think for a while would be lovely. Then I'll ring for you and Minna when I'm ready to eat and dress for the day," Rennora shyly explained.

"Milord?" Stelna addressed Alleron.

"The same for me, please," he responded. "Perhaps a bite in another hour or so as well. And worry no more. I will personally see to Lady Rennora's every need while she's in my care."

Rennora felt a tingle in her body and blushed again at the sound of her name from his lips. He tenderly squeezed her hand briefly. She returned the gesture with a shy smile. Stelna gave them a knowing gaze and turned to descend the stairs as Kestin and Minna ascended into view. Stelna snatched an arm of each servant and half dragged them back down. Their protests and confusion echoed within the stone tower's walls, then faded.

"Is Stelna usually that forceful?" Rennora asked, curious.

"Not that I've ever seen," Alleron replied, his face revealing his puzzlement at the maid's behavior as well.

He guided her inside, clear of the door, closed it, then shifted her hand from his and wrapped it around his arm.

Beastly Cycle

"Now that we have some peace," he began as they walked slowly around the corner, past the dried up fountain, and deeper into the vast corridor. "I hope that you can forgive me, but I was able to catch most of what you were muttering over. I believe that we may find that we shared the same dream somehow. You were mulling over the lion – Correct?"

She stared at him in astonishment! "Yes, I was! A boar man was before him."

"And the first was a white tie— ma—."

"Amazing! B-but how?"

"I don't know myself. You seemed to be having trouble with the first one I mentioned, I believe it was."

"Yes," she replied as they entered the somber royal apartments together and headed toward the doors to the right. "I finally remembered that the lion man had said something about being hidden, but nothing else. Do you know what it was? I feel like this is very much something I need to know. Please."

"I heard his exact plead both last night and another time pas… when I had the dream myself." Alleron gestured toward the double glass doors within the dusty windows before her as he explained, "This balcony was built for the royal family's use. It overlooks the courtyard from last night and the garden beyond. Feel free to linger as

Dagger Lessons

long as you wish. I will be on the other side of the room, near the mantel, to sort through my own thoughts. I'm at your service should you need anything at all."

"Thank you. Do you happen to have any thoughts on who he meant?"

"I'm not permitted," he explained. "Sorry. I hope that you will find this a pleasant place to mull things over."

He smiled as he opened the one door that was still attached for her, then took up his position on the other side of the covered mirror. She thanked him, stepped outside, and pulled her robe a little snugger. A cool breeze blew gently. The sun slowly rose, tinting the few scattered clouds overhead a soft orange and pink. She found the sight quite relaxing and gazed out at the vast landscape while she finally recalled the lion man's full words, wondering who could possibly be hidden, how, and where. The gaping chasm, like a huge maw ready to swallow the entire grounds whole, then caught her attention. She did not understand how anyone could possibly live so close to such a monstrous thing without being terrified every single day! She studied it for a moment. She could have sworn that it was closer and bigger across by several yards than when she had first arrived…

She tore her eyes away from it and peered down at the grounds to calm herself. She smiled

Beastly Cycle

fondly at the empty courtyard and the tiny people crossing it. She thought of the dance and secretly hoped for another one this evening. She wondered if it would be rude of her to request one… Her attention shifted to the garden between the courtyard and the chasm. There were various paths winding their way through a blend of green, brown, and minute dots of bright colors. She noticed a few different shades of red amongst them. She then sharply recalled the ring of deep red roses around both the prince's feet after he turned into a tiger and the man in the floor's.

She vaguely heard a knock at the hallway door behind her as her heart raced in excitement! Alleron informed her that their meals had arrived, pulling her out of her private musings. She rushed into the doorway and clung to it to steady herself!

"That garden below!" she exclaimed. "Does it happen to have roses?"

"Yes, many different colors of them."

"Red ones?"

"Yes. Why do you ask?"

Rennora grinned widely. "That has to be it then! The prince is hiding in the garden among the roses, just like the entrance hall's floor image!"

"You think that he's the man in the floor?"

"Who else could it be?"

Alleron thought in silence for several minutes before he slowly responded, "Fair point."

Dagger Lessons

He handed her breakfast to her and took his back to his place on the floor by the fireplace in silent reflection. She quickly devoured hers, most eager to be on her way. She stepped toward the door. She then suddenly remembered her day's plans from within her elation.

"I would like to explore the garden this morning, if that's alright," she hesitantly stated.

"You don't require my permission for that," he explained. "You may come and go as you wish. I think you may also be trusted to explore the fourth level. All I ask is that you don't come into these royal apartments without my personal permission."

"With pleasure."

"Do you still wish to have lessons today?"

"Yes, please! Will an hour and a half from now be alright?"

"I'll be waiting at the forge."

She smiled in delight and rushed back to her rooms, ringing her bell as she entered the tower. She quickly dressed in a simple, pale blue gown that would allow her full movement, explained that she had already eaten, and insisted that her hair be simply braided. She thanked both her maids as she tucked her bell into a hidden pocket within the skirt's folds. She then asked Minna to guide her to the courtyard.

Once there, Rennora dove down one of the two paths leading into the greenery, hoping to locate

Beastly Cycle

the missing prince and, no doubt, another part of the tale. She soon found stone benches of varying degrees of decay and sparse clusters of roses amongst the various other flowers and shrubbery. However, not a single one was the blood red that she was seeking. She returned to the mossy stones of the courtyard in deep thought, wondering if she had been mistaken in thinking that the roses would lead to the hidden prince, when she noticed the older man from last night as he approached the garden, his hands full of boxes with tools for tending the various plants. She curtsied and smiled politely. He bowed with a surprising grace, considering how full his hands were. His face was quite stern. She spied an immense sadness in his dull eyes as he stood there, staring at her, patiently waiting.

Feeling awkward, she glanced around her to avoid his intense gaze. She then had a thought.

"Are you the groundskeeper by any chance?" she asked him.

He silently nodded.

"Wonderful! Is this the only garden with roses, or do you know of any others?"

He nodded again.

She wondered why he was refusing to speak. She tried again. "So there are other roses?"

He nodded.

"Would you be so kind as to tell me where, please?"

Dagger Lessons

He set one of the boxes down. He pointed to the top of the castle behind him, then somewhere to the west on the ground level. He gazed at her, nodded in approval, carefully scooped his load back up, and silently plodded into the garden using the other path.

She peered at the empty walkway, curious about the mysterious man. She soon shifted her attention to the fourth level. She wondered if the plants and prince could possibly be hidden up there. She was grateful that she now had Alleron's blessing to explore it as she wandered to the west side of the grounds first. She headed around the tower, near the crystal statues, when she noticed the massive hedge ahead, blocking the way to her destination. She changed her course to where she hoped the hidden gate was and passed between the statues' garden and the huge rose tangle. She glanced to her side. She promptly froze in her tracks, staring at the mass of deep red roses and lush green foliage, mixed with touches of brown, a few feet taller than she! She felt such the idiot for not remembering the tangle sooner!

"That's what he meant by hidden in plain sight," she muttered aloud as she circled around, searching for a way into the mess.

She did not see an entrance anywhere, so she tried again at a much slower pace, studying the bottom of the plants where they met the ground

Beastly Cycle

more closely for any possible hints. Glimpses of some pale stone peeking between the leaves caught her eye on the far side. She cleared what she could of the half-decayed plants and fallen leaves from the objects. They turned out to be a set of large, stone vases about four feet apart. She then noticed that the roses formed a narrow corridor between the vases, which opened to the sky. The tall grass surrounding the tangle and the placement of the opening made it quite difficult to see it.

Delighted with her find, she carefully picked her way through, taking great care not to catch her clothing on the huge thorns. The corridor twisted to the left and then to the right. She forced her way through the last two feet of the overgrown grasses and stumbled into a sizable clearing in the center. Before her was a pair of crystal statues on a moss-covered stone pedestal with a ring of flat stones, like a small courtyard, around it. A large crystal tiger sat beside a hunched down crystal man, who had his back to her. The only other thing in the secret garden was a small, covered, stone block on the side edge of the ring, which turned out to be a hollow box. Inside was a long, sturdy, leather box with circular ends, like a closed tube. She carefully retrieved it, then shifted around the area for a closer examination of the statues, taking care not to step too close to the stones. The man turned out to be kneeling. He had one hand on the pedestal to steady

Dagger Lessons

himself, with a single crystal rose beneath it, while he held his face in the other. She could make out the grimace on his frozen mouth and a trail of tears on his cheeks, but little else of his facial features. The poor man seemed like he was in total agony and torment. She examined the tiger next. There was not a single tear anywhere on the intricately detailed statue. She wondered why the man was facing toward the castle instead of the corridor, while the animal faced the opening. It was like the tiger was a silent protector over the man, in an eternal vigilance.

Suddenly, she heard a couple of worried voices calling for her! She yelled in return, letting them know her location and that she was safe! She then heard a man grunting as he made his way to her through the rose corridor. Alleron rounded the corner and entered into the clearing. He opened his mouth to say something, when he noticed the statues over her shoulder.

"Is that really him?" he asked as he indicated the man.

"I believe so," she replied, perplexed at his astonishment. "You mean you've never seen this one?"

He shook his head. "It never occurred to me that a person could even enter here. My hunt took me to another place instead. I wonder…" He gazed up at the castle looming over the top of the rose tangle. "You were right about this, perhaps you're right about her as well…" he mumbled to himself.

They both carefully made their way out in contemplative silence to see Stelna waiting outside of the entrance. Rennora glanced at the tangle, her heart breaking for the prince and everyone involved.

"Um…" she said to no one in particular. "Do you know what's going to happen to all of the crystalized people once the curse is broken?"

Alleron thought for a bit before he shook his head.

"I do not think there is an answer to that one, milady," Stelna replied. "But then, no one has thought to ask either. Something to ponder though…"

Rennora began to hand over the leather box to Stelna, when she remembered her suspicions about the missing scroll. Stelna gazed at her, slightly confused.

"Is there something else, milady?" the maid asked.

Rennora held onto the box a little tighter as she replied, "Never mind. I'll tend to it myself."

Stelna noticed the box. Something soon dawned on her. She dropped into a deep curtsy before them as she apologized, "I beg both of you your forgiveness. I was the one that took the missing scroll of beasts' names from you, milady, so

Dagger Lessons

I could return it to its proper place before it was noticed."

Alleron asked Rennora, very curious, "Where did you find it?"

Rennora replied, "It somehow found its way onto my personal shelves, with the parts of the tale I've already found."

"I believe you," he assured her. He leaned in and whispered to her, "However you discovered my name, I'm still glad that you did."

She fought back a blush as he beamed at her. A minute passed by of warmly gazing into each other's eyes. Stelna then coughed, shifting the pair's attention back to her.

The servant fought back a delighted smile before she swore, "I will *not* do it again! I give you my word, milady."

Rennora studied her maid for a moment before she nodded. She was forgiven yesterday for her deception after all. Stelna rose to her feet. Rennora opened the box and peeked at the scroll nestled within the wooden lining. She saw the prince's handwriting, but unfamiliar content. She closed everything back up and handed over the box without letting go.

"I'm holding you to your word, and the same will go for Minna. I really do wish to save everyone, but I need the freedom to figure out how, and the ability to trust the people around me. Please add this to the other volumes in my room. Also, leave the chest at the foot of my bed alone." She released it.

Stelna curtsied and replied with a smile, "Yes, milady. It shall be as you command."

"Oh! One more thing. I no longer need the painting. Would you see to it that it's returned, please?"

"Of course, milady."

Stelna quickly curtsied and hurried off. Alleron and Rennora headed through the hidden hedge gate in silence.

As they reached the practice poles, Alleron turned to her and asked, "Out of curiosity, would you happen to know the name of the one before me?"

She wondered who he could possibly have meant. She then remembered the list!

"You mean the hawk lady before you?" she inquired.

He smiled.

"Her name's Soramilda."

"Interesting… My name for her was close."

"What was it?"

"I'm afraid I cannot speak it. Now then, shall we begin with your daggers?"

"I wish I had known, I would have brought them," she replied as she rung her bell. She turned the beautiful piece over in her hands and asked a

Dagger Lessons

question that had been gnawing at her, "How do the servants hear our bells when they're out of range?"

"I don't know... I do know that your maids will always answer yours and Kestin mine, unless we're concentrating hard on one of the other servants. If that's the case, then the other person will respond instead. No one else can hear it that hasn't resided here at some point for at least a day. However, I believe that if you don't wish for me, or others, to hear it, you have to include that desire in your concentration."

"How do you know all of this?"

He looked a little embarrassed. "I did a lot of testing as I took over the forge."

Minna made her way to where the pair waited.

Rennora addressed her, "I'm terribly sorry to do this, but would you fetch both of my daggers for me please? I didn't know that I needed them until now."

Alleron added, "The fault is mine entirely. I didn't choose today's weapon until after her ladyship left for the garden this morning and failed to inform her. Oh! Would you bring her sheath as well, please?" He turned to Rennora. "You might as well begin wearing them both, if you're going to be serious about mastering them."

Rennora nodded her consent. Minna glanced between the two, slightly irritated at them, curtsied, and left.

Beastly Cycle

Alleron addressed Rennora, "While we're waiting, you can begin learning with a couple of the other daggers from the shop."

He soon returned with a pair of daggers about the same size and weight as hers. He instructed her on various holds, attacks, and defenses with a single dagger, when both her maids returned with the requested items. Alleron presented her with a second sheath. Stelna and Minna took Rennora into the forge's storage room for a little privacy and assisted her with positioning and securing both of the weapons, the medium one on her upper thigh with access through a pocket, while the smaller was angled alongside of her chest, hidden very discreetly with a secret slit, so she could still reach it. She felt slightly odd, being so armed, and ended up walking slightly stiffly back outside. Alleron tried to bite back his mirth at her plight as her maids left.

"You'll get used to having them on with time, especially if you wear them every waking moment," he assured her through his grinning. "Just relax and move with your usual grace. Can you draw them easily?"

It took her several attempts before she grew comfortable with them both. She grinned in delight as he complimented her efforts. They returned to her dagger lessons with the addition of a surprise dual dagger block and strike. One particular defense, she could not seem to coordinate the steps

Dagger Lessons

correctly, and his dagger kept slipping past her! He explained it a little more slowly and even stood beside her to show her yet again. She picked up how to halt the attacking blade with her dagger now, but was lost with how to twist both her attacker and herself so the person would be thrown to the ground, allowing her to attack or to flee. She became rather flustered with herself!

He hesitantly asked, "May I come closer? With your permission, of course."

"To better assist me?" she clarified. "Yes, please!"

He repositioned her hands, then stood directly behind her and guided her through the movements with his own hands, while he explained things, step by step, in her ear. His closeness made it quite difficult for her to focus as she went through the movements herself, with his hands resting on her shoulders. She forced her focus on her task at hand, just managing to complete the sequence, to her joy! She did it a second time, to ensure that she had everything correct. He delighted in her progress as well! She gazed over her shoulder at him, quite pleased with herself, and met his eyes. Her heart began to pound in her ears. She scarcely drew breath as she remained frozen in place.

Chapter 26
~ Beast ~

Hesitantly Happy

Alleron stood frozen as well. His eyes were locked onto hers. His hands rested still on her delicate shoulders. His heart raced. He could hear hers beating just as hard. An eternity passed before he forced his eyes closed, breaking her hold on him. He slowly released her and took a few steps back as she turned to face him. His heart was a chaos of joy, hope, fear, and agony. He was not sure how to respond when she asked if he was alright. He heard her worry for him within her tone.

    He forced a casual smile and set Rennora to practicing her thrusts and strikes on a pole. He grabbed a sword and several throwing daggers for himself and worked at his own skills to calm and refocus himself for a while. He discreetly glanced at her, wishing that the curse was already broken so he could court her properly, instead of in small spurts as his heart got the better of him. He redirected all thoughts back to his task at hand and away from his miserable musings. He did not want to make her unhappy or worry any more. When he

Hesitantly Happy

felt in better control of himself, he checked on her progress. She still needed a bit of assistance, so he pulled her from the log and sparred with her, keeping his focus on her training. They continued until she finally managed to land a strike on him, as well as trip him. He had her do it several more times until she could do it with ease and a decent speed. He sat on the ground where he had last stumbled, grinning at both her success and her delight in it! They then moved onto weaponless fighting. After another two hours, she was able to land several blows on him and learn a few more techniques for tripping him and wrenching his arms.

"Always remember that your attacker has no concern for your safety, unless you're practicing like we are," he cautioned. "You must *not* worry about the person's safety, or you *will* be harmed, or worse. A real attack isn't a game."

Rennora gazed down at the fresh scarring on her hands, saddened. "You don't have to tell me twice," she sighed heavily.

Alleron took her hand and assured her, "Those that truly care about you would *never* harm you in any way."

She blinked back tears as she gave a slight smile. He gently squeezed her hand before he noticed Kestin and Minna arriving with their noon meal and reluctantly released her. They rested

Beastly Cycle

themselves by the pool as they ate and enjoyed each other's company.

"May I ask your plans until dinner?" he inquired politely.

"Nothing special, honestly," she responded. "Some exploring, then reading. Why do you ask?"

"Curious is all. Why not make time to enjoy the lovely day as well?" he suggested, hoping that she would not see through his intent until he completely declared his secret hope.

She considered this for a while. "Perhaps a lovely place to read would be a good idea, since I already know where the tale is headed…"

"And perhaps I may be allowed to join you afterwards, if you would permit?" he shyly asked. He held his breath for a moment, partly afraid of what her answer might be.

"Thank you!" she beamed. "It would be my pleasure."

He rose to his feet, grinning widely, and bowed as he bid her, "The pleasure is mine as well. I wish you well in your exploring and will meet with you later."

He meandered with his hands clasped behind him toward the front of the house without looking back, delighted with himself, but also wondering if his actions were wise, or terribly foolish and dangerous for them both. He dismissed the idea, since it was a little late for such somber musings.

Hesitantly Happy

Everything was now arranged. He wandered into the front door of the entrance hall, intent on passing the time in his garden, when his eyes fell on the floor image. He paused in front of it. He studied the man and the woman with the feeling that he was seeing them clearly for the first time. He focused on the woman and the tree carefully as the otter man's words rang in his ears. He wondered if that was who he had meant was hidden in plain sight as well. He felt the question gnawing at him as he dashed off toward the lake, beyond the crumbled stables, hoping to find an unknown thirteenth crystal statue, either around the willow tree or somewhere near it, and a better answer to the curse than the ones he currently had.

Chapter 27
~ Beauty ~

The Fourth Floor

Rennora watched Alleron disappear around the other side of the tower before she wound her way to the fourth level, wondering if he would ever declare his heart plainly to her. The huge corridor formed a 'U' just like the other levels, with just a few doors down the two ends. A dried up fountain sat in each area in front of both north towers, with a small sculpture adorning the top of one. She stood before the immense windows that almost touched the ceiling along the wall that connected the towers. The clear, sparkling glass gave her a complete view of the budding front grounds, the stone border wall, and the vast forest beyond. She savored the beautiful sight for another minute before she took out a clean handkerchief and set it beside the doors that she was sure led to the royal chambers. She was tempted to enter them, to see more into Alleron's private side, but forced the idea back. She had no desire to satisfy her curiosity at the cost of his trust.

The Fourth Floor

She tried the double doors between the northeast tower and the corner near the royal chambers. Strangely, they were locked securely. She made a note to request entry later, if she was not able to locate the last part anywhere else. Next, she moved around the corner to the double doors directly across from the windows. They seemed vaguely familiar to her. One of the doors was barely hanging on its hinges. She carefully opened the other one and slipped inside. Everything was coated in a blanket of dust several inches thick. Two sets of footprints in a thinner dust traveled along the wall to a small area, where more dust had been disturbed, and back to the doorway where she lingered. She could see the gray stone slabs of the floor peeking through. A heavy sheet of some kind covered a large, wide, lumpy object in the far corner. Grime-coated windows lined the wall opposite her, with a pair of dingy glass doors, framed in rusty metal, in the center. Huge chandeliers hung low on their chains, almost touching the floor, and were wrapped in layers of thin cloth. She forced open the rusty doors, to let in some fresh air, as she finally recognized where she was. She felt like she was the first to trespass within the royal ballroom in a very long time. As she hunted under the cloth and amongst the warped, neglected instruments, she imagined all of the nobles and royalty dressed in their finest, dancing gracefully across the floor to

Beastly Cycle

the most beautiful music. She searched both of the chandeliers, wondering if the castle would ever see such grandeur again. Would any of the people trapped here even wish to continue to reside in a place that had known such horror and heartache? She examined the balcony that was beyond the glass doors. How would the crystal people be able to resume their lives after being frozen for so long? What about the prince? Did the kingdom even belong to him anymore? She examined both fountains in the corridor next. She wondered if Kestin and Alleron would be able to aid and shelter all of the people, both crystal and servant, until each could work out what to do with their lives. Perhaps the prince could assist them as well. It would be the least he could do, since he was the reason that everyone had been cursed in the first place, or at least, part of the reason…

    With a heavy sigh, she headed around the next corner and entered the double doors on the same wall as the northwest tower. It contained a vast room with several low pedestals and raised stone slabs which were dispersed throughout the floor. Thick nails were embedded high on the walls. Heavily curtained windows were opened, allowing the sunshine in. However, the warm rays did little to dispel the feeling of despair that enveloped everything. She quickly searched the room, then quietly left as she wondered what it had been used

The Fourth Floor

for, if it had always been so empty, and what had happened to give it such an air.

    The next set of doors was on the adjacent wall. The huge room within almost mirrored the royal chambers. It was neatly kept and sparsely furnished in faded brocades, silks, and cracked wood inlayed with gold. The wall of windows gleamed, showing the balcony outside as well as the other two beyond. There were three sets of double doors on the wall opposite the balcony, while two more sets, one on either side of a large fireplace, stood in the wall opposite the outer door.

    She did a quick search of the balcony. Nothing. The rooms to the left of the mantel were next. They were generous, clearly built for those of noble or royal blood and their servants. Yet, the only things in the rooms were a massive, intricate headboard that was broken in half and a faded, tattered rug on the wardrobe room's floor. She found no book or scroll in them either. The double doors to the right contained a single, extensive room that had been devastated. Benches and chairs were shattered, expensive fabrics shredded, and the mantel of the fireplace was pitted with large chunks torn from it. One bookcase was smashed apart, while another had a few shelves cracked and was half tilted against the wall. All the books in the room were ravaged, and the pieces lay scattered on the floor. Everything was coated in dust, but not as

Beastly Cycle

thick as the ballroom's. Heartbroken over the devastation and overwhelmed by the thought of sifting through it all, she decided to save it for last, hoping that the remaining rooms would not be quite as bad.

 The next two sets of rooms along the last wall were spotless, but completely empty. The third set had a beautiful cherrywood bed frame that was still intact and skillfully carved. However, the mattress for it was on the floor beneath the bed chamber's window with some blankets draped across it. Curious, she peered out the window and saw the village nestled below. She noticed that Alleron was not at his forge, nor was there any smoke drifting from the chimney. As she searched the other rooms connected to the bed chamber, she wondered where he was and what he was doing.

 She returned to the doorway of the ruined room still empty handed. She tightened her resolve and reluctantly set about her task. First, she propped open the doors to the main room, the balcony, and the ruined room to help with any dust that she was certain to stir. She then forced open the room's windows to let some fresh air carry away the stale odor that persisted. Finally, she cleared the room one small portion at a time, using the main room to stack and organize things into different piles to be dealt with later. After she emptied it of pages, torn fabrics, and smaller debris, she shifted the medium

The Fourth Floor

items into a pile in a far corner of the main room, separating out any that could possibly still be salvaged into its own area. Tired, she then flopped down beside the doorway and scanned the room. All that was left were a few large, heavy pieces of unrecognizable furniture and the massive, tilted bookcase. She examined inside and between the pieces carefully. Then, bracing herself against it and using the strength in her legs, she moved each of them out of the way so she could search the area they had sat as well.

    She approached the remaining bookcase last. Its craftsmanship must have been exquisite! It had the appearance of once being very grand and a beautiful place for books and scrolls to rest. Now, the outside of it was deeply scratched in several places, marring the elegance of what carvings remained. She stood on tiptoe, and even hopped a bit, so she could better scan the upper shelves. However, she did not see anything on the medium brown wood. She then examined the narrow gap between its back and the stone wall behind it. It looked like there was something huge, flat, and dark there, but she could not make out what it could possibly be. She tried to slide the case in any direction she could, but it was just far too heavy for her to budge. She reached for her bell to summon some additional assistance when she noticed a movement in the main room.

Beastly Cycle

"Hello?" she called out.

Alleron appeared in the doorway, looking flustered, unhappy, and slightly panicked. He scanned the newly cleaned room.

"Did I do wrong by coming here?" she asked, apprehensive of his expression.

She became terrified that she had offended him by her presence there, even with his permission! She prayed that he would not fiercely berate her just like Mistress LaZella loved to! She tried to swallow back the rising lump in her throat as she trembled in anticipation of his wrath that she was certain was building in the silence. She gazed fearfully at the confusion in his eyes and waited, ready to flee or hide. However, his face softened at the sight of her. He kneeled down with his fist on his chest and his other hand on the floor.

"Forgive me if I seemed out of spirits, belle mademoiselle," he gently apologized. "You are correct to be here and have not trespassed nor done anything wrong in the slightest. I am the only one that I'm upset with, I assure you."

He cautiously smiled at her as he straightened, but she just stood there, stunned at his reaction, not knowing what to do or say once again.

"Did you find what you were seeking?" he politely inquired.

It took her a minute or two for his question to sink in, then to remember her task.

The Fourth Floor

"N-no actually," she stammered. "Well, not yet. The first room I tried was locked. The others yielded nothing, and as you see, I'm still working my way through here, but it was an awful mess and quite a task to sift through everything."

He rubbed his neck nervously and grimaced as he gazed around.

"Apparently, each takes his or her rage out somewhere in the castle, or on the grounds, and well…" He looked quite embarrassed. "I hope that you can forgive me," he humbly apologized.

She caught on! "You mean that you destroyed this room after you transformed?!" She peered over his shoulder at the piles she had created, saddened. "Such anguish in your heart… From the dust, I take it that no one has set foot in here since then?"

He slowly shook his head. "It's like an entirely new room in here now," he commented forlornly as he rubbed his arm.

She slipped to his side, worried about the hurt that was surfacing on his face, her own troubles forgotten. She tenderly placed a hand on his arm.

"Will you be alright?" she carefully asked.

He closed his eyes, tilted his face upward, and took a deep breath as he placed his hand over hers and gently squeezed it in return. "You're too good to me. Eventually, yes. I will be one way or another. Right now… Well, let's not worry about that for now. Is there anything I can do for you?"

Beastly Cycle

She smiled warmly at him, happy with his desire to be useful, and indicated the obstacle. "Would you mind helping me move this thing, please? I think there's something behind it."

He crossed over to the bookcase and ran his hand along it until he halted in a particular spot on one of the upper shelves. He smirked. "Just like the other one," he muttered.

She wondered what in the world he was talking about. "Can you help me with it?" she persisted.

He studied her for a moment before he replied, "What you're hunting for isn't behind here. That I know for certain."

She was quite disappointed. "Do you happen to know what is there?"

He fell into a contemplative silence for several minutes. He then pressed a hidden something near his fingers. She heard a metallic click as the bookcase lurched forward slightly. Surprised and startled, she leapt away from it!

"Stay back," he warned as he grabbed near the bottom and heaved upward. The end of the case inched forward a little more. He let it tumble from his grasp, scanned the other end of it, and heavily sighed as he returned to his position, "The hinges on this are bent, which will make shifting it much more difficult than I thought."

"I can help with that," she offered.

The Fourth Floor

"Fine ladies don't lower themselves to moving heavy objects," he teased playfully. "They are far too delicate for such weighty tasks."

She promptly rolled up her sleeves as she stubbornly declared, "Then it's a good thing that I'm just a simple scullery maid! Where do you want me?"

He smirked merrily as he returned to the task at hand. "I'm going to get a better hold on this. Guide it from behind this side once I have it opened enough that you can fit your hands in safely, milady."

She curtsied and playfully replied, "Yes, milord," with a chuckle.

He braced his shoulder against the lower part, heaved upward, and slowly hauled it forward.

"Helping to push!" she hollered over the groaning hinges as she saw her opportunity.

She squatted down against the wall, braced her back, and used her feet to push with the strength of her legs. Their combined power shifted the case open until Rennora's legs straightened fully and Alleron's strength gave out. He quickly set the load down. They dropped to the floor, surveying their efforts as they caught their breath. Hidden behind the case was a circular room that contained a set of stairs, which twisted upward out of sight around a central stone column. Cobwebs clung to every surface within the dusty room. Rennora grabbed a

Beastly Cycle

lit candlestick and some tattered cloth from the other room. She wiped the back of the case clear of the webbing, then burned any that was still blocking the secret doorway. Satisfied that they could enter safely, she turned to check on Alleron.

"Very useful trick," he commented. "Unless of course, there are things near the webs that easily catch fire."

"True," she replied. "You do have to be very careful with it." She peered into the room. "Have you any idea what could be at the top?"

Before he could answer, they heard a shocked gasp from the other doorway! Alleron scrambled to his feet at the sight of Kestin and Minna standing there.

"W-what have you done to your clothes, milady?!" Minna exclaimed, horrified.

Rennora noticed for the first time all of the dust and dirt coating both her body and her clothing. She reached up to find her hair rather disheveled. She quickly re-braided it to neaten it back up as she noticed Alleron similarly messy and attempting to smooth his fur a bit. He then gazed at her and began to mischievously grin. Unable to help herself, she burst out laughing at them being caught like naughty children by the servants! Alleron laughed heartily along with her! It took them a minute or two to regain control of themselves. Rennora wiped the merry tears from her eyes with the back of her hand.

The Fourth Floor

She apologized for their state as she accepted a clean handkerchief from Kestin to wipe the new grime from her face. Alleron used the inside of his sleeve to clear his tears as he chuckled one last time. Both servants were gazing at the pair in shock and sadness. Suddenly, Minna burst out sobbing and buried her face in her hands! Kestin tenderly wrapped his arms around her and patted her shoulder to soothe her.

Minna snapped as she gazed up at him, "I *cannot* go through this again! I just cannot bare to lose another—" She cut the rest of her thought off as she returned to weeping on his shoulder.

The steward nodded his head respectfully toward Alleron and Rennora. "Please forgive her. She has been through so much. It sometimes gets the better of her."

"No need to apologize," Alleron assured him.

"We're really sorry about our appearance," Rennora added. "Will she be alright?"

"Some peace and rest should aid in calming her, I think," Kestin replied.

"Then I'll only ring for her if I need both of my maids this evening. I'm sure Stelna can manage me, so Minna won't have to worry."

Kestin respectfully nodded again and gently guided the distressed maid away.

"I wonder what that was really about," Rennora mused aloud.

Beastly Cycle

Alleron shook his head. "I don't know... Now then." He took her hand and placed it on his arm. "My guess is that this is the top of the southwest tower and leads to the roof top, same as the other one in the sitting room of the royal chambers that I use."

"Is there anything up there?" she asked, quite curious, as she held the light up and they entered.

"If I'm correct..." he began while he brushed away the webs barring their way with each few steps.

He left the thought unfinished as they worked their way to the landing at the top. A single, heavy, metal reinforced door stood in the rounded wall. He tried to open it, but it was stuck fast. He shoved the bolt hard to break it loose enough to shift it. He then rammed into the door a couple of times to free it. She was blinded briefly as a bright light was revealed on the other side. It took a second for her sight to return. Alleron peered through the doorway, relieved her of the candlestick, and then took her by the hand.

"It isn't much, but this is a little place that I like to call home right now," he humbly explained as he shyly guided her through.

Chapter 28
~ Beast ~

Decision

Alleron watched Rennora continue forward, slipping her hand out of his. He saw her awe and delight as she absorbed the incredible view around them, while he set the candlestick by the door. She whipped around to face him, positively beaming! She tried to put words to her thoughts, but failed.

"Now you see why I chose this as my personal sanctuary," he explained. "Only Kestin and I freely traverse here. The others do as they wish with the rest of the castle."

An immense, cylinder structure of glass and metal that stood in the center, with a dome top, caught her attention. It had vertical, rectangular glass around the walls and a rectangular glass than angled toward the flat, multi-sided top with angular panes that connected them, all supported by sturdy, steel frames around each one. Some of the angular ones near the top were detached at the upper, smaller end and tilted outward, away from the dome, allowing air into the room within.

Beastly Cycle

"What is that?" she hesitantly asked, indicating it.

He hesitated for the space of a minute. He then decided that sooner was better than later as he took her hand again. "Let me show you," was all he said as he guided her toward it.

Once they reached the closest glass doors, he ushered her inside. She gasped at the sight before her! The glass room was filled from floor to almost the ceiling with plants of all shapes and sizes, from full trees to delicate flowers no bigger than a newborn baby's smallest fingernail. Each was in its own pot, or a massive shared box, inside a low stone wall that encircled massive individual sections, well-tended and carefully arranged. She stepped forward slowly, taking it all in as she went, until she halted in the center of the room near a small raised pool and faced him.

"H-how do you like it?" he hesitantly asked, hoping for her approval.

"I-it's…" she stammered, grinning broadly, "more beautiful… like a dream… How did all of these get up here?"

"That's a question for someone else. I found it, sorely neglected. Kestin and I spent quite a lot of time reviving the different plants, clearing away all of the dead foliage and debris. This is the inner ring. There's another that follows the wall. Come. There's something I want you to see…"

Decision

He eagerly led her out of the inner ring and around to the outer one that housed larger plants. He stopped her short, deliberately blocking her view, nervous for her next reaction.

"Sorry for the mess," he apologized, slightly embarrassed. "I tend to sleep here when the weather is pleasant."

He stepped to the side, revealing his bedding on the stone path's floor and half kicked to the side. A chest with his clothing and more personal items, along with a small stack of books and scrolls, sat under a large stone bench that was built into the curve of the wall which surrounded that half of the plant ring. He waited patiently, hoping for her to notice one particular detail about her surroundings. She slowly scanned around and nodded approvingly.

"I can see why you chose this place inside here. It's a gorgeous—" Her words failed as her eyes fell on a very special bush on the outside of the inner ring and directly across from the bench.

Its dark green leaves beautifully enhanced each of the pale blue rose blooms on it. Her eyes widened at the sight of it! She took a hesitant step toward it. She suddenly froze. Her stunning, slate blue eyes silently begged him for permission to continue.

He beamed, delighted for her. "Go ahead. They're quite real. Be careful of the thorns though. They're long, fine, and very sharp."

Beastly Cycle

Tears filled her eyes as she gently caressed a petal. He seized the opportunity to pull out two items from his chest while she was distracted. He carefully cut a rose that was not fully opened yet, but no longer a bud either, from the far side of the bush with his well sharpened dagger that he kept for tending to the plants. He then quietly and hesitantly presented her with it. Her face betrayed her astonishment at the gift as she gazed into his eyes. His heart melted. She shyly accepted the rose with a whispered thanks. He thought its allure a very pale comparison to the one who was now drinking in its unique and intoxicating fragrance. He seated himself on the bench and brought his spare ocarina to his lips. He softly played a song from his heart of beauty and love, just for her. She made herself more comfortable on the floor and savored each note of it as she carefully fingered the soft petals of her rose. He completed his song. A heady silence fell on them.

"Beautiful," she whispered.

"Which one, the flower or the music?" he inquired, curious.

She gazed lovingly into his eyes, then into the rose as she blushed. "Both…" she softly answered.

He grinned foolishly as his heart leapt, immensely pleased with how things were going! He then heard soft footfalls approaching them on the stones within the room. He recognized them

Decision

immediately and silently cursed the steward's timing.

"What is it, Kestin?" he called out, trying to keep the irritation out of his voice.

Kestin dashed up and skidded to a halt, startled to see Rennora there. After a minute, he caught his breath and bowed quickly.

"Please forgive my interruption, milord and lady," he apologized, "but I need a word with his lordship if you please, and I am afraid it cannot wait, milady."

Alleron composed himself as he assisted his beloved Rennora to her feet.

"Well then, I believe I will return to my task," she reluctantly replied as she dusted herself off. "Till later then?" she directed at Alleron.

"Of course," the fox man assured her.

He walked her back to the west doors and watched her gaze back at him, a little wistful. She headed toward the northwest tower. He quickly redirected her to the correct one that would take her back to the fourth level instead of the one that housed his other sleeping chamber. She thanked him, then stumbled for a few steps as she quickly crossed the roof. She laughed at her own clumsiness before she checked around to see what had tripped her. She discovered another leather box lying out in the open! She scooped it up, peeked

Beastly Cycle

inside, looked at him ecstatic, and darted off with both of her treasures.

    He leaned against the metal door frame with a heavy sigh. He no longer had any doubts in his mind on whether she loved him. He felt the responsibility of such knowledge weigh heavily upon him. She loved in ignorance as to the possible consequences. He alone of the pair held the burden of the beastly cycle. If only she could just leave on her own! Why did she have to be so stubbornly determined to help them?! Worst of all, why did his resolve to keep her at a distance always crumble to nothing whenever he laid eyes on her? Why did his heart's voice of love and pursuit always overrule his mind's one of warning or to maintain silence at the sight of her shy beauty, both inside and out? He cursed himself for his weakness toward her. He heard Kestin approaching from behind. He gazed longingly at the closed southwest tower door, hoping that there was another way to fix this mess than the two before him, since his scan of the island had yielded nothing.

    "I can't do this anymore," he told the steward. "I can't let her risk herself. The price is far too high! I've been back and forth on this for too long. It's past time to stand firm."

    "Forgive me, Lord Alleron, but I do not agree and believe that you are worse than a fool if you let Lady Rennora go," Kestin firmly replied. "What of

Decision

the curse? What about the rest of us? Would you continue to doom us all to this frozen existence?"

"Fear not. I am by no means abandoning your people. I'll take care of the curse myself. Look after everyone when I'm gone."

"Milord! You would *not*!" Kestin exclaimed in horror!

Alleron gave a mirthless chuckle. "Nothing like that, I assure you. What I have in mind will take much longer, but still work. Many years in fact…"

Kestin stood in silence for several minutes. "Then you would doom yourself to save her… May I ask why? Why not put your trust in her?"

Alleron turned to look Kestin straight in the eye with a cold gaze. "Because she's far too precious to me, and I will *not* simply stand around and watch helplessly as her trust, her heart, and possibly her mind are crushed forever! I love her too much for that." He walked past the stunned servant and paused to ask, "What was it that you wanted to tell me?"

"Yes, of course. Jes has disappeared from the kitchens! She knocked the servant that was guarding her unconscious and fled! We were searching the castle and grounds, including the tree and prince's roses, but I fear that she is already beyond our borders by now."

Beastly Cycle

Alleron nodded. "Have a female servant, that's skilled in protecting as well, stay with ma belle mademoiselle at all times until Jes is found. Maintain a guard over both armories, just in case she tries something with them as well. Also, discreetly inform everyone that her ladyship will not be staying with us for much longer, and I have the curse well in hand." He rubbed at his chest as he felt his heart shattering within it. "Brace yourself, Kestin. Tonight is going to be most unpleasant for all of us. I only hope that she can forgive me in time…"

Chapter 29
~ Beauty ~

Attempt

Rennora eagerly flew back to her chambers, where she found Stelna preparing her things for later.

"I found it!" Rennora exclaimed, joyfully! "The last part of the tale…" She saw a worried look on Stelna's face. "Is there something wrong?"

Stelna shook her head and smiled. "No, milady. Will you be wanting a cozy fire to read by after your bath?"

Rennora considered it as she set the new scroll next to the previous one. "No thank you. I'll be reading by the lake today, after a quick change. Oh, would you bring the rest of the tale please and meet me there? I think I would like to reread everything in order after I read these. Perhaps I'll be able to glean some additional information that way."

Stelna curtsied. Rennora quickly cleansed and changed, then collected both of the scrolls from Minna and launched through the door, heading down and out of the castle by way of the northeast tower. She slowed as she skirted the ruined building

Beastly Cycle

and crossed to the lake. She settled herself in and promptly dove into the second scroll which had the Queen's elegant handwriting.

I stood there by my mistress, whose name I am forbidden to write, as she thoroughly berated my son and heir, terribly ashamed in what he had become and in my neglect that aided in his selfishness. Once I threw off my cloak and revealed myself, I demanded that he answer her immediately! He seemed so lost and confused for a moment. His eyes then hardened like steel. He refused to answer, quite defiant.

My mistress raised her hand to summon his punishment. I quickly halted her, insisting that I bare that particular burden. She studied me with a questioning gaze, but I stood firm. She

Attempt

then yielded with a nod, declaring that she would deal with the other two herself, and promptly left us, entrusting him to me.

I braced myself for the task ahead and closed down every emotion within myself. I threw a quick enchantment that froze his shoes to the floor. He flinched. I took my time weaving the full enchantment of the next, drawing all of the elements from around me and combining them with my own power and strength, as I had been taught. Small specks of water, earth, fire, air, darkness, and light began gathering around me in a stream, quickly gaining speed. The tip of the stream swirled up my body, touched between my whirling

Beastly Cycle

hands, and churned into a large, loose ball. Once the last of the stream entered the growing ball, I completed the last of Vindan's portion of the curse. I condensed the ball until it was no bigger than a walnut.

    I took a small pinch of it in one hand, while I held it aloft in the other. I steeled my heart one final time and pronounced sentence on him. I informed him sternly that his wife still loves and weeps for him. If he did not permanently fix himself and return her affection once the curse was broken, then he needed to set her free or pay the consequences most dear. His face went from horror to genuine confusion. I hovered the ball for a second before me as it gained more and

Attempt

more speed. I then released it, spinning... hard!

It flew at Vindan and vanished halfway there. I could see a wisp of a trail wrapping around his feet as I waited patiently. Suddenly, he was thrown backwards off of his feet as the invisible curse slammed into him, leaving his shoes frozen to the floor! I collapsed to my knees as my strength left me, gasping and barely holding on to the pinch of curse. I watched as Vindan sat up slowly, looking for the first time in a long time like himself and through clear eyes.

"What have I done?" he asked as a single tear trickled down his cheek.

Beastly Cycle

The first stage of the curse then hit, and he fainted, giving us time to complete the remainder of it and tie everything together. All of a sudden, I felt a mystical surge to the east, along the ground level. I rose shakily to my feet and worked my way to the lake, my steps growing stronger with each I took. I found my mistress with her one hand outstretched and Jesseva hovering before her, frozen with a look of both hatred and horror! A steady stream of darkness, laced with bright purple and green flashes of light, drained from the girl and formed a thick cloud above my mistress's other hand. Once the last of it left Jesseva, the girl fell to the ground and fainted, mercifully. Amheer was already

Attempt

unconscious not far from where he had already collapsed. Poor Belnisa was sobbing silently near the lake's edge behind my mistress.

My mistress then summoned a stream of light and used it to dispel the darkness by balancing it. She noticed my presence, looking weary, but resolved to finish this.

"Is it done?" she asked me.

"Yes," I answered, still numb.

"Do you have it?"

She inspected the tiny piece of curse I still held and nodded her approval. "Very well done, and the opportunity for one that truly selflessly loves to break it, if Vindan fails, is the perfect touch, my dear. It will unite everything together

Beastly Cycle

quite nicely. Now for us to continue, then rest."

I gazed at the heartbroken princess, wondering what would become of her.

"Leave her to my care," my mistress insisted. "We have much to do and precious little time."

I peered at the small, grassy island that stood in the center and the bridge that connected it to the lake's opposite shore, hoping that the beautiful girl that I had come to love as my own daughter would be safe and know happiness once again. I then left for the entrance hall and trusted that my mistress had things well in hand as I felt another mystical surge from behind me.

Attempt

I glanced at the cloud that coated the sky in every direction as a result of Vindan's curse, touching the tops of all four boundary walls, just before I entered the castle to wait with my emotions and thoughts still under tight control. Time seemed like it was slowing down for us. How long it actually took for my mistress to join me, I could not tell. She did not say a word to me as we stood in the center of the solid, stone floor. We both held out our hands as we faced each other. I released the piece and gave everything I had as my mistress chanted the final part that would set and seal the entire curse. The clouds above came to our aid and coated every inch of everything, both inside and out, including

Beastly Cycle

ourselves. We did not waver until the last phrase passed through both of our lips, and we collapsed, weakened and winded.

It was soon after that when we heard a scream of pain and terror! Vindan scrambled out of the ballroom, clutching his head, then fell to his knees near the threshold. I have no words to describe what happened next. I could only watch as he transformed before my eyes into part man and part white tiger that he had treasured so much once. He roared so loudly that everything in the room shook for a moment! His eyes then rolled to the back of his head, and he toppled over, unconscious. Everything that I had been holding back broke

Attempt

through like a flood. I wept like a little child into my hazy hands over everything! I cried until I had nothing left, my heart felt like it was bleeding from within.

"Rest yourself a bit more," my mistress gently urged. "We still have a few more tasks to complete before we can take care of ourselves, so we can safely watch over the others. You did well, and all will be made right. Have faith in them."

Rennora dried her eyes at the poor queen's ache and the prince being cursed by her own hand. She then noticed another phrase written sideways about midway down the scroll.

Beastly Cycle

Heart of a beast beats in your chest. Open it to love, your prison will shed.

She wanted to check the previous parts for the other phrases she had seen, but Stelna had not caught up with her yet, so she dove into the last scroll. The writing was very neat and looked exactly like the hand, in which the list was written. She wondered if she had the wrong one, until she began reading it and realized that it was Vindan's words in someone else's writing.

I sit here near the smallest garden between my ring of the deepest red roses and the hedge wall, waiting for milady to make her appearance at midnight on this warm, clear night, under the full moon, where she will openly declare her love and kiss my muzzle. I can no longer even hold a quill, let alone write with one, so my

Attempt

ever faithful steward records this instead.

The moment the curse hurled into me, Jesseva's hold on me fell away. I was finally able to recall everything for myself. I accepted my prison as punishment for my folly without a fight. I do not blame my mother, or the sorceress, for what has been done to me. This is my mess and mine alone to fix. Jesseva, thankfully, lost her powers. Amheer lost his voice. They are still around, with an opportunity to fix their own damages. However, they can cause no more trouble.

Soon after I recovered, I eagerly sought my dearest to begin there, but no one could tell me what had happened to her. I have carefully searched everywhere within our boundaries for her. I even had the

Beastly Cycle

bottom of the lake scoured thoroughly as well. Her scent ends by the remnants of the bridge to the island where we used to sit for hours on the grass, gazing at the sky overhead, talking and laughing together, before the willow tree was placed there as a symbol of each tear I caused her heart. The surviving servants that did not give in to horror or melancholy during those first months of adjustment, wish for me to hold a ceremony of mourning for her, but I refuse to believe that she is dead! It is not just stubbornness on my part. I can feel it within the depths of my soul that she is alive still somewhere. She is simply where I cannot see her, just out of my reach...

    I pieced together the hints left behind by the others and in the correct order. I feel that this is my best course

Attempt

for freeing us all and finally returning my heart's delight to me. I live for the day when I can fall to my knees before her and do everything within my power to set things right, even throwing myself into the growing chasm that has opened up along the rear wall behind the castle, if need be. I will do anything and everything she asks of me to mend us, even let her walk out of my life forever, if that is her wish...

I wait beneath the full moon's light for one that is not my precious beloved. I care about the lady enough to let her break the curse, but my heart will always and forever belong to my Belnisa. I will accept whatever the results of this that come. I am hoping for the best as I hold a deep red rose for my precious one, and a different one as

Beastly Cycle

a sign of my gratitude for the lady who aids our freedom. I do not know what I will do if this fails. However, I do know that I will never <u>ever</u> give up...

Rennora heard someone approaching her. She looked up from the scroll to see both of her maids working their way toward her with their loads, tears streaming down her face. They rushed to her side, distressed.

"Milady?!" Stelna exclaimed. "Are you well? Have you been injured in some way?"

Rennora dried her eyes on the offered handkerchief as she shook her head, then returned it.

She swallowed the lump in her throat before she found her voice, "I'm just fine, thank you. No need to fret over me. I finished poor Vindan's tale is all."

She relieved Minna of the rest of the tale and scanned through each part until she found the other two hints. All three were written in the sorceress's handwriting.

She drew her maids' attention to it as she asked, "Do you know the name of the person who wrote this by any chance?"

Attempt

Both maids studied the writing for a moment. Minna then gasped in surprise and suddenly looked to Stelna!

Stelna declared firmly, but sadly, "We are terribly sorry, milady, but we are not permitted to say."

Rennora was getting quite frustrated at hearing that for an answer.

Her face must have shown her thought because Minna replied, "It is very frustrating for us not to be able to give the answers that we truly wished to as well."

Rennora was humbled. "A lot of frustration all around."

Both maids sighed in agreement.

Rennora peered at Minna. "Are you any better?" she asked her.

Minna looked slightly perplexed, then mortified, and finally greatly embarrassed. She curtsied low as she apologized, "I am so terribly sorry and ashamed that you saw my outburst like that. Can you ever forgive me?"

Rennora shook her head. "You have nothing to apologize for."

"B-but a servant must remain composed at all times, milady! She must never, ever lose control like that!"

"Servants have hearts, not just nobility, and sometimes they hurt or get the better of us like any

Beastly Cycle

other person. So I ask you again, are you better now?"

Minna nodded. Rennora smiled warmly at her.

"If you need a little more time for yourself, then I can dismiss your services until I retire for the day…" the girl offered.

"That will not be necessary, milady, but thank you for thinking of me. I am quite able to resume my duties."

"I'm glad," Rennora replied as she noticed Stelna's load. "What are those?" she asked her.

Stelna laid out a board, several empty parchments, an ink pot, and a quill beside her mistress. "We thought that you might need these," she explained.

"Perfect!" Rennora exclaimed, delight with her maids' foresight!

She thanked them both. Minna smiled, curtsied, and returned to the castle, while Stelna remained behind.

"If I may, you will need assistance with carrying everything back inside, milady," the maid explained. "I wish to keep you company and aid you however I may until then, if you please."

Rennora nodded her approval. She turned her attention back to the sorceress's hints. She rearranged them several times until they made sense and felt right to her. She quickly copied them down

Attempt

on a blank parchment. She then rose to her feet and read them again to ensure that she had them correct. She gazed at her companion, a little puzzled.

"What is it, milady?" Stelna inquired.

Rennora's attention shifted to the top of the castle as she suddenly got the feeling that she was being watched.

"There has to be more…" she declared as she stared at the figure gazing down at her. Somehow, she knew that it was Alleron watching over her.

"What makes you say that?" Stelna urged.

Rennora tore her eyes away from him as she insisted, "I don't know. The words just feel like they're missing a very important piece or two to them. I can't explain why." She tore off most of the blank parchment, folded the remainder up, and tucked it into her pocket. "It doesn't seem like this is meant for me, to be honest. Perhaps it's for Alleron instead. I just don't know. It's all so confusing. Maybe the tale holds more insight to the verses than meets the eye."

She scooped up the prince's final lament and got no further than the first three words when Stelna interrupted her thoughts.

"I beg your pardon, milady, but if you are going to dress in time for dinner, then we need to begin on you soon," she tactfully stated.

Rennora glanced up, bemused for a moment. "Oh, is it that late already? I forgot about that… I

Beastly Cycle

believe that Alleron will be joining me here shortly. Let's wait until afterwards, please."

"Forgive me, milady, but I bring word that his lordship is unable to enjoy your company at this time. He will, however, still be able to dine with you this evening."

Rennora could not pretend that she was not disappointed with the news. "Would you kindly help me with this, and we'll go now then."

Before Rennora could gather more than two scrolls and the board, Stelna scooped up everything else and marched off toward the castle. Rennora gazed up at the roof, hoping to see Alleron again, only to discover that he had already vanished, so she shook open the prince's scroll as she slowly followed. She came to the end of the first paragraph and froze in her tracks a few feet from the tower door where Stelna waited with it ajar.

"That's it!" Rennora exclaimed, her excitement escalating until she could hardly stand it! She showed the opened scroll to Stelna, demanding, "Quick! What's the moon like tonight?"

"It had barely a sliver missing last night, so it should be whole this time," Stelna replied.

Rennora grinned widely with hope filling her body, as she realized that the weather had been pleasant all day, so tonight was the perfect night to break the curse!

Attempt

Stelna sighed heavily at her. "Please do not become too dismayed if things do not work out as you hope," The maid whispered to Rennora as the girl darted inside.

Rennora halted, her heart sinking fast, "Why?"

"No one has succeeded yet, milady, so it is difficult for us to get hopeful at the prospect of yet another try is all. Please have care…"

They climbed the tower stairs and returned to Rennora's chambers. The girl was enveloped in a somber, reflective silence, saddened by her maid's words. Did the others not have faith that this time would be different? She truly loved Alleron and he her. She was absolutely certain of it! All those other tries were missing that one simple element. She just knew it! She was confident, as she surveyed her dress selection, that she would succeed where others had not! Midnight was the time the prince had declared. She decided on a simple dress of a fine, deep blue silk with a silvery stitching along the neckline only. She requested an extra lovely dress be set out when she returned after dining. She wanted to surprise Alleron with the breaking, without giving her intent away too soon by her level of care in her appearance. She pondered how she could lure him to the garden without arousing his suspicions, as she entered her bed chamber and transferred her parchment to her new dress. Her eyes then fell on her chest, giving

Beastly Cycle

her an idea that she was certain would work! She sat down to allow her maids to dress her hair, delighted with her plan!

Once she was completed, she slipped downstairs, escorted by Stelna, hoping for an enjoyable evening. Dusk was falling by the time she reached the entrance hall. She waited patiently for Alleron to join her. Time slipped by. She grew uneasy. After thirty minutes or so, Kestin entered and ushered her into the dining hall instead, looking stiffer and slightly grimmer than usual. Rennora wondered what was going on as the steward assisted her with her chair, putting her directly across from Alleron, who was modestly dressed, fur clean and neat, and already seated. He had his face resting on his propped up fist. His eyes were intent on the blazing fire near them. She greeted him with a warm smile. He glanced her way and barely returned it, seeming distant. They ate in silence.

"Um…" she began hesitantly. "May I ask you something? You don't have to answer if it doesn't concern me, or you don't wish to…"

He stopped eating, rested his hands on the table, his gaze still focused on his plate, but said nothing.

She was now more anxious then ever and charged ahead before her imagination could suggest all kinds of horrible things! "Are you alright?"

Attempt

"I suppose you have a right to know," he sternly stated. "Jes has gone missing, and it has everyone on edge, especially for your safety."

"Oh…"

That explained Stelna's insistence on accompanying her downstairs, but not Alleron's current dark mood. She wondered if there was more to it than had remained unsaid, as he cleaned his hands, rose to his feet, thanked her for her company, and turned to leave. Surprised at his rush, she quickly begged him to stay! He obeyed, but maintained his back to her.

"Would you mind meeting me later tonight, please?" she timidly requested. "I still have something of yours that I would like to return to you, if you don't mind."

She waited in silence, wondering if she should wait until he was in better spirits.

Finally, he asked "Where?" as if he already knew the answer.

"By the crystal garden, if that's alright," she replied.

His shoulders dropped as he lingered there with one hand on the doorway. As Kestin entered to attend to his duties, Alleron left without another word. Her appetite was deserting her rapidly, so she quietly asked the steward if he would see her back to her rooms. He delivered her safely there without incident. She thanked him, disheartened. Alleron

Beastly Cycle

had not been as thrilled about meeting her as she had hoped. As she gazed over the beautiful gowns before her, she resolved to make him smile again once he was freed. She returned her focus to looking her best.

The three dresses were all absolutely stunning! She decided against the delicate gold one, all in satin brocade with a fitted bodice and full skirt. It was a little too regal for her taste. The next was a black velvet one, with fitted sleeves and flared at the hips. It was soft as butter and seemed to absorb the light instead of reflecting it. It had subtle, intricate, silver beading along the neckline, cuffs, and skirt hem with single, tiny beads sparsely scattered all over it, like miniature stars in the night sky. She was afraid that she would vanish into the darkness while she declared herself with that one, so she dismissed it as well.

Her heart fluttered joyously at the next! It was a pale hint of gray, like the moon, with a soft velvet bodice that felt just like the black one, flowing sleeves, and a skirt in several layers of sheer fabric that would whisper with her every movement. She dressed with great care and asked her maids to do their utmost best with her hair without overdoing it. They gave her a little bee's wax to soften her lips for the final touch afterwards. She was stunned by the results in the looking glass! She never thought that she had ever looked so well in her entire life!

Attempt

  She stashed her bell and the parchment in hidden pockets within the folds of her skirt, double checked her daggers were in their proper places, even though they still made her feel silly wearing them, and retrieved the tunic from her chest. She wondered if she should request a guard to guide and remain with her until Alleron arrived, since Jes was on the loose, when she heard a sharp rapping at the outer doors.

  She allowed Minna to answer it for her as she threw on a cloak to cover herself and hoped that it was Alleron on the other side. She hid her disappointment well at seeing Kestin there with a torch in his hand. She accepted his offer graciously to accompany her. Rennora fought back her nervousness as they wound their way to the darkened garden where a large, well-armed man stood guard. She checked the moon. It was still a few hours before midnight. She seated herself on the tower steps and resigned herself to the long, agonizing wait, determined to maintain her composure.

  She attempted to engage Kestin in polite conversation to pass the time and take her mind off of her task ahead, but he said very little, preferring to keep a careful watch around him, along with the other man. She gave up after a while and kept a close watch on the moon as midnight drew closer and closer. The final hour then approached. She

Beastly Cycle

began to pace with impatience. She continuously scanned for Alleron, muttering what she wanted to say over and over to herself. Midnight came and still no sign of him. She decided to give him a bit more time, just in case his own preparations were taking much longer than either of them expected. The time dragged on. She soon had the feeling that he never had any intension of meeting her at all…

"Kestin," she called, her voice breaking slightly.

She was fighting not to think the worst as Kestin came to her side and bowed.

"Milady?" he politely inquired with a blank face lit by the torch he carried.

"Do you happen to know what's keeping Alleron?" she calmly asked.

Sadness and pity appeared on the silent steward's gentle face. Her heart plummeted as she realized the truth behind the fox man's demeanor as he had left her earlier.

"He's not coming… is he?"

Kestin refused to meet her gaze, as he remained silent. She felt betrayed, hurt, and robbed of her chance to finally set everyone free.

"Very well," she replied, shaking as angry tears welled up in her eyes. She set her jaw firm. "I demand that you take me to him at once. We'll just do this the hard way…"

Chapter 30
~ Beast ~

For Her Own Safety

Alleron pumped the bellows to the forge, sending the flames soaring into the chimney as the coals flared a bright red. The heat spilling from the furnace did nothing to warm his soul. He examined the color of the iron bar within, fished the white hot metal out with a firm grip on his tongs, and transferred it to his anvil. He began beating on it with a steady, even rhythm. His sharp ears told him that Kestin was leading a very unhappy Rennora his way. He braced himself and turned his heart cold as ice in preparation of what he knew was coming, as he spied their movement approaching the smithy out of the corner of his eye. He lowered his gaze a little further and refused to even glance upward from his work. Kestin's shoes then stepped into view, and the simply dressed fox man could shut them out no longer.

He paused his pounding just long enough to calmly address the steward, "Thank you, Kestin. I'll take things from here."

Beastly Cycle

The man bowed respectfully, but remained where he was, hesitant to obey.

"Thank you, Kestin," Rennora snapped, quite angry. "That will be all. We'll summon you if you're needed."

Alleron could feel Kestin's gaze on him. He nodded as he finally looked up. The steward slowly walked away, glancing back at the pair one last time, most apprehensive, before he disappeared into the night. Alleron raised his hammer to resume his striking.

"Why didn't you come?" Rennora asked softly, her voice quivering slightly.

He stuffed the cooling bar back into the hot coals and built the heat back up, ignoring her in hopes that she would leave on her own if he neglected her enough. She stubbornly stormed over to him.

"I don't understand," she insisted sternly. "You know that I'm here to set you and everyone else free."

He turned away from her.

"Will you at least look at me?!" she demanded.

He did as she said with a grim look on his face, his heart cracking at the sight of the anger and frustration toward him contained within her breathtaking beauty.

For Her Own Safety

He cursed her stubbornness as she continued her tirade. "Don't you even want to be human again?! I thought that that's what you truly wanted most! Was I mistaken in this?" She waited for an answer, but he refused to speak. "I take that as a 'no', so why won't you let me even try? I love you, and I know that you love me in return! Let me do this, please. I'm the only one who can break this horrid curse on you!"

He could take it no more. He could feel her working herself up to try despite his resistance, if not tonight, then she was determined enough to stay as long as it took to catch him unawares.

"No," he firmly stated. "If you truly believe that, then you're a fool." He gazed into her eyes and saw the shock and hurt as something fell from her hand and landed by her feet. "You keep declaring how much you want to help, but you have *no* idea what that will cost you!" He took half a step closer and snarled at her, "That pathetic existence, as you called it, in your town is a far better fate than what awaits you here."

"I DON'T CARE!" she shrieked at him, her tears flowing freely.

"YOU HAD BETTER!" he fumed in return. "You'll end up dead or worse if you stay!" He thundered back to his anvil, distancing her from his rising fury. "Just go…" The words were like a sword to his heart as he began to tremble.

Beastly Cycle

"*NO!*" she screeched at him! He heard her follow huffily to the other side of his anvil. "I *will* fix this, whether you like it or not!"

He snatched up his hammer and threw it behind him. "*IT'S NOT YOUR PROBLEM TO MEND!*" he exploded, his own frustrations getting the better of him. "DON'T YOU UNDERSTAND?! YOU'VE SERVED YOUR TIME HERE! YOU'RE NO LONGER WELCOME! GO!"

She stepped back, truly afraid of him now! He threw anything within his reach at the back wall as he roared at her one final time, "*GO!*"

He then watched her hopes, her love, shift to horror and agony in her tear stained eyes in that one brief moment before she turned and fled toward the front grounds, and no doubt, the road beyond. He crumbled to his knees and howled his rage at himself as he beat the stone flooring with his fists until his hands bled. He was disgusted with himself for what he was doing to her! He had betrayed both her heart and her trust. He loathed his own existence as tears streamed unchecked. He collapsed completely and stretched out a hand toward the empty doorway as a few snowflakes drifted down along with a little frozen rain. His pain was far worse now than even when he had transformed. He clutched at his chest. A gaping

For Her Own Safety

hole felt like it was growing where his heart once beat.

The minutes slowly crawled by. He heard Kestin's footsteps crunching in the collecting snow. Alleron had lost the will to even move. He felt a blanket drape over him, but felt no warmth from it. Kestin carefully tended to his master's hands, then somberly left.

"Be safe, my precious treasure…" the creature whispered to the darkness as another tear fell.

Chapter 31
~ Beauty ~

Town and Life

Rennora raced as fast as she could across the grounds! Alleron's fierce, animal cry echoed behind her in the darkness! She threw open the torch lit gate and fled into the shelter of the forest to the east. Deeper and deeper she ran until she began stumbling. She tumbled into a tree trunk, her strength gone. She clawed at the rough bark as she slowly collapsed at its base. Her chest was racked with pain! She fell apart with no one to hear her heartache. She clenched her fists, scraping her fingers hard onto the bark, feeling lost, betrayed, and abandoned. She had given him her heart, but he had coldly shattered it, just as if he had taken his hammer to it, leaving her in tiny pieces of a hollow shell! She laid there in the darkness, the tears streaming continuously, until she slipped into a fitful slumber. She no longer cared what happened to her anymore…

She awoke the next day, blinded by the sunlight streaming down on her. She shielded her eyes and lay there, still feeling broken inside, but

Town and Life

also numb and sore. She rolled onto her side as the memories surfaced. The tears returned. She could not think of what she could have possibly done to turn him against her like that! The answer had to lie in the time between lessons and dinner. She stared at her scabbed fingertips and filthy hands, thinking very carefully, but could not come up with a single hint. She did not want to let him go, in spite of things. Meeting and loving him felt so right to her, like they had been courting for several months instead of a few days. Yet, she could not go back to where she was not wanted either.

Not knowing what else to do, she rose shakily to her feet and began wandering aimlessly away from the castle and the road, allowing the forest to decide for her. The question of why he did it persisted with each step, threatening to consume her, body and soul, until she pushed it away. She felt numb, once again, as she wrapped her arms around herself, trying to hold what was left of herself together, even a little.

Hours later, a familiar sight broke through the forest. She halted just short of the dense brush that bordered the town's ditch and stared at Mistress LaZella's diminutive house. It looked more cold and unwelcoming than ever. The plants had wilted without her there to care for them. She felt a part of her dying inside at the thought of returning to that nightmare, her body trembling in fear. No! She

Beastly Cycle

retreated further into the safety of the woods. She did not know what she would do, or where she would go, but she refused to put herself at those two's mercy again. *That* she knew for certain.

She carefully worked her way further on for several yards and crossed the dry ditch there, taking care not to tear her clothing. She drew her hood to cover her face. She then quietly slipped to the road. She meandered automatically to his lordship's grounds where she rested against the other side of her favorite tree, hoping she would be less likely to be noticed there, and mulled over her situation. She had no money to start fresh somewhere else. She had no friend that could take her in. She could ask Madam Tisza if she could live at the lord's house until she found a home or someone else to take her in. However, it was already overflowing with servants that resided there. Next, she lowered her hood and checked her hair for any combs or precious ornaments that she could sell to aid her, but found nothing. They must have fallen out during the night. Disappointed, she wondered what else she had when she heard heavy footsteps approaching her from behind.

"Pardon me, milady," Quorrick said, until Rennora hesitantly turned to face him. "Rennora?!" he exclaimed, unable to believe his eyes! He then pulled her into a tight hug as tears of relief streamed down his cheeks. "We thought you were lost forever to us, child, when that boy told us you had vanished into the woods!" He held her at arm's length. "Thank heavens you're safe. You look terrible. Are you alright? What happened to you?"

She had no answer for that, so she shrugged her shoulders, not trusting herself to speak of her pain quite yet.

"Well, you're here now. But tell me, how did you break the enchantment and escape?"

"What do you mean?" she shakily asked, caught off guard and wondering what he was talking about.

"The enchantment that monster put on you to lure you into its clutches."

"Who said that?"

"The boy I watched pursuing you before you returned to the kitchens."

She stepped back, unable to believe what she was hearing! "You mean Wescar's been telling you that I was trapped this entire time?!"

"Well, weren't you? He's been very insistent, more so since yesterday."

"*No!*" she shrieked.

He folded his arms across his chest, quite upset with her. "Then tell me where in the world you've been, because your little surprise journey has made some people worried sick over you. Myself and my wife, Tisza, for starters!"

Beastly Cycle

"Y-you mean th-that someone actually noticed I-I was missing?" she stammered, stunned and touched.

"Of course! Even Wescar—" His eyes widened for a moment. "Come with me! Quickly!" He rushed out of the grounds and to the road with Rennora in tow. "Wescar's gathering everyone possible in the square to mount a search and rescue for you! He has to be stopped!"

"Why aren't you with him?"

"His heart's in the right place, but I don't agree with how he's persuading them. He's got half of them terrified of what's happened to you, while the rest are terrified of him! He's been secretly threatening them into following him all day. I heard him myself. I was planning on gathering those of us left with good sense and searching for ourselves. You just saved a lot of trouble for everyone. I just hope that we get there in time… Hurry!"

They maintained a fast pace until they finally reached the town's center. A huge crowd was gathered with Wescar standing above them, waving his hands in different directions while he was passionately explaining something. Quorrick searched for a minute as everyone was listening to Wescar insisting on avenging Rennora, and her sacrifice not being in vain. The groundskeeper pulled her along the back of the crowd and halted. He placed his hand on the shoulder of a woman.

Town and Life

    Madam Tisza turned around and squealed Rennora's name! All talk halted as the townsfolk turned to look. People parted until Rennora had a clear view of Wescar standing on the base's edge of the town statue, shocked, with Mistress LaZella and Thevesta lingering on the ground nearby, staring at her in astonishment and dismay. Madam Tisza squashed the missing girl in a tight hug, relieved that she was alive! Arissera came running up from the front of the crowd and hugged her tightly next. Wescar tried to pulled her into his arms as well, but she pushed herself free with a gasp from the sharp pains in her hands and took a couple of steps back from him.

    Suddenly, Mistress LaZella and Thevesta were there, patting Rennora on the back, both insisting how worried they had been! Rennora gazed at everyone, still in disbelief that she had been missed so dearly. Mistress LaZella told her that all was forgiven, and that she was welcome to her old room anytime that she wished as Thevesta pulled Rennora's cloak slightly opened. Rennora's heart stopped! Everything was happening too quickly! She noticed an odd person, cloaked and mysterious, standing on the edge of the town square as her knees buckled out from under her.

    Quorrick scooped her up before she had a chance to hit the ground. She could hear people moving closer as they demanded to know what had

Beastly Cycle

happened to her! Madam Tisza roared that they all give them some room, effectively silencing them at the same time! Quorrick carried a limp Rennora away. Rennora kept her eyes closed as she fought back the tears, thoroughly embarrassed. She heard some people following them. It was not long before she felt Quorrick halt. A door creaked. He took several more steps onto wood, it sounded like. He then gently set her down on a long, wooden bench.

She opened her eyes to a large, modestly furnished room, that was cozy and neatly kept, as Quorrick and Wescar rushed to throw open the windows. Arissera joined her on the bench, looking worried. Madam Tisza closed the outer door behind her. She took in Rennora's state for a minute.

"Right, something warm and nourishing for Rennora, I think," she declared. "Quorrick and you, young man, will you see to it, while this girl and I tend to Rennora's other needs?"

Wescar introduced himself to the couple just before he and Quorrick headed through one of the interior doors.

"Now then," the kindly cook addressed Rennora. "Let's get this off of you and see what I'm working with."

Rennora rose shakily to her feet and allowed Madam Tisza to undo the intricate silver clasp and remove her cloak. Both of the ladies gasped at her clothing! Rennora glanced down. Her beautiful

Town and Life

gown, pale as the moon, had somehow managed to survive her journey back with a touch of dirt along the skirt's hem, but otherwise, unscathed. She teared up at the sight of it, a reminder of what could have been. She heard movement around her as she slowly sat back down, heartbroken once again. All of a sudden, a damp cloth slipped into her view.

"To clean your face," Arissera explained.

Rennora whispered a thank you. She reached to take it, but as her fingertips touched the moisture, pain shot through her hand! She ripped it back, grimacing. Madam Tisza gently turned both of the girl's hands over. She quickly grabbed several things and had Arissera assist her as she carefully cleaned, applied a stinging salve, and bandaged each finger in turn. Quorrick and Wescar returned, glaring at each other and baring a steaming tankard of a very fragrant drink. The groundskeeper noticed Rennora's poor fingers and became angered.

"I think that it's past time that you told us the truth, child," he sternly groaned as he seated himself across from her and handed the tankard to his wife, since Rennora was unable to hold it. "I promise that you're safe with us, and nothing that is said will go beyond these walls, if you wish."

Rennora avoided looking at them, until a womanly hand touched her chin and tilted her face upward to meet Madam Tisza's gaze. The cook took the cloth from Arissera and gently cleaned

Beastly Cycle

Rennora's filthy face and remainder of her hands as Arissera tackled brushing her mess of hair. Rennora let them, tears trickling down her cheek. She missed Stelna and Minna. She wondered if the servants were alright, or were they paying for her folly. The cook helped her take a few drinks of what turned out to be a hot, delicious broth.

"There," Madam Tisza said as she and Arissera finished their tasks. "Nothing like cleaning up to make things a little better, child."

Rennora did not respond as she dropped her gaze again. She never thought that she would ever find herself in the same place as Conadora. She allowed the memories to flood her, when she realized that the merchant's daughter's stay had been very different than her own. The other had made no mention of any music, or a forge, or gardens…

"Take your time, child," Madam Tisza said as she tenderly patted Rennora's arm.

Rennora knew that she needed to tell them something. Yet, it all felt too private and precious to share. She also feared for what would happen to the people, if her fellow townsfolk discovered what was really there. Tears began to well up again. Arissera dried them for her. She smiled sadly in response.

"I, uh… got lost in the woods," she began. Her voice then became shaky. "T-then a stranger

Town and Life

kindly took me in for a few days, and I got lost again on the way back…"

"Someone of means by the look of your dress," Wescar commented.

Rennora quickly shook her head. "Not really. H-he's more of a caretaker."

"With access to the wealth in his care perhaps?"

"No. This dress was loaned to me, not given." She leapt to her feet, not liking where the conversation was going. She swallowed back the rising lump in her throat. "I need to change, so I can return this somehow."

"What of the monster or the prince?" Quorrick questioned. "Did you see anything of either?"

She shook her head. "There is no monster," she firmly insisted.

"And the prince?" Arissera asked.

Rennora just shook her head as she stepped away from them, refusing to speak.

"Then who's been plaguing the town and taking the ladies?!" Quorrick exclaimed, exasperated! "It has to be someone, prince or not!"

"I'll get to the bottom of this myself," Wescar heatedly volunteered. "I *refuse* to allow one more person to be harmed by that *thing!*"

He stormed toward the outer door as Rennora screamed, "NO!" desperate to stop him!

Beastly Cycle

Wescar darted out the door, ignoring her. The remaining eyes were on her. She could see the questions and shock within each set.

"My dear," Madam Tisza directed at Arissera, who introduced herself. "Do you know where Rennora lives?"

"With me," the girl replied.

"Perfect. Would you be so kind as to fetch her fresh clothing, so that she may change as she wishes, please?"

Arissera hesitantly obeyed. Madam Tisza sat herself heavily on the bench beside Rennora.

"Now then, child," she began. "We really do need to know the truth, for the safety of others, if not your own. What really happened, my dear?"

Chapter 32
~ Beast ~

Final Lament

Alleron slowly opened his eyes. He ached so much, both inside and out. A strong fire was crackling in the small fireplace of his tower bed chamber. Kestin was slumped in the wooden chair in front of it, his head propped up in his arm and his elbow on the arm rest. A small trickle of drool trailed from the corner of his mouth. Alleron vividly remembered that he had fallen asleep somewhere else… He fought back the pain that threatened to surface from the memories. Kestin shifted, waking himself up in the process.

"Milord?" Kestin tentatively asked.

"How did I get here?" Alleron asked, his voice cracking and throat quite dry.

Kestin poured him a tankard of water from the waiting pitcher and handed it to him. "Our strongest man carried you through the castle and well, partially tossed you onto your bed. I slid you the rest of the way."

"That couldn't have been easy."

"The snow and ice aided greatly."

Beastly Cycle

"I was hoping that I had imagined it. I'm truly sorry for all the trouble I've caused since I first set foot here."

Kestin bowed deeply. "These past years have been a delight, I assure you, milord. Now, time for you to rise and bathe."

Alleron rolled away from him, not wanting to face the cold light of her absence just yet, and pulled the blanket tighter around him, when suddenly, Kestin ripped it off! Alleron was shocked at such a bold move!

"None of that! You *will* get up, and you *will* get cleaned. Either you will go to the bath, or the bath will come to you," Kestin calmly declared, sternly.

Alleron did not know what to think at first, as he stared at the determined steward. "You know," he finally replied. "I do believe that you would actually dunk me or dump the water on me…"

"It is your decision, milord. Your odor has grown a bit strong overnight, and you will feel much better once you have changed as well."

Alleron reluctantly rose to his feet and shakily headed outside to find that the snow had mostly melted. He entered the bathing chamber at the top of the northeast tower. He did feel mildly better as he obeyed, then dressed in a simple pants and shirt, instead of the fine nobleman's clothing that Kestin

Final Lament

had laid out for him. He nibbled a little on the fresh breakfast tray, but did not have much of an appetite.

"Kestin, has Jes been located yet?" he inquired.

"Not yet, milord, but no one is giving up." Kestin began to leave, when he paused to add, "Her ladyship slept in the forest last night and has returned safely to her town. Stelna kept a hidden watch over her until she crossed the boundary."

Alleron was relieved. However, he tried not to think of her beyond that. The pain was still too new. He wandered down the southwest tower, avoiding the royal chambers with the mirror, and out onto the grounds, as the sun barely shone between the heavy clouds with little warmth to his soul. He found himself at the forge near his anvil. He could not stand the sight of it at the moment. Working on anything was out of the question right now. He began to walk away, when he spied a cloth object rumpled on the floor. He picked it up. It was one of his tunics, specifically the one that he had given her to stay warm that night. Tears flowed as he caught a touch of her scent still lingering on it. He thundered away, throwing it into the pool as he passed, to rid himself of the foul thing. An occasional drop of frozen rain bounced off of him. He slowed as he reached the outside of the northwest tower and front grounds, when he spied the still opened gates. He took a hesitant step back. He did not want to know

Beastly Cycle

what the metal image had shifted to this time. He figured that he should probably close and lock it. However, he did not have the heart to fully shut her out. He decided that he would deal with it later. He turned around and headed behind the rear flower garden and on to the eastern grounds, avoiding the castle as he went. He would answer to the servants before dinner, and if they chose to imprison him for what he had done, he would not fight them.

  He came to a halt at the edge of the lake. He gazed forlornly at the place where he last saw her reading from the rooftop without a care in the world. He clutched at his chest, a sharp ache striking at his heart, as snow began to mingle with the rain. He forced himself to think of something else, anything else! He turned to make his way to the solitude of the northeast corner, on the other side of the lake, when a gale of wind suddenly buffeted around him! He covered his face with his arms as he widened his stance to steady himself. After a minute, it lessened. He lowered his arms a bit. He saw the branches of the willow dancing in the wind, just like he had years ago when he first explored the grounds. He then dropped them completely as he noticed the strange, ovular area on the trunk in the fading shadows of the clouds. It looked just like a human face to his sharp eyes! The gust died down completely, concealing the trunk once more.

Final Lament

Alleron felt a tiny twinge of hope flutter within his chest. He backed up a few yards in the breaking sunshine to give himself some room. He then dropped on all fours and charged straight for the tree! Inches away from the water's edge, he launched himself into the air using the added strength in his animal hind legs! He landed on the island and slid to a halt, just short of tumbling into the water on the other side. Excited and nervous, he parted the curtain of branches and entered. The smooth area on the tree was definitely a face, feminine and graceful as any noblewoman could dare hope for. A single tear of hardened sap lay frozen on her cheek below her closed eyes. He thought to the prince in the rose tangle and the floor image. He then slowly kneeled with one hand on the ground and the other on his chest.

"Your highness," he humbly whispered as he bowed his head in respect for what he was certain was the missing princess. "The bat lady and otter lord hinted at your continued presence. Please…" His voice began to shake. "Grace me with your wisdom, so we can be free of this waking nightmare."

He sat back on his heels, gazing at her loveliness and despair, not sure what to expect. Nothing happened. Determined, he scanned around him, paying close attention to the base and trunk of the willow. On the ground directly beneath the face,

Beastly Cycle

nestling the base of the trunk between a pair of large roots, grew a single blood red rose with several crystal tears attached to some of the petals, but nothing else. He gazed at her wooden face.

"I know you have your part in this," he said to the tree, desperate. "I just need to know where, please!"

A gentle breeze rustled the leaves and thinner branches. His eyes shifted upward to the closest branches above him. He spied something pale wedged between the base of a branch and the trunk, well beyond his reach.

He whispered eagerly, "At last!" and thanked the princess. He scrambled back to give himself some room. He then charged right up the tree and leapt as high as he could! He quickly grabbed the branch with one hand, as he knocked down the object with his other from its hidden perch. He dropped to the ground and claimed the lightly oiled cloth wrapped scroll. He carefully unrolled the aged, crackling parchment to read Princess Belnisa's words in her own hand…

My world is no more, and yet, she insists that I make an account of myself in the short time I have left before I am granted my desire.

Final Lament

I, Belnisa, was thrown in the dungeon at that Jesseva's command, I am certain. Happily, there are people still loyal to me and the throne who prevented those bewitched by Jesseva from doing anything to me beyond that. The days melted together, so I do not know exactly how long I was trapped in that wretched place. Today, I remember that I heard a commotion and something heavy falling outside my door! The lock then rattled and turned. The door opened. I snatched the small stool within the room to defend myself, when my faithful maid, Minna, stepped into view with torch in hand. I could see our steward, Kestin, just over her shoulder. I dashed to her and wept, relieved! They had a plan to quickly secret me away to a safe place! I demanded to know of my family's fate. My beloved Vindan was still firmly in Jesseva's mystical grasp. His

Beastly Cycle

mother, whom I called Mother as well, had already left a month ago to summon aid in freeing us all.

 Kestin handed Minna and me a lit torch. We quietly made our way up the secret stairs, through the rear servant's hall, and out the southeast tower. We almost made it to the chapel, when the guards found us. A pair of unfamiliar faces ordered the others to seize us, but I countered it, firmly reminding them who still wore the crown! The unknown captain, by his uniform, sternly reminded them of the prince's decree, removing any and all of my power. I stood tall, despite my fear tying my stomach in knots. Kestin stepped forward and ordered them back to the castle. There was no question of his authority. Most of them took several steps back, looking lost and quite

Final Lament

baffled. The unknown two remained where they were.

In that rising tension within the silence, Minna glanced back and whispered a single word to me. I stood there, looking braver than I felt and ready to take action.

Minna then spoke a little louder. "Flee, your highness."

My dearest friends were going to sacrifice themselves for me! I did not know how long they could hold out, but I did realize that I could give them whatever additional time I could. I had them part and slowly stepped forward, looking every inch the royal I was, despite my filthy appearance. As I passed by Kestin, I quickly whispered for them to guard my retreat. I then halted just beyond them with my still burning torch in hand. I saw a flash of triumph in the captain's cold eyes and a smirk

Beastly Cycle

on his lips. I took a deep breath as though I was about to speak. I then hurled my torch at that captain and charged as fast as I could back between Minna and Kestin, toward the stables!

I vaguely remember a scream somewhere behind me. I did <u>not</u> look back, however. I focused on my path ahead and got as far as the lake before my cursed skirts tangled up my legs, tripping me! I scrambled, trying to regain my footing, when someone slammed into me and pinned me down. I then was forced to my feet and turned to face Amheer and Jesseva herself, with no sign of either of my loyal servants. I steeled my gaze at her and remained defiant, thinking fast.

"What a lovely betrothal gift," she sneered as she drew closer.

Final Lament

Amheer tried to stop her, but she shrugged him off, then glared at him until he stepped back. I waited for her to take just two more steps and promptly spit in her eye! Terribly unladylike, but fitting and quite satisfying. She slapped my face! It stung. However, I refused to let it show. I promptly kicked her shin! She punched me in the stomach! I collapsed to my knees, unable to properly draw breath as I wheezed and gasped.

"Enough of this!" she snapped.

I gazed up as she slowly whirled her hands in a circular motion, and darkened specks gathered around them.

"Vindan's mine entirely," she triumphantly laughed. "This kingdom is mine, and you will not live to see my power completed."

Beastly Cycle

I was forced to my feet. I glared at her with furious tears streaming. Then without warning, I felt myself released! The next thing I knew, Jesseva suddenly froze, and Amheer was hovering in the air, with no sight of my other captor! I saw Mother's friend swiftly approaching us with her hand outstretched, palm facing the advisor, looking enraged and <u>not</u> a person to be crossed! She demanded to know what had happened! I shakily informed her.

She halted in front of a terrified Amheer. She placed her other hand over his mouth and pulled it back. A thin, pale fog emerged from his gaping mouth and streamed into her open palm. She clenched her outstretched hand. Amheer dropped to the ground, then collapsed unconscious! She

Final Lament

stashed the small ball of fog that had formed into a pouch on a belt at her waist.

I watched numbly, thinking she had to be a mighty sorceress, as she turned her attention to Jesseva, who was scrambling frantically to retreat! Suddenly, that hag flew upright into the air and floated closer to the sorceress's outstretched hand. The sorceress then turned her palm to turn Jesseva slowly around. The girl soon halted, still hovering three feet off the ground and facing her captor.

"M-mercy!" Jesseva pleaded! "I-I beg of you!"

Her nerve at even <u>thinking</u> of mercy for herself after all she had done lit an inferno within me!

"How <u>dare</u> you!" I shrieked. "You have stolen <u>everything</u> dear to me! You were

Beastly Cycle

even arranging my death at my beloved's own hand, and you desire mercy?!"

I tried to lunge at her, to claw at her face, my sanity deserting me, but my feet were stuck fast to the ground! I tried to continue my tirade at her at least, but my mouth refused to obey! Everything that had built up inside me broke through. I sobbed hysterically for the loss of my people, and especially for my poor Vindan, as I crumpled to the ground. My mouth was freed, but I was too caught up in my sorrows to do much else. I felt a surge of power rip around my body for a moment. I refused to look up from my hands as my tears flowed, terrified at what I might see within my grief.

I then heard Mother's voice in conversation with her friend. I did not pay much attention to all of their words. However, I did hear the sorceress mention my beloved's

Final Lament

name. Everything soon fell quiet. I finally brought my gaze up and noticed Mother returning to the castle. The sorceress knelt before me with a groan.

"Tell me your heart's desire, my child," she gently urged.

I said nothing.

She placed a hand under my chin and tilted my face to meet hers. I was too weary and pained to resist.

"If you would have me grant your soul's one true wish, what would you ask of me?"

One thought, one desire alone, filled my thoughts. "Free him from Jesseva's foul hold..." I whispered with fresh tears.

"And what of you? What is to be your fate?"

"To share in his, whatever it will be."

"To what end?"

Beastly Cycle

"To happiness or ruin, as he wishes. If the later, I will try my best to aid him in returning to the good man I know is still in him. If I fail, then I will personally request that you do with him as you choose, and I will vanish from these lands in shame, never to be heard from again…"

"You have much faith in him."

I nodded.

"You love him still, in spite of everything…"

I wept again.

"May your faith and love not be misplaced. He has his chance to still prove his worth. I will grant your desire and tie you to his curse as well. Come, dear child."

She rose to her feet. Her hand came into my view. I accepted it and rose shakily to my

Final Lament

feet. As I braced myself for what was to come, my eyes fell on the unconscious pair.

"What will become of them?" I hesitantly inquired.

"Jesseva has lost her powers, which she had stolen from one of my other apprentices by trickery. Amheer has lost his voice. Both have a chance to aid in fixing what they sought to destroy. Fear not for the rest of your people, they will be protected until they are freed."

She took a firm hold of my hand. I thought her surprisingly strong for one so elderly. I closed my eyes as I felt myself rising upward. I moved forward several yards, then gently settled back to the ground. I opened my eyes as I startled at the sound of wood creaking, then shattering! The bridge to the island that we were standing upon had been blasted apart! The sorceress produced a single dark red rose,

Beastly Cycle

that was my darling's favorite color, from a different pouch and presented it to me. I fell apart into its fragrant petals, praying that we would one day know happiness and love once again.

Her final words to me were, "Freedom, like love, will require the true hearts, bravery, and actions of two, not just one alone, if it is to endure and break free."

Chapter 33
~ Beauty ~

So Stupid...

Rennora blinked back more tears.

"I-I fled," she stammered. "Blacksmith, not prince. R-returns everyone safely."

"You mean a simple tradesman stole the eight ladies from us all this time?!" Quorrick snapped, outraged.

"No!" Rennora insisted, mortified at the idea. "That's not what I meant in the slightest!"

"Then what *do* you mean?!" he demanded!

"It's so terribly complicated! There *is* a curse, but they aren't monsters. They need help! Or at least... they did..."

Quorrick rested his head in his hands, infuriated.

"What changed?" Madam Tisza dared to ask.

Rennora shook her head, weeping again. "I don't know! Things were going so well. Then h-he... I-I..."

Quorrick leaned in closer and carefully held her hands. "Did the blacksmith do this?"

Beastly Cycle

"No!" she exclaimed. "H-he would never hurt me like that… Rough bark on a tree last night."

The married couple watched her intently. Rennora had the feeling that they did not fully believe her. She slowly stood, unsure of what to do. She was not going to try to convince them any further. No one in town listened to her anyways, so she gingerly donned her cloak and headed toward the door.

"Where are you going?" Madam Tisza inquired, her worry evident in her voice.

Rennora halted with one hand barely touching the handle, but failed to answer.

"Stay with us," the cook urged. "Just one night in a warm bed is all we ask. Give your hands a chance to heal further. You'll find tomorrow a better day after that. Agreed?"

Rennora began to ask if they were sure she would not be too much trouble, when *his* heart felt response to a similar question of hers from a few days past flashed in her mind. She tried to dismiss it before the pain started. However, she clenched at the door as she dropped to her knees, devastated again. She felt herself being swept up into Quorrick's arms, carried into another room, and gently laid onto a soft bed. Her tears were dried for her as Madam Tisza brushed Rennora's stray hair out of the way. The kindly woman checked each of the bandages, then slid a chair closer and seated

So Stupid...

herself without a word. Exhausted, Rennora drifted off with no strength left to fight it.

All thirteen beasts stood before her again, with seven of them already transformed. Six were still cloaked in shadows. The second in line floated out about halfway, then turned toward Alleron. It hovered in a swirl of blue, white, and dark gray for a few minutes. It then drifted to its place in line, just like some of the hazes from the last time. The fourth in line came before Rennora and shifted into a large woman of grace, dressed most simply. She then transformed into part badger with a heart rendering scream!

The badger lady's words were more humble and gentler than the others' had been. "Don't let him do it," she urged. "No one deserves that fate."

She returned to her place and stood patiently. The sixth shadow faced Alleron, turned a very dark gray, and returned.

The seventh one floated before her and changed into a taller slender man with well made clothing in muted colors. He then crumpled to the misty ground and rose to his feet in his beast form. The animal portions of him reminded her of the lean, wild hares that she had seen trappers return to town with, rather than any of the fat, domesticated rabbits that people kept on their land for food and companionship. His ears were quite tall with rounded ends. His face was long with a nose that came to a point and joined with a line that ran to his upper lip, like a 'Y'. His arms and massively powerful feet had very short, light tan fur on them. His body had slightly longer fur of the same color running down his neck, with a combination of light gray, soft cream, and pale tan colors everywhere else.

He echoed the prince's plea for help, then took his place.

The tenth one addressed Alleron in a mirage of reddish orange. The twelfth one came before her and shifted into a girl, about a year or two younger than Rennora, with long brown hair, green eyes, a flowing gown of brown, and a bitter expression on her face.

"Soramilda," Rennora whispered as she realized who stood there.

The girl screamed in horror as she stared at her hands and transformed into a partial hawk. Feathers covered her body, including her arms. She had yellow, thick-skinned fingers, with a sharp black talon on the end of each. White feathers coated the front of her neck with scattered brown ones among them. The rest on her body were brown. She had a sharp, gray beak that curved into a point. A yellow stripe ran across the base of her beak, near her face, and had two small nostrils. She had no wings.

So Stupid...

"I don't deserve this!" the hawk girl snapped! "I only did what the others before me chose to. Why didn't it work?! Free me now!"

Alleron remained where he was and refused to look at her at all. A tear trickled down his cheek. He had an angry and lost look to his face...

She woke up, gasping! Two ladies were right there to calm her. Rennora recognized them after a minute and accepted the offered tankard of water. She slowly remembered where she was as she drank and repeatedly apologized, embarrassed at being seen like that. Madam Tisza and Arissera assured her that she was safe and had nothing to be ashamed of. Rennora sat there, quite broken.

"How long was I asleep?" she softly inquired.

"Not more than an hour, dear," Madam Tisza gently replied.

Rennora whispered her thanks, wondering why the other beasts were begging her to return, when she noticed her change of clothing draped on the end of the bed. She silently gestured toward it. Madam Tisza glanced at the items and brightened.

"Yes, let's get that off of you," she offered.

Rennora rose to her feet with one hand on the small table beside her to steady herself. Madam Tisza assisted her with removing her cloak. The girl turned around so she could be unlaced, when she felt something within the folds of her skirt lightly

Beastly Cycle

bump her leg. She reached into one of the pockets and carefully pulled out the parchment. She stared forlornly at it, until Madam Tisza politely requested if she could see it. Rennora passed it over. The cook read it in the tense silence.

Arissera inquired, quite curious, "What does it say?"

Madam Tisza asked, "May I?"

Rennora nodded her consent. The woman read it aloud,

> *Heart of a beast beats in your chest. Open it to love, your prison will shed.*
>
> *Four tries must honestly attempt, if your prison you choose to keep instead.*
>
> *Imprison another, and your cold heart turns to stone.*

"What does it mean?" Arissera asked, puzzled.

Rennora turned to explain what she could, when something fell into place for her! She quickly snatched the parchment back and reread it! The second part entranced her, burning itself into her memory.

So Stupid...

"I am such a complete imbecile..." she muttered to herself.

"What was that?" Madam Tisza inquired.

Rennora held it out. "*This* is what she meant! I'm number four!" She threw on her cloak and fumbled with the clasps as she felt her strength rushing back to her! Quorrick came to the doorway as she insisted, "Don't you see?! That stupid fool drove me away, so he could break it himself by dying all alone and not risking it imprisoning me!"

She pushed past the groundskeeper, but he caught her arm, halting her in her tracks.

"Where do you think you're going?" he demanded of her.

She begged him as she tried to free herself, "You have to let me go to him! Please! He's dooming himself to protect me! I just know I'm right!" She threw off the cloak, slipping out of his grasp in the process. "I'll be fine!" she assured them as she threw herself at the door. "You'll see!"

She launched outside, her hope renewed, and dashed across town with her skirt lifted enough to free her legs, until she could not run another step! She then slowed to a quick trot that she could easily maintain. She soon found the place that she had crossed out of earlier. She was surprised and dismayed to see it as dense as the rest of the forest on either side of it! She followed the ditch along until she found the area that she had originally

Beastly Cycle

jumped across days ago, but it was impenetrable as well! Determined, she continued onward, searching frantically for any way through. Suddenly, she heard someone calling her name as she worked her way behind the last house and onto the edge of a field. She turned and saw Wescar leading several men toward her, all around their age. She noticed a lot of stubbornness, rope, and weapons between them!

"NO!" she sternly shouted at them as she increased her pace! She alternately shifted her focus from the crowd to the forest and back again. "I'm fine on my own and don't need your help!"

Wescar ignored her and maintained his same insistent pace. However, the others slowed briefly. She half ran, hoping to discourage them by out distancing them! Wescar and his friends, unfortunately, matched it. She shifted her focus solely on the forest as she now ignored Wescar's persistent calls, fervently praying for a way in for her and her alone. She then spotted it! Several yards ahead was an arched opening through the thick foliage! She promptly trotted toward it. She heard Wescar closing in on her. She madly dashed the last few feet and into the bottom of the ditch! She threw herself up the side and through the opening, when a hand seized her arm and pushed her forward several feet into the woods before releasing her! She caught herself on a tree in time to

So Stupid...

see Wescar and some of his friends resting for a moment within the forest, as the branches and brush wove swiftly together to reseal the opening with much groaning and creaking. While they had their attention on the mysterious underbrush, she quickly fled toward what she hoped was the castle, desperate to warn the people of Wescar's presence before he could find them at least! Beyond that, she did not know what she would do... Suddenly, someone snatched her, throwing her off balance a few steps before she could regain her footing! She glared venomously at Wescar as he held her securely!

"Why did you not answer me?!" he snarled, confused and enraged.

"Release me!" she insisted through gritted teeth as she fought to free herself, her sore fingertips protesting her every try.

"Not until you answer me!" he heatedly persisted, tightening his grip.

"You're hurting me!" she snapped. He loosened his hold, but did not let go. She stubbornly insisted, "I have nothing more to say to you! Release me and find someone else to court!"

"Surely, you do not mean that," he half laughed.

She looked him straight in the eye with steel in her own as she dared, "Try me."

He was shocked! "She was absolutely correct!" he muttered. He then smiled warmly, yet

Beastly Cycle

it did not reach his eyes. He gently explained with sweetness laced into his pleasant tone, "Come, my dear Rennora. Let us get you safely back home to Mistress LaZella, where you will be cared for and watched tenderly over, until I can break the enchantment on you," as he firmly hauled her back the way they had come.

"*NO!*" she screamed furiously.

She tried desperately to break his grip again, but he increased his hold and snatched her other hand! She bit him! He finally released her, mortified and furious!

"You *will* listen to me for a change," she demanded as she wiped the foul taste from her mouth and backed away. "I'm under no such thing. Your presence is *not* welcome in the slightest. There's nothing here for you. Leave me alone forever, Wescar! I want no more of you! GO!"

He shook his head sadly. "She told me that you would say such things. It is no use getting you to see reason as you are, so we will talk more tomorrow. Come…"

She backed away faster, absolutely livid that he was still not hearing her!

"Do not do this," he gently urged as he reached for her and slowly stepped closer. "Come with me, and it will all be over soon…"

"*NEVER!*" she shrieked.

So Stupid...

She fled deeper into the woods. She heard him roar for his friends as he closed in on her again! She darted this way and that, trying her best to lose him, but he persistently stayed with her. Suddenly, he snagged her skirt just as she entered a large clearing. A few of the outer layers tore as she stumbled to the ground. She tried to scramble to her feet, but he latched onto her arm, forced her to her feet, pinned her arm behind her, and placed a large hunting knife at her throat.

"I did not want it to come to this," he whispered angrily in her ear, "but you left me no choice. You have become a danger to yourself and others around you. You need to be secured until you can be freed."

Just as his five friends caught up with them, they heard the monstrous snarl of a large animal echoing around them!

"*NO!*" she screamed at the top of her lungs. "THEY'LL KILL YOU!"

Wescar thrusted her to two of his friends who held her securely with a hand over her mouth and a dagger to her neck. He traded his knife for his sword, while another man readied his pitchfork and moved to the side. The remaining two scanned the forest with weapons in hand as they took up their individual positions.

Chapter 34
~ Beast ~

To the Rescue

Alleron's eyes were drawn to the last few paragraphs, especially the princess's response to the question of her own fate. She was willing to do anything, including be cursed herself, to free her husband… He honored her for loyalty and bravery, but wondered how that could aid them, as he noticed a small line at the bottom that was written in a different hand. Then suddenly, he heard people rushing around and calling his name frantically, pulling his attention away from the scroll! He stepped out from under the willow to see the cook, Mistress Cavina, dashing through the drying field along the castle. The large woman was searching desperately as she roared for him! He caught her attention with a wave and asked what the trouble was.

"Master, Kestin is seeking you urgently, milord!" she exclaimed as she crossed the grounds. "It is about her ladyship! He said that she is in a very bad way!"

To the Rescue

He rolled up the parchment and secured it to himself. He then backed up, leapt over the water again, and firmly landed, only getting the tip of his tail wet. He dusted his hands off as he joined the distressed servant.

"Where is he?" he demanded.

"Your forge, milord," she replied with a curtsy.

The pair of them quickly wound their way through the grounds.

"Explain," Alleron commanded, when they came within hearing range.

"She is being besieged by a group of ruffians!" Kestin explained. "She has fought back admirably up to now, but is outnumbered!"

Alleron felt his blood begin to boil as an ominous cloud formed along the boundary wall. "Where?"

"The forest east of here, about halfway to her town and a mile in from the road's edge."

Alleron handed over the scroll. "Look after that." He promptly armed himself, thankful that his hands had completely healed overnight due to his curse. "Secure everything and shut the gate, just in case the worst should happen. Maintain a watch on us using the mirror."

"The curse will keep us hidden."

"That's about the only good it's done… Well, aside from her."

Beastly Cycle

Kestin placed a hand on Alleron's shoulder. "Look after her, milord. She is very precious."

Alleron swore, "With my life." He noticed Stelna and Minna standing close by, seeking comfort in each other and extremely worried. He bowed to them. They curtsied in return. "Now, let's hope that the enchantment on the forest works with us," he stated as he tightened his last buckle.

He began in a swift trot to the front grounds, then launched into a dead run on all fours toward the eastern wall. He sprang into the air with his powerful hind legs and easily cleared the tall stone. He saw a wide path open for him in the dense foliage as he quickly covered the cleared lands beyond in seconds.

"Thank you," he whispered as he charged along, weaving around the trees with a prayer that he would reach her in time!

As he bounded through the forest, he heard a faint whisper of Rennora shrieking "Never!" from somewhere ahead in the bright sunlight. He snarled fiercely in response! He then heard her frantic scream of "They'll kill you!" from close by!

The terror in her voice cut through his heart like a white hot blade as he adjusted his course. He then caught the scent of men and a flash of color between the trees! He skid to a halt behind a tree, pausing to catch his breath for a moment. He carefully peeked around it. Four men had their

To the Rescue

weapons ready and were scanning around a large clearing. They formed a ring around two others who were holding Rennora firmly with her mouth covered. He noticed her heavenly fragrance mingled with unfamiliar ones that reeked of the unwashed. He then inhaled a whiff of another odor that he would recognize anywhere. The filth that had been stalking his precious lady was one of the six men! He had to free her quickly! He slipped a bit further back, then padded his way around to the far side of the ring, thankful for his quiet animal feet. He closed in, little by little, keeping low and in short, sporadic bursts of movement that blended with the shifting shadows of the forest. He then settled in to wait for the tension to rise to an almost unbearable level. Suddenly, the man holding Rennora's mouth drew his hand back in disgust! The man with the sword directly in front of her snapped at him to be silent!

"She licked me!" the captor whispered as he childishly wiped his hand on his tunic.

Without a moment's hesitation, Rennora stomped on the foot of the other while the first captor was distracted. Alleron suddenly launched himself at the man in front of him, slamming into his throat with an outstretched arm. He continued his charge past the fighting girl to the man on the other side of the ring. One of the men cried out to kill him! He came in low and rammed into the next

Beastly Cycle

man's stomach, hurtling him off his feet. They tumbled further into the forest. Alleron regained his footing and snatched the man by the arm. He promptly slammed him against a nearby tree by his arm, knocking him unconscious. He then slipped around to the front of the remaining men and used the greenery to conceal himself. He had not recognized any of the men's scents that he had just dealt with or passed. The filth must be one of the other four still holding their position in the ring.

    He gave the center trio a quick glance. One of her captors was groaning on the ground, doubled over. The other had his arm across Rennora and his blade on her elegant neck. Some of her fingers were bandaged! He fought back an angry growl at her continued predicament. He could smell fear hanging thickly in the air, along with blood. With their numbers thinned, he was now ready to be serious. He rose to his full height and calmly strode into the clearing. All the men gasped in horror at his sudden appearance as he halted before the swordsman. He glanced at the girl. He was delighted and saddened at the same time for a single moment, behind his blank face, at the sparkle in Rennora's slate blue eyes gazing back at him. He forced his attention back to the task at hand.

    "Release her," he commanded as he drew his unusual weapon free from the harness strapped diagonally across his back.

To the Rescue

The blade was about thirty inches long. Two thirds of its length formed a large, flat, elongated oval that had a single straight blade running inside its open center, while its outer edge, where it met the crosspiece, did not curve quite as much as the rest. The remaining third of the blade created a small, closed oval with a sharp point at the tip. The outer edges of the entire blade were sharp, while the center of the upper and the inner edge of the lower ovals were flat. The wide crosspiece had curved ends to protect his hands, without getting in the way. The sturdy hilt was long enough for him to wield it comfortably with either one or two hands, and it had two small grooves that ran from the crosspiece all the way through the pommel. A tiny latch sat across one of the grooves, just under the crosspiece and near his thumb. He held it easily in both of his hands due to the weight, relaxed, but ready.

The swordsman confidently declared over his shoulder, "Do not worry, widdle wady. I will protect you from the hideous demon."

"I *hate* it when you speak like that, Wescar," Rennora snarled.

She then winced as her captor's blade pressed against her skin. He whispered something in her ear.

Alleron maintained his calm composure, despite his powerful urge to rip the monster holding her to shreds. "Terrible way of protecting her," he nonchalantly stated. "Do you usually let your friends harm the ones you care for?"

Wescar glared at him with a slight touch of guilt. "That is *none* of your concern!"

Alleron lunged forward as he struck. Wescar managed to block it quick! Alleron locked their blades.

"I'm making it my concern," Alleron snarled with eyes of steel as he sampled the man's scent and realized that *he* was the filth that had been plaguing his dearest belle mademoiselle!

"Keep her secure!" Wescar barked at his companions.

Wescar thrust him back and retreated a step. Alleron noticed the rear guard joining Rennora's other captor. He forced his focus on Wescar so he could end this quickly before anything far worse could happen to her. They struck, thrusted, and blocked in the ancient foe's dance, each seeking to gain the advantage over the other, as Wescar re-angled himself, step by step with a smirk, until Alleron's back was almost toward Rennora's captors. Alleron realized his opponent's intent and pressed Wescar in return to protect his back. He noticed an occasional footstep encircling them in the forest, out of sight between the clanging of the swords. Wescar struck, slid his blade along the flat of Alleron's, and locked them together again, using his upward curving crosspiece end. Alleron shifted

To the Rescue

his weight to side step, to break the lock, when he spied only one man with a panicky Rennora! He then heard a single step behind him. He forced himself not to reach to the sound just yet. A perfect time for his little surprise!

He released the latch on the hilt and drew a second hidden sword free from the core of his first. He turned sideways with a twist of his feet and met the ambush strike from the missing man with his twenty-inch sword and a shorter crosspiece, to everyone's shock, especially the men!

"Two against one is hardly an honorable fight," Alleron stated in a conversational tone. He then snarled vehemently for all to hear, "Of course, I would expect no less from an unsavory piece of *filth* who hunts ladies from the shadows in his cloak of gray!"

Rennora gasped, horrified! Alleron ripped down both of his swords, freeing his blade, and leapt back to bring both opponents in front of him.

"Better than a *demon* that lures and enchants innocent girls into falsely loving him!" Wescar snapped fiercely as he and his friend doubled their efforts.

A few of their attacks slipped through Alleron's defenses. He found himself hard pressed. Yet, he managed to cluster his opponents together, keeping pace with both of them, and connect with some of his own attacks on each rather well, as they

Beastly Cycle

circled around. His keen ears caught the soft whisper of metal against leather from behind him. A twig broke with a faint pop a couple of yards away. They then heard a roar of pain! Lighter footsteps charged in! He heard two people struggling. Wescar shoved his opponent toward his friend and darted backwards, quite distracted. Alleron brought both swords to bear against the man and soon had him disarmed. The man dropped to his knees, sniveling for mercy. Alleron's stomach turned at such a pathetic sight. He quickly knocked the man unconscious. He then returned his attention to the frozen Wescar. He paused as he noticed Wescar watching Rennora's battle, mortified! She grappled for control of the man's pitchfork. The man was attempting to stab Alleron as he fought to free the weapon. She jerked her knee up toward a tender area of his, but he leapt back beyond her reach. She then shifted her grip and threw all of her strength in a single twist, slamming the handle into the side of the man's head. He staggered back, releasing the pitchfork and clutched his wound. Her former captor, well behind her, was kneeling and focused on stemming the flow of blood from his leg as he gritted his teeth and glared at her.

  Rennora proceeded to storm over to where Alleron and Wescar stood. She halted at Alleron's side, much to both opponents' surprise! Wescar took a step closer to her. She raised her weapon to

To the Rescue

his chest, keeping him at bay! He shifted toward Alleron with his sword ready. She darted between them, shielding Alleron.

"No!" she snapped. "You will *not* take him from me!"

"Then how can I possibly free you?!" Wescar demanded hotly in return.

"You're *still* not listening!" she shrieked. "A rock wall hears me better than you do! Go home and take your lackeys with you! Leave us be!"

"You're not returning with me to the castle," Alleron whispered to her.

Rennora half faced him and resolutely declared, "Try me."

He returned her obstinate gaze with a stern one of his own as he dared, "Try it…"

Alleron spied a sudden movement beside them. He blocked a strike from the one Rennora had stabbed as he cried out, "Watch out!" to her.

She darted out of the way and engaged her former captor using the pitchfork against his sword. Alleron returned to engaging Wescar, when he noticed one of the men that he had wounded at the neck earlier carefully slipping up behind Rennora with a raised club, as the other kept her distracted! Wescar must have seen the additional attacker as well. He suddenly turned reckless in his fighting techniques. One particular thrust went a half an inch too far than he had intended. Alleron let it slip

Beastly Cycle

to the side of him. He then snatched Wescar's arm. He twisted his body as he pulled the man over his shin with the added momentum, sending Wescar crashing into the ground. He rushed to her aid, but the unseen attacker struck true! She collapsed into a heap. Alleron's heart stopped! He slashed to the sides. Both men scrambled back, well out of his range! He dashed to the fallen girl and dropped his inner sword to check her. She was alive, thankfully.

    Pure venom filled his mind toward the three remaining enemies as he slowly rose to his feet. His vision flashed red! They stepped back, trembling slightly. He charged at them, fighting wildly! He blocked with the outer sword and slashed with his claw at Wescar. His hand then caught the other man's club and ripped the foul thing out of his hand. He swung it across Wescar, who ducked, and hurtled it into the forest. The other man fled! He snatched Wescar's sword arm and forced it high as he tore his sword free. He slammed his sword against the third man's blow, the power of his sheering the other sword in two! He stepped past Wescar and wrenched the man's arm almost to the breaking point, forcing Wescar to release his sword. A movement caught his eye! The third man was gathering Alleron's beloved into his disgusting arms! The fox man threw Wescar down and charged a couple of steps before a crippling pain flashed on his back! He crumpled to his knees as

To the Rescue

multiple blows rained down on him, driving him further to the ground. All of a sudden, they halted. Alleron braced himself shakily on his hands and knees as he focused on a way to turn things to his advantage. Wescar then stepped into his view with the club in hand.

"For Rennora…" he muttered before he swung hard at Alleron's head.

Alleron knew no more.

Alleron slowly awoke, aching all over. Thick ropes bound his body and muzzle tightly! An animal panic at his predicament rose within his chest! He closed his eyes and breathed deeply to regain mastery of himself. He carefully worked himself upright within a heavy cage that surrounded him, with little room to move. He then scanned around him. The cage was situated on the edge of the forest beside a wide, dirt road. About four yards or so further up the road, and in a small, cleared area beside it, was a crowd of people around a roaring fire. They seemed to be far too busy with tending to the injured to notice him. Five of his opponents were alive, but in varying states of wounded. One lay on the ground, covered in a large cloth with only his feet showing. Wescar was seated slightly apart from the others, fuming. Alleron wondered why the men had not finished him when they had the chance, as he wriggled to see if his hidden daggers were still

Beastly Cycle

on him. They were gone. He was not entirely surprised. He pondered how to turn his misfortune around, when he heard a soft groan. Near him, but well out of his reach had he been free, was Rennora, tied up and sleeping fitfully against a tree. It was not long before she awoke as well, frightened, but wisely made no sound. Her beautiful eyes then met his.

Chapter 35
~ Beauty ~

Escape

Rennora's heart broke at the sight of Alleron, caged and bound like a feral animal!

"I'm so sorry that you were dragged into this mess," she whispered to him. "I discovered why you pushed me away. I can't simply live my life while you lock yourself away to die alone, even if it is to free everyone else."

His gaze dropped.

"Please," she softly pleaded. "Let me stay and keep you company, at least, so you don't have to face it alone."

He struggled to respond, but all he could manage was an awkward mumble of, "Why?"

She began to explain. However, Wescar and many others approached them before she could utter a single word.

"Are you alright, child?" Madam Tisza inquired, quite worried, yet maintaining her distance as well. "Wescar here told us what had happened. Don't fret, my dear. We'll have you freed tonight."

Beastly Cycle

"What do you intend to do to me?" Rennora questioned, calmly. Her heart sank as she waited, terrified of the answer.

The cook assured her with a gentle smile, "Nothing, my dear."

"Then why am I bound?"

"So you don't go injuring yourself again."

"What of him?" Rennora nodded toward Alleron.

"We thought it best to keep you together for now, so you'll remain at ease. Just a few more hours, dear, and it'll be nothing but a bad memory."

"The only bad memory was Wescar and his friend's daggers to my throat."

"What's this?" Quorrick demanded.

"Wescar and his people—" Rennora began to explain, until Mistress LaZella cut her off.

"Silly girl!" the older woman insisted with a knowing smile that felt false to Rennora. "You imagined that part! You were fighting him so hard, because of your enchantment, that you slipped from his grasp and poked your neck on a branch. You just think you remember it differently is all."

"No," Rennora calmly replied, determined not to let the woman get the better of her. "You weren't there. I promise that I have all my senses and know what I'm speaking of."

"So you say," Mistress LaZella gently stated as she smirked. "But Wescar and the others tell a

Escape

very different tale, plus there's the parchment that he received that declares the same as he."

Alleron softly growled.

Rennora quickly asked, "Who sent it?" to keep their attention on her.

"A poor, frightened soul that worries so for you," Mistress LaZella explained.

"And what exactly did the person have to say?"

"It matters not." The woman's half hidden grin showed that she was secretly enjoying herself.

"It does to me, and I would very much like to hear it."

"No," Wescar sternly replied.

"I think it a reasonable request," Quorrick insisted, firmly.

His wife heartily agreed with him.

"I haven't heard it yet, either," Thevesta added. "I have to admit that I'm very curious why you haven't finished off that thing." She pointed at Alleron.

Wescar glared into the determined faces around him for several tense minutes. Reluctantly, he pulled a small scroll from his pouch and read it aloud.

"Your heart's dearest, Rennora,

has been captured by a powerful creature

Beastly Cycle

of mystical abilities. He has enchanted her into believing that she cares most deeply for him so that she will willingly allow him to drain her life and her heart from her on the dawn of the third day. A spear with a silver tipped point driven into its chest when the moon is at its zenith will break the spell and return her to your arms. You and all that aid you will be rewarded handsomely for this deed from the royal treasury when the demon's heart has beat its last."

    Rennora managed a calm exterior as her heart plummeted into her slippers! They were going to kill Alleron! She *refused* to let that happen while she had breath in her body! She did some fast thinking. She then forced out a chuckle that soon turned into roaring laughter. Everyone gazed at her like she had lost her mind, and their worst fears were just confirmed! Alleron had curiosity dancing in his handsome brown eyes, while he quietly

Escape

watched. Her mirth died down as she managed to apologize.

"Do you honestly believe that you'll be richly rewarded for this?" she asked, incredulous. "There's not even a throne, let alone a single brass coin or minute shard of a jewel in that place. The people that remain there are paupers from a forgotten realm that has no ruling beyond the grounds they sit on. I seriously doubt that the ruler of our kingdom will pay what he never promised. The creature certainly can't do it! I mean, he's the master and a simple, unpaid blacksmith! Where are you hoping the reward will come from?"

Thevesta stomped forward and yanked at Rennora's tattered sleeve, tearing it further. "This dress tells a different story!" she snapped. "That's no course weave of a peasant! Tell to me how you came by that again."

"And the only of its kind," Rennora explained. "It's quite worthless with the shape that it's in, but I'll be happy to hand it over, if I'm permitted to change out of it. Surely the blacksmith will have no objections."

"There I know that you are wrong," Wescar snapped, his irritation showing. "That demon is no blacksmith nor nobleman! He is a lowly guard from some lord in a vast town near the mountains that ran off five and a half years ago when he was caught running his sword through his lord's personal soldier over a girl!" He smirked superiorly at the caged fox man. "What do you say to that?"

Alleron sat there, looking bored.

"I hate to point out what's staring each of you in the face, but he can't exactly respond with his mouth bound shut," Rennora explained.

"It speaks?!" Thevesta gasped, shocked.

"Yes, he does, and quite intelligently as well."

Quorrick moved toward the cage, until Wescar stopped him.

"Better that you do not," Wescar declared. "It is quite dangerous and still an animal, even if it can speak."

Quorrick shrugged him off and knelt by Alleron. He whispered something to him. Alleron shook his head. Quorrick whispered something else. Alleron hung his head and nodded. He then glared up at Wescar. The groundskeeper rose to his feet and meandered a few yards away, in deep thought.

"How do you know what that thing really is?" Mistress LaZella voiced the question on everyone's mind.

"My family was visiting a friend of his lord's," Wescar indicated Alleron, "and this thing was practicing his swordsmanship on the grounds near the barracks. I recognized his fighting style as I captured him."

"How?"

Escape

"He is one of two that I have ever seen wield two swords at once. The other was a master. He is not…"

"And?" Rennora replied. "He never claimed to be nobility, and there's nothing shameful about being a guard or a blacksmith, however many swords he fights with."

Wescar glared at her calm face and took a deep breath to retort, but was interrupted before he could get a single word out.

"Enough, children," Madam Tisza scolded. "Dusk is setting very quickly, and I'll need everyone's aid if we are to eat in a timely manner. Come."

Everyone followed the cook. Wescar trailed behind reluctantly. Quorrick dragged further behind, then halted near Rennora.

"Wescar, would you mind if we spoke for a minute?" he asked.

Wescar paused for the groundskeeper to join him. As they left, Rennora noticed a cloaked figure standing behind where the group was, with its back to her and Alleron. The person made no sudden movements, but seemed to be absorbing everything around it. Wescar and Quorrick soon returned with a pair of torches that they stuck in the ground well out of reach on either end of Alleron's cage in order to light the area. The light fell on the person's face as she turned. Rennora's eyes widened, and her

Beastly Cycle

heart stopped at the sight of Jes studying the group, looking quite pleased with the situation! Rennora dropped her gaze quickly. Jes' presence made their predicament even worse! The two men took position on opposite ends of the small area around the captives. She thought hard for any way possible for Alleron and her to escape without drawing attention to themselves, but nothing came to her immediately.

All of a sudden, she felt the ropes biting into her ankles slightly, pulling her from her thoughts. She shifted as best she could, when she heard a soft, silvery tinkle as something solid slid against her leg briefly from within the folds of her tattered skirt. Her heart leapt with joy! Her bell! She had forgotten all about it. Its presence gave her an idea. She scanned around to see if anyone else heard it. The men still had their backs to her. Jes was intently watching Wescar. Alleron's ear was angled in her direction. He barely nodded once, then squirmed until his back was to her, with a lot of rattling against the cage. It took her a bit of effort to work her legs under her. She prayed fervently that her plan would succeed. She then thought hard of Kestin, remembering to exclude Jes, as she tossed herself onto her side and Alleron kicked the cage hard once at the same time to cover the sound from Jes' hearing! Thankfully, the bell in her pocket sounded! As the men rushed to right her, she

Escape

explained with a wince, and a brainless look on her face, that she had carelessly lost her balance as she had attempted to make herself more comfortable. Satisfied that she was fine and still secured, they left her in peace and returned to their places. She hoped that the summons sang out, even though it had not been her hand that actually rang the bell.

    She watched Quorrick pace slightly as delicious smells wafted over from the fire, and she waited. She rested her hands on the bottoms of her feet with a sigh. She felt the rough rope fibers brush against her sore, bare fingertips, making her grimace for a moment. She then realized that there was something else that she could do, even if aid never arrived! She slipped her shoes off, then carefully went to work on the ropes around her ankles, despite her raw fingers. She paused in her meager efforts to rest as Wescar accepted a spoon and steaming bowl from a playfully pouting Thevesta. He gingerly carried the hot meal to Rennora, knelt beside her, and eagerly offered to feed her. She coldly refused him, wondering how he could possibly expect her to be friendly after everything he had done! He sincerely apologized for her rough treatment with a playful pout of his own. She did not think the look on him, or anyone else for that matter, appealing in the slightest. She refused to even look at him. He rose to his feet, quite irritated with her. Her eyes fell on Jes and a very horrid thought popped into her head! She took a deep breath to steady herself before she spoke.

"Wescar," she gently called as he shifted to leave.

He returned his attention to her. She noticed Jes' interest in her. She would have to be wary.

"You mentioned something earlier about 'She was right'," Rennora said with a soft, demure look. "Who did you mean?"

He smiled tenderly at her. "Just a wise woman that has taken an interest in our plight and is helping in every way that she can. Nothing for you to worry over."

"What's she like?"

He placed a finger on his lips. "That is a secret. She is very particular about who is allowed knowledge of even her existence."

"Why's that?"

He smiled as he insistently shook his head. "Are you sure you are still not hungry?" he inquired as he impishly wafted the food's delectable aroma toward her.

Her refusal was slightly more polite this time, but no less determined. He stormed away as he flung the food from the bowl into the woods. She wished that he was not so childish and persistent. She noticed Jes watching her intently, so she forced her gaze elsewhere. She was absolutely certain that the servant was behind Wescar's accusations and

Escape

deeds. She peered over at the people surrounding the fire as she waited for Jes to lose interest in her. Suddenly, she saw Wescar leap to his feet! He studied the forest behind him for several minutes. He then returned to his guard position with a torch in hand. Jes meandered a little closer and spoke to Wescar. He neither responded nor gazed in her direction.

She screamed near his ear, "KILL THEM!"

He still gave no reaction. She gritted her teeth, quite flustered. Her attention then shifted to the pair of captives. She smirked knowingly at them and savored their predicament for half a second. Then suddenly, she gasped in shock as she vanished mysteriously into the night! Rennora gasped softly in terror! Alleron froze with his ears rotating furiously!

She wondered what was happening when she heard a familiar voice whisper from behind the tree she was resting against, "Do not move, milady. We are here to free you."

She could have wept with joy as Kestin worked quickly at each of her ropes. She whispered, "What of Alleron?"

She felt a thick key pressed into her hand.

"Stelna is returning Jes to the castle," he explained. "I will keep them busy and meet you both in the forest where Minna awaits. Just keep

Beastly Cycle

moving. We will find you. Look after him, milady."

"With my very life," she promised.

She sat calmly and struggled to keep her face blank. Something then softly clattered in the forest on the other side of the fire! Wescar shifted closer to the others and intently scanned the tree line. Rennora quietly slipped over to the cage and tapped Alleron's shoulder. He turned his head toward her. She freed his muzzle, then fought with the ropes around his wrists.

She managed to loosen his restraints when suddenly he whispered, "He's returning."

She darted back to her position, sat on her legs, held her hands behind her back, and steadied herself. Both torches on the other end of the area suddenly fell and went out with a fit of sparks! Quorrick soon emerged from the darkness with a slightly smoldering torch in hand. He halted near Wescar and requested another torch since his burned out. He assured the younger man that he would keep Rennora quite safe. Wescar frowned for a moment and examined the moon's location overhead. He then thrust his own, still burning torch toward the groundskeeper with a look of quiet disdain.

"I need to prepare myself now anyways," Wescar replied, grumpily.

Escape

Wescar headed toward a large wagon on the edge of the road near the camp, when Quorrick suddenly ripped the other torch out of the ground beside him and smothered it in the dirt with a small splash of sparks! A branch snapped deeper in the forest on the far side of camp! The people leapt to their feet and snatched up their various weaponry! Quorrick remained where he was. Another stone clatter sounded, closer this time!

The groundskeeper then softly insisted over his shoulder, "Hurry, child! You don't have much time!"

Alleron scrambled to free his hands. Rennora carefully unlocked the cage with as little noise as she could manage. Alleron moved on to his feet. She held out her last smaller dagger to speed his efforts just as he whipped the rope off. He gingerly wriggled out and rose shakily to his feet. She snatched his hand with a whispered thank you to Quorrick. They stayed low as they picked their way into the forest. He stumbled on a protruding root for a couple of steps after they passed the tree line. She draped his arm over her shoulders and wrapped her other arm around his waist to steady him.

"Can you see in all this?" she inquired, a bit nervous at the pressing darkness and shadows. "I'm rather blind right now."

"I can guide us through with ease," he assured her. "Let's hope the forest will keep our pursuers

Beastly Cycle

confused and lost long enough for me to get you to Sennelton. You'll be safe there until we locate you a new home and position somewhere far from here."

"You're a complete idiot if you still think that I'm abandoning you."

"You're not much better if you think that I'm going to let you waste your life tending to me as I wither away over the years."

"It's my life to do with as I choose. I love you, and I'm staying at your side whether you like it or not, you silly fox."

He fell silent. She heard him hiss through his teeth as he leaned on her more and his limping grew steadily worse. She halted them and carefully eased him against a large tree to rest. The moonlight was gently streaming down through the canopy overhead, giving her scattered light in which to see. She flopped down ungracefully across from him, quite weary herself. He shut his eyes against the pain and said nothing.

"They'll be hunting us by now," she commented, for lack of anything better to say.

"Give me another minute or two, then I'll be ready," he panted.

She was mortified! "Forgive me! I didn't mean to make you feel rushed. Please, take your time."

She gazed up at the moon peeking out from the leaves, bright and gently caressing the sky, and

Escape

marveled at its quiet beauty, framed by the softness of the foliage around them. She wished that the peaceful moment could last forever... She heard Alleron shift. She noticed him clench his teeth from the effort. She slid closer.

"Will you be alright to continue on?" she asked, quite worried about the few wounds that glared at her from his upper arms, and the probably vast number on his body that she could not see.

Suddenly, they heard hurried footsteps approaching.

He inched his way to his feet and braced himself against the tree. "What choice do I have?"

She supported him again and helped him take a tentative step forward. He halted her, shaking his head as he started to sweat.

"Go," he whispered. "Save yourself and get to the castle."

She gazed at his frustrated face, wishing that she could relieve him of his agony somehow. She then placed her hand on his chest to better steady him upright. The feel of him so close sent her heart pounding. She leaned in to kiss his muzzle. He panicked for half a second as he turned his face away from her.

"Please don't," he softly begged, his voice trembling.

She quickly kissed him on his furry cheek anyway. He stepped out of her arms and leaned

Beastly Cycle

against the tree with his hand on his cheek, looking horrified!

"What have you done?!" he hissed as Kestin and Minna stepped into view.

The tension mounted. Time slowly passed. Everyone watched her and waited for something to happen. After a while of listening to the owls hoot and crickets chirp in the stillness, Alleron heaved a sigh of relief.

"Don't *ever* do that again," he scolded her as he motioned for Kestin to assist him. "You just scared several years off of my life, ma belle mademoiselle."

Rennora stood there, enraged and frustrated. "I-I don't understand! I confessed my love and kissed you! The curse is supposed to break now!" She gazed into his pitying eyes as the tears welled up in her own. "Y-you're supposed to be free…"

Heartbreak at the sight of her pain filled his eyes. "I do love you too, dearest Rennora, but I'm glad that this is how it turned out. I never want you to know the torment of my prison. Come. Let's return to the castle before we're found, and that idiot runs me through."

She dried her eyes as she nodded, her stomach a little queasy. "Knowing my luck, the curse would have passed to him, and he would lock me away with him permanently."

Escape

She moved to take up Alleron's other side, when suddenly, she felt something slam into her stomach, throwing her off her feet! She rolled onto her knees as she clutched her abdomen, unable to give voice to her terror! She gasped to catch her breath, but her chest felt tight and was fighting her with every heave.

"*NO!*" she heard Alleron roar in horror.

She gazed up to see his fur falling away from his body gradually, revealing pale, smooth skin and well calloused hands beneath it. She grunted and curled up even tighter as searing pains stab at her face and stomach. It spread throughout her body in a matter of moments, then sank deep inside her. She collapsed, the world vanishing before her eyes.

"This wasn't supposed to happen!" Alleron softly shrieked as his voice shook in fury and shock.

She sank completely into the depth of the void, her pain and thoughts fading into the stillness…

Chapter 36
~ Beast ~

Not Alone

Alleron could only stare, sickened and enraged, as he collapsed to his knees! His worst nightmare was unfolding before his very eyes! Her legs reshaped themselves into an animal's hind legs. Palest gray fur sprouted from her forehead and ran down her back. Touches of light tan and soft white fur appeared along her shoulders and down the sides of her body. Shorter fur coated her arms to her clawed hands and legs to clawed feet. A soft white fur ran down from her lower lip down the front of her neck. Her nose and mouth shifted into a longish, narrow muzzle, with a black nose on the end. Light gray fur coated the outside of tallish, pointed, triangular ears that stood on the top of her head, with soft white fur lining the inside. A sudden rip of fabrics, then a long, bushy tail of palest gray made its appearance out the back of her dress.

He slammed his fists onto the ground and roared, "*NO!*" He sobbed, tears falling onto the grass blades as he clawed them, "Not her! Anyone

Not Alone

but her... Give it back to me! Make me a beast again, just free her! Please..."

An icy crackle softly echoed in the trees.

"Milord?!" he heard Stelna suddenly exclaim.

He looked up through his furious tears. Stelna was standing apart from the other two servants, studying him intently.

"Are you absolutely sure?" she cautiously, but sternly asked.

"Tell me how to take it back!" he fiercely snarled at her, hatred in his eyes! He gazed at the unconscious, pale wolf girl. His heart shattered to pieces as he desperately whispered, "Please..." and gathered her close in his very human arms, weeping through clenched teeth.

A soft breeze caressed them for a second, carrying within it the aroma of fresh roses and the delicate whisper of creaking wood. He then felt a tingle begin in his fingers. It inched its way up his hands to his arms. He lowered Rennora gently to discover fur like hers creeping up his flesh and firmly attaching itself to him! His skin crawled as he forgot how to breathe for a moment! It halted and began to flow quickly back to her, filling in the thinner patch that had briefly formed.

"No!" he gasped in horror as he held her to his chest. "Make me a beast again! Spare her. Make me a beast again. Just spare her," he pleaded over and over again as he buried his face in her silky fur.

Beastly Cycle

The tingling inched its way throughout him. He felt his body shifting painlessly, and a tail growing as his strength returned to him and his wounds faded. It then halted. He sat up, feeling more invigorated than ever. Rennora moaned for a moment, then fell still again. He carefully laid her down and slid back a bit to better examine his newest changes. To his surprise and confusion, he found that he was covered in a blend of medium gray and white fur that was slightly longer than his fox's had been! His tail was bushier and coated in the same. His muzzle was a bit wider. His fangs were slightly longer as well. His ears felt the same height, but furrier. He wondered why he had not returned to a fox man, when he caught the scent of fear from the forgotten servants. Stelna had left while Kestin and Minna were trembling nearby.

"Tell me," he began, delighted that his voice was unchanged. "What animal am I this time, please?"

Kestin managed to swallow back his horror and reply, "A-a wolf, milord. Same as her ladyship."

He sighed heavily as the wolf girl began to stir. His misery increased at the thought of her reaction to her new form, but one thing lightened his burden. He resolved to remain at her side and aid her with adjusting in any way he could until she banished him from her company forever. Rennora

Not Alone

opened her slate blue eyes up toward the sky. She carefully loosened the laces on her now tight bodice and took a deep, steadying breath. He could see her shaking as she raised her hand to examine it.

"You're part wolf now," he gently informed her.

Tears streaked down the side of her face.

"At least you're free though," she whispered.

"Not quite," he replied.

Her eyes widened in surprise and bewilderment. She slowly gazed over at him and promptly clapped her furry hand over the end of her mouth as she gasped in horror!

"Not what I thought would happen either. However, I'm still me, fox, wolf, or human." He studied her for a moment. "Can you sit up, or are you too sore from your transformation?"

She shut her eyes and breathed deeply again. He did not blame her in the slightest for being enraged, torn apart, and frightened out of her mind! He admired her all the more for her little composure.

"You're handling this much better than I did the first time," he pointed out. "I threw myself into the pool and rubbed my skin raw trying to wash the fur off."

She could not help but chuckle for a minute, then quickly apologized for her rudeness.

"No need," he assured her.

Beastly Cycle

Her triangular ears began to twitch. It must have been a very bizarre sensation to her, because she promptly clapped her clawed hands over them to halt it.

She apologized, clearly embarrassed. "I thought that I had heard something, then my ears moved in all directions on their own," she explained.

He listened intently for himself, but heard nothing unusual. He softly whispered to the forest surrounding them to protect both of them and the residents of the castle. He was far too exhausted for any other adventures tonight.

He addressed the forgotten servants, "Where did Stelna vanish to?"

Kestin swallowed back his fears enough to reply, "She has returned to the palace to bring word of and prepare everyone for both your coming. We have agreed that we will remain loyal and protect you both for as long as you wish or require it."

Alleron was most grateful for the declaration. He then noticed Rennora trying to sit up. He urged her to remain where she was. "We're safe for now," he assured her. "You're still very weak and need to rest." He then returned his attention to the steward. "Would you and Minna keep watch for the remainder of the night, so we can be ready for what surprises tomorrow may bring?"

Not Alone

The servants quickly agreed and shifted to new positions surrounding the creatures. Alleron then settled in, determined to watch over Rennora until she dozed off. The female had other ideas.

"May I ask you something?" she barely breathed as she lay, gazing up at the few stars peeking through the canopy overhead.

"I'll do my best to answer," he replied just as softly, knowing that her keen hearing would catch his every word.

"Why weren't you freed? I thought that once I did my part, you would be free permanently."

"I was for a moment…" She gazed at him, astounded and quite puzzled at his response. He continued, "However, I couldn't let you remain trapped. I tried to take the curse back on myself, so you would be free entirely, but it seems that we now share in it instead… I hope that you can forgive me for not being more stubborn or trying harder."

She returned her attention to the sky for several silent, tense minutes. He wondered if she would ever speak to him again. She then closed her eyes and breathed deeply.

"At least we're the same animal now," she shyly stated as she hesitantly slid her furry hand toward him. "That's a start…"

She turned her lovely, slate blue eyes toward him once more, full of hope. His heart leapt! He slowly slipped his hand over hers and gave it a

Beastly Cycle

careful squeeze as he lay in awe of her abounding beauty, grace, and heart. A delighted smile danced across his lips as they both drifted into a peaceful slumber, serenaded by the soft song of the forest.

Suddenly, Alleron's eyes popped open! Dawn was less than an hour away. The area around them was calm. However, a foreboding feeling was settling in the pit of his stomach. He then caught Wescar's scent as a soft breeze stirred the leaves around them! He growled.

"What is it?" Rennora asked as she eased herself stiffly into a sitting position.

"We have company. Your suitor refuses to give up, and you're in no condition to deal with him quite yet." He called to the servants, who quickly responded. He then explained to them, "The hunt has been taken up once more. We need to split up, and now. Both of you get yourselves to safety and stay there until Wescar and the others lose interest. Then return to the castle, if we aren't under siege. If we are, keep away no matter what happens. I'll take Rennora back to the castle myself and protect everyone."

"But you will get killed if they see you at the gate!" Minna exclaimed.

Alleron gazed at her with a mischievous grin. "I never said that we would be using the gate…"

Not Alone

Kestin replied, "Be safe, milord, milady," as he bowed respectfully to each. He then grabbed Minna's hand, and they darted off into the forest.

Satisfied that they would be fine, Alleron lowered himself with his back to her. "Forgive me for this, ma belle mademoiselle, but I need you to climb onto my back. You're unable to even stand right now, let alone run." He felt her grab his shirt for a moment as she hesitantly obeyed. "Hold tight," he urged her.

She clasped her hands across his chest and wrapped her legs around him. He was thankful that her clothing was tattered enough to grant her a secure hold.

"Now, *don't* let go," he insisted as he dropped to all fours.

He swished his tail for a moment to gain a feel for it as he listened for Wescar's position. He heard him and the others crashing through the forest to his right. He launched into a full gallop straight ahead! Rennora squealed in surprise! He whipped easily through the maze of trees, barely making a sound in his flight on the forest floor. He almost lost her as he made one of the turns a bit sharper than he had intended. However, she maintained her grip admirably well and stayed with him. They broke through the forest and onto the cleared grounds surrounding the castle's boundary wall. He spied the top of the willow tree peeking above it! He

Beastly Cycle

bounded several yards to the left of it, sped up with all of his strength, and leapt over the wall gracefully! His landing was slightly less so. His feet slid as he fought to maintain his footing under the additional weight. He then slowed to a walk, near the lake, to catch his breath.

"Thank you," Rennora whispered to him.

"For what?" he asked as he straightened and headed toward the southeast tower, still carrying her.

"For not screaming in horror, and fleeing at the sight of me…"

"I should be saying that to you. After all, you battled through your terror and disgust to keep me company at dinner."

"I wasn't disgusted by you!"

"You were terrified though."

"Yes, I was…" she reluctantly admitted.

"Are you still?"

"Not anymore! Well, last night when you lost your temper, I was more frightened than I had ever been in my life."

"I hope that you can forgive me. I loathe myself for doing that to you. You already know why, at least…"

He felt her snuggle her face into the back of his shoulder.

Not Alone

"Don't ever do it again unless you truly hate me and wish me gone permanently… please," she softly pleaded.

"That won't be a problem, I swear," he assured her as he gently leaned his head on hers briefly. "Now, we need to find the others."

As he skirted the tower, the sun slowly brightening the clear sky overhead, wondering if Kestin and Minna had returned safely, he caught the sound of people in a loud, heated argument. He rushed past the courtyard and found all of the servants gathered near the southwest tower with torches in hand. He spied Kestin, Minna, Stelna, and Mistress Cavina by the edge of the crystal garden, with Jes bound at their feet. He carefully let Rennora down and helped steady her, until she could manage on her own.

"What's going on here?" he demanded as they approached.

The rest of the servants recoiled in horror at the sight of two beasts, leaving the way clear for them!

"Steady," he told them. "Lady Rennora and I have changed some because of the curse, but we haven't given up. Kestin, what's the trouble?"

"Mistress Cavina wanted to send a search party for you both when she heard what had happened!" the steward explained. "However, the

Beastly Cycle

townsfolk are headed here by way of the main road!"

"How did they find the way to the castle?"

Kestin indicated Jes. "*She* had been giving one of those men messages, and even a map, before we retrieved her, milord!"

"Wescar…" he heard Rennora whisper from beside him.

"The damage is done now," Alleron stated. "Will the forest keep them away?"

Stelna answered gravely, "I'm sorry, milord, but as long as they stay on the road, the forest cannot touch them."

Alleron thought for a moment. "Kestin, arm everyone and be ready for the fight of your lives. Protect those who cannot protect themselves."

Rennora clung to his arm, her gray-blue eyes brimming with worry as clouds began to slowly form along the boundary wall.

"What about you?" she demanded.

"I'm going to hold them back for as long as I can to give Kestin as much time as possible. You need to lock the gate behind me. That should give another layer of protection from the curse. After that, you need to follow Kestin's orders."

Her eyes grew wide, then hardened. A small ball of ice fell by her foot.

"Someone else will have to do that," she declared. "I'm coming with you."

Not Alone

"No," he firmly stated. "Now is *not* the time to be stubborn!" Another ball plummeted beside his foot as the clouds strengthened overhead. He silently fumed over the curse's control over the weather. With two beasts now, things were about to get interesting…

"I'm a beast too now, the same as you," she insisted. "I may not do very well with a blade, but I'm light on my feet and can strike and run to help keep them off balance as you take them down! I *know* I can do at least that much!" More ice began to bounce on the ground surrounding them.

He gazed at her, loving her more than ever in that moment, stubbornness and all.

"Are you sure you feel up to this?" he asked, his worry for her laced in his gentle voice, the weather easing.

"Don't worry about me," she assured him, confidently, as she took his hand in hers. "Let's go."

The clouds promptly drifted apart. Sunlight fell in golden beams, melting the ice with its gentle touch. He gave her hand a tender kiss. Her fur was soft on his lips.

"Together?" he inquired, with a pleased grin and joy fluttering in his chest.

She shifted closer to him and gazed lovingly into his eyes. "Together."

Beastly Cycle

Alleron promptly demanded fresh weapons. They quickly strapped them on as Kestin promptly gave orders to the servants, and Stelna dashed off to lock the main gate. The wolf people took a moment to strategize. Alleron then pulled Rennora onto his back once more. They headed back around to the willow, intent on taking cover and striking stealthily from the forest. Alleron took a minute to catch his breath, then dropped to all fours, charged hard over the drying ground, and leapt back over the wall. He heard Rennora's gasp of dismay as they cleared the top of the wall! There, in the dry clearing and approaching the wall was Wescar, several other men of various ages, and the large man that had aided in freeing them from Wescar's grasp earlier! Alleron skid for several yards upon landing, turning as he slowed to a halt to face the intruders. Rennora slid to her feet and quickly drew her sword. He saw her nervousness as he drew his own.

Alleron gently whispered under his breath to her, "Together." He saw her ear angle toward him. "If they begin to overwhelm, I'll keep them busy, and you flee to the shelter of the trees. They'll aid you. Strike fast and hard from there as you see openings. Don't fully engage any of them. I'm counting on you, ma belle mademoiselle."

"Together," Rennora promised just as softly. "Don't die on me. I'm not done with you yet, you infuriating fox!"

Not Alone

He fought back a foolish grin as she quickly steeled herself, while the humans cautiously approached with Wescar in the lead.

Wescar promptly drew his own sword and demanded loudly for Rennora to be brought to him, or he'll raze the castle to the ground! He was rather arrogant, since they outnumbered the pair of creatures before them in both numbers and strength.

Alleron's hackles shot up as he stepped forward, snarling. How *dare* that filth demand a rare jewel of a queen that he would *never* truly appreciate! Alleron suddenly felt a hand on his chest, blocking his way!

He turned his head to see Rennora, quietly and gently asking him to calm himself. He steeled himself to protect her anyways, when she softly whispered that Wescar was her problem, not his, and it was well past time that she pounded some sense into his thick skull.

Alleron desperately wished to run his sword through the filth and be done with it! However, he did see her wisdom in her fully standing up for herself and handling it on her own. *However!* If the filth harmed even a single hair on her lovely body, no force in the *world* would stop Alleron from tearing Wescar apart with his bare hands! He calmed himself for a moment as she wished, then shifted to the side to allow her to pass.

Beastly Cycle

Rennora quietly stepped forward and calmly halted. He watched as she steeled herself to speak, when Wescar's impatience got the better of him.

"*NOW! OR YOU BOTH DIE HERE AND NOW!*" he vehemently roared.

She raised her hand to halt any further tirade. She then calmly declared, "I am she…"

Astounded, Wescar stared at her in complete disbelief! Alleron could hear her heart beginning to pound in anticipation of a fight.

"Easy…" he whispered in caution.

She immediately calmed herself as she proceeded to tell of several events concerning the filth before her. Alleron guessed the events to be very private in deed! Wescar stepped back, mortified! The nameless man that aided them gazed questioningly at Rennora. She subtly nodded. The other men quickly looked to Wescar for direction, but he had fallen silent and unmoving. The wolf people waited, calm, but ready. The tense minutes ticked by…

Then suddenly, Wescar's eyes filled with hatred and fury! He roared, "*WHAT HAVE YOU DONE TO HER?!*" as he charged toward Alleron.

Just as quickly, Rennora leveled her weapon at Wescar's chest, promptly halting him. He stood there in utter shock at her protective move for the space of a single heart beat.

Not Alone

Genuinely perplexed, he softly demanded through gritted teeth, *"But why?!"*

Rennora calmly, but firmly explained, "This form is my *own* doing and mine alone. I chose him…" She then shyly added with her heart in her voice, "…and he chose me."

With his own heart attempting to joyfully pound out of his chest at her words, Alleron lightly rested his hand on her shoulder to assure her that she was quite correct.

Chapter 37
~ Beauty ~

True Answer

Wescar's eyes hardened. He then suddenly whipped up his sword and pointed it at Alleron, just past Rennora's shoulder. "Do not *dare*," he snarled as a fierce rage filled his body again. "She is *not* yours to claim! She never was and never will be! Moon or not, I *will* free her of you *permanently*, then break her curse myself, no matter how long it takes. Then we will promptly wed, and she will find great happiness for the rest of her life with *me*. I will soon make her forget that you ever *existed*." He emphasized the last word with a small thrust toward Alleron.

Rennora's eyes widened in horror! She realized that Wescar was going beyond stubbornly ignoring her words and wishes. He was blatantly deciding her life for her! She had a momentary flash into a crushing future of complete misery with him, if she did not do something and *now*! A unison of low growls from both her and Alleron promptly snapped her to the present.

True Answer

"Give me *one* good reason to forget that there is a lady present, foul thing," Wescar challenged Alleron through gritted teeth. "I beg you," he added with a cold laugh.

"NO!" Rennora snarled as she knocked Wescar's sword away with her own. Wescar dared to side step closer, ignoring her completely! Rennora stormed fully between the two, screaming stubbornly, "*NO!*" at the idiot before her. "You will *not* touch him!"

Wescar reached to shove her out of the way. She promptly slapped him! All her frustrations, all her anger, all her hurt within that single blow sent him spinning away from her, then collapsing to the ground, with four deep slashes across his cheek from her sharp claws! His sword lay fallen between them. He gazed at her, hurt, furious, and determined. He carefully touched his cheek and grew even more enraged at the sight of the blood on his hand!

"You *stupid* girl," he hissed. "Why can you not understand that I am simply trying to save you from both that demon and yourself?!"

Rennora dropped her sword and lunged at him to strike him again with her bare hands, further infuriated at his stubborn, unfeeling stupidity! A pair of strong arms suddenly threw themselves around her and ripped her off her feet before she could take more than two steps!

Beastly Cycle

"*Release me!*" she shrieked as she fought Alleron's firm hold!

"No," he calmly insisted. "Your next blow will surely kill him with your new strength, sharp claws, and intense fury in your heart." She eventually halted her struggle as he continued, "Calm yourself before you continue. Please, ma belle mademoiselle."

She saw the sense in his words through her rage. She breathed deeply several times, as he carefully released her and stepped away a few paces.

She then addressed Wescar, her tone firm and full of forced politeness. "The only fool here is you for not listening once again to me. I have told you more times than I can count that I will never wed you. Not now, not *ever*. Now, leave us in peace and find yourself a girl that will treasure you as I never shall. My heart has been freely given to another. I can honestly say that I am happy. Worry about me no more, for I am no longer your concern…"

She then waited a minute for Wescar to do something. He sat there, fuming and glaring at Alleron. He then suddenly lunged for his sword! Rennora darted forward and firmly stomped both her feet on its blade. As she figured, her new body was considerably heavier. Wescar was unable to get a hold of his sword at all!

True Answer

"Leave us…" she stubbornly insisted as she looked him straight in the eye.

She could see his determination flaring once again for a single second, as he eased his one hand on his lap and his other behind him. Then suddenly, he whipped his hand out from behind him and continued to extend his arm straight in front of him, releasing a dagger in one smooth motion! Rennora's heart stopped as she threw herself into its intended path, while Alleron roared in horror at what was happening! Without warning, Rennora crashed into the ground as the dagger flew past her and tumbled onto the ground near the road. The earth trembled slightly beneath her as she felt herself hauled to her feet, while her stunned gaze remained locked on the dagger.

"Are you alright?!" both Alleron and Quorrick demanded in turn!

Rennora nodded numbly, certain that where the dagger had landed was not in line with the direction that it had been thrown. She had just enough time to wonder at it for a moment, when she spied Wescar about to hurtle another dagger! She cried out and began to shove Alleron out of the way, when he threw his arms around her and twisted himself so that she was out of harm's way instead! This time, she saw the dagger flying through the air, directly aimed for her love's back! Then suddenly, a mysterious wind, narrowed and focused, hurtled

Beastly Cycle

behind Alleron, redirecting the weapon sharply, then carrying it away to tumble beside the first…

Rennora felt the wind slowly and gently wrap itself around her and Alleron. She heard him gasp, stunned!

Frightened, she whispered, "Don't let go!" as she felt the wind strengthen and their feet leave the ground!

Alleron held her tighter as he fiercely whispered back, "Never again!"

As they floated over the heads of their baffled pursuers, a huge gale suddenly ripped through the forest surrounding the castle, shaking all of the vegetation! Three massive trees snapped near their bases, hurtled though the air, and slammed into the ground around the men below, effectively pinning them within. She could hear several other trees snapping deeper in the forest. As they carefully cleared the top of the wall, she noticed Stelna at the outside corner near the road with her arms calmly stretched parallel to the ground, as the wind tore continuously at her clothing. The soft breeze that surrounded her and Alleron gently carried them over the castle ground. As it set them down behind the castle, Rennora saw the gale then rip through the grounds, carrying dry, green and light tan-tinged willow leaves and blood red rose petals with it, as it uprooted the entire hedge wall near the prince's roses and half the tangle! It then sought out and

True Answer

engulfed the pair of wolf creatures! They clung tightly to each other and knelt to the ground to steady and protect one another as their clothing whipped against them! She felt the wind tearing painfully at her, down to her flesh! She shut her eyes as they pulled each other even closer, fearful that they would be hurtled apart from the sheer force of the wind surrounding them! Then all of a sudden, it faded away…

Chapter 38
~ Beast ~

Shattered

Alleron carefully opened his eyes. Everything the wind had gathered was whirling around in the air above them, along with a faint gray and white blur! The debris froze for a moment, then dove into the chasm! The fear in his chest eased as he released her. He watched the others rising to their feet, safe as well. He felt lighter, freer somehow. He gazed down at his beloved still in his arms. His heart skipped a beat in delight! Their eyes met. She covered her entire mouth and gasped in shock and awe at what was staring back at her! He grinned widely as his eyes teared up at the sight of her, very much human again. She wept with joy, touching his face briefly. He caressed her hand. He then examined his other hand, overwhelmed to see it human and pale, without a single strand of fur anywhere on him.

He laced his fingers in hers, praying that all of this was not a dream, when a sharp crack pierced the stillness! He leapt to his feet as another sounded! He slipped Rennora protectively behind him. She

Shattered

passed him a dagger. He eased a few steps closer to where he believed he had heard it last. A third crackling betrayed the source. Fractures marred the otherwise flawless surface of the prince's statue, each one shimmering in the light, like webbed lines of starlight! Another appeared across his face with a crisp pop! Then, the crackling ceased. Alleron and Rennora halted at the corner of the crystal garden. The next sound came from near them! First one statue, then another, and another until each and every one, human and animal, had fractures coating their entire surfaces! Each pairing of statues then inched toward each other before suddenly smashing together and shattering into an icy dust, revealing a beast person within!

 Minna and Mistress Cavina quickly snatched Jes up and hauled her to the side! The other servants drew nervously back, clustering together for safety. Twelve beasts clamored off their stone pedestals and stiffly eased their way out of the garden. Alleron was pleased to see them all alive and well as he tightened the ties on his now loose pants, but failed to understand why they were still creatures, as the tiger prince meandered apart from the others, with his hands clasped behind his back. Perhaps he and Rennora still had more to do to completely free everyone. He felt Rennora cling to him a little tighter. He wrapped his arm around her to calm both of their nervousness. Then again, like their portion of the curse, maybe the answer lay with those still imprisoned…

One of them noticed Alleron and Rennora mulling on the edge. Her short, black fur had touches of a warm brown underneath. She had small, rounded ears perched on the top of her small head with a patch of soft black curls draping down between them. Her small muzzle ran smoothly to her forehead with no definition between the two. Her small black nose twitched. She had fine claws on the ends of her slender hands. A great, bushy tail lay against the back of her clothing and curled almost in half at the top. The squirrel lady hobbled over and crushed Rennora in a tight hug as tears streaked down her cheek fur.

"You did it!" the creature squeaked in delight as she held the girl at arm's length. "I knew you could do it!"

Rennora's confusion matched Alleron's as another lady gracefully glided to him and hugged him. Her smooth, reddish-orange scales made his flesh crawl from the touch! Small, black dots were scattered all over her slender body. Her eyes bulged slightly as she beamed at them both. Her arms were shorter and ended in short, fine claws. She had a long tail that dragged the ground behind her faded skirt. Her lack of hair gave her an exotic look.

"All of our thanks to you," the salamander lady beamed at them both.

Shattered

"B-but why are *we* still cursed?!" a younger, swallow lady demanded from nearby as she gazed heartbrokenly at her exposed arms beyond her rumpled sleeves.

"I believe I'll concern myself with that later, my dear," the salamander lady gently replied. "I'm content for now to move and speak." Her gaze fell on the other beasts gathered around poor Kestin and loudly attempting to gain his attention. "Pardon me, if you please. There is something I promised I would do, if I was ever freed."

Alleron watched her hesitantly approach the otter lord, steel herself, and tap him on the shoulder. The creature turned with a mild curiosity, until he noticed her presence. His face became blank as he waited. She tried to speak, but he shook his head and pointed to his small, rounded ear. He then motioned her to follow. He led her near Alleron and Rennora, where it was much more quiet.

"Forgive me, milady," the otter lord apologized with a brief bow to the salamander lady. "I could not hear a word you were trying to say over there."

Stelna whispered to Mistress Cavina as she indicated the pair. The motherly cook nodded in agreement. They dragged Jes between them to join the smaller group, while Minna hurried to Kestin's side.

Beastly Cycle

"That is alright," she assured him. She then eased into a deep, graceful curtsy as she continued, "I just wished to humbly beg your forgiveness for turning you into a beast all those years ago. I was eager, foolish, and most selfish. I beg of you to tell me how to fix this…"

He gazed down at her with a blank face for several minutes. He then heavily sighed. "Rise… please," he urged her as he assisted her to her feet. "I stupidly fell into the same trap, as you can see. Being a statue, only able to see and hear, allowed me ample time to reflect on both of us. I ask that you don't deceive a single soul like that ever again, and I will swear to do the same. Oh! That reminds me…" He scanned the group as he asked, "Have you seen Soramilda, by any chance? She's the wingless hawk."

Rennora gestured toward her on the edge of the crowd.

He thanked her. "My turn to make things right and now." He then headed toward Soramilda.

Stelna commented, "And so it begins…" with a satisfied smile as others began to pair off with much bowing, curtsying, and talking. Even the prince fell to his knee in his grimy finery before the swallow lady, with one fist on the ground, and spoke an apology from his heart.

The maid then gazed harshly at Jes. "And what of you, Jes?" She nodded toward the tiger

Shattered

prince standing a few feet behind Alleron again. "Will you follow suit?"

Jes glared back at the maid and said nothing. Soramilda came over and muttered her apology to Alleron. She then darted away without waiting for an answer from him. Suddenly, someone broke away from the cluster of servants. As he drew closer, Alleron realized that he did not recognize the person. The manservant halted in front of Jes, enraged. Mistress Cavina moved protectively between them, until he motioned her back sternly and folded his arms as he glared at Jes silently.

"Do you know him?" Alleron asked Rennora in a whisper.

She nodded, softly replying as she snugged down the laces on her bodice's sides, "A groundskeeper, I believe. He's never spoken to me though."

The servant furiously pointed over Jes' shoulder at the tiger prince.

"Speak!" Jes jeered at him. "I cannot understand you, dear uncle."

He pointed insistently at the prince again, but said nothing. She glared back at him.

"Are you certain that you wish to continue like this?" Stelna dared the servant.

Jes refused to shift her gaze or her stubbornness.

"Very well..." Stelna sternly declared.

Beastly Cycle

The maid walked over to the empty space on the other side of the crystal garden and what was left of the wilting rose tangle, with the grace and elegance of a queen. She threw a single hand into the air on the other side of the rear flower garden. A gentle breeze wrapped itself around her as her clothing fell away, like shedding leaves from a tree, revealing a simpler, elegant gown of a very fine weave and belted at the hips. Her skin withered as she aged rapidly before their eyes, the wrinkles enhancing her growing beauty rather than tarnishing it. Her hair lengthened to her waist and turned pale as moonlit snow.

"*LORD AND LADIES OF THE BEAST!*" she roared out, her voice magically amplified and unchanged. "COME TO ME, AND WE WILL END THIS!"

Alleron stood, stunned and in awe of the former maid. Yet, all twelve of the creatures did as they were bid, with expressions of curiosity very evident on their faces. Only the tiger prince joined the silent ring that had formed with no reaction to the maid's mystical transformation or emotion on his face. His eyes betrayed that his thoughts were consumed elsewhere. Alleron wondered if the prince would ever find peace, when the bat lady and the lion lord shifted apart, exposing Stelna in the center.

Shattered

"Will you join us as well?" she asked as she beckoned toward Mistress Cavina and the rest.

Mistress Cavina roughly hauled Jes into the center, while the groundskeeper trailed behind. Alleron and Rennora tentatively moved closer, but halted just outside the ring's opening, uncertain if they were included in the invitation or not.

"A bit closer if you would," Stelna gently urged the pair.

They took each other's hand and shyly obeyed, taking their place in the open space of the ring. Stelna nodded her approval.

She addressed the groundskeeper in a firm tone, "Amheer, you have proven your remorse for your actions and changed for the better since that day. I have seen you aid and protect each beast in turn with my own eyes. I return this to you…"

She reached into a small pouch on her belt and pulled out something small, clutched within her fist. She carefully opened her hand to reveal a diminutive ball of thick, swirling gray fog. She brought it close to her lips and gently blew on it. It slowly glided out of her hand, halting just before the groundskeeper's face. Joyous tears streamed down his grateful face. He licked his lips eagerly for a moment. Fear then crossed his eyes! He hesitated as he looked to Stelna for final permission.

"Go on," she assured him with a matronly tone. "You have earned it back."

Beastly Cycle

The older man smiled for the first time. His expression softened, exposing the handsomeness of his chiseled features. He then carefully took the fog into his mouth. He strained for a minute, clenching his teeth against the unpleasantness of it. Finally, he took a deep breath and, somehow, managed to swallow. He opened his mouth to speak. However, nothing came out! He tried once more with the same results. He glared venomously at Stelna, mortified and betrayed!

"Allow it a few hours to settle in," Stelna instructed. "You have been without it for a very long time, but your lovely voice will ring out again. Be patient with it."

Amheer nodded silently, bowed with respect and grace to her, and turned to leave when he noticed Rennora standing there. He bowed deeply to her, then to Alleron. He mouthed a few words to them as he straightened, but Alleron did not know what they were. The humble advisor left the circle to join the other servants, his demeanor no longer hunched with a heavy burden.

"Now, my faithful apprentice," Stelna addressed the cook. "Leave Jes to me. Tend to the boundaries until I am finished. The fallen trees will only hold them back for so long, and the time for secrecy is over."

"Yes, mistress," Mistress Cavina replied with a curtsy.

Shattered

The cook handed the disgruntled servant over. As she darted away, Mistress Cavina's clothing and portliness fell away with each step. Her gown beneath mirrored Stelna's. Her body gained a regal gracefulness and unspoken power as she took charge of the uneasy servants. Alleron studied the maid watching from the center of the ring, with thoughts of the prince's tale drifting through his mind. He then realized who Stelna truly was as she flicked her hand toward Jes' feet before she released her hold! She took a deep breath and raised her hand, palm outward, toward the swallow lady.

"Your actions here tonight weakened your curse, until it is the thinnest of layers on your person," the sorceress explained. "These two," she indicated Alleron and Rennora, "have cracked it enough for this to be possible. Never forget that honesty and love are powerful forces. Now then…"

The creature flinched as Stelna clenched her hand, then acted like she was dropping something as she softly chanted, her eyes swirling a tender white and fierce gray, like rolling storm clouds. All of a sudden, the swallow lady clutched at her head with a wince! She had large wings on her back. The underside of her flight feathers were dark gray. Fine, soft white feathers ran from the base of her neck and down her chest, from her arms to her wrists, on the underside of her wings near her shoulders, and on the underside of her tail feathers

Beastly Cycle

as they fanned out briefly behind her. One of the feathers on both of the outside edges of her tail were twice as long as the rest and a dark gray. Sapphire blue feathers coated the top of her wings, sides of her neck, sides of her head, and forehead. Coppery orange feathers lay between her eyes, along her cheeks, around her small, dark gray beak and nostrils, and down the front of her neck. She had rough, dark gray skin on her claw-like hands, with thick talons on the ends of her fingers.

    Her feathers quickly ruffled up, then exploded from her body, falling to her feet and melting together into a small disk of the clearest crystal before her! A younger lady, a few years older than Alleron, straightened, staring at her human hands, her clothing hanging looser on her featherless frame. She wept, overwhelmed and stunned that her prison was finally shed for good! She stammered her humble gratitude as she collapsed to her knees.

    Stelna turned her attention to the boar lord next. His chest and arms were thicker than the prince's were. Coarse, black-ish brown hairs coated his body, with shorter ones on his face and stunted snout. Stout, white tusks peeked out from his mouth, against his upper lip, on either side of his flat, oval shaped snout, which had a rounded point at the top and a large, round nostril on either side of the center, giving him a wild pig-like appearance. Furry, oval-ish ears, with a point on each, sat on the

Shattered

top of his head. Thicker, darker hair grew longer on the top of his head, between his ears. Four of his fingers had fused together into two thick ones on each hand, giving his remaining three fingers a hoof-like appearance, along with the slight ridge-like, dark gray texture that ran from his wrists to his pointed fingertips. His legs were curved as well, and ended in large, cloven hoofs. Soon, another small disk formed on the grass from the beast's hair and tusks as the now barrel-chested man stepped back, fumbling over his whispered thanks as he clung to his now too large pants.

    The badger lady was next. Her muzzle was longer and the fur on her cheeks flared out a bit, giving her face a triangular shape. A pair of twin white stripes ran on her black furred face from just above her oval nose to the top of her head, near her smaller rounded ears that sat there. A longer blend of black, gray, and white fur coated her neck and outer parts of her arms. Black fur lined the front of her neck and inside of her slightly shorter arms. Long, white claws were attached to her stouter fingers. The large woman of grace's eyes teared up in gratitude as the disk formed at her feet as well.

    Then the hedgehog lord. The squirrel lady. The hare lord. The bat lady. The lion lord. The salamander lady. The otter lord. Finally, the hawk lady. Eleven disks lay in a circle as Soramilda stepped back as well, with grateful tears streaking down her cheeks.

"You have been granted a second chance to prove your heart true," Stelna explained sternly. "If you trick another into falsely giving you his or her heart to your own selfish gain, the punishment will be far more dire than fur, scales, or feather… You have been warned."

Stelna dismissed the freed humans. Once they were clear and tending to their clothing, she raised her hands in front of her and thrust them apart. The ropes still binding Jes fell away. Stelna then gave a twist of her wrist. Jes whirled around to face her.

"Jesseva," Stelna sternly commanded as she straightened to her full height. "You used stolen mystical powers to entice and enchant Prince Vindan to your will and to gain his royal powers as well. You plotted and enchanted others to carry out the execution of his wife, Princess Belnisa, in order that he should wed you. You tried to deceive and twist many of the hopefuls seeking to break the curse into slaughtering the current beast. You tricked an outsider into believing that Lady Rennora was in grave danger to aid you to this end as well. Your heart is *still* an icy stone, even after having over a hundred years to mend your ways and make things right with all." She curled her hands into claws and turned them toward each other. "For your

Shattered

crimes and your cold heart, your life will be forfeit, as *you* tried to forfeit others'."

"*NO!*" Jesseva shrieked, petrified! "I *am* sorry! I swear that it will not happen again! Please believe me!"

"Too late…" was all the response Stelna gave.

She clapped her hands together in the tense silence as she chanted, her eyes full of pity and raging fire! Rennora clung to Alleron's tattered sleeve in fear! The disks shook for a second, then began swirling around the terrified girl along the ground, drawing closer and closer to her feet. They then rose and slammed flat against her body as Jesseva let out a gut retching scream! She tried desperately to rid herself of even one of the monstrous things! They flattened further as they rapidly spread and molded to her form with an icy creaking. Her movements became stiffer and slower until, with a final wail, she transformed into a crystal statue. Stelna threw her hands apart, her incantation complete! The statue exploded, shattering into a fine, glassy dust! It then gathered into a stream, swirled up into the air, and slipped into the chasm behind the castle. Stelna collapsed to her knees, panting with one hand on her chest.

Chapter 39
~ Beauty ~

Free At Last

Rennora released her fearful hold on Alleron and took a few hesitant steps toward the tired woman, a persistent suspicion gnawing at her since the first beast was returned to human.

"W-who are you?" she shyly stammered.

"I am who you think I am," the woman stated. "We will talk more later. I need you and Lord Alleron to tend to his highness, while I aid her majesty. Meet us in the front grounds by the gate when you are done."

"What do you mean?" Alleron asked.

Stelna ignored him as she stiffly rose to her feet, then limped toward to the front grounds. Rennora stared after her, stunned and unsure what to think of the girl that dressed and cared for her, being the very person that aided in the curse in the first place! She noticed the new humans savoring their freedom with much cheering amongst themselves. Her eyes then fell on the silent tiger prince. She wondered why he alone still remained a beast. Had he not fixed his ways like the others? What possible

Free At Last

task could be left for him to complete to prove his worth? He glanced at her as though he had sensed her musings. She politely curtsied, for lack of a better response. The prince dropped his gaze, staring at the ground, quite lost.

"It did not work," he softly muttered as he fought to keep his voice calm.

"We'll discover how to free you, your highness," Rennora assured him.

The beast shook his head. "I no longer care about that." He remained quiet for a while. He then explained, "I was hoping that if I was freed from my icy prison, that I could be reunited with my Belnisa…"

Alleron spoke up. "I found her, your highness."

The prince stared at him, eager and desperate. He snatched Alleron's arm and demanded, "Where? When? Take me to her!"

Alleron winced from his strong grip and was quickly released.

The prince apologized as he regained his composure. "Would you take me to her, please?" His long, striped tail swished briefly, betraying his continued eagerness.

Alleron bowed briefly. "With pleasure. I must warn you, your highness. She was affected by the curse as well."

Beastly Cycle

  The prince looked mortified for a moment, then quite determined. "Shall we?"
  The three of them quickly made their way to the lake. Rennora gasped at the sight of the withering tree. Over half of its leaves had fallen away, and the remaining were dry and laced with an orange-ish brown, leaving its trunk exposed. Several of the thinner branches were scattered on the grass. The prince inched closer, his face blank.
  "She has been hidden in plain sight the entire time," he whispered miserably. "How did this happen?"
  Alleron replied, "She chose to tie herself to your curse, in hopes that she would be able to free you from it and restore you to your senses."
  "You spoke with her?!" the prince gasped, astounded!
  Alleron shook his head. "I found her final words before she was turned."
  The prince hung his head in shame and gazed into the blood red rose that he had been concealing behind his back. "I no longer am worthy of her love, but she does not deserve this either…"
  Rennora stepped forward, her heart full of sorrow and pity for him. She gently urged, "Speak what's in your heart to her, your highness. Real love doesn't easily shatter or disappear without cause. It takes a lot to break it forever. It can be

Free At Last

hurt, but it can also be mended. Be honest and tell her everything."

Alleron wrapped his arm around her as they took a couple of steps back. The tiger prince took a deep breath and hesitantly kneeled a few yards from the water's edge.

"I know that I do not deserve to be heard," the prince began as a soft breeze blew from him to the willow. "I cannot begin to describe how greatly ashamed I am of everything that has happened, and so, *so* very sorry for this mess I dragged you into." He began to tear up, and his voice cracked slightly. "For all the pain, misery, and heartache I caused you… For each tear you shed, because I *stupidly* let my guard drop with Jesseva, which allowed her to slip a hold on me…"

The prince clutched his head with one hand and braced himself with the other, the rose resting beneath it. A gentle wind enveloped the willow. The fallen branches, remaining leaves, and bits of bark swirled into the air as the tree uprooted and was carried over the lake. Rennora prayed that this would be it! Everything whirled tightly together for a moment as the bottom of it carefully touched the ground before the prince. The wind then carried the vegetation up into the air and into the chasm, leaving behind a woman of breathtaking grace and beauty, gazing at the tormented creature at her feet.

Beastly Cycle

"I know that I do not deserve your forgiveness, and I would not blame you if you walked away from me," he continued, refusing to look up, "but I beg of you to tell me how I can make this right again!"

The woman dropped to her knees, placed a hand on the back of her husband's head, and rested her forehead against his. She whispered something to him. He shook his head.

"How can you forgive me so easily?!" he demanded. "I was a complete beast to you!"

The princess kissed his forehead and sat back on her heels. "Some of the hopefuls over the years could not read, so they would have Kestin or Minna read the scrolls and books aloud to them here, by the lake. You knew that you could have easily ordered my execution within two weeks of my capture, but you delayed it. You fought them in small ways, whether you knew it or not. You never stopped loving me or searching for me once you were free of that creature's hold, my precious Vindan."

All of a sudden, the wind returned. It carefully wrapped around the tiger prince. Princess Belnisa stepped back. The wind gathered speed into a full gale. Blurry streaks of white, with touches of black, fluttered within it. The entire wind froze for the space of a heartbeat, still holding the prince hidden in its center! It then dove into the chasm and left behind a very human Vindan. He was quite careworn, but handsome. He gazed up at his wife

Free At Last

through teary eyes and presented her with his very battered rose. She lovingly accepted it with a gentle glow on her face. Prince Vindan pulled Princess Belnisa into his arm as he rose to his feet and clung to his pants with his other hand. Rennora's heart leapt in delight! It was several awkward minutes before the pair broke apart. The princess chuckled for a moment at her poor husband's plight as he attempted to secure his tattered, loose clothing. She gently assisted him with his troubles. They turned to rejoin the others, when they caught sight of Alleron and Rennora. They then bowed deeply in respect and gratitude before their humble attendants. Rennora had never been so caught off her guard! Should she curtsy in return? Should she bid them to rise? She gazed at Alleron in hopes that he would know what the proper reaction was. However, he was as much at a loss as she was!

"Y-you shouldn't be bowing to us, your highnesses!" she managed to stammer. "We've done nothing to deserve such honor."

The prince shook his head. "That is where you are wrong, dear Lady Rennora. You discovered how to truly break the curse. How?"

Alleron explained with a playful grin, "Lady Rennora stubbornly persisted, despite my resistance."

Beastly Cycle

Rennora returned his loving gaze. "Lord Alleron took the curse back on himself and finally allowed me to remain at his side."

Princess Belnisa nodded sagely as she said, "I take it that you found the last part of the poem."

Both Alleron and Rennora were bewildered.

Rennora pointed out, "I was only able to locate three parts to it."

The princess shook her head. "The sorceress wrote the last part on my scroll and read it to me just before she transformed me into a tree." She then recited,

"Take back your prison and never be alone."

Alleron seemed quite embarrassed. "So that was the part that I missed. I noticed the writing, but didn't have time to read it because I was rushing to ma belle mademoiselle's aid…"

Rennora blushed. "I'm glad that you figured it out without the last part."

"I don't deserve such praise. I was just doing everything to stop my prison from becoming yours. I didn't care what happened to me."

Rennora held him close with all of her heart. She savored his embrace, his arms, warm, strong, and gentle. They then heard a loud boom from the

Free At Last

front grounds that jarred them! She remembered the angry townsfolk that were in pursuit, thanks to Wescar. She reluctantly released Alleron and reminded him of their next task.

Alleron sighed heavily. "I have no desire to harm them, if it can be helped."

Rennora thought for a moment. She then assured him, "If I have my way, you won't have to…"

"Then let's end this, once and for all."

The four of them made their way toward the hedge between the tower and the ruined building. As they stepped within a couple of yards of it, a huge gale flooded out of the chasm, split into two, and surged along the boundary walls, ripping up every stone and hedge until it touched the front gate! It changed course and slammed into the castle, leveling it along with the village! It then hauled all of the rubble away, leaving the people unscathed. The ground suddenly began to quake and heave! The tremors intensified as the wind dove into the closing chasm. Then, just as the last of the debris vanished into the chasm, the opening slammed shut, leaving behind only a scar of fresh dirt along its entire length as a mute testimony of its existence.

Rennoa and the others cautiously rose to their feet. They gazed at the empty lands around them in awe of the curse's final deed. She noticed every person from the castle lingering together in silence on the front grounds, near the road. She lightly touched Alleron's arm as she proceeded to join them, with a determination that she *would* make herself heard this time. The servants turned and made way for the stubborn girl. She halted near the still standing gates of iron, the center of the rose displaying a man and a woman hand in hand, facing each other. No watchful eyes, no animals, just happiness shared between them. About thirty people, including the ones that had held Alleron and her captive, stood in the main road. Then suddenly, the front gate gave a warning creak and fell flat at their feet. There was a long pause. Each group of people then softly spoke amongst themselves. Minna whispered something to the royal couple hovering just behind Rennora and Alleron. They nodded in agreement. The maid soon gathered the remaining eleven of the former beasts around her, and off to the side. Rennora wondered what Minna was doing, when she spied a bandaged Wescar thundering toward her, with his lackeys and Quorrick close behind. She took a moment to steel herself to finish what she had begun, as she noticed Kestin quietly joining them, very curious. As Alleron began to explain things to him, Rennora calmly walked over to meet Wescar.

"Dismiss them now," she firmly insisted before he could utter a single word. "This is between you and me. Quorrick only can remain, if you wish, but the rest go, or *I* will leave, and you'll *never* find me this time…"

Wescar's eyes narrowed and hardened. He slowly folded his arms across his chest, licked his teeth for a moment, then stubbornly replied with a defiant, resounding, "*No.*"

Rennora promptly turned to leave without another word, when Wescar snatched her arm as he began to speak. She calmed herself, turned to face him with a false smile, halting his words and surprising him, then quickly slammed her fist upward into his stomach with all of her strength! He doubled over, winded and grunting for air. She drew her dagger and pointed it at his face. Several of his lackeys drew their swords and pointed them at her. Suddenly, three more swords joined in, two from near her arms and one from Wescar's side, shielding her. Wescar did not look quite so confident anymore, as he gazed upward and behind Rennora.

"Release me," she calmly demanded.

He hesitated as he straightened. She emphasized her wishes by suddenly stabbing at his arm! He winced as blood slowly bloomed though his sleeve from the shallow wound, then reluctantly obeyed.

"Good," she declared. "Now, call them off and dismiss them."

Beastly Cycle

He glared at her, then nodded to the others. They hesitantly obeyed, moving several yards away, but still within view. Her additional assistance shifted around until Alleron stood beside Rennora, with Kestin and Quorrick flanking Wescar. Satisfied, Rennora had her protectors lower their swords. They reluctantly did so, but kept them in hand and ready.

"Glad to see you're finally listening to me," she observed to Wescar.

He glared at the men. "You are giving me little choice…"

"You should have listened sooner then." She straightened slightly, more confident. "Now. You *will* leave me in peace. There are plenty of other girls for you to choose from and who would be delighted to have you. Turn your attentions to them and find willing happiness there. *If* you dare to pursue me, or even live wherever I choose to settle, I *will* run you through. Am I clear?"

Wescar stubbornly said nothing. Rennora whipped her dagger threateningly toward his arm. He jumped back a step! Kestin and Quorrick promptly halted his further retreat. The groundskeeper menacingly stepped closer to the very determined, younger man.

"The lady asked you a question," Quorrick rumbled.

Free At Last

Wescar continued to remain silent, a mischievous and daring smirk playing across his lips.

"Go with her," Quorrick directed Alleron and Kestin. "See that she's settled happily and safely far from here. I'll ensure that this child returns to town and doesn't cause her any more trouble."

"I am a *man*, not a child!" Wescar indignantly sneered as he took a step toward the older man and raised his fist.

Quorrick promptly rammed his fist into Wescar's gut! Wescar collapsed to the ground entirely, clutching his stomach and fighting desperately this time to breathe.

"Then behave as such," Quorrick sternly commanded.

Rennora graciously thanked Quorrick, then calmly walked toward the servants, feeling that the groundskeeper had things well in hand. She was relieved more than words could say to finally be free of Wescar! She halted a few yards short of the other groups, breathed deeply, and allowed a true grin to break through, until she noticed the frightened looks on the servants and the mutinous ones on the townsfolk. She turned to locate Kestin. He and Alleron were a few paces away, beaming proudly at her. She quickly motioned them over.

Beastly Cycle

"We need to do something about them," she urged Kestin as the men joined her, and she indicated the lingering people.

"I agree," he assured her. "What is the question. I can take care of my people, but the townsfolk will hardly listen to a stranger like me."

"May I try?" Rennora hesitantly asked. "I'm at least a familiar face…"

Kestin considered it for a moment before he agreed. "Do your very best persuading, milady, or things will probably turn quite ugly for my people."

She gave the steward's arm a reassuring squeeze. She then walked over to the townsfolk with a confident air that hid the massive knots of fear in her stomach.

"My fellow townsfolk!" she called out as she came to a halt on the grounds in front of them, with Alleron a yard behind her. "You have seen for yourselves that there is nothing here! No monsters, no castle, no riches, nothing but a people that were frozen in time, who are now free to find and make new lives for themselves somewhere else. Our assistance is wasted here! Return to your homes, please."

Mistress LaZella and Thevesta shoved their way to the front of the crowd.

"What of the riches that we were promised?!" the older woman demanded.

Free At Last

Rennora pointed at the former castle inhabitants behind her, grateful that everyone from servant to nobility's clothing was in tatters and quite filthy from their ordeal. "Look at them! Do any of them seem like they have a single coin between them all to pay even one of you for something you didn't do! They have the clothing they wear, just like me, and even that is worthless!"

"What about the lands?" Thevesta snapped. "Surely that wind took all the gold with it when it buried itself."

"You are free to search all you wish," Prince Vindan declared as he emerged from the crowd of servants with Princess Belnisa on his arm. "We give these grounds to whomever desires it. Kestin. Minna. Stelna. We call upon you as witnesses to this. My wife and I relinquish our claim upon it from this day forward and on through the generations to come. We had received this place years ago shortly after we were wed, as a gift, so it is truly ours to do with as we wish."

The sorceress declared from the side of the castle road where she and Mistress Cavina were sitting on the grass, "It will be done. I warn everyone though, there is nothing to find, because there never was any wealth here in the first place, hidden or in plain sight, and I have been here since the beginning."

Beastly Cycle

All of the servants nodded and murmured in agreement.

"THEN I CLAIM THIS LAND AND EVERYTHING ON IT AS MY OWN!" Mistress LaZella quickly bellowed! She then pointed to everyone. "Each of you are a witness to my claim. All of you have one hour to leave my lands!" she declared, quite pleased with herself.

The townsfolk reluctantly obeyed, complaining of a wasted night as they vanished down the main road toward town, taking a sulking Wescar and his lackeys with them. Quorrick, Madam Tisza, and Thevesta remained behind. Thevesta gazed, enraged and tired, at the empty grounds. Her eyes then fell on Rennora, looking content, and she smirked for a moment.

"Mistress LaZella," the larger girl said in a fearful tone. "Since you command these lands, I respectfully demand that you have *this* girl," she pointed at Rennora, "seized for attacking me six days ago!"

Mistress LaZella nodded approvingly. "Yes, I had forgotten about that. You!" she pointed at Kestin. "Yes, you. Seize that girl near you and bring her here."

Kestin stood silent for a moment. He then shrugged his shoulders and seized Rennora's nearest arm as he whispered something behind her back to

Free At Last

Alleron. Alleron grabbed her other, despite the protest of some of the servants.

"Trust in him," Alleron whispered to Rennora as the three of them maneuvered to the main road behind Mistress LaZella and well out of her easy reach.

"Now then," the older woman declared as she clasped her hands behind her back and surveyed the captive before her.

"Just a moment," Princess Belnisa interrupted. She beckoned everyone to follow and they all shifted to the main road and just to the side. The royal couple then stepped forward as the princess continued, "You say that this girl attacked you several days ago. Correct?"

"Yes!" Thevesta insisted. "I was at the well when *she* viciously hit me with a rock! I didn't touch her at all. I still have the lump on my head!"

Rennora stood there in terrified silence, until Alleron softly encouraged her to speak for herself.

She calmly retorted, "You ripped the water bucket out of my hands twice, scraping my knuckles in the process, then slammed me into the ground, which wounded me." She raised what was left of her sleeve to show her fresh scarring still on her arm. "Then you were about to strike me with your fist, so I struck to stop you from further harming me."

Beastly Cycle

"THERE!" Thevesta exclaimed joyfully. "You see! She struck me first!"

The princess nodded sagely at this. Rennora felt her stomach sinking, wondering if her worst nightmare was about to come true.

"Are there any witnesses to this event?" Princess Belnisa inquired.

"No," Rennora reluctantly admitted.

"I see... Anything that anyone else wishes to declare concerning this?"

"We do," Quorrick spoke up as Madam Tisza nodded. "Yesterday in the town center, Mistress LaZella informed Rennora that all was forgiven, and that she was welcome to return to her old room."

"I *never* said any such thing!" the older woman exclaimed.

"I heard you as well," Madam Tisza firmly assured.

"That matters little!" Thevesta snapped. "*I* didn't say it, and *I* am the injured one here!"

"Exactly," Mistress LaZella insisted. "For your crime, Rennora, I hereby declare that you'll serve Thevesta here, until such time that I feel your offense has been worked off. You can begin by building us a temporary place to live, until we can manage something more permanent."

"Just a moment, if you will," the prince spoke up. "There is one problem with your decree..."

Free At Last

"This is *my* land!" Mistress LaZella shrieked. "You have *no* say here!"

"Therein lies the trouble," he explained calmly, stepping forward. "You see, this land is in fact yours, but also falls into the current ruler's kingdom, where he holds the ultimate say in this dispute."

"And he's not here, or he would consider it to be not important enough to be worth his time!"

"I do agree with you there. So it falls on the next titled nobility to resolve this. I doubt I have much claim to the throne as I once did, but I am still a prince of this realm and well within my rights to step in."

Mistress LaZella's eyes widened, then narrowed shrewdly. "So you claim, but what proof do you offer?"

"None that you would care to acknowledge at this time."

Mistress Cavina stepped up beside him and sternly stated, "He is what he claims to be."

"Stay out of this!" Mistress LaZella snarled at the woman. "You have nothing to say about this!"

"Oh, but I do," Mistress Cavina declared. She stood regally before the other. "I am the Queen Mother, and he will have his say."

The prince stood startled for a moment at this news, as though he was seeing her clearly for the first time in many, many years! He then pulled himself together and bowed briefly to her. "Thank you, Mother. I wish to discuss your concealment from me over the years with you later, but at the moment…" He returned his attention to the older woman who stood trembling with fury. "I have this to say instead, you have no right to enforce such a punishment on this girl."

"THIS IS MY LAND, AND I WILL DO AS I WISH ON IT!" she screamed at him.

"Yet again, that is correct. *However.* You will find that she is no longer *on* your land. She stands in the road that was claimed and created by my grandfather, King Hoshdor the Fourth."

Everyone stared at Rennora, a few in rage and others quite intrigued.

The prince continued with his face void of emotions, "She stands on the king's lands, and *I* hereby banish her from *your* lands permanently, never to set foot there again on pain of banishment from the kingdom."

"*NO!*" Thevesta shrieked. "WHAT ABOUT ME?! What about the wound that *she* deliberately inflicted on me! I demand punishment!"

Prince Vindan gazed at the girl sternly for several minutes. He then responded, "Very well, since you insist… Rennora, I hereby banish you from the town that this girl," he indicated Thevesta, "currently resides in as well. Should she move, or linger outside of that town for more than two

Free At Last

months, then the banishment is lifted, and you are free to return as you wish. Kestin, would you inform the ruling lord of this. Tell him that he can also expect a written decree of this above my personal seal for him to keep."

"*NO!*" Thevesta screamed, furious. "Throw her in the dungeon! Have her beat until she can't move!"

Prince Vindan glared her into silence. "Are you attempting to give me suggestions for your own punishment instead? I have spoken. If you disagree with this, take your complaints to his current majesty, and we will deal with it further *there*. As for now…" He wrapped his wife's arm around his. "I have my people to tend to. Shall we?"

Rennora could hardly believe her ears as she was released! The judgement was just and generous, within its harsh words. She watched in stunned silence as the other servants trailed behind the royal family, while the remaining townsfolk headed down the road in the opposite direction from the town, leaving Mistress LaZella and Thevesta to the newly claimed land. Rennora then felt someone take her arm and gently guide her as she tore her eyes away from the pair, baffled and relieved at the same time. Alleron then wrapped her arm around his.

Chapter 40
~ Beast ~

Question for Her

"He won't trouble you anymore," Alleron assured Rennora as they and Kestin followed the rest down the road, his exhaustion threatening to catch up with him. "You did quite well."

"Where are we going?" she asked.

"Just around a couple of bends, then to rest with the others until the wagons and carriages I sent for take us on to Sennelton," Kestin replied as he stumbled a step, quite tired himself.

"What's going to happen to everyone?" she inquired.

"We will look after all of them until they decide what to do with their lives, and where they wish to go. If they choose to remain, we will find a home for them and continue to assist them."

"What of the royal family?" she asked, her words begun to slur.

"He is going to relinquish his claim to the throne and see if he can be granted a more humble title and a bit of land to call his own, so he can

Question For Her

spend his time being married and working toward their happiness together."

Rennora suddenly tripped and crashed into the ground. Alleron scooped her up into his arms and carried her into the forest. He set her down under a massive, silver maple tree, just in sight of the road, then flopped beside her, his own strength spent. Kestin tiredly offered to bring a carriage to retrieve them while they remained there. Alleron barely raised his hand in consent. The sunlight caressed the vegetation around them as they rested, enhancing the natural beauty and peace of the forest.

"Tell me," Rennora whispered. She leaned her head on Alleron's shoulder. "What did Quorrick say to you when you were in that cage?"

Alleron rested his head on hers. "He asked me if I was the one that had injured you, then if I would give my life to keep you safe once he figured out a way to free you from Wescar's clutches."

Rennora smiled and gave his hand a quick squeeze and settled in a little closer. "Now that you're human, I hope that won't be a problem."

Alleron chuckled, "Most definitely not, ma belle mademoiselle. Tell me, what will you do after we reach Sennelton?"

She sighed heavily. "I'm not entirely certain. Probably seek out a new place and be a scullery maid again until I marry. There's nothing left for me back in that town…"

Beastly Cycle

"Why not try for a better position, now that you have a fresh start? Surely there's something else that you would rather be doing than endless dishes…"

"Secretly, I would love to be a cook, but who could I possibly ask to teach me? If I send a message to Madam Tisza, Wescar may be tempted to follow."

"You could speak with the Queen Mother for assistance in locating someone, or she may surprise you and offer to teach you herself. Then you could leave for a new home after your training is complete."

She thought about it for a bit. "Yes, I think that could work. Thank you!" She gazed at him, a little worried. "What about you? What are you going to do?"

Alleron sighed, pondering over his secret hopes. "If I can, I believe that I would like to continue with blacksmithing here for a while after I've visited with my family, then open up my own shop in a sleepy town by the sea. I've had enough of soldiering for his lordship back there, and endlessly loading and unloading others' goods isn't what I want to be doing for the rest of my life."

"What happened with the lord?"

"A captain was trying to take advantage of one of the local girls, and I brought his intentions to a swift halt. The lord was going to have me shamed

Question For Her

and imprisoned, but another captain saw what had happened. I was only dismissed, while the other was stripped of his rank and thrown in the dungeon." He grinned widely. "It feels great to actually be able to answer as I choose, instead of the curse forcing me into silence."

"It's really nice to finally talk freely as well." She smiled warmly.

Alleron felt his knees turning to melted butter. "You, uh, said you had nothing left for you in that town. Are you certain that you have no one that you'll regret leaving behind?"

"No."

He was a little reluctant to remind her, but he wanted to be sure that her heart was free of others. He plunged ahead, "What about the man from the mirror?"

She glanced at him, slightly puzzled, then realized who he was hinting at. She replied, "I had completely forgotten about him. Fistorick's found his happiness, and I can honestly say now that I am truly delighted for him and his bride. I wish them well and much joy throughout the years." She lowered her gaze shyly to the ground as she blushed. "I only hope that I can find such happiness with someone dear to me…"

She glanced at him, and a small demure smile danced across her lips. He hoped that he was reading her hints correctly as he shifted to kneel

Beastly Cycle

before her, to her surprise! He took her hand into his.

"I realize that we've only known each other for a short time, eight days at most, so I humbly request permission to court you, with the intent of marriage, or not, if we find that we aren't well suited with each other," he asked, hoping that she could see past his nervousness to his heart.

She gasped and covered her mouth for a second. She then gazed into his eyes, looking concerned. He began to wonder if he had just made a serious blunder, when she whispered something that he did not quite catch.

"I'm sorry," he said. "I missed that…"

She hesitantly spoke her thoughts a bit louder. "If you truly wish to court me, then all I ask is that you give it your all, heart and soul. None of that pulling me close, then pushing me away. I will give it my all as well."

His heart leapt at her words! He kissed her hand and, with his hope shining in his eyes as he gazed into hers, he assured her, "I will do exactly that for as long as you allow me to remain by your side, my beautiful Rennora."

She teared up with joy, beaming broadly at him as she held his hand tenderly in both of hers.

"Now, who do I have to see in order to formally request permission to begin courting?" he happily inquired.

Question For Her

Her face promptly fell. "I-I have no family. My parents died when I was small. I was given to a lady to raise until I was old enough to work. Then Mistress LaZella took me in and found me my position. Madam Tisza, Quorrick, and Arissera are the closest I have to a family. Well, Minna and Lady Stelna as well now, I suppose…"

Alleron did some fast thinking on how to fix that, when he spied Kestin, Minna, Lady Stelna, and the royal family riding in a large, fine carriage toward them.

Perfect! he thought. He then asked Rennora aloud, "Would you consider Kestin family, then?"

She was startled at his question! "Oh! I… suppose so… Why?"

"Here he is now." Both Alleron and Rennora rose to their feet to greet the people joining them. Alleron then addressed the steward with a nervous smile, "Kestin, may I have a moment of your time, please?"

"Of course, milord," Kestin answered as he scanned around them for a suitable place.

Alleron bowed low as he continued, "My Lady Rennora has no family living, so I ask that you accept the responsibility of speaking in their stead. Would you grant me the honor of allowing me to court this beauty, with the intent of marriage, if we are suited well for each other?"

Beastly Cycle

He heard the ladies gasp in delight as he straightened and waited for an answer as a moistness began to coat his palms. He discreetly dried his hands.

Kestin thought it over, nodding sagely. "And what is her ladyship's response to your request?" the steward inquired.

Rennora shyly whispered with tears welling up in her slate blue eyes, "You really wish to court me that badly?"

"With all my soul," Alleron whispered back as he took her hand.

Tears streamed freely down her cheeks as she beamed at him. She threw her arms around him as she declared for all to hear, "Yes! I would love for you to!"

His heart leapt as he wrapped his arms around her.

Kestin responded, "Then yes, you may from me as well! Well done, milord!"

Alleron savored her embrace as he whispered in her ear, "I love you, my stubborn wolf."

"I love you as well, my infuriating fox!" she happily whispered back!

Epilogue

A New Life

Five years later in a small town by the sea, twenty-four-year-old Rennora held her sweet, little three-year-old in her arms as she carried both the young child and the sack of food from the house, across the large garden, and to the smithy next to it. The steady clanging of the blacksmith hammer told her that her twenty-five-year-old husband was still hard at work on improving a piece to repair his lordship's carriage. She came around the forge to the front and lingered in the doorway as Alleron paused to reheat the metal and stoke the fire, shaking his head in dismay.

 She gently smiled at the scene and waited patiently for him to notice her. It did not take him long. His return smile lit up his handsome face at the sight of her. He checked the fire one more time, then scooped her into his arms, baby and all. She kissed him soundly and drank him in. His lips lingered on hers. When they broke apart, he relieved her of their child and promptly reduced the small one into a fit of delighted giggles with his tickling. He then settled on a cleared bench so they

Beastly Cycle

could enjoy their midday meal all together. Rennora busied herself with passing out the food from the sack. She then read to him the letters that she had received from both Belnisa and Madam Tisza as he tended their little one.

    The royal couple had been granted a duchy, which included Sennelton, just had their first child, and were doing quite well in marriage. Kestin had finally asked Minna for permission to court her! Her exact answer was playfully demanding to know why he had taken so long to ask! She then delightedly answered 'Yes'! Amheer was living in a small cottage and very dedicated to tending the grounds around the minor lord's manor in Sennelton. The Queen Mother was away, completing her training, then both her and her mistress would visit soon. Most of the uncursed humans had accepted their loss of title and lands, and left Sennelton, eventually, to seek new lands and fortunes on their own terms. Some were fighting long and hard to reclaim what they had lost. A very few had decided to remain in the protection of Vindan and Belnisa's good graces, still unable to cope with everything that had happened to them… A ceremony had been held to remember and mourn those that had lost their lives over the course of the curse. Wescar had moved to a new town, much further inland, with his lost ancestor, Lord Dunfelkar, and both were in the process of charming

A New Life

the various ladies, causing the local menfolk much distress! Fistorik and his wife were about to welcome their second little one and were happy as ever. Arissera was being courted by a minor lord's son, a humble and steady man, to her delight! LaZella had a very small cottage built on her new land and was seen digging various holes all over it, complaining all the while. Thevesta was happily seeking a better position, and Wescar's attentions, in the same town as he. Both writers sent their love and promised to visit soon.

    Rennora set the letters aside and started in on her own meal. So much had happened since they had parted company. She delighted in everyone's happiness, saddened for those still lost, and resolved that her family would hold their own little ceremony as well that evening… Once their stomachs were full, Alleron brought her wedding gift to him to his lips and played a merry tune. Rennora promptly retrieved his to her and quickly joined in. As the three of them danced together to the dual ocarinas, she savored her happiness and blessed that day, so long ago, when she jumped that silly ditch and took a chance on a trapped beast.

~ Pronunciation Guide ~

Alleron – {Ah-l-er-oh-n}

Amheer, (Advisor) – {Ah-m-hee-r}

Arissera – {Ah-rih-s-air-uh}

Belnisa, (Princess) – {Beh-l-nih-suh}

Cavina, (Mistress) – {Kah-vih-nuh}

Conadora – {Koh-nuh-d-ore-uh}

Dunfelkar – {Duh-n-feh-l-k-are}

Ella – {Eh-luh}

Fistorik – {Fih-st-ore-rih-k}

Honrik, (King) – {Oh-n-rih-k}

Hoshdor (the Fourth, King) – {Hoh-sh-d-ore}

Jes – {Jeh-s}

Jesseva – {Jeh-seh-vuh}

Kestin – {Keh-s-tih-n}

Kilda – {Kih-l-duh}

LaZella, (Mistress) – {Luh-zeh-luh}

Minna – {Mih-nuh}

Quorrick – {Kw-ore-rih-k}

Rennora – {Reh-n-ore-uh}

Sennelton – {Seh-neh-l-toh-n}

Soramilda – {S-ore-uh-mih-l-duh}

Stelna – {St-eh-l-nuh}

Thevesta – {Theh-veh-st-uh}

Tisza, (Madam) – {Tih-z-uh}

Vindan, (Prince) – {Vih-n-dah-n}

Wescar – {Weh-sk-are}

Many thank yous go out to the many people over the years that have helped me answer the strange random and oddball questions that have struck me as I've been writing this book and more, including family, friends, a good friend that kept driving me to finish it, a weapons guild member, and a blacksmithing professor…

This twist was inspired by Beauty and the Beast. It is a very special one for a variety of reasons, one of which is it is one of my favorite fairytales since I was a child. As a result, I have been pondering some of the twists for quite a few years, such as the rebounding curse and taking a share in it as the answer. For additional inspiration, I watched many, many versions of the tale and even tracked down an English translation of the original French tale by Gabrielle-Suzanne de Villeneuve. Well worth the read! I also found some things that I did not agree with in each version that I saw and read, which I addressed in my own way.

May the results of my writing journey between this cover bring joy and find a special place with its readers...

This story and its characters are fictious. Any resemblance to any persons, living or dead, or real life situations are purely coincidental.

    Leeanna R. M. Pilcher started this project as just something to aid her in working through her on and off depression at the time. It worked quite nicely! Once she was back to her cheery self many months later, she had no intention of finishing it, until she shared some of the details with others, who then begged her to complete it. How could she refuse such enthusiasm? Through the ups and downs, she felt that the tale was worth it to the last word, giving a quiet part of her imagination and creativity for others to enjoy…

Made in the USA
Middletown, DE
11 December 2023

44000682R00307